THE BEST LAID TRAPS

Other books by Philip La Croix

Aperture Eats

THE BEST LAID TRAPS

PHILIP LA CROIX

Cover design by MiblArt

Interior print design and layout by Sydnee Hyer

Ebook design and layout by Sydnee Hyer

979-8-9869147-0-1 paperback
979-8-9869147-1-8 eBook

ACKNOWLEDGMENTS

I want to extend a huge thank you to all my friends who have beta read and powered through my punctuation and spelling errors. Your efforts are greatly appreciated and were instrumental in the creation of this story.

Special thanks to my editors, Sabine and Anna, at Eschler Editing for not pulling any punches and helping me present the best final product possible.

Thanks to Steve and Savannah D'alo at S&S Productions for their expertise in helping me create my first audiobook.

Finally, I'd like to thank my best friend, Alec Voorhies, for being my automotive expert for this project and would like to state to the reader that if you notice *any* inaccuracies when it comes to the cars, it's his fault! Love you buddy!

Chapter 1

HAPPY BIRTHDAY

Edward Dalton trudged his mountain bike the third and final mile of his commute to school. Large, sharp thorns stuck out every which way from his once-plump tires. They always sagged a bit under his ample weight, but all life had finally gone out of them, a sad end for tires that had worked so hard for so long.

Georgia's May morning sun caused sweat to run freely down his face and pool in his shirt. It dripped into his eyes, and he ran a large hand up his forehead into his curly black hair to wipe it away.

He was going to be late for school, but all he could do was keep moving and ponder how his birthday had gone so far. Today was supposed to mark him becoming a man. Eighteen and just weeks from graduating in the class of '14, he was about to start his life out in the real world. He even had an upcoming interview with Johns Hopkins University, his dream school, with hopes of entering the medical field, and he felt strongly about his chances. Today so far, however, had only been one disappointment after another.

This morning, his father had tied giant Mylar balloons in the shapes of one and eight to Edward's place at the kitchen table. In the middle of the table, still in its protective plastic bubble, was a chocolate birthday cake and next to it a card with *Eddie* written on the front.

The card had a picture of a classic Ford Mustang—one of Edward's favorite cars. He'd opened the card, hoping to find either a green or white slip of paper, but instead, he found a note from his father:

> *Happy Birthday, E! Sorry, but money is a little tight this year. I was thinking that I could take you out to Steely Phil's after school as a celebration! I'll pick you up as soon as you're done. Until then, have an awesome day at school, and I'll see you real soon!!!*
>
> *Love,*
>
> *Dad*

Although the sentiment was there, Edward couldn't help but feel a little disappointed that his birthday present was going to be a dinner. Not much for what most call the biggest birthday in a young adult's life, but he thought to himself, not for the first time (or even the thousandth), that it was what it was. His father was always concerned about money. He even made Edward use his old Nokia brick of a cell phone instead of buying one of the newer models, any of which *had* to be better.

After breakfast, Edward had gone into the garage to get his bike and start the three-mile ride to school. As he opened the large door, a huge blast of warm, humid air billowed in, and he immediately began to sweat. Halfway through his ride, he failed to see the sharp stickers in the road in front of him, forcing him to walk the rest of the way.

Gonna be one of those days, he thought.

By the time he got to school, class had already started. He walked into his first class, interrupting the lecture, which came to a screeching halt at the disruption of the door swinging open.

All eyes gazed at Edward as if he was the surprise subject of today's lesson.

"Sorry, had some trouble getting here," he stammered apologetically.

Mr. Myerhoff, a no-nonsense, eighty-three-year-old man who had plenty of cantankerous pep left in his step, scrutinized Edward's sweaty, red face. "Well, I trust you should have no trouble finding your seat, Mr. Dalton."

The class gave a collective laugh, which turned to murmuring and snickers as Edward made his way to his seat.

Myerhoff cut them off with a sharp "Quiet." Immediately, the attention returned to the teacher, and he continued the lesson.

Edward, meanwhile, still huffing and red, made his way to the only open seat in the classroom. The desks had not joined the rest of the twenty-first century; each was an individual chair with a small attached wooden slab, just like when his dad had gone here. All were lined in five columns spread across the room. The seats were not assigned, but despite this, students usually kept to the same seat every day . . . *usually*.

Today was one of the rare occasions when the class had shifted, and in accordance with Edward's luck, the one open seat was right in front of Zack Roe.

Edward had been picked on the majority of his life, both in the flesh and on social media by most of the other kids, for his weight and complexion, but Zack was the worst bully of them all.

Walking to the open seat, Edward noticed a sharp, malicious grin spread across Zack's angular face. Zack raised his eyebrows toward his spiked blonde hair.

Unconsciously, Edward raised his eyes, as if to beg the heavens for mercy he knew he would not receive. With a heavy heart, Edward plopped down in his seat and tried to put his attention forward.

It wasn't long before he heard the tearing of paper behind him and began to feel bits of crumpled wads hitting him in the back of the head. Edward did his best to ignore it.

On and on it went. With each passing minute, unable to pay attention to the lecture, he feverishly wondered why Myerhoff didn't notice, but the strikes were too well timed, thrown at the exact moment the teacher looked down to check his notes.

Edward's temples pounded, his heart raced, and his skin grew hot. Finally, when he could take no more, he jerked his body around and said in a loud, harsh whisper, "Dude, stop!"

Now Myerhoff noticed. In an agitated voice, he said, "Mr. Dalton, is there a problem?"

Edward didn't want to make the situation worse, so he clenched his fists until they were bone white. "No, sir. Sorry."

Myerhoff returned to his lecture as Zack, in a mocking, hushed tone, said, "Dude, stop."

Small giggles popped up all around.

Edward's face grew redder.

Zack, obviously elated by the reactions he got from his surrounding audience, began fresh torment for Edward.

This time, it was almonds instead of paper that pelted Edward in the back of the head. After one well-placed shot, Edward lost control of his senses. Before he even knew what he was doing, he spun up and out of his seat until he was standing in front of Zack. Edward's large frame blocked Zack's view of the rest of the world, and his sharp, blue eyes stared daggers down at him. In a firm, deep voice, he said, "STOP!"

From the look on Zack's face, Edward could tell that he took this as a challenge. Before Zack could respond, however, the real world came crashing down around them as the firm voice of Myerhoff cut through the air.

"Mr. Dalton! That is the third time you have interrupted my class today. It is only because of how well you normally conduct yourself that

I've even considered tolerating the first two. I hope you have a good explanation for this abysmal behavior."

Edward was many things, but a snitch wasn't one. Say what you want, but his large frame was supported by a thick moral fiber. He also knew "tattling" on Zack would be looked on by all as a childish breach of the high-school code of conduct and would just get him picked on even more.

He bit his tongue and remained silent. Tears of frustration welled up at the corners of his eyes.

Myerhoff looked between Edward and Zack, putting two and two together. However, instead of calling Zack out, he gave a small sigh, turned his gaze toward his papers, and said, "Goodbye."

The cue was known all too well by anyone who had sat in his classroom. If you were unlucky enough to hear this word directed at you, you were expected to pack your things and leave the room, not to return until the following day. Until you left, the class would remain in complete silence.

With a feeling of severe injustice, Edward began his walk of shame.

A small huff of laughter escaped from Zack's mouth, and due to the silence surrounding it, it had not gone unnoticed. Edward glanced back just as Myerhoff said, "You too, Mr. Roe."

A look almost to match Edward's fell across Zack's face as he managed to stammer out, "But—"

"Goodbye," Myerhoff said without even a glance up from his notes. There was no emotion behind it, only the chill of the word itself, which made it incomparably worse for all who heard it.

Edward saw the look on Zack's face and took advantage of the fact that he was already packed to make a hasty retreat. He didn't know where he was going, and he didn't care, as long as he was away from Zack.

Instead of one large building, Peach Creek High resembled an outdoor mall with classrooms instead of shops. On one corner of the plot was the cafeteria. Edward sat at the very edge close to the dumpsters, with Westley, his best (and only) friend. Westley was a skinny blond boy who stood about a head shorter than Edward and wore thick, black-framed glasses. His noticeably crooked smile was nevertheless very bright and warm. Although he was bullied just as much as Edward, he kept an infectious, upbeat attitude.

"No offense, man," Westley said, "but you look like hell! What happened? You get a turd caught sideways?"

"Nah," Edward said. "Rough morning."

He related all that had happened, and when he got to the part about him and Zack getting kicked out of class, Westley said, "Aw, man, that sucks! But at least he got a little of what's coming to him."

"I wish it would've just been me. He looked pretty angry."

"Man, that guy is so ugly, I didn't think he could look 'pretty' doing anything! Guess you just have horrible taste in men." Westley nudged him slightly.

Edward couldn't repress a snort of laughter. "Could you not? People might hear you and get the wrong idea."

"Why, Edward," Westley said, emphasizing the *h* and turning the *y* into an *ah*, "do you mean to say you're ashamed o' little ol' me?"

"Stop it," Edward said, betraying his words with the crack of a smile that widened to both ears.

"There! That's the face that you should have on your birthday, bro! You should wear that thing more often. Maybe it'll turn your gloom to boom!"

Edward cocked an eyebrow at him. "Gloom to boom?"

"Shut up," Westley said with a smile. "You know how hard it is to come up with stuff on the fly?"

"Well, let it fly right back in the toilet, 'cause that was *shit!*"

The two laughed freely and heartily until they were jerked back into the world by a soft voice.

"Hi, guys."

Brittany McLaren was always considered out of their league. The small and demure girl with her blonde hair braided into two French braids was considered very attractive by all who beheld her. Although she had been approached by the self-proclaimed "popular" clique, Brittany would have nothing to do with them and chose to focus on progressing herself through learning and discipline rather than relying on her looks. She was in a class all her own. But still, her class didn't belong on the dumpster side of the cafeteria.

As if driven on by the awkward silence and stares, she continued. "Look, Eddie, I just wanted to say it was wrong that you got kicked out for what happened in Myerhoff's class today. I saw the whole thing and thought it was really brave of you to stand up to Zack like that."

Westley, being the more sensible of the two, regained his senses first and attempted to bring his friend back to life by giving him a nudge to answer. When that didn't work, Westley gave a quick and painful elbow to the ribs. Edward coughed as if to clear his throat.

"That guy's all talk. I'm sure anyone would've done the same in my shoes." As soon as the words left his mouth, he cringed. What was he thinking? What if someone heard, and it got back to Zack? He tried to swallow the bile that rose in his throat.

"Well," Brittany continued, "I'm glad to see that you won't let him push you around."

When Edward didn't answer, Westley came to his aid again. "Ah, yeah, that's Eddie. He won't take crap from anyone. You should've seen him this one time when I couldn't find my cat, and my neighbor was looking all suspicious—"

Edward was jerked from his stupor at Westley's words and finally regained his senses. "What he means to say," he said, nudging his friend equally as hard, "is thanks for telling me. Makes me feel like today didn't suck as bad as I thought." Edward gave a nervous laugh.

Brittany smiled. The sight of that smile melted Edward until he was once again incoherent.

"Well, I hope the rest of your day gets better." Brittany bit her bottom lip, covering her smile, and Edward felt as if the world had just been deprived of something wonderful.

Westley, noticing that Edward was lost again, tried to keep the conversation going. "I hope so too! I mean, it *is* his birthday, after all!"

"It's your birthday?" Brittany said in surprise. "That sucks you had to be in school for it, but I'm sure you can make the best of it."

Just the fact she had decided to talk to him made this the best birthday ever. Still stupefied, however, all he managed to get out was a dreamy, "Yeah."

"Well, I gotta go, but I'll see you around?" she said.

"Yeah." He sighed again, staring mesmerized through drooping eyelids.

"Awesome. Happy birthday, Eddie!" The color rushed to her cheeks, making Edward even more caught up in her beauty. He couldn't help but continue to gape as she turned and walked away.

The two friends watched until she was out of sight. Edwards's heart beat so hard and fast that he felt its rhythm in his ears. Brittany McLaren had talked to *him*. She'd wished him a happy birthday. It *was* a happy birthday! He was swiftly brought back to his senses by a sharp pain on the back of his head and realized Westley had smacked him.

"Ow! What was that for?"

"Snap out of it. If she catches you staring at her like that, she's gonna think you're a major perv. Also, what the hell is wrong with you?"

Edward stared at him, confused. "What do you mean?"

"She's into you, bro! You should've said something to try and keep her talking."

"You're crazy."

"*I'm* crazy? She came all the way over here just to talk to you, and all you could do was say 'yeah' and stare at her like you'd never seen a girl before. Then you let her go without even trying anything!"

"Like what?"

Westley smacked his hand to his forehead. "I don't know; ask her about herself, let her know you're interested too, see if she might want to hang out sometime, maybe even ask for *her number*." He pronounced the last words as if he was referring to the holy grail.

"Yeah, right. Like someone like her is gonna give me"—he gestured to his large frame with an up-and-down sweeping motion—"their number."

"Stranger things have happened."

"Oh yeah? Like what?"

"She called *you* brave."

The wide grin on Westley's face drew out a hearty laugh from Edward.

Westley joined in. "Dude, just promise me if you ever get another chance, you'll *try* to talk to her. Live like the Frizz, man: 'Take chances, make mistakes, GET MESSY!'"

"Did you seriously just quote *Magic School Bus*?"

"Hey, just 'cause it came from a cartoon doesn't mean it's bad advice!"

Edward, thinking he'd sooner get an apology from Zack before getting to talk to Brittany McLaren again, just smiled. "Fine. *If* I get another chance, I'll try." Then he considered his words, and beads of sweat sprang up on his palms as he realized he meant them.

Chapter 2
PRIDE AND JOY

Edward enjoyed his last two classes. Both seemed to fly by with the memory of lunch playing over and over again in his mind. After the final bell, his feet, out of habit, started him toward his bike, but for all the attention Edward paid, he could've been walking to the moon. His head was so far in the clouds that he didn't notice the three boys walking toward him. By the time he saw their shadows bearing down upon him, it was too late.

Edward stopped dead in his tracks.

There in front of him were none other than Zack Roe and his two cronies: Brent Wheaton and Cory Mar. All three were on a school sports team of some kind or other. Peach Creek was a small town, and they had all grown up with one another. Edward and Cory were even friends once, but ever since the boys had started adolescence, the two had grown apart, and eventually, Zack and Cory had become buddies. After that, Cory acted as if he never knew Edward, and not only turned a blind eye to Zack's bullying but also jumped in whenever told.

Before Edward knew it, the three surrounded him. He looked around frantically in hope of seeing a teacher.

Not a single soul in sight.

Trying to keep a calm voice, he said, "What?"

Brent's low, scratchy voice said, "Oh, look. Dalton's got a spine after all." His face cracked into a malevolent grin.

Zack started to circle Edward as the other two smirked and chortled. "I don't like being disrespected. 'Specially not by a fat-ass like you."

"How have *I* disrespected *you?*"

Brent, usually more of the silent, stupid type, surprised Edward by chiming in once more with, "You got him kicked outta class!"

Edward knew there was no arguing with stupid and that they were just looking for an excuse, *any* excuse, to cause a problem, so he kept silent, waiting to see how this scene would play out.

Without warning, a sudden pain exploded in Edward's lower back where Zack kicked him, and his legs gave out. Edward was left on all fours in front of his attackers, gasping in pain.

Zack knelt to get closer to his ear. "Why?"

Why what? Edward thought, still trying to grasp the entirety of his situation.

"Why," Zack continued, "are you still around? Hmm? No one likes you. How is it that you can get up and lug that tub of lard you call an ass into public where the rest of us are forced to look at it? For years, I've had to put up with your stupid, fat face. Occasionally, I try to help by giving you a lesson." He punctuated this point by hitting Edward square in the jaw. "Hoping you'd be inspired and either lose some weight or just go away, but you just *can't* take the hint."

Zack stopped directly in front of Edward, lifted his already-swelling face with his hand, and made him look into his eyes.

"How can you go on living knowing that everyone hates you? Why don't you do the world a favor and just kill yourself?" he said, almost quietly enough to be just between the two of them.

Brent, after seeing Zack get two licks in, decided he didn't want to be left out of the fun, so he came in and kicked Edward as hard as he could in his left side. Edward gasped for breath in between painful dry heaves.

Zack continued to speak, but his voice was just a buzzing, white noise to Edward. When Edward finally gained enough control over his breathing to feel like he wasn't going to suffocate, he looked up at Cory, silently pleading for help. Cory wouldn't look at him; instead, he looked down at the ground in disgust.

Zack saw where Edward was looking and said, "Hey!" Cory looked up immediately into Zack's face. "You just gonna stand there all day?!"

Cory fixed his gaze upon the eyes of his old friend, and with a look that was half disgust, half hatred, he punched Edward's eye as if to silence its pleas for help.

Edward lost hope. Every muscle went slack as he resigned himself to the beating. His body felt as if it was on fire. The side of his lip and his eye began to swell even more. A warm trickle of blood fell down his face from a cut by one eye, and tears fell from the other.

Just then, a curious thing happened. Edward began to feel cold. His ears weren't working right, but their sense was starting to return as he heard and felt a loud whooshing sound. At first, he thought he was going blind. He looked around to see his frame of vision being enveloped by a large, white cloud.

Edward was not waiting at his bike when school got out for the day. Something was wrong; Westley was sure of it. He walked toward where Edward's last class was and stumbled upon the three jocks cornering his best friend. Once he saw the first blow, a powerful need overtook him, and he knew he had to do something.

He looked all around and saw no one. His eyes frantically searched for something, *anything*, to help. That's when he saw it: Hanging on the wall next to a classroom door was a large, dry-chemical fire extinguisher.

A moment's thought was spared to the idea that he might be suspended or even expelled, but this was an emergency, and he didn't see much of an option. In the time it took for Westley to formulate a plan, Edward ended up gasping on all fours, trying to dislodge remnants of lunch from his throat. Westley ripped the red tank out of its box on the wall and ran as fast as he could toward the bullies, yanking the pin out as he went.

When he was close enough, he pointed the nozzle toward all four of them, took a deep breath, and clamped down hard on the trigger, spraying all around to spread confusion and disorientation. Once he released all its contents, Westley dropped the empty tank on the ground, got Edward to his feet, and dragged him off as fast as he could.

Even in the chaos of coughing and choking, Edward recognized his chance of escape and allowed Westley to pull him away.

At the end of the schoolyard was a steep, grass-covered hill about twenty feet above the level yard and just before the main road. Normally, the students would walk down this hill to get to the street, but Westley, wanting to get as much distance between them and their attackers as he could, threw himself down the slope, pulling Edward to the ground, and they both tumbled down. Two masses of flailing limbs and backpacks went spiraling down toward the street.

When the two reached level ground, they stopped. More than a little wobbly, they found their way to their feet to see the three bullies starting to run down the hill. They were in no condition to run from Zack's crew, so they opted for the safety of the gas station across the street.

It was a well-known fact to all the students who visited Abe Wilkins's shop after school that he was a no-nonsense old man whom pretty much everyone suspected of being crazy. Everyone knew he kept a double-barrel under the front counter because he would often mention it as a warning to those he felt had sticky fingers. It was said he even pulled it out from time to time to remind folks he had it. Westley was hoping today would be one of those days.

Mr. Wilkins, startled by the sudden jerking open of his front door, immediately knitted his face into his signature scowl. The look was aided by the large wrinkles piling up on top of his brow all the way up his balding head, which was accentuated by small wisps of white hair on the sides. He was just beginning to open his mouth to lecture the two for their conduct when they immediately started to babble out story.

"Whoa, whoa, whoa there, fellas; slow down. One of you take a breath and tell me what you need to tell me."

Westley explained what was going on while Edward waited near the door to see if the three would enter. He needn't have worried. It *was* well known what one could expect from Mr. Wilkins, and none of the other three dared enter the shop once Westley and Edward had made it inside.

Edward jumped as his pocket vibrated. He pulled his small brick of a phone out and saw *Dad* on the screen.

"Hello?" he said tentatively.

The voice on the other end was so loud that it rang out into the store. "Eddie, where are you? I waited by the car for twenty minutes, then I went to check the bike rack at the school. What happened to your tires?"

"Look, Dad, I just ran into a bit of trouble—"

"Are you okay?"

"Yeah. Can you just come get me?"

"Where are you?"

When Edward got into his car, Steve Dalton immediately noticed the grass stains and blood his son was covered in. His eye and lip were swollen and beginning to turn purple.

"What the hell happened?"

Edward's face contorted as if deciding how much he wanted to tell. "I was trying to get away from a couple of bullies, and I fell down the hill over there."

"Are you all right?"

Again, it looked like Edward was choosing his words carefully. "I'll be fine. Can we just go to Steely Phil's?"

"Son, I don't think you're in any state to go anywhere except for home or the hospital."

"I know, but can we go, please? I just think it'll help get my mind off of"—Edward paused as if he'd almost said too much—"things."

Steve looked at his son with pity. He'd never been bullied, but he'd definitely seen and done his share. Maybe life was getting back at him for having partaken when he was in school by forcing him to watch his son go through it and not being able to do a damn thing about it. He did pity him, but he also felt a pang of pride in his son for not wanting to let it get the better of him. It was his birthday, after all, and there was still the surprise waiting for him at home. A surprise Steve was sure would overshadow any bad memories this birthday was trying to leave Edward with.

He shook his head slightly as the ghost of a smile crept onto his face. "All right, Steely Phil's it is." He started the engine, and they made their way as quickly as possible to their favorite restaurant.

Steely Phil's was the best barbecue the two had ever come across, and they visited every chance they got. Steve didn't pester his son to tell him any more about what had happened, and Edward didn't offer. Instead, they sat in silence as they ate clear to bursting.

"I'm sorry your birthday didn't turn out as you planned," Steve said on the drive home.

Edward let out a small *humph*. "Yeah, it was a bit rough, but it did have its high points."

"Well, just remember that life has many things in store. Who knows; some things might even be so good, you didn't even think them possible before they happened." Steve kept his eyes on the road, but a smile crept onto his lips. He couldn't change what had happened earlier in the day, but his surprise might be able to make Edward forget it. "You're growing up fast, and I'm proud of the man you're becoming. I just wish your mom could've been here to see it."

Edward tensed and didn't say anything. He always got that way when talking about his mother. Cancer was a bitch. Edward and Steve never really talked about anything well except for cars. That seemed to be the one thing Edward had inherited from him.

As they pulled into the driveway, Edward let out a small groan. "Dad, we left my bike at school. Could we go to Wally World to grab some tires and go get it?"

"Son, I don't know about you, but I'm full and tired. Let's just get home for a bit, and if you feel you need to, you can borrow my car and go grab them yourself."

Edward sighed. "Okay."

Steve tried to suppress his laugh. Edward was in for the surprise of his life. Steve put the car into park and looked over at his son.

"You mind opening the garage?" he said.

They always went through the garage to get into the house, but this request was odd, and a puzzled look furrowed Edward's brow.

"What's the matter; you got a broken finger?"

"Never mind the sass, boy. Would you just push the button, please?" Steve took the clicker down from the sunshade and handed it over.

Edward, with one eyebrow cocked, took it. He pressed the button, and fluorescent light flooded out from under the door as it slowly rose upward.

Just as the object inside began to take shape, Steve said, "Happy birthday, Eddie."

The door came to a halt, revealing the all-American muscle of a 1971 Chevrolet Corvette. The sleek, long-nosed two-seater was silver-gray with chrome accents around the bumpers.

Edward sat still for a moment before slowly opening his door and circling the car. He ran his fingers up and down the sleek lines and gentle curves as if trying to convince himself it was real.

"Eddie!" Steve said, jerking Edward out of his trance.

Edward looked up to see Steve toss something at him. A glint of flashing metal arced its way through the air. Edward reached out and caught it, then stared down at the keys lying flat in his palm. He looked up, stupefied. "How . . ." was all he got out.

"Well, a couple of things. I've been saving up for this for quite some time, and Mr. Dobson from across town was planning on selling it and owed me a favor, so I got a *really* good deal. Now, I know it looks shiny and new, but it has its original engine. It runs, but it definitely needs to be replaced. I was thinking you and I could get an upgrade for it and install it together. Whatcha say?"

Tears welled up in Edward's eyes. "That sounds perfect, Dad." He walked toward Steve and gave him the biggest hug he'd given in years. "Best birthday ever!"

"Just remember, this is also your graduation present. I can't exactly top this." He gave a small chuckle that sprang from the deep pain in his wallet.

"Understood! Can I give it a try?"

"It's yours, ain't it? Besides, you're gonna need to get used to it if you're gonna drive it to school tomorrow."

Edward's attention turned back to the car. "Why's that?"

"Take a look in the cockpit."

Edward made his way over to the driver's side door and opened it. The black leather and the wooden accents making up the interior, although clean and vibrant, bore the unmistakable signs of a well-used car. In the middle of the two bucket seats was a four-speed manual gearshift.

Steve had taught him how to drive stick, but he'd barely gotten the hang of it. Now, Edward hopped in the driver's seat, running his hands all over as if still trying to convince himself this wasn't a dream. He placed the key in the ignition and twisted it. The whole car gave a lurch forward, then died and sank back. Steve, realizing what had happened, laughed.

"You know what you did?"

"Yeah," Edward answered sheepishly. He took the stick out of gear and let it hover in neutral. Then he placed his foot on the break and once more turned the key. This time, the engine roared to life. Steve nodded approvingly as he shut the door for his son. He knocked on the window, and Edward grabbed the lever to roll it down.

Steve leaned down through the window to point out the mechanism to turn on the headlights, and Edward activated them. Where there was only a smooth hood before, two squares popped up and illuminated the world outside the garage.

"It's getting late, and this is an unfamiliar car, Eddie. I want you to stay close to the house tonight, okay? She may not have a lot of muscle in the engine right now, but she's a beast, so be careful. She also burns a lot of fuel, so keep an eye on the gauge."

Edward looked up at his father, waiting for more. Steve had so much more he should've shared, but tonight, that was enough. Let the boy go have his fun. He smiled, jerked his head sideways toward the open garage, and said, "Go on, get outta here."

———

Edward had texted Westley the night before to tell him he got a car for his birthday and had offered to pick him up for school. Now, as Westley waited on the street in front of his house, he couldn't help but wonder what type of car Eddie had gotten. A truck, or maybe his dad had turned over the family sedan and gotten himself a new car instead. Whatever he was expecting, it certainly wasn't a sports car. He stared in amazement as the Corvette made its way down his street and stopped in front of him.

Edward got out and looked over the roof. "She's a beaut, ain't she?"

Westley shook his head to clear it, jostling his thick-framed glasses. He took them off, wiped the lenses, and put them back on as if this would reveal a much humbler car, but the Corvette remained unchanged.

"No way. No freaking way!"

A large grin stretched over Edward's face, and he bounced with an excitement that Westley felt. "I know, right?!"

"How the . . . Where did . . . Who'd you have to . . . How?!"

Edward explained, and Westley just stared, open-mouthed, trying to comprehend it all.

"Man . . . I wish my dad was that cool."

"Yeah, he's great, ain't he? Now c'mon, we gotta get going, or we're gonna be late!"

"Dude, it's right down the street."

Edward did his best impression of their favorite animated show and said, "LET'S GO ALREADY!"

Westley laughed and got in. When they pulled into the school lot, every head, every face, every eye followed the Corvette's progress. All who saw it couldn't help but admire its beauty. Even Zack, who was hanging out by his 1986 A70 Toyota Supra, couldn't help but stare.

The shock of seeing the car itself was nothing compared to the reaction people had when they saw Westley and Edward emerge. A few people made comments to Edward, telling him how nice his car was, and some even said they were jealous. Many, however, just kept silent and inwardly painted themselves green.

Word of Edward's Corvette spread like wildfire throughout the school, and people who grew up with him, but had never said two words to him, were suddenly complimenting him on it.

Later on, Edward and Westley sat at their usual table, enjoying their lunch. A new video game trailer had dropped recently, and they were discussing the future prospects of the game when it came out the following September when once again, they were blissfully sidetracked.

"Hey, Eddie! Hey, Westley!"

It was Brittany McLaren again, her bright blonde hair down and flowing in the breeze. This time, Edward found his voice before any prodding was needed.

"Hi, Brittany! How you doing?"

"Horrible," she groaned. "I'm pretty sure I just failed my AP Calc test. I swear Mr. Michelle is the worst teacher in the world."

"That sucks," Westley said.

"It really does. It's a wonder anyone passes his class."

"I'm sure you've got it in the bag, Britt," Edward said, trying to cheer her up.

Her blush was alluring. "Thanks. I hope you're right. I've never had a class so frustrating. Anyway, I heard about your car. Congrats; that's awesome!"

Edward's face grew hot. "Thanks! My dad and I are really into cars, and I guess he decided he was gonna go all out for my eighteenth-slash-graduation."

"That's so sick."

Edward blushed even harder.

Thankfully, Brittany didn't seem to notice or care. "What type of car is it?" she asked.

"It's an old one, a 1971 Chevy Corvette."

"I thought cars like that were called 'classic,' not 'old,'" she replied, smiling.

Edward was pretty sure that she couldn't get any more perfect, and neither could today, until she added, "I'd love to see it sometime, if I could."

Edward felt as if he'd been whacked in the back of the head. His entire body quaked with nerves. Brittany McLaren wanted to see his car.

"Um, sure. You could pop by the parking lot after school . . . if you want."

"I'd like that. I'll meet you by the stairs after class, 'kay?"

He swallowed. "Yeah, sounds good."

"Great! I can't wait!" Her bright smile spread wide across her face before she quickly turned and walked away.

The duo once again stared, dumbfounded at what had just taken place. Westley recovered himself first. He punched Edward's shoulder softly.

"Way to go, man. You are so in."

Edward's face changed alarmingly fast from beet red to a pale, rancid green.

"I think . . . I think I'm gonna throw up."

"Don't be so dramatic. You're gonna be fine."

"What if I can't think of anything to say?"

"Honestly? I was surprised at how well you did just now. I don't know what well you tapped, but do it again."

Edward was filled with half dread, half elation. The dread made him plead with his best friend.

"You'll be there, right?"

"Not a chance." Westley grinned at him. "Trust me; this is good. This is your chance."

"I know it is, but I feel like my lunch melted down into a lead weight."

Westley laughed hard. "That's normal!" And he slapped him on the back.

The next hours flew by. Once the final bell rang, Edward started on his way to the stairs that led to the student parking lot. His body felt like it was filled with butterflies, yet his feet were like lead. He didn't know if he was walking to an adventure or an execution.

When the stairs came into view, his heart skipped a beat. There she was, sitting on the wall, looking down into one of her textbooks. Her golden hair fell in a sheet on one side and was elegantly tucked behind her ear on the other. Edward knew he wasn't in the best shape and vaguely wondered if all he was feeling might be signs of a heart attack, but he decided this was too important to give up now and pressed on until he got right up in front of her.

"Hi!" he said, trying in vain to keep the nervous quake out of his voice.

Brittany looked up from her book and smiled. "Hey, Eddie! How were your classes?"

He stopped to think about this. The truth was he had no idea because he couldn't remember a thing about them. Actually, now that he came to think about it, he couldn't remember anything other than the reason why he was here.

"They were all right. Nothing super memorable." Which was perfectly true. "You?"

"A lot better than grading that stupid test, thank God. But yeah, I guess nothing special either." She gave a small, nervous laugh. "So, where's this famous car of yours?"

Edward felt another blow to the head as he remembered his car in a sudden rush. "Oh yeah. I'll show you."

Brittany hastily closed her book, shoved it in her bag, and placed one strap over her shoulder as she got up. He waited until she was next to him, and they walked side by side through the parking lot, not noticing the looks they were getting.

When they finally got to the Corvette, Edward swelled with pride. "Welp, there she is!"

Brittany took one look and said, "Whoa!" She walked all around it, taking in every aspect as the lot emptied itself of students.

Edward just watched her in silence, marveling at his luck not only to have what he reckoned was the coolest car in school but also to talk with the prettiest girl, and now the two had come together.

He was suddenly struck with inspiration. "Do you want to see inside?" he said as he rushed forward with the keys. He opened both doors, and Brittany moved her ogling to the interior.

Within a few seconds, she saw the gearshift and popped her head up to look at him.

"You can drive stick?!"

"Uh, yeah, my dad taught me."

"Your dad seems really cool! I wish I knew how."

Edward seemed to have lost the filter that checked his words before they passed his lips, because he sputtered out, "Maybe I could teach you sometime."

To his surprise, her face lit up. "Really? I'd love that!"

Emboldened by his success, he decided to press his luck. "Sure! Would you like to go for a ride? We can probably find an empty lot somewhere and start right now."

Her face fell the tiniest fraction. "That'd be awesome, but I gotta check with my dad. He's usually pretty cool about things, but he wants me to ask him first."

"No problem," he said, forcing a smile, but he couldn't help but feel a little downhearted that she'd said no.

A little of what he was feeling might have shown in his face, because she said, "I'll check with him tonight and get back to you about it tomorrow. Sound good?"

His heart soared once again, though he wasn't sure he could wait for tomorrow. "Yeah, that works." His face beamed.

Brittany continued looking around the car, and then, to his astonishment, she got in the passenger side and sat down, leaving the door wide open, dangling one leg out and resting her foot on the asphalt. In a bold move, Edward decided to do likewise in the driver's seat. He wasn't sure where he got the nerve; maybe it was the car, maybe it was the soft tilt of Brittany's lips when she looked at him, but whatever it was, soon he was sitting next to her, and it felt right.

Neither of them spoke for a minute, but then Brittany broke the silence.

"Hey, Eddie?"

The tone in her voice had changed from car enthusiast to something more solemn. *This is it*, he thought. The moment everything would come crashing down.

"Yeah?" he said nervously.

"Are you gonna go to prom on Friday?"

"I'm not sure," he said, not at all having expected the change of topic. "I thought I might go. I mean, it is the last school dance we'll ever be able to go to, isn't it?"

"Exactly what I was thinking. This is the last chance for us"—she tripped over her words and said the next part really fast—"to do a lot of things before heading off to college and stuff. You should definitely go."

Edward's mind felt like Jell-O again, and all he could utter was a dreamy, "Okay. Will I see you there, then?"

"Actually . . . I was sort of wondering . . . like . . . Would you maybe want to go to the dance . . . *with* me?" Her face immediately turned bright red, and she looked anywhere but at him.

Edward, meanwhile, tried to make sense of what she'd just said. Did she just actually ask him out? Like, on a date?

He must have taken too long in answering because Brittany started to get up.

"It's fine if you don't want to. Just thought I'd ask. Thought it'd be nice, you know . . ."

A little voice at the back of his brain started shouting at him to hurry up and say something. Without his brain fully working again, he said, "I'd . . . I'd love to!"

Brittany gave a quick huff of relief, as if in shock that he'd said yes. "Really?"

"Absolutely!"

"Great!" She smiled her brightest smile yet and stared straight into his eyes, as if lost there.

After a few seconds, Edward asked, "What?"

She gave a little jump. "Nothing. I was just looking at your eyes. I don't think I've ever seen that shade of blue in eyes before. They're so pretty." She gave a nervous chuckle.

Edward, taken aback, laughed. "My mom used to tell me they were my best feature—said I could stare right into your soul." He laughed again, as if dismissing what he'd said.

"She was right." Blood crept back into Brittany's face, but Edward was certain all the blood had drained from him. Had this just happened? He wished he could really see into her soul to know what she was thinking, but his boldness had reached its limit.

"Well, I'd better get going," she said.

She rummaged in her bag and pulled out a notebook. She opened it up to a blank page and hastily scribbled something, then tore off a small slip and folded it.

"Here's my number. Send me a text later so I have yours, and we can plan for Friday."

He took it and held it like it was a gift from the heavens themselves. "Sure."

"I'll talk to you later, Eddie." She got up, still smiling, slung her bag over her shoulder, and started on her way home.

Edward sat there, dazed. The scene that'd just transpired played over and over again in his head, and each time, he felt more and more like it had happened to someone other than himself. Then, as if slowly awakening from a dream, he felt something in his right hand. He looked down to see the little piece of paper and unfolded it.

Here was the proof that yes, it'd been real. She'd even dotted her *i* with a heart. Edward's heart soared.

The following day, while Edward, Westley, and Brittany ate their lunches and enjoyed each other's company, another trio sat shaded from their view at a table under the overhang of the cafeteria. This trio could see them perfectly and were paying close attention to the scene acted out before them by the fat kid, the twiglike four-eyes, and, to their astonishment, Brittany McLaren.

"Look at that," Zack said to Brent and Cory, thrusting his chiseled jaw toward the unbelievable sight. "Who the hell does he think he is? It's one thing hanging out with that skinny freak, but where does he get off thinking he's got the balls to talk to any girl, let alone her?"

Cory felt like he could guess at what was going on behind Zack's scowl. Truth be told, Zack had always had a crush on Brittany, but despite many attempts to get her to join their group, she constantly rebuffed his advances, making him only want her more. Now she was talking to Chubby Fat-Ass. The sight of him alone was enough to make Zack see red, especially after what he and the skinny freak had done on Monday, but those two in the company of Brittany sent him into a fit of anger he couldn't stand.

Brent chimed in to try and cheer Zack up. "She's always signing up for those charity events, yeah? Maybe the freaks are her next project."

This got a small chuckle from Zack, but he shrugged it off. "She's probably only talking to him because of his car."

Cory nodded. "Yeah, you gotta admit, it *is* pretty nice!"

"I don't gotta admit anything!" Zack snapped. "Still, it's a shame that a car like that should be in the hands of a fat-ass loser."

"Agreed," Brent said while Cory nodded.

Something started to nag Zack. "Corey, take a pic of them and send it to Sara. Ask if she's heard anything about why Brittany McLaren is sitting at the reject table."

Cory reached into his pocket and pulled out his phone. He snapped a picture and quickly sent it to his twin sister. A soft ping came from his phone seconds later.

"Sara says, 'Lauren overheard Brittany talking to her friend Steph and says that she and Edward are going to Prom on Friday.'"

Zack looked like he was choking on his own vomit.

Smiling, Brent added, "That is disturbing."

"Yeah," chimed Cory. "Somebody ought to do something about that."

"No." Zack slammed his hand down on the table, causing everything on it and the people surrounding to jump. "Not *somebody*. *We* need to do something about it."

It felt like the temperature dropped instantly. Cory had only meant it as a joke, but the look that took over Zack's face made his own drain of color. He looked at Brent, neither of them daring to speak for a moment.

Finally, Brent asked, "Are we gonna get back at him for Monday? Give him the beating he deserves?"

"That is exactly what we are going to do." Zack's words were crisp and final. They hung in the air, waiting for the other boys to contradict them. They didn't.

Cory, who had forgotten to breathe, took in a gulp of air. "What did you have in mind?"

"We need to find a way to keep him from getting to the dance."

Brent laughed. "We could tie him up somewhere."

Zack smiled. "Yeah. Take him to the trees at the edge of the football field and leave him there until after the dance. The gym is far enough away, no one will hear his cries."

"Sounds good," Cory said, relaxing at the idea of a harmless prank.

"Yeah, I like it!" Brent grinned ear to ear.

"Plus," Zack added, the evil glint in his eye turning to a more mischievous flicker, "Brittany will think he stood her up. I'll have to save the day. And we'll be sparing everyone the sight of Fatso being at the dance while bringing Brittany McLaren back into the light and saving her reputation. We'll be big damn heroes!"

The tension in the air lightened as the three were spurred into fits of laughter.

Chapter 3

EDDIE TAKES THE FALL

On Friday night, Edward outdid himself with his attention to detail. Everything was perfect, from the all-black suit with the lone shimmer of a silver belt buckle and two spurts of white that were his tie and pocket handkerchief to the corsage he'd picked up earlier at the local florist. He'd even taken extra care to trim and clean his nails, slipping the clippers into his pocket just in case the grime found its way back under the tips as it so often did. He folded his coat in one hand as he said good night to his father and walked out to his car.

The sky was dark, but the warm glow of the garage door lamp spilled out onto the driveway. Edward opened the driver's side door, bent inside, and placed his jacket on the passenger seat, then jammed the key in the ignition. He was just about to sit down when a voice came out of the darkness.

"I'm surprised you can even fit in that thing."

Edward's head jerked up and smacked the ceiling. He reached his hand up, trying to soothe the throbbing that shot outward. A cold chill ran down his spine and froze his hand as he realized who owned that voice. He steeled his nerves to prepare for what was coming.

Like something out of a horror movie, Zack walked from the darkness and into the light, as if materializing out of thin air.

Edward tried to control the tremors wracking his body. "What do you want, Zack?"

"We have some unfinished business."

Edward stepped forward toward Zack and away from his car. It was a mistake. As soon as he cleared his car door, Brent and Cory appeared from either side from behind Edward, each grabbing an arm and forcing it behind his back.

"So, what's the story here, Fats? You get a semi-decent car, and all of a sudden, you think you're hot shit?"

Zack slammed his fist straight into Edward's gut. The blow knocked the wind out of him, and he would have slumped forward if not for the two holding him up.

Edward stood there, head spinning, gasping for air. He felt like he was going to puke but couldn't.

Zack had something in his hands. It wasn't a rope, but it was long and thin like one. The eye of a large, metal tie-down hook stared threateningly up at him. Something clicked in his head, and he understood not only what it was but also what they were going to do with it.

Without thinking, he raised up his right leg and stomped down as hard as he could on Cory's foot. Then he dipped his head forward and brought it up and back hard into Brent's face. He felt the crunch of Brent's nose, and the pain from smacking his head earlier reignited.

The moves had done their job, and both cronies let go. Edward pushed Brent hard and jumped backward to reach his car. Zack was frazzled for just a second, but that was all Edward needed to get in and slam the door. Zack ran forward to grab the handle, but it was too late. The engine roared to life, and the car peeled out.

Edward felt a thrill of excitement at getting away, but as the seconds caught up to him, panic crept into his brain. His head replayed the last few moments, and he suddenly realized he was driving. It took even longer for him to recognize where he was. Then he saw two headlights in the rearview whip around a corner and swell in size. Unreality washed over him for a second. This couldn't be happening. Were they really following him?

He looked around, pleading to find a way out. To his right was the turnoff for a little-used road that had many twists, turns, and junctions. If he could just get far enough ahead, he might be able to give them the slip. He took the turn.

With no surprise, he saw them follow. Something about this particular turn cemented the situation in his mind. Fuel drenched the already roaring flames of panic. What if they caught up with him? What would they do to him?

Aside from the road immediately in front of him, the world was black, and behind him was a pair of yellow eyes getting ready to pounce. Edward remembered his brights and immediately flashed them on, but the bulbs were so old that they did next to nothing. He only saw glimpses of the world outside as he pushed his car to go faster. He still hadn't mastered driving stick, and the constant twists and turns caused him to switch gears back and forth.

Every time he saw a quick turn, he'd take it in hopes that they might accidentally speed past, but Zack seemed to know what he was doing and kept right on after him.

After what seemed like hours but may have been only minutes, the road straightened out for just long enough to let Zack come up and take a bite out of Edward's backside. It was little more than a tap, but it was enough for a bolt of terror to seize Edward and almost cause him to overcorrect.

Were they insane? They were trying to run him off the road.

Edward's iron grip tightened to the point where he was in danger of breaking the steering wheel or shift knob clean off. On and on, the two pools of light twisted down the road, a strange game of firefly tag. Try as Edward might to distance himself, Zack stayed right on him. Despite all the turns, he was just too fast for Edward's inexperience and lesser horsepower.

As fatigue set in, Edward's right shoulder burned, both legs shook violently, and what little skill he had began to leave him. Zack started toying with him, pulling up next to him as if he was going to pass but never going farther than window-to-window. Once, Edward chanced a glance over and saw all three either laughing or flipping him off. He decided after that to keep his eyes on what was in front of him.

Zack got bolder and bolder as time and scenery flew by. He forced his way over until Edward's right side was on nothing but gravel and had only inches between his passenger side door and the trees whipping by at an alarming rate. When Edward couldn't go off any farther, Zack didn't press but held his position until he finally allowed him back on the road, but something grew, and Edward could feel it. After a while, Zack backed off of Edward just enough to get his front bumper in line with Edward's rear. He eased his front over until it was touching the other car, then he increased the pressure, trying to take Edward's back out from behind him. This caused Edward to swerve until contact was broken. Zack struggled to regain control of his own car, while Edward was able to pull out and keep driving.

Zack pulled out of the swerve and made his way back up to Edward's tail. This time, Zack waited until there was a sharp curve in the road to start pushing Edward's back out. Once the Corvette started to swerve, Edward had no chance of correcting in time and slammed on his brakes.

Edward tried to regain control, but it was no use. His car lost contact with the pavement and slammed face-first into one of the numerous trees that encased the road. The impact was swift. He never lost consciousness, but when he saw the tree coming, he clenched his eyes shut as if doing so could protect him. When he realized he'd stopped, he opened his eyes. The front of the silver hulk had crumpled around the tree. His focus came in closer, and he saw the dashboard had come inward, and the steering wheel was now much closer to his face. He had just enough time to reflect that he supposed there were no airbags while his hand found his stinging right eye and came away bloody.

As his brain started working again, he first gave thanks that the car had so much nose to go through to help cushion his impact. Then a small burst of panic worked its way in when he saw the headlights behind him. He started to remember all that had happened and felt the need to get out of the car immediately. He found the handle, and to his relief, the door swung easily outward.

His shaking leg somehow made its way out of the cab and onto the ground. The sound of car doors opening caused a fresh pump of adrenaline. He had to keep moving—what were they going to do if they caught him? He knew they were awful, but this was a whole other level. He was certain all humanity had flown out the window.

He was able to pull himself to his feet, but he immediately collapsed. Clutching the swinging door for support, he pulled himself upright. He looked back toward the blinding headlights of the other car, and movement stirred as shadows appeared in front of them. Edward started to put weight on his legs and found he was able to stand. The surrounding forest felt like his best means of escape.

He took one last look at the mangled mess that had been his pride and joy just moments ago, then tore himself away and shambled off into the trees.

"Where do you think you're going?" Zack called. "Come back here, and we can finish this." He paused for a moment to give Edward a chance to answer. "This is stupid, Fats. We're gonna catch you. You might as well turn and face me."

With each step Edward took, he felt heavier. As much as he hated to admit it, Zack was right. Where could he go? He chanced a look back to see that he hadn't gone more than a few yards into the tree line. The world was illuminated by the broken streams of Zack's headlights.

Edward continued to walk away from the road until his back found a tree, and he leaned into it to keep himself standing. He looked at the shadowy figures making their way toward him. His face was bathed in light and blood, which continued to stream down the side of his face.

"Why? Why are you doing this to me? What did I ever do to you to deserve this?"

"You exist," Zack said simply.

Brent and Cory looked at each other. Edward felt for a moment that they would finally come to their senses and talk Zack down, but they remained silent.

Zack continued to make his way toward him, so Edward moved away from the tree and began to walk backward.

"Look, if you just go, I promise I won't tell anyone about this. I'll even find my own way back into town. Just please, for once in your life, *leave me alone!*"

Zack paused to consider this, then once more began to creep forward. Edward did all he could to stay out of reach.

"Think about what you're doing, Zack! I can't just 'go missing.' People are gonna ask questions. You'll go to jail. You'll—"

What exactly would happen to Zack, Edward couldn't say. He'd taken one step too far, and his heel found nothing but air. Edward fell backward off a drop in the forest, then sank into the trees below and out of sight.

⌐══▷

Zack looked over the edge of the steep slope into the darkness and trees beyond with an odd smirk on his face.

"That didn't just happen. That did not just happen." Cory's hand found his mouth and chin and rubbed compulsively.

"He just . . . fell. I . . . I can't believe it. What are we gonna do?" Brent asked as he stared wide-eyed at the place Edward had been just moments before.

Cory gripped his hair and tugged frantically. "We gotta go get someone. Maybe they can still do something, you know? Maybe he's just hurt; maybe he's not . . ." He trailed off as if the utterance of the last word would engrave what they'd done in stone.

"You mean, you think he's . . ." Brent also couldn't bring himself to say it. He didn't need to; Zack finished for him, for all of them.

"Dead? I don't think *anyone* could—"

Brent cut him off. "No, he's probably just hurt! Hey, Eddie!" he hollered. They stood silent for a moment. There was no response.

"We have to call someone!" Cory said.

"And tell them what?!" Zack yelled. "'You see, Officer, we were just trying to pull a joke on him. We were chasing this guy down the road, ran him off, and then followed him until he fell off a cliff? Yeah, that'll go over *real* well. They'll go down there, find his body, and next thing you know, you're strapped to a table with a needle in your arm."

"He might not be dead," Cory stammered.

"Oh, and that's better?" A small huff of laughter forced its way out of Zack. "Excuse me, then. No needle; you just get to spend years staring out from behind bars, maybe for the rest of your natural life. That sounds *loads* better."

Pleading crept into Brent's voice. "What should we do?"

Zack turned to look over the drop once more. The silence seemed to stretch for miles.

"*We* don't do anything. I'll drive us back. You two go to the dance and act like nothing happened. I'll take care of this and join up with you later."

"What are you gonna do?" Brent asked with raised eyebrows.

"Don't worry about it. The less you guys know, the better. You just let your pal Zack take care of it, and you never have to worry about a thing." He walked over to Brent and patted him patronizingly on the cheek.

"Then what? Go about the rest of our lives pretending this never happened?" Cory spat.

Zack smiled, and a visible cringe went through the other two. "Exactly." He said it with such utter calm that they were struck dumb. "In fact, I want you to swear that no matter what, you will never speak of this again. I'll take care of everything; all I want back is for you two to swear."

"What about you?" Brent asked.

"I'll start if it makes you feel better." The smile still carved on his face, Zack put his right hand over his heart and raised his flat left hand next to his shoulder as if about to give testimony. "I swear to never speak of what happened tonight ever again, so help me!"

"I swear!" Brent blurted without hesitation.

Cory looked at the two faces now staring at him, both illuminated by the broken light from the headlights. One face smiling, the other slack-jawed and wide-eyed, both looking back at him, waiting.

With no other choice in sight, Cory made his pact with the devil. With a dropped gaze and a voice just audible to the other two, he swore.

Zack drove them home to get dressed and get a move on. He knew what he had to do and didn't want to waste time. Before his house came into view, he was worried about what he might find. His father worked for a towing company that was subcontracted with AAA. Zack's father came home most nights with one of the company trucks on the off chance he'd be called into action. Still, there were nights when he'd bring the beat-up, old Ford pickup home instead. Wouldn't it just be his luck for that to happen tonight? The one time Zack needed the tow truck.

He held his breath, then let out a huge sigh when he saw the large white cab with the blue machinery sticking out the back. Zack pulled up to his double-wide and opened the small screen door slowly to minimize the rusty squeak. Once the first door was open wide enough for him to get behind it, he inserted his key as gently as a burglar picking a lock.

His father had two rituals after arriving home. First, he would sit down to eat the pitiful meal Zack's mom had thrown on the table and yell at her for doing a piss-poor job. After, she would usually knock herself out with the pills she always managed to get her hands on, and his dad would drink himself into oblivion in front of the forty-inch screen they had in the living room. Hopefully, he'd already done so.

Luck seemed to favor the wicked. Zack opened the door and saw nothing of his father but the back of his chair. The kitchen and den were lit by the soft orange glow of the ceiling lamp, and the ever-changing flashes coming from the TV had hypnotized his father.

Zack's way was clear. He crept over to the little counter that protruded from the wall where a long strip of dirty metal on the floor separated the linoleum and the carpet. Once he reached the green Formica counters, he saw the large, full keyring and quietly snatched it up.

The hard part was over. A lightness worked its way into his step as he made his way to the truck, opened the door, and climbed in the cab.

The entire town of Peach Creek rolled up its sidewalks around 8:00 p.m., with the exception of its one saloon and, tonight at least, the high school. Zack was certain no one would see him. Without a care in the world, he made his way back to where they had left the fat-ass's car.

The first, and only, pang of fear came when he thought he forgot exactly where the crash had been. A cold sweat broke out on his forehead, but it vanished immediately when he turned the corner and saw the smashed Corvette in his headlights.

Zack's father had taken him out on the job many times throughout his life. Every time he got suspended, after his father finished working on him with his belt, he wouldn't let Zack stay at home where he could fart around and have himself a grand vacation. Oh, no; Zack would have to accompany his father all day, every day, until he'd served his time. Consequently, Zack had learned all he needed to know about working the controls.

With ease, he was able to pull the car away from the tree and load it up. He drove for as long as he dared away from the spot. He had to get the car far enough away that no amount of searching would lead them to the body. If Edward really had survived the fall, by the time his car was found, he'd be dead for sure. Zack chose a similar tree and did his best to recreate the damage with the crowbar kept under the seat. When he felt it was good enough, he brushed his hands off on his jeans and unloaded the car. He was done with that fat-ass forever. He couldn't help but hum a happy tune as he drove back to town. Life was good.

<hr />

Brittany did her best to enjoy herself at the dance, but mostly she just sat at a table in the corner, her phone bouncing nervously in her hands as she checked and rechecked it for the millionth time. She'd waited for him by the stairs for an hour. With each passing second, her heart had sunk a little further, and after a while, she'd felt embarrassed waiting outside the party for someone who didn't show.

Many thoughts whizzed through her head; some gave plausible explanations, but none offered any comfort. At first, she thought he was just running late, but an hour? What if something had happened to him? But that was crazy; wouldn't he have texted her? Wouldn't he send some sort of notice or explanation if he was interested in her?

And there it was. The doubt in the pit of her stomach: What if he didn't feel the way she felt?

Tears threatened to make an appearance, and she hid her face in her hands. All she wanted to do was go home, but darn it, she didn't want to let anyone keep her from enjoying her prom. She decided to stick it out as best she could, but she still had that gnawing feeling at the back of her mind.

She watched the happy faces out on the dance floor moving to the beat. Multicolored lights and lasers flashed across different styles and moves, none particularly good; it was more just a huge mass of bobbing heads and flailing limbs, all still having a wonderful time.

Brittany looked down at the back of her phone and thought about when she'd first moved to Peach Creek. Her father had moved them out here halfway through her kindergarten year. How she'd cried to let her stay in Atlanta where all her friends were. No amount of tears would change his mind, and she had been forced to change schools and start anew.

On her first day, she wanted to join in with the other kids at recess, but the girls on the swings weren't using them right. They were either barely moving, or worse, just sitting on them and not moving at all. One of them saw her looking and started whispering to her friend, so Brittany turned away quickly.

Other kids were trying to go down a slide, but one of the big kids was sitting at the top, not letting anyone go down. Off in a corner of the sandbox, two kids were digging a hole that looked like it might go all the way down to China.

Brittany's eyes drifted off to the field behind the playground, where some boys were playing catch. Brittany loved baseball; her father would watch the Braves games with her every chance he got.

"Can I play?" she said in as loud a voice as she could.

Everyone stopped dead in their tracks as the ball dropped and lay forgotten on the grass. They stared at the girl in the yellow dress and the unicorn backpack.

"Ew!" one said.

"No girls allowed!" another chimed in.

Brittany felt her face grow hot as one of the boys came up to her.

"Everyone knows girls can't throw. Why don't you go over there with the others and play dollies?"

They all started to laugh.

Tears welled at the corners of her eyes. She shouted, "I don't play dollies," as if this was the biggest insult in the world, but they just kept laughing.

"Look at her stupid pony bag. Why don't you go play catch with it?"

"*You're* stupid!" she shouted as she clutched at her bag, still trying hard not to cry.

It became too much to bear. She turned and stomped off while they just continued to laugh.

She huffed all the way back to the sandbox, tears spilling out now, unable to be contained. Not long after, she felt a hand on her shoulder. She looked up and saw a boy standing there. At first, she prepared herself for another shouting match, but he was smiling.

"Those guys are just stupid," he said.

Brittany smiled at someone else having the exact same thought. She realized this was one of the two boys that had been digging.

"My name's Eddie, and that's Cory over there." He pointed over to the other boy, who was smiling with two missing front teeth. "You wanna come play with us? We only got one shovel, but you can use it. We don't mind using our hands, honest."

Brittany had had a secret crush on Edward since that day. But it made her incredibly nervous whenever they were in close proximity. It had taken her years to finally get the courage to ask him out. When he'd said yes, she'd felt that all was finally right with the world. Until about an hour ago.

She scanned the gym, hoping to find Edward looking somewhat like he did when he came into class late: a little wind-tossed, a little scatterbrained. He'd probably be carrying a clear plastic box with a flower in it.

Sorry I'm late! he'd say. *Most of the stores were out of corsages, and I had to hunt this one down, but—*

The front doors opened, and her insides twisted, but it wasn't Edward. Brent Wheaton and Cory Mar came slinking in, trying their best not to be noticed. She frowned at them and saw Brent had something silver in his hand. He drank from it, then handed it to Cory.

Ugh.

Brittany tried to push them out of her mind, but her eyes kept wandering back. They were swaying their way across the room and onto the dance floor, bumping into everyone who crossed their path but not noticing them. Brittany hoped they would be equally as good at not noticing her until Brent slapped Cory in the chest and nodded in her direction.

Shit, shit, shit . . .

With a speed she wouldn't have thought possible in their drunken state, they came up on either side of her and sat down. A sharp, stabbing odor like rubbing alcohol assaulted her nostrils and made her cough.

"Heeeey, Britt. How you likin' the dance?" Cory asked with half-lidded eyes.

Brittany sat in silence, arms crossed, trying to ignore them.

Brent leaned closer to her as if inspecting her face, then leaned back. "Looks to me like she's not having fun, Cory."

"What a shame! Whassa matter? D'ja get stood up?"

Both boys fell into uncontrollable fits of giggles and snorts. Brittany gave a look of deep disgust to the pair, got up, and started walking to the door.

"What? C'mon, don't be a bitch! If someone left you all alone, it's their loss," Brent called after her.

A sudden chill replaced the utter revulsion in Brittany. They'd touched on exactly what had been going through her mind. How many people knew she'd been planning on coming to the dance with Edward? It was a small town. Everything was everyone's business; you couldn't avoid it. But that didn't mean she liked having her personal life under a microscope. All night, she'd been getting pitying looks. Cory's comment cemented her suspicions.

She decided she'd had enough and wanted to go home. Outside, the air was cool, and the noise was muted. She texted her dad to come and get her, and then leaned against the brick wall of the school. She just wanted to be alone, but the smell of cigarette smoke told her she wasn't.

She looked around at the darkness, which was broken only by the small throws of individual lamps that tried in vain to illuminate the school. Yet another unwelcome visitor made his way up to talk to her. Once he was finally in the light, Zack Roe took the cigarette out of his mouth, threw it onto the sidewalk, and stomped it out. He was dressed in a blue, short-sleeve button-up and jeans. It was nowhere near his usual clothes but could hardly be called formal. In fact, it looked like he was wearing a work shirt that was just missing a name tag.

"Sorry," he said while grinding his foot down. "Disgusting habit, I know, but I got hooked when I was thirteen and haven't been able to quit."

"Awfully gutsy to smoke on school property," she replied.

"True, but there hardly seems to be anyone around to catch me . . . 'Cept you, of course. What're you doing out here, anyway?"

"I don't feel well. I'm waiting for my dad to pick me up."

The corners of Zack's mouth twitched but then lay flat and unreadable. "Kinda chilly out here; you can't be comfortable in that." He gestured to the thin, pink material of her dress.

"Look who's talking. You really think that's appropriate for prom?"

A small laugh escaped. "Unfortunately, this is the nicest shirt I own. Some of us can't really afford much."

She paused for a moment to try and decide if he was being serious. After all, he did have a pretty nice car, but then again, his dad towed cars for a living. Maybe it had been one that went unclaimed.

"Sorry," she said, somewhat abashed. "I didn't mean to insinuate anything."

"No worries. Nobody's perfect." He shrugged. A smile that she didn't like crept onto his face. "I got a jacket in my car, if you want to borrow it."

She recognized the gesture, but a shudder ran through her all the same. "No, thanks."

"You sure? I can run and grab it real quick. I'll even wait here with you until your dad gets here."

At that moment, a pair of headlights turned into the parking lot and started making their way toward the gym. She'd never been so grateful for anything as she was to see her dad's sedan.

"That's him right there." She tried to flash a smile but couldn't muster one. "Thanks anyway. Hope you have more fun than I did." She made her way to the car and got in, and they drove away.

Steve Dalton went to bed already in the mindset that his son wouldn't be home until late. He slept in the following morning, and when he finally awoke to find his son not at home, a pang of unease went through him. He quickly dismissed it, thinking he'd probably gotten up early and was with Westley. Worry didn't really settle in until later that night when he tried to call Edward to see when he was coming home, only to get no answer. By the time nine o'clock rolled around, Steve decided that either Edward was in trouble, or he was going to be.

He found Westley's home number and dialed. Westley's father picked up, and Steve explained that he was trying to get ahold of Edward. No, he hadn't seen him there, but he would grab Westley to see if he could get some answers.

"Hello?" a tentative voice called across the line.

"Hello, Westley? This is Steve Dalton. Have you heard from Edward recently?"

Without much pause, Westley answered, "No, last I heard from him, he was about to leave for the dance."

"You didn't go with him?" Steve asked, trying to keep the mounting fear out of his voice.

"No, he had a date with Brittany McLaren, and I wanted to give them some privacy. Why? What's going on?"

Steve tried to move the massive lump in his throat. "He didn't come home last night or today. I'm trying to get ahold of him."

"Are you sure?" Westley asked, and Steve heard a note of panic that he himself was feeling. "I'll see if I can find him right now."

"Thanks, Westley. Let me know if you hear anything."

"Of course," Westley said hurriedly before the click.

Steve decided to call one more number after that. When he finally got ahold of Sheriff Alders, he told him the situation, and although Hal took his feelings seriously, he tried to reassure Steve that it was probably nothing. Edward may have just wanted some time alone. Nevertheless, he'd keep an eye out for Edward's car.

Chapter 4

THE FOREST

Heat seared off Edward. He couldn't remember a fever ever being this bad. Thankfully, his mother was nearby. When the sweat started to bead on his forehead, she dabbed at it, trying to wake him.

Edward didn't want to wake. He wanted to stay asleep until he got better, but his mom dabbed at his head with a rough washcloth, saying his name over and over.

She dabbed harder.

Jesus, what was the rag made of, broken glass? Then the pain came, not from the fever but from the force she applied. Her voice grew high-pitched. It felt like she was trying to take off some of his skin, screaming as she did it.

Edward's eyes opened wide as he sucked in a loud gasp of air. The sudden movement and sound sent the huge, black bird that'd been pecking at his head screaming off as fast as it could. He tried to figure out where he was and how he had gotten there. All he saw was trees stretching to the sky and dead leaves and moss covering the ground.

Then the pain returned.

His head felt like it was going to explode. His right hand shot to his temple as if trying to keep his brains from spilling out. He sucked in air through clenched teeth and was startled to find that when he lowered his hand, it came away bloody.

He clawed his way up into a sitting position, his body screaming in pain with every inch. He took inventory of himself: Except for his bleeding head, nothing seemed seriously hurt.

Once standing, he found he was able to walk. He moved around slowly, trying not to aggravate his sore body more than necessary.

A large stone wall traveled upward to his right. He backed up and saw at the top of this wall was a large, steep hill that rose as far as he could see. And then he remembered.

Falling; he remembered falling. He must have hit something, and it had knocked him out—maybe a lot of somethings, judging by all the aches and pains. But what had happened before the fall? Edward tried to rack his brain, but it was in no condition to be worked so hard.

More important than what had happened was where was he? How was he going to get home?

Every time he tried to calm down, another question would arise. All he really wanted to do was lie down and take a nap. He knew doing so after a traumatic head injury could be dangerous, so he resisted.

Great, he thought. *How is it that I can remember that but not anything else?*

He took a deep breath and closed his eyes. He kept breathing deeply, hoping that doing so might silence the banging gong in his head.

No such luck.

Another sound registered. Water. He headed off in that direction and came upon a small river. Sudden and immediate thirst swallowed him, and he dropped to his knees to scoop some of the crystal-clear liquid in his hand. Just before it reached his lips, another survival instinct came to mind and he wondered if it was safe to drink, but the thirst won out.

He dipped his hand back in the freezing water over and over, feeling a little better each time. After many scoops, he started to come back to himself and paused with his hand in the stream, watching the caked blood moisten and flow away in dark red wisps.

He started scooping again, this time not to drink but to wash his face. The cold water felt amazing, but each time he lowered his hand, he saw a good amount of blood go with it. He needed to stop the bleeding, and he needed to get out of here. He took his cell phone out of his pocket and held it up, moving it around, hoping for at least one bar.

There were none.

He marveled that the little brick was completely undamaged, but big whoop if it couldn't get a signal. He immediately shut it off to save the battery.

Edward stood up and took another look around. For all the many things he knew about different subjects, nature was not one of them.

He followed the river against the current, hoping it might lead him to a bridge.

The way was long, and he often had to pause and sit on one of the large, moss-covered rocks along the way. He was so tired, and soon, he began to feel woozy. His head was still bleeding, the blood stinging his eye before he could wipe it away.

He unbuttoned and removed his shirt, then pulled off his under-shirt and put the first back on. He bent down to the river once more to rinse sweat off the white tank, then wrung out as much moisture as he could and tied it around his head. After the initial wince of pain from the pressure, the coolness of the shirt started to relieve it. Still, any motion was enough to make him lightheaded. His foot slid on the rock he was standing on, and he barely managed to keep himself from going into the river. Movement seemed pointless, and with no help in sight, he sat and propped his back up against a rock. His breathing wasn't labored, but no matter how he tried, he couldn't take in enough air to catch his breath.

He sat there until the sun made its way over the trees and the warm rays hit his cheeks. Something shiny twinkled in the lower part of his vision, and his eyes reflexively darted for it. It was his belt buckle. Edward hardly ever wore a belt. Every pair of pants he owned were so tight that he had to suck in his gut in order to just be able to button them, yet there it was, staring up at him from his lap.

Part of my suit.

The recognition combined with the solitude of the moment was all it took. Huge chunks of information started flowing into his brain.

Being chased in his car played over again, and then the sight of it smashed on the tree; then stumbling through the trees, hunted by three shadowy figures backlit by a blinding yellow light. And then the fall.

He was suddenly grateful that he was alive at all. There was no question: Zack had meant to kill him. A surge of furious energy ripped through him. He had to get out of here, had to tell people what they did. They had to pay for this. He stood up again. Still woozy, but not enough to pass out. He had to find a way back into town.

An unbidden, unwelcome voice sprouted in his head: *You exist.*

That was it, wasn't it? He existed, and it pissed them off.

"Well, it didn't work, did it? I'm still here, assholes, and as soon as I get outta here, you're all going to jail. If you aren't already."

The idea puzzled him. How long had it been? He was hungry, but not to the point of starvation—maybe hours, possibly a day; he couldn't be certain.

How long would it be until someone came looking for him? Someone would have to come across his car eventually and send out a search party. If only he could find a bridge or a campground. He continued on, hoping for a miracle, but soon came to an abrupt halt.

Blocking his way at the end of the river was a towering waterfall. His spirits crashed. There were only two ways to follow the river, a fifty-fifty shot. Edward had gone the wrong way.

His head hurt, he was tired, and his stomach was empty, but moping about it wasn't going to help him in any way. He couldn't give up.

At the far side of the river next to the wall, he saw a pile of trash. Things that had washed down with the current but were now trapped.

He found a plastic grocery bag, three empty beer cans, a bit of grimy plastic rope, a pair of sunglasses with one of the lenses missing, and what appeared to be a full bag of potato chips. His heart began to race. He didn't care how stale they were; he was hungry enough to eat them. When he looked inside the bag, however, he saw a bunch of crumpled paper towels, and his heart sank. He didn't think he really expected to see chips in there, but hunger does funny things to the mind.

He was on the verge of throwing the bag back down when he saw that the inside of the bag was shiny. He pulled the paper towels out and jammed them in his pocket, then tore open the bag and tried to see his reflection in it. The bag was so full of wrinkles that all he could see was indistinct shapes. When he pulled the bag tight and angled it just right, however, there was his face staring back at him. It wasn't as good as an actual mirror, but it was a start.

He checked back around the sides of the pool to see if he could find anything else. He was about to give up when he saw what looked like a bug sitting on top of the water.

Was he really *that* hungry?

His growling stomach assured him he was.

He reached down, expecting to have to catch the insect as it tried to escape. To his surprise, the bug stayed stock-still. He grabbed it only to find it wasn't a bug at all but a bit of fishing line poking above the water-line. He pulled until he met with resistance. He wanted to get as much line as he could, so to avoid it snapping, he followed it down below the water with his hand to find where it was snagged.

His fingers met with even more tangled line, and then it seemed to go under a rock. Edward kept tension on the line as he lifted the rock. Something was set free, causing him to pull up, and a sudden, sharp pain sank into his pointer finger. As much as it hurt, this pain meant he had fishing line *and* a hook. It'd been years since his father had taken him fishing, but it wasn't hard. All he had to do was untangle the line and maybe find a nice stick for a pole. He removed the hook, gathered up the other found articles, and found a place to sit with his back propped up against a tree. He set everything but the fishing line down and started working his way through untangling it. As he did, his mind wandered, looking at all his newfound possessions and trying to figure out what he could use them for.

His eyes fell to the sunglasses. With a regular lens, you could start a fire by focusing the sun's rays into a beam of light, but could it be done with a shaded lens?

It was worth a try. He put down the fishing line and grabbed the glasses. He popped out the remaining lens and went to grab a bunch of dead leaves. He took them over to the river where the sun was still beating down, took up the lens in one hand and a leaf in the other, and held the lens above the leaf.

Nothing.

He fiddled around with the lens, trying new positions, but no matter what, all he got was a translucent shadow that fell upon the leaf. He twisted the lens, and a bright flash whizzed across his vision. He immediately stopped and reversed his movement until again the flash came. Instead of using the light passing through the lens, he used the reflection of the sun and pointed it toward the leaf.

Bingo!

He now had a bright beam of light focused on the dead leaf. He stood absolutely still, resting the hand holding the lens on a rock while pointing the beam at the leaf he held upright in his other hand. He waited and watched.

Nothing happened.

He stood there, holding his position, staring at the bright dot on the leaf until his eyes hurt. He knew this took time, but damn, not *this* long. Just as his mind was forming the conclusion that it wouldn't work, a small wisp of smoke arose. Edward was so surprised that he removed the beam to see what it had done. A little brown burn had been left behind.

So, it *was* possible, but now he had to start all over.

He grabbed a bunch of rocks and set up a stone ring on top of a large, flat rock by the river. He pulled the paper towels out of his pocket, and as he did, his fingers brushed up against a small, metal something. It was the nail clippers he'd left in his pocket before leaving his house.

He gathered a bunch of dead leaves and sticks to add to the flame along with the towels, if he was able to get one going. He gathered a bit of wood but paused to check the sky before he'd gathered as much as he'd wanted. By the look of things, he didn't have very long before the sun dipped below the tree line again. It was now or never . . . or at least until the sun reappeared the following day.

It took a while before his next leaf began to smoke, but when it did, he held it still until he saw the hole burn wider. Gently, he blew the smoke. It went away for just a second, then sprang back thicker as he took in another breath.

Suddenly, the leaf caught. It was all Edward could do to put it down to join its fellows before it burnt up. He blew onto the burning leaf to help the others catch flame.

"YES!"

He rushed over to his meager wood supply and began snapping twigs and placing them in the fire, then went in search of bigger logs that he could use to keep it going.

When night fell, he was still incredibly hungry, but the fact that he was warm helped quell his insides. He'd made fire! His mind was now free to dwell on seeing Zack and his cronies put behind bars when he got out of here. The thought warmed him even more than the fire.

Edward stared at the flames while untangling the fishing line to keep himself occupied, wrapping the untangled coils around a small log. Morning had come, and with it, no sign of rescue.

His fingers traveled upward to prod his forehead. It hurt worse than ever. When he removed his undershirt, it still came away bloody. He grabbed the chip bag and held it up to inspect the damage, but it was too difficult to hold it in place while keeping it wrinkle-free.

He placed the bag down and looked around for something to help him. He settled on a flat rock, wrapped the bag around it, and tied it down with some of the old rope. After it was tight enough, he breathed on the surface and wiped it down with a bit of his shirt.

He held his mirror up as he gritted his teeth and dabbed the wound clean. After he got a good look at the gash, he had no doubt it needed stitches, and soon, if he wanted the bleeding to stop. His mind flew to his hook and line.

He could do it. When you got right down to it, it was nothing more than a mixture of sewing and tying your shoelaces. He propped his mirror up on a rock next to the fire, then pulled out the clippers, cut a length of line, and washed it as best he could in the river. He placed a small stick in the flames until it caught, then held the stick up to the hook in his other hand, sterilizing the metal as best he could without burning himself.

When he was certain he'd done all he could to prepare, he turned toward the mirror and got down on his knees to peer into it.

His chest heaved, forcing air in and out in an attempt to blow up his courage. Finally, he held the hook up to the first bit of flesh and pushed.

Pain exploded in his mind, and he let out a huge yelp. Once there, however, he knew he had to keep going, and he hooked both sides of the cut and pulled the line through, screaming all the way.

He tied a quick square knot and pulled until it was tight enough. Once he clipped off the excess line, he sat himself down and stared at the fire to prepare to do it again.

Over and over, he hooked the metal through both flaps of skin and pulled them together. He ended up with six stitches and prayed they were enough.

When the pain moved from sharp to just a low throb, Edward decided to go on the move again. He had to get out of here. He made his way back downstream until the river split in two. He had a choice now: One way he knew would at least bring him back the way he'd started, but the other led to who knew where. He decided that it would be best to keep to the path he'd been following, but with his luck, the other way probably led straight to a town. There wasn't time to worry; he had to keep moving.

The farther he went down the river, the more the trees and bushes encroached upon the banks of the river. Once or twice, he had to go in the water in order to progress. After one of these encroaching patches, he saw a bright lighted area further down as the forest widened up. A spark of hope went through him. Maybe he was about to figure out where he was or even find a way out. His feet became lighter, and he moved quickly to the mouth of the river.

Welp, he thought to himself, *I'm out of the forest, all right.*

That's what he told himself, anyway, to try and cope with the new development. The river did lead out into a clearing. He had wandered his way onto a beach in front of a small, crystalline lake that formed at the base between two steep mountains. The shoreline was pockmarked here and there with other beaches, but at least 90 percent of it was nothing but dense trees.

It was then he really started to suspect where he was. The car chase must have led him into the national park; he'd gone partway up and fallen into some sort of crevasse in the Georgian portion of the Appalachian Mountains. He was in the middle of nowhere. Worse, if he picked the wrong direction, he could walk as far as Maine without hitting civilization.

He walked out onto the beach and scanned his surroundings, looking for any trace of human life.

There was nothing.

His mind spiraled as he walked along his stretch of beach. How was he going to get out of here? *Would* he ever get out of here? Every thought that whizzed through his mind led up to one undeniable reality: He was lost.

The beach was maybe a half mile long, and if Edward walked up it, maybe he'd even find something useful. He then remembered his phone. There was little chance of getting a signal, but he decided to power it up and check anyway.

No such luck.

But as he moved to turn off the phone, his eyes caught the overgrown remnants of what looked like a trail. With no better idea, he followed it through thick patches of trees. In the distance, an old shack came into view. It looked like a large outhouse that you'd see in kitschy old towns or Western movies, minus the crescent moon on the door. Moss and vines crisscrossed the front door.

"Hello?"

He waited a few moments. Then, louder, "Hello?!"

He walked up to the door and knocked. Once. Twice. A third time. Nothing.

He opened the door and took a look inside. The shack had no windows, and the door opened into darkness as a whiff of old, musty air billowed out. Once his eyes had time to adjust, he saw it was a dingy, small room, complete with plank flooring. In it was an old wooden chair, a table, what looked like the broken remains of a bed frame, and a big, black, rusted wood-burning stove.

His eyes roamed over to the chair lying on the floor next to the table. He picked it up, set it right, and eased himself down into it. The old wood was thick and apparently strong, at least enough to hold his weight. Once he was sure it wasn't going to crumble out from underneath him, he let out a long, low sigh of pleasure.

What was this place? Everything in here looked ancient. Especially that stove. If it hadn't been as thick as it was, it'd probably have rusted out years ago. Whatever this place was doing here, Edward was glad to have it. Who knew how long he would be stuck here before help came? He wasn't sure in his condition—or shape—that he would make it much farther than he already had. At least this way, he had shelter. His eyes fell on the broken bed frame. Three sides were still intact, with the fourth drooping lazily onto the floor, where a large pile of dirt and leaves had collected. If sitting felt this good, he could only imagine how being in an actual bed would feel. He would have to try and fix that. If only he weren't so damn exhausted.

That was the other big problem. He had to get some food. Every effort cost him a ton of energy that he wasn't able to replenish.

He put all of his belongings on the table to take inventory. The whole of his possessions consisted of his cell phone, a plastic grocery bag, one busted-out sunglasses lens, nail clippers, the makeshift mirror, fishing line and hook wrapped around a branch, a bloodstained undershirt, a bit of old rope, and three beer cans.

His best bet would be to go back to his beach and see if he could find anything useful that may have washed ashore, but he didn't find much. His beach was made of smooth rocks that looked like the kind you'd see people in movies skip across the surface of the water. He decided to give it a try, but the rock just dropped with a single *plunk*.

As he looked for another to try again, he saw a flat rock the size of his palm that resembled the head of a hatchet. It was thick on one side and tapered down to a thin edge. With a little bit of effort, he figured he could use it in place of a knife.

He continued to look around, but aside from his new tool, it seemed that the day had given all it meant to, and he headed back to his shack. On his way, he saw a long, gnarled branch that caught his interest. He picked it up, and it was almost as tall as he was. It reminded him of a wizard's staff from *Lord of the Rings*, and he decided that he could use it as a walking stick.

He paused in thought for a moment to think of how long he had been in the forest, pulled out his newly acquired ax head, and carved two lines near the head of his staff.

Right as he was about to move on, he spotted movement on the ground. A rabbit flashed its fuzzy, white tail and rapidly diminished in the distance. It was like it was taunting him. If he could just catch one.

For a moment, he thought that maybe he could make a bow and arrows.

This didn't last long, as he remembered that if by some miracle he was able to make a bow, he'd have to train himself to use it.

He followed what he figured to be the rabbit's path through the trees. Spread across the floor was a number of long, thin, grasslike needles that sprang up in patches all over. He saw clear indentations in some places and what looked like little tunnels in others. He disturbed the tunnels with his stick, hoping to either frighten a rabbit into moving or discover a nest of some sort. All to no avail. The grass was soft and yielded immediately to the touch. No animal bigger than a beetle would use this as shelter.

If he couldn't have food, he at least needed a way to warm himself. He made his way back to the cabin, and once again, it took all he had to turn the beam from the sunglasses lens into flame. Although it was slightly easier this time, he didn't dare risk losing his hard work now that he had a place to stay. With the fire slowly burning, he went into the cabin and pulled on the door of the stove until it creaked open. Pushing out a little dirt, he created the perfect spot for his fire to go.

The sun began to set. He slumped heavily in his chair and reveled in the small relief of being able to get off his feet. Except for the small crackle of flames in the stove, all was silent, leaving Edward alone in his cell with nothing but his thoughts and the occasional growl of his stomach to keep him company.

It'd been Friday night when he'd gone missing. Two days had passed since he had woken up here, so it was at least Sunday evening. Surely, they were looking for him by now, right?

His father was probably worried sick. Someone would have to find the car eventually, and finding no body inside, the next step would be to form a search party. It didn't matter, then, if he didn't know where he was, right? He couldn't have possibly gone that far away from the crash. If he was to wait right here, maybe build up a signal fire or something, someone was bound to find him. In the meantime, all he had to do was wait.

The thought of having to resign himself to this plan didn't lift his spirits. Instead, pawing over how long he might be here until someone found him made him feel abnormally tired. His eyes drifted to the broken bed frame and stared longingly at it. He got up and pushed around the leaves and dirt that were in the middle of the wreckage, and some of the dirt vanished through cracks in the floorboards as the remainder of the clutter was brushed aside. Moving the debris exposed some old, torn fabric that might have been a stuffed mattress many years ago.

He pulled it up, showering his lower half and the floor in loose dirt. He held the tattered cloth in front of his eyes, and it stretched all the way down and collected on the floor. He was just barely able to see a faded pattern of white and blue stripes.

A thought occurred, and he rushed outside, gathered a bunch of fallen leaves, and placed them in a long pile by the bed frame. Then he covered the pile with bunches of the wispy grass the rabbit had gotten away in. He took the balled-up remnants of the mattress and placed them at one end. There was only one thing left to do now, and that was to test it.

Chapter 5

LIFE GOES ON

About the same time as Edward carved the third notch in his staff, Steve awoke to the phone ringing. It was Hal letting him know Edward's car had been found two counties over, smashed into a tree. There was blood in the cab, not enough to have been fatal, but he had at least been injured. He'd probably hit his head and gone wandering off, not knowing what had happened.

The disembodied voice at the other end of the phone said they were gathering up efforts to search the area around where the car was found. To Steve, although he was elated by finally having some news of his son, the voice sounded mechanical, and he felt he couldn't hope for much more.

Edward became increasingly desperate for food. He devoted the entire day after waking up in the shack to finding a way of getting it. When he started to feel bad for laughing at Wile E. Coyote all those years for trying and failing to catch his dinner, he knew the hunger was beginning to affect his mental capacity. He needed to eat, and taking some inspiration from the cartoon, he decided a snare might be his best bet.

Obviously, he knew he couldn't bend a tree down, attach a snare to it, and have it magically stay in place until some poor, unsuspecting creature came along, but people had been trapping animals for thousands of years. Surely, he could figure out one of the ways they did so.

The simplest way that he could think of would be making a kind of noose, attaching it to a branch or tree root, and hanging it on the ground where something could walk through and catch on it. *Simple enough*, he thought, but the execution was much more difficult.

He started with his fishing line and made a loop that could tighten. Then he attached the line to an exposed root and placed the loop in a small path between the trees where he'd seen a rabbit go. He even tested the snare by placing his hand through the loop and pressing forward until it tightened.

The trap set, he decided to work on a way of fishing and possibly find sustenance that way while waiting on a rabbit. Since he didn't have any bait to use, he figured he'd have to make a lure out of something. His first thought was to make something out of a piece of the chip bag that'd been serving as his mirror. It was shiny and would certainly attract the attention of fish, but it was too soft and wouldn't be able to move through the water very well. His attention then fell on one of the beer cans. It was certainly strong enough to be used as a lure, and the inside was still shiny. The main obstacle would be cutting out a piece of it without cutting himself.

The end product somewhat resembled a child's drawing of a fish, only cut out, shiny, and about the size of a rectangular eraser. Edward poked two holes (nose and tail) and strung his line though, holding the lure in place with a couple knots and tying his hook at the end. He looked at it for a moment, admiring his handiwork, and hoped to the gods of fishing he could not only catch something but also not lose his hook in the process.

Given the fact that all he had to work with was nail clippers, a sharpened rock, and his own hands, the effort had taken most of the day; but he was so excited that he had to try it out. The sun had already left the sky, leaving its residual oranges and pinks mixing with the darkening blue above and making him think of cotton candy. His father always said that the best time for fishing was right when the sun was coming up or going down. Edward had also learned from experience that this rule was not absolute either way. Proud of his ingenuity, he strolled to the mouth of the river with his head held high.

He came back about an hour and a half later with it considerably lower.

The only thought able to get him out of bed the next day was the prospect of finding something in his snare. He went out to check, hoping wildly that something would be waiting for him. Not only was there no rabbit there to greet him, but when he bent down to inspect the trap, he also found that the whole line was gone.

Edward went into a blind rage, swearing up a storm, picking up rocks and branches and chucking them as hard as he could in any direction. He knew all he was doing was wasting precious energy, but he didn't care. It felt good to finally uncork his feelings and let them spew all over. What had he done to deserve this?

Nothing!

This whole situation was the result of someone else's problem, and now *he* was paying the price. He was sick of it! He wanted to go home, he wanted to eat in his own kitchen, but the face of Zack was burning red in his mind, laughing at his struggles while perfectly comfortable continuing life back home. Thoughts of how he'd like to wipe that laughter off Zack's smug face filled him up with a fiery rage.

After a few minutes, he started coming back to himself. Though self-satisfying, his rant didn't bring him any closer to food. He stared down at the ground below him where he'd set the first trap, his gaze slack like it always was when he thought hard. Pushing away the hunger and frustration, he concentrated, looking for anything that would help him, but all he saw was his shoes.

"You idiot!" he said, smiling to himself.

He bent down and tore the laces from one shoe. The previous snare had been too light; the heavier weight of the shoelace might just do the trick. He set it up the same way as last time and even partially obscured it with dead leaves and grass, then took a step back to admire his handiwork. One shoe considerably looser than the other, he nodded his head in approval, then looked down at his other shoe. He shrugged his shoulders as if to say "Welp, can't have that," then proceeded to remove his other lace and found another place to lay a second trap.

Once both traps were set, he went to retrieve one of the strands of the plastic rope to make new laces. The strand as a whole was too thick to fit through the holes, so he pulled it apart until he had two good-sized replacements. His first attempt snapped with the tightening and he had to start over.

He wasted so much time getting out of bed and fiddling around with the snares that by the time he made it out to fish, the sun was shining in its late-morning glory. Still, he had to try. His strategy was to throw the lure into the middle of the mouth of the river and let the current take it out as far as it could, then slowly pull it back toward him, wrapping the line around the stick in his hands.

Over and over, he sent the lure out and slowly, methodically reeled it back in. He did this for over an hour before he felt a tug. His heart raced as he brought the hook inward. It was hard to tell which was moving faster.

The fish got away, but he was relieved to see that it hadn't taken anything with it.

"So close!" he said with glee and quickly sent it out again.

Not long after that, he felt that little tug again. More carefully this time, he pulled just slightly, then let the current take the lure out again and waited. Again, he felt the tug, this time a little more violently, and he yanked the line back as hard and fast as he could and relaxed it.

It worked.

He felt the fish at the end of the line. The hook was set, and all he had to do was bring it in.

When he pulled the slimy, wiggling thing out of the river, he felt a small pang of disappointment. The fish was hardly bigger than the lure. Still, it was food. He placed it under a rock far away from the shoreline and tried again, but the little guy was the only one biting that day.

It took some effort, but he was able to gut the fish, and once done, he left the head and guts on the table and placed the body on top of the stove, where it immediately began to sizzle.

He waited a few moments, and the smell, that heavenly smell, wafted toward him, inviting him to take a bite. He forced himself to resist. Edward knew a fish that wasn't fully cooked could give you parasites, and he could not afford to get sick. He had no idea how long he would need to wait for someone to find him, but he didn't plan to do that while puking his guts out.

Still, waiting was complete agony.

Finally, he pronounced it good enough. He scooped it up with a sharp rock and shoved the whole piece of meat in his mouth. It burned his mouth instantly, and he had to juggle it with his tongue to cool it off before he chewed and swallowed.

That one little bit of protein and fat was enough to warm his heart. It made him feel that maybe things weren't so bad. For at least a while.

When the hunger set back in, it was razor sharp. Still, he was able to pass the night with hope, and when thoughts of those three living their lives in the outside world descended upon him, it wasn't as bad as it had been.

The next morning, he walked the short distance to his first trap. At first, he thought he was hallucinating. There on the ground in front of him lay a rabbit, stiff and still. He bent down beside the furry creature and touched it to make sure it was really there. He removed the lace from its neck held it up in front of his face and marveled at it. Here was not a mouthful, but a full meal. His throat tightened, and his eyes welled up in tears of joy. He couldn't contain them, and he didn't want to.

"Thank you!" he said over and over. "Thank you, thank you, thank you." To the rabbit, to the forest, to God, if he really existed.

If the day had ended there, he would've been happy, but when he reset the snare and checked the other, he found another rabbit, even bigger than the first. Elation flooded all other thoughts from his mind, and once he reset the snare, he walked back to the cabin with a newfound spring in his step.

If the fish was good, the rabbit was heaven. He ate every bit of it right down to the bones, then placed those on a heap outside with the entrails.

It was only midday, so he spent the rest of the afternoon making as many snares as he could with the remaining rope; testing their strength before using them. When finished, he set out along the trees beside the beach and set the snares in places he felt would give him a good chance of catching more. While setting his last snare, he found a new path. He was feeling pretty good with his large lunch resting comfortably in his stomach, so he decided to explore a little more to get a better sense of his surroundings.

The path was small but easy enough to follow. After a distance, however, he found that it widened up considerably and was covered with enough crunched leaves to give the impression that someone was using this path on a regular basis.

His heart leaped at the possibility of another human being. Maybe it was a path that eventually led to a road. He followed it all the way to a cave carved out of the hillside and curiosity took hold.

He paused at the opening. "Hello?" His word echoed far into the distance before it finally died out. "Anyone in here?" The cave asked the question back in his voice.

He took a step inside. Everything was pitch black at first. Then, slowly, things came into focus. The light trickled in from the opening just enough to see the first part of what looked like a tunnel. He had no idea how far it went and wondered if he dared trying to find out without a light.

He felt something charging in the air, as if a bolt of lightning was approaching the critical limit before it had to strike.

Somewhat more timidly, he called, "Hello?"

When the sound of his own voice died out, he sensed something move. The hairs on the back of his neck stood on end, and a shudder trickled down his back. Then he heard it, far in the distance, but the acoustics brought it right to him.

A long noise that sounded like someone dragging their feet on gravel. He heard great, deep sniffs and huffs that came from something enormous, definitely not human.

The shuffling and chuffing continued, and Edward felt a cold sweat bead up all over as his heart raced. He had already started to back away slowly when whatever it was gave a great, loud roar that sounded as if the cave itself was bellowing for him to leave. He did not need to be told twice.

Edward bolted the rest of the way out and stumbled through the trees, trying to make his way to the shoreline. He slid as a squishing sound came from something underfoot. He looked down at what could only be a pile of fresh droppings. It was large, moist, and red. Dear God, it was red! What had it been eating?

He didn't want to find out.

He slammed the door to his cabin hard with a loud crack and leaned his back against it. He slid down until he sat on the floor, his breaths coming heavily.

He waited.

That was the worst part: waiting to hear sounds telling him that whatever it was had given chase. He tried to control his breathing and calm his heart, which was trying to leap right out of his chest. As the moments passed and no sounds of large feet crashing through the forest were heard, he relaxed and laughed in relief.

When he finally calmed down, he found he was hungry again. Suddenly, his nostrils flooded with the smell of his lunch still lingering in the air. From his position on the floor, his eyes drifted up to the table, where he knew the second rabbit lay waiting for him.

He let out a huff of air. "Well, never too early to start thinking about dinner."

He groaned as he pushed himself up and went to work cleaning up the second rabbit. Although he cleaned the animal considerably faster than the first, night descended upon him, and the only light available to him while cooking billowed out from the flames in the stove. He stood in front of the stove as the fire gave a particularly loud snap. He paused for a second, then realized the sound came from outside. He closed the door on the furnace, plunging the cabin into darkness.

He fumbled and groped around until his eyes began to adjust and noticed little slits of light coming through where the planks of the walls didn't touch. The moon had come out enough to throw some light on the world outside. He peered between the slats and waited.

The silence spun out, and Edward started to feel funny until he realized he was holding his breath. He let it out but almost immediately sucked it back in when he heard shuffling off in the distance. He looked through his little slit but saw nothing.

Then the sniffing started.

He cursed himself. Whatever he'd met earlier had followed him back and was now sniffing him out.

Steadily, the sniffing and shuffling grew louder until it sounded as if it was right outside. Edward didn't want to move for fear of making a sound, but he needed to know. He switched his position to a few feet over and looked out again.

At first, this view was no better, but then the big black spot at the corner of his vision twitched slightly. Then he realized it was a giant, furry foot. The foot itself, leading off and out of his field of vision, looked like it was the size of Edward's head. His stomach plummeted, and his heart leaped into his throat.

He moved over again to get a better look at his visitor. Mere feet from the cabin was the biggest black bear he'd ever seen. Granted, the only ones he'd seen were from a distance in zoos. But this one was enormous, like it could swallow him whole. It was just feet away, and the only thing that separated it from him was about an inch of ancient wood.

Its nose was doing something. Feeling immensely stupid, Edward realized it was eating the remains of the fish and rabbits that he'd tossed so carelessly aside. He silently cursed himself again before realizing he still had the current rabbit cooking on the stove. What would happen if the bear finished out there and decided it was still hungry? He'd heard stories, even seen pictures of the aftermath of hungry bears looking for food. Cars ripped open like they were peeling off the top of a soup can. That was sturdy metal designed to withstand crashes; the wood of his shelter didn't stand a chance.

He made his way over to the stove where broken branches lay ready to be added, picked up two of the longest, and placed his hand on the stove door, concealing the fire. Ever so slowly, he inched the door open, but with every microscopic nudge, the hinges screamed out into the dark as if calling to the bear for help.

The sweat was no longer in little beads; it flowed freely down Edward's face, collecting in his shirt or splashing onto the floor. His heart beat so loud that he was sure it could be heard over the door's squeals. Slowly, the vertical slit of red-orange glow widened until the wall adjacent was bathed in the dancing flickers. Edward dipped the tips of the branches in and waited for them to catch.

All the while, he kept his gaze on the wall between him and the bear. It seemed incredible that it hadn't come to investigate the smell or sounds coming from inside. All was quiet, and the only movement came from the fire bouncing off the walls.

Perhaps it was just a trick his mind was playing on him, but Edward thought he saw a coin-shaped flash move past one of the open slits in the wall. Now, Edward's heart seemed to be holding its breath. His ears tried to reach out beyond the wall to gain a sense of what was going on, but he heard nothing in return for his efforts. The silence became maddening.

Minutes dragged on as the silence continued. Edward was a statue—a grotesque, frightened take on the Statue of Liberty, one hand clutching his heart as if trying to muffle it and the other grasping the base of his torch, the tip of which still gathered flames.

He couldn't take it anymore; he had to do something or lose what grip he held. He pulled his torch from the fire like he was King Arthur and walked silently to the wall. Holding the flames away from the wood, he peered through the cracks.

Nothing.

He tried another crack: still nothing. Then another, and another, mechanically working his way through each crack in the wall. When one wall ran out, he moved on to the next until he made his way full circle, and still there was no sign of his furry neighbor.

Edward felt like he'd been holding his breath the entire time and finally let it out in one long, sighing blow. Then, for the second time, he began to laugh, heartily and maniacally.

The days dragged on into weeks as Edward cut notch after notch into his staff. He tried making signal fires out on the beach, but either no one saw or no one cared. One day, he made a fire so large that the wind blew the flames backward, and some of the brush behind it began to catch. Edward was just able to put it out before the forest caught fire around him. He decided to just have one ready to burn on the beach in case he saw a search plane or chopper.

Edward continued to explore his surroundings to look not only for a way out but also for other items he might find useful. Things continued to wash down the river—fishing line, water bottles, even a gallon jug—and Edward was more than happy to find uses for them.

He traveled back up the river and forged his way across to explore where the second arm of the fork stretched to. As he followed, the trees began to encroach on the river and slow down the water's progress until it became green and murky. The trees grew out of the water in gnarled clumps with huge patches of moss hanging from them. The twinkle of fireflies pocked the air, and Edward could hear the calls of frogs in the distance.

He'd only gone to Disneyland once, but that one time had left an impression so great that he would never forget it. When he saw the swamp for what it was, his mind immediately went to the *Pirates of the Caribbean* ride where you had to travel through a dark swamp before taking the plunge into Davy Jones's Locker.

It was a place that, despite being a swamp, lifted his spirits for a precious few moments, reminding him of happier times. He tried to memorize this feeling for the next time the depression of being alone gripped him.

Each day was a constant physical struggle in order to stay alive, but the silent battle that went on in his brain was hardest of all. He would have to try and keep a grip on his mind at least once a day, if not more. The thoughts of how he'd been bullied throughout the years before he ended up here gripped his heart and squeezed. He'd been picked on all his life, mostly for being overweight. Zack and his cronies were the worst, but plenty of others had done their share.

Fat! Say it, fat boy, you tub of lard!

Pizza face!

Why do you go on existing knowing everyone hates you?

It seemed that at this point, even his own mind felt compelled to bully him. And just when he felt he was starting to move on with life, Zack and his lackeys put a stop to it.

His thoughts soon turned to hate and what he would do to them if he ever got the chance. At first, he was sated by the thought of them in jail, but soon, that wasn't good enough. He began to think of ways of making them suffer until they knew the heartache they'd caused him.

He found the best way to combat these feelings was to keep his mind occupied: fish, make new traps, improve his shelter, make new tools, stitching his rabbit skins together to eventually have a blanket, and so on. These things would grant him brief respite, but it was only a matter of time before the silence of his surroundings would press in on his ears and the internal struggle waged war on his heart and mind. Thoughts would spring from woe and pity to hate and anger, then back again, forever cycling. Sometimes these episodes would last minutes; others would go on for hours, leaving Edward a sobbing mass curled up on the floor, praying for mercy, whatever that might entail.

Right about the time Edward was starting to have faith in his new food-gathering abilities, he awoke one morning to find no rabbit in his first snare; instead, his trap was torn to shreds, covered in blood and hair. Something had gotten to the rabbit before he did.

At first, he shrugged it off, but as he continued checking his snares, he either found nothing or more hair and blood.

A flare of white-hot anger lit in his chest, and he could just barely keep it in check. All he could do was reset and hope for a better tomorrow.

When he found that the next day brought only more of the same, his stomach tightened about twenty notches, and the flare of anger sprang up again.

He looked all around the traps that had been stolen from to try and find some sort of clue. When his eyes fell upon a paw print that looked like it may have been left by a small dog, an image of a sly, pointed nose and a furry face popped into his head.

He had a fox.

The creature had taken to walking his trap line instead of searching for its own sustenance.

Edward decided to reset only one trap that day, as close to his cabin as the thought he could get away with, and attached one of his beer cans with a few pebbles inside to the line. He placed his hand through the noose and struggled around for a bit until the amount of noise was satisfactory to him.

He spent the rest of the day fishing.

When the lake gave him only one fish, he knew he'd better fix this situation fast.

Edward lay awake all night with his ear cocked in the direction of his trap. Early in the morning, he heard the can and rushed right out to get the rabbit, but he arrived just in time to see the fox making off with the kill.

He spent the following day fuming and thinking of ways to solve the problem, and he decided to set one more trap, this time for the fox.

After catching a fish, he cut off a small portion to use as bait, then ate the rest and tried thinking of a trap suitable for the fox.

Edward found a boulder just light enough for him to move and tried to attach the bait in such a way that the boulder would fall when the fox took it. He settled on anchoring one end of a string underneath one side of the rock and tying the other end to a stick that was just strong enough to hold the other side of the rock up. He fiddled with his contraption until he got it weighted to the point that a touch of the string would cause the stick to slip out and let the rock fall on whatever was underneath.

After testing the trap many times by slightly nudging the string with his calendar staff, he set it once more and placed the bait carefully over the exposed string. After all was set, he went back to fishing and was only able to catch one more fish.

The next day, Edward went out and saw the trap looked like it had been completely untouched, but the bait was gone. He took his staff and set off the trap easily, but apparently not easily enough. He reset the trap, this time placing the bait closer to the rock.

When he came upon the trap again, he saw that it had been sprung, but no fox corpse was dangling out. He lifted up the rock and saw that his bait had been stolen again. The fox must have come in from the side and snatched the bait up.

After much thought, Edward reset the trap. Once again, he placed the bait on the string close to the rock, but this time, he plunged a bunch of sticks all around the side of the trap to hopefully force the fox to come at it from the front. The trap reminded Edward of an alligator's mouth that would hopefully snap shut on the fox.

The next day, he found the trap sprung, but again, no body. He lifted up the rock to once again find the bait gone. Then he saw that some of the sticks on the side of the trap had been gnawed through. The fox had bested him again.

Edward's stomach growled in protest at the thought of giving up more fish to try and stop the fox. His mind had already started fogging over again with lack of nutrients. He decided to stop setting traps and just fish for his sustenance.

That day's haul was a good one: five mouthwateringly big fish. Edward cooked them all but only ate one. He knew he had to be more careful about rationing his food since he was now depending on the lake.

The next morning, Edward woke up to a grim surprise: Every single fish he had stored from the day before was gone.

He looked all around his little space, but no trace of the fish could be found. In a crack between the door and the wall, he found a small scattering of ginger-red hairs.

The lack of nutrition over the past few days, the loss of his cache of food, and the realization that the fox had come into his space and taken the fish sent him screaming at the top of his lungs. He went over to his table and started grabbing things and throwing them against the wall. All the while, he felt his remaining energy draining out.

When there was nothing left to throw, Edward spun around and clocked his hand against the corner of his stove. He heard a quick sizzle when his bare flesh hit metal. The pain from the impact and the burn screamed and fought against each other for Edward's attention. In an attempt to soothe both, the affected part of his hand made its way into his mouth.

Rather than sending him spiraling even more, the pain brought him back to his senses, and he went to the lake to dunk his hand and think of his next move.

Over the next few days, Edward was only able to grasp two thoughts: get more fish and keep the fox from entering his space. He tried his best to devote his energy to the two, but his mind was becoming foggier. The lake wasn't giving him much, and what he did catch he had to eat immediately to make sure it didn't go to the fox.

Finally, the lake blessed him with a particularly large fish, and he decided to eat the whole thing. It was the largest meal he'd had in a while, and he was now feeling sluggish while his body digested. He needed to rest while his body took care of the fish, and right before sleep took him, he knew the fox had to die.

The fish had done its part, and Edward felt more like himself again. He stared into the belly of the stove, watching the flames sway and jump as he thought.

He thought about all the times he'd set a trap to catch the fox. How every time, it found a way to get the prize and escape. How was he supposed to set a trap good enough to combat a mind that had all the rest and nourishment that he himself lacked?

Then it hit him. If he had food, he knew it was only a matter of time before the fox would try to get at it. So why not make the fox come to him?

Immediately, he looked around his cabin for inspiration. The room was small, easy enough to keep watch over. He let his gaze travel upward and saw the many gaps in the wood roof, and an idea began to form in his mind.

He gathered up all the rope he had left from what was once his rabbit snares and the ragged bit of cloth that had once been a mattress and got to work. Once he was satisfied with his trap, he set aside a large piece of firewood next to his bed and went out to catch the bait.

The lake had only provided him with one fish that day. He took it home and prayed that by this time tomorrow, his fox problem would be resolved.

Later that night, Edward lay on his bed, one eye barely open and watching the fish on the floor as it was bathed in the firelight from the open furnace. Hours passed, and the flames died down to a rosy glow. Still, Edward remained motionless.

Sleep began to threaten with the lack of stimulation and nourishment, but Edward held fast. Just when the fire began to die completely and white patches of moonlight crept in, Edward heard a muffled movement. He knew it wouldn't be long and kept his eye on the fish. Movement formed at the edge of his vision. It was eerie how utterly silent the fox's tread was.

Just as the muzzle reached out to grab the fish, Edward pulled with all his might on the piece of rope in his hand.

Immediately, the fox and fish were engulfed by the mattress fabric being hauled upward to the ceiling, where Edward had threaded the rope between the slats.

The fox wasted no time in trying the one thing that could possibly save itself and began to gnaw at the fabric.

Holding on to the rope with one hand, Edward grabbed the large piece of firewood and began to strike the struggling mass hanging in

midair. Blow after blow fell on the fabric until it turned red and the struggling lessened. Edward let the rope drop, grabbed the wood with both
hands, and continued to strike down at the heap on the floor. The fox had
given up the ghost long before Edward gained enough control to stop.

Once he calmed down, Edward placed new logs in the stove,
unwrapped the reddened fox, and began to clean it.

He cooked the animal for a long time, just staring at the hunks of
meat on the stove in hatred. When he finally ate the pieces, he felt sated,
not only in his hunger but also in his thirst for revenge. Revenge at this
animal that had done its best to leech off of all his hard work. Who
would keep on feeding until Edward died of starvation and, even then,
would feed on his remains.

Well, not this time. I got there first, didn't I?

The next day, Edward took the bloody fabric and fox pelt down to
the water to rinse them as best he could. He was sure he could still use
both, and now he had a trophy to remind him of his victory.

He spent the rest of the day setting snares for the rabbits he was sure
to catch now. In the following days, as Edward cut more notches into
his staff, he found himself feeling very lucky with the number of rabbits
and fish he was obtaining. As time wore on, his hopes of being rescued
any time soon started to fade. He decided to set up a smoker on top of
his chimney to preserve all the meat he didn't eat, knowing that he may
need it when winter's chill set in.

During one afternoon walk, Edward found himself back up the
river, passing close to the seemingly endless high wall and steep slope
that kept him trapped in his prison.

Why not try to climb it? He was not nearly as woozy as he had been
when he'd first entered the forest.

He went over to the large rocks that made up the wall and began
to climb. Not being so tired and confused, he was having a much easier

time of it than he thought. He was even able to hold on to his walking stick, which was good because the steepness of the hill required the extra stability.

There were trees all around him, making it hard to see where he was or where he was going. The only direction he was aware of was up.

He hadn't gone for very long before wondering if he might climb a tree to possibly see beyond the canopy. He sat at the base of a particularly large tree, breathing a moment before exerting himself. That's when he heard rustling in the distance. His eyes snapped over to where the sound came from just in time to see a long, furry tail slip out of sight.

His heart sank at the thought of another fox, but then he was struck by a new thought: What if he could follow the fox to its den? Would that even be possible? The thought of nipping this particular thorn in the bud was too tempting not to try. He slowly made his way up to where he'd seen the tail.

The leaf-covered ground gave no clues to the fox's whereabouts. It was hopeless; he was no tracker. All he saw was leaves, dirt, and rocks.

Then he heard movement again and, without thinking, moved toward the sound. When he felt he was approximately where the sound had been, he stood stock-still, hoping to hear another.

He was rewarded with the fox bursting into view as it bounded off to try and get away.

Edward did all he could to follow, paying heed to nothing but the last spot of movement, but the fox was much better adapted to the terrain, and the hill was too steep for Edward to follow quickly. Edward's foot slipped, and he went tumbling down the hill. He spun faster and harder, bumping against trees and rocks as he rolled. He had to grab on to something, or he'd just keep rolling. He clutched at his walking stick, not wanting to lose it, but there was no need. Edward's descent was stopped with a sudden jerk as his back smacked against something surprisingly soft, yet still firm enough to hurt.

He opened his eyes to see a large mass of black fur. The creature let out a surprised roar of outrage before its paw smacked against Edward's side, and he began to slide again. He stuck his stick down in front of him and gripped a tree to stop from sliding any farther. As he gained his footing again, his side felt like it was on fire. His hand went to probe the area and came away bloody.

Another roar sounded from behind him, and without looking, he knew the bear was pursuing him. He tried to do a controlled slide down the slope, but no matter how fast he went, he heard the bear gaining. Edward turned around in time to see the bear standing at its full height, swiping a large, furry paw down on him.

Instinctually, Edward leaped back. He had avoided the brunt of the blow, but he felt the claws make contact with his chest, and he hit the ground and rolled. He tumbled and rolled, feeling the pain with each tree and rock he hit. He slid, trying to hold on to his stick and keep conscious, knowing he couldn't stop. To stop was certain death; he could only hope that this way had a different outcome. The one comforting thought was that he had survived this fall once.

Finally, he felt the absence of ground and the falling sensation of gravity pulling down. His body tensed in anticipation of the final blow that meant he was back at the bottom, but to his surprise, he was met with a splash and an immediate encasement of cold water. He had been dropped back in the river, the current already taking him down toward his lake.

Edward didn't dare look to see if the bear had followed; rather, he kept as still as he could, clinging to his walking stick as he floated down the river.

When he finally decided to get out and walk, all of his adrenaline had worn off, and the pain settled in. Blood collected in what remained of his shirt, and every bit of him ached. Lightning shot up his leg from his right foot. He looked down and saw that his ankle had already begun to swell. He clutched at his walking stick and forced himself onward. It was all he could do to drag himself back to his cabin and begin the arduous task of caring for his wounds. The cuts were shallow and stopped bleeding on their own, but his ankle was certainly sprained, if not worse.

The next day, Edward was too sore to get off the mound of grass he called a bed. He lay there, unable to move, drifting in and out of consciousness.

The following day, he wanted to do the same, but he couldn't ignore the sharp howls in his stomach and the scratchiness and clicks from the dryness in his throat. He got up and forced himself to drink, eat a little of his food, and tend to his fire. Just before returning to bed, he scratched two more notches in his stick; they were light but enough to distinguish them for later.

The following days were much the same. He fought the pain in his leg and scratches just long enough to tend to his food, water, and fire. The most he could manage beyond that was marking another day on his walking stick. When he started to feel better, he passed the time by attempting to carve images into it.

As time passed and Edward slowly began to heal, he wondered more and more at the many notches on his stick. By his count, he had been out here for almost two months. Why hadn't they found him yet?

Surely, they were looking for him, right?

But were they? If they *were* out looking for him, wouldn't he have heard overhead sweeps of a plane or a helicopter?

Then the thought that had been lurking just below the surface ever since he'd first woken up out here rose up and burst with an almost audible pop: *Who would really care that I was gone?*

His father, sure, and Westley, but what was that? Two people out of the entire world population.

Brittany?

His mind reeled for a moment over that one. She'd been warming up to him before his accident, but Zack had seen to that, hadn't he? Knowing Zack, he'd probably made sure she thought Edward stood her up. She probably hated him now. Would she even believe him if he tried to explain?

So, who would actually be out there looking for him? If his father had gone to the police and had them form a search party, wouldn't they have found him by now?

Ah, came that horrible voice again, *but who would be a part of that search party? Members of the town, people who have shown you over the past twelve years of bullying in school that they don't give a damn about you?*

He considered this. Even the adults in town would make comments on his weight, not as baldly as his classmates, but they stung all the same.

Did they care if he was gone? If they didn't, even if they were part of a search party, they wouldn't find a pine cone if they weren't really trying.

These thoughts and more spiraled in a mind already made fragile by the large quantity plaguing Edward through the silence of his isolation. The thoughts had gone away slightly with one immediate problem after another, but they had grown in their absence and were back in full force. All he could do was try and keep his mind occupied with acquiring food and fixing his shelter.

One day, while fishing, he looked at the tree-covered mountains. If he could actually make it to the top of one, he would probably see where to go in order to find his way back. But did he really *want* to go back?

A touch of a smile cracked at the corner of his lips. He'd lasted two months out here on his own. He survived plummeting down that mountain twice, avoided starvation multiple times, lived through a bear attack, and even stitched himself up when the occasion called for it.

Why not stay out here? It felt like the world had turned its back on him, so why not turn his back on the world?

That night, Edward sat on his chair in the firelight, looking at all the notches marking his time out here. He was lost in poisoned thoughts of a world that had left him behind.

With a sudden jerk, he rose from his chair and stormed outside to the first tree he came to. In one swift motion, he swung his walking stick against the tree trunk and snapped it in two. Then he took up the pieces one at a time and snapped them against the tree. When he was satisfied, he brought the pieces inside and threw them in the furnace.

In the weeks that followed, Edward didn't regret his decision, but the thoughts and unbidden voices never went away; in fact, they grew. It drove a spike into his brain, slowly but unceasingly. He didn't want to go back, but his mind ran rampant in the constant silence. So, what did that leave?

It wasn't long before his mind began to flirt with the idea of suicide. Just thoughts at first.

He started toying with the idea of hanging himself. At first, this was ludicrous; he couldn't if he tried, unless he hung himself with his pants, but the thought of someone finally finding his body like that deterred him. But then more and more plastic rope began to wash up, sometimes a good amount of it. He made snares for rabbits, but that voice that started to speak up again in the back of his mind, whispering at first, but steadily growing louder, and he eventually made a noose for himself.

He didn't use it after he finished but left it hanging from a crack in his door as a dark reminder of a sure way out.

Chapter 6

SIX WEEKS LATER

Time passed, silent and still. Soon, the noose by the door was not enough, so he moved it to the bed, hanging it loosely around his neck as he slept in his own version of Russian roulette. He would pull the line taut until he passed out. If he woke up the next morning, he would endure another day. If he didn't? Well, at least his troubles would finally be over.

Tonight, Edward was tired, too tired to pull himself into unconsciousness. Instead, the rope stayed around his neck, a reminder of a fate that called to him, while he dozed fitfully. A loud crack sounded from beside him. He rolled over to see embers bursting outward from the stove door in a spray of sparks. Instead of fully waking, Edward gave a loud grunt and rolled over to face the wall.

The air soon became thick, and Edward finally awoke, choking madly. He turned over to see that flames had leaped out of the fireplace and were spreading on the floor. Even though death had been on his mind these last several nights, this was not the way he'd planned it. As quickly as he could, he flung his blanket on top of the fire and stamped out the flames. The smoke in the air became worse, and it was all he could do to make it out of the door and fling himself to the ground. Choking, gasping for air, he began to retch.

It took some time before the bulk of the smoke made its way out. He stared into the darkness of the doorway, preparing himself for the damage he would find. He strode over to the blanket and checked to see if it was smoldering. He'd smothered the flames just in time. Although he now had a big soot mark on the skin side of his blanket, it had no real damage. He took one side of the blanket and began to fling it up and down to try and get rid of the extra smoke.

As the smoke cleared and his eyes adjusted, he looked down to see that the air he was moving was breathing new life into the embers left on the floor. He slammed the skin back down and grabbed his jug of water. He pulled up the blanket to reveal black scorch marks on the floor and hastily poured water onto them.

A little hiss of steam issued out as the last of the heat was drawn from the wood. Edward kept pouring out the water, but another, more curious sound struck him. He bent down and put his ear to the floorboards. It sounded like water striking ground, but from far away.

Edward grabbed the most serrated knife he'd made and picked the part of the floor where the fire had burned the deepest. The wood was old and made more fragile by the fire. He stabbed down and knocked some of the damage away until he had a hole big enough to get his fingers underneath.

He heaved up with the intention of breaking the board off, but to his astonishment, a great portion of the floor seemed to want to go with it but was held back under his weight. The sudden movement of the floor startled him. He dropped the board and scrambled back. When nothing else happened, he moved in to have a closer look.

Now that the dust had been disturbed, he could see the faint outline of a seam. Taking care to stand on the opposite side of the crack than before, he reached under the board and lifted. A two-foot square of the floor lifted all at once and fell flush on the floor behind it. A hole now yawned in the middle of the cabin.

Edward stared at it, unblinking. The opening sat and waited. He looked in the stove to see if there was a log he could use as a torch. Found wanting, he was forced to wait as another lit.

When he finally had light, he lowered it down. A wooden staircase led into the darkness. Cautiously, Edward put one foot on the first step, testing it, slowly putting more and more of his weight down, ready to jump back at the first sign of trouble. The stair didn't budge. He continued his descent, and things started to materialize around him. He was in a room that was taller than the cabin above and at least twice as wide. Big wooden barrels were stacked up on the far side of the room, opposite the stairs.

The only distinguishing mark on the first barrel he inspected was faded black paint that made up a big letter *B*. He checked another and another and found the same *B*. Then he came to one exactly like the others, but this one had the letter *W* on it. He checked the ones next to it, and they had more *W*'s.

He cracked open one of the *B* barrels, and an odor that reminded him of dirty socks wafted up out of the liquid inside.

"Beer?" he asked the room. "Then that must mean that . . ."

He went over and opened one of the barrels with a *W*. The strong odor of alcohol shot up his nose and burned his nostrils, making him cough.

"Whiskey!"

He dipped a finger in, tasted both, and found that he didn't have much of a liking for either, but he'd never been drunk before; maybe *that* was worth a try. Loads of people drank out in the sticks; it couldn't be because it tasted great.

He moved his light around and followed the wall to the area behind the staircase. There in the corner were stacks upon stacks of books. He ran over to them, hardly daring to believe it. They were all hardcover and leather bound. He read title after title. Works of all history, both myth and fact, were there, as well as all the works of Shakespeare, Homer, Sir Arthur Conan Doyle, Mark Twain, L. Frank Baum, Jack London, Robert Frost, Alexandre Dumas, and so on. Histories of the rise and fall of many empires, histories of technologies, encyclopedias all the way up to about 1930, and the list went on and on.

The books themselves must've been worth a fortune if they were half as old as they looked, yet they were still in fairly good condition. But to Edward, what lay between the pages was absolutely priceless.

The same emotion he'd felt upon catching his first rabbit came back tenfold knowing he would have this seemingly endless source of information to occupy his mind until death finally came. He wept, long and hard, thanking God for bringing him this bountiful feast for his starved, half-crazed mind.

Edward wanted to drop down and start into it right then, but he suddenly felt as if he were being watched.

His head swiveled around, and he gazed out, trying to see through the dim light. In the opposite corner was a long, plush, reddish-brown leather couch with many dimples in it from strategically placed buttons. On it lay a complete and clothed skeleton, grinning up at him with one arm laying across its dress shirt rolled up to the elbows and its pinstriped button suspenders, the other arm drooping lazily to the floor.

Edward looked around and saw a side table next to the couch, and on it, an ornate handheld lamp. He opened the lamp to see the remnants of a used candle inside and lit it.

It was then that he got a good look at the skull. A large hole was visible on the side. He moved his torch around on the floor next to the couch and discovered a gun feet away from the hand.

The sight unnerved him. It was bad enough that he had a humongous bear as a neighbor. Now, he was cellmates with a man who'd seemingly gone through the same situation that he himself had landed in.

Edward had to do something to ease both this specter and the feeling that its last remnants represented. How was he supposed to make it through the day when beneath the floorboards existed a shrine to giving up?

He picked up the revolver and opened it, pulling out all the remaining casings. Only one had been discharged. Realizing it may come in handy one day, he decided it was worthwhile to sacrifice one bullet to see if it still worked. He pointed the barrel at the far wall and pulled the trigger. He heard the telltale click, but nothing more.

He hadn't expected it to work, but it was another blow all the same. He placed the gun on the table next to the lamp and thought about the best way to get the body out. The rib cage and leg bones beneath their cloth casings moved with absolutely no resistance as he worked his hands underneath the corpse. Nevertheless, he lifted a little only to see the bones dislodge from where they had been positioned for so long.

The skull rolled and hit the floor with a sickening crack, the lower jaw separating from the top. He bent over to pick it up but immediately felt woozy. He tossed the skull back on the sofa like it was scorching hot.

A grim idea came to mind, little though he wanted to; he figured the best way to go was to wrap the body in his blanket and carry it up. Although he knew it would not stay in one piece, he could finish the job in one go.

Once all of the remains were situated, he carried the almost-weightless mass over his shoulder. Edward took the bundle far away from the house to a clearing in the trees and set to work. Using repurposed rocks, he dug a grave for the cabin's previous occupant. The ground was hard beyond the topmost layer, so Edward resolved that it would be a shallow grave. Once finished, he placed the remains down as respectfully as he could. When the time came, he hoped the next person would be just as respectful to his body.

He pushed the thought from his mind.

That was for later. When he would play his nightly game of "Eddie Roulette." That was the deal, anyway. If he lived, he would pursue the next day as best he could to preserve himself. That way, it was more fate than suicide.

More out of habit than anything else, Edward checked all his snares and the multiple fishing lines he set with either found hooks or ones he made from aluminum cans before he went back. It'd been a good haul. Three rabbits and two fish. When he brought them back, he was tempted to leave the cleaning and storing for later. He wanted to get started on the treasure trove of books downstairs, maybe indulge himself in some alcohol. But he knew this would be a mistake. If he didn't get lost in one, he was sure to in the other. The last thing he wanted was to let meat start to spoil or, worse, attract the attention of his nosy neighbor.

Once finished with his catch, he nearly flung himself on the books, wondering what he would choose first. He decided to let fate decide and pulled a book up at random. *Treasure Island* by Robert Louis Stevenson.

He'd never actually read the book, but he'd seen many different versions of it on TV. His mind went straight to the character of Ben Gunn, and he couldn't help but laugh at their similarities.

He looked over at the now-vacant couch and thought, *Why not sit down to a good read with a drink in hand?*

He retrieved one of the empty water bottles from upstairs and cut the top off. He chose the whisky because, although he didn't like the burn of the alcohol, the smoky aftertaste was more pleasant than the bitterness of the beer. He sat down on the couch, book in one hand, whiskey in the other, and began to read.

It wasn't long before he forgot about the whiskey entirely. He delved deeper and deeper into his subconscious as the harsh world of reality dissolved around him, and he became engrossed with the characters that were so beloved they withstood the test of time.

Edward sat and read until the entire book was finished. To his dismay, he found that the sky outside was pitch black. How long had he been down there?

At the sight of the blackened sky, his eyes immediately began to droop. He was hungry but thought that it could wait until tomorrow when his eyes found his bed. The blanket lay tossed on it with a good portion of his mattress exposed, as if inviting him in. He climbed in and was asleep almost as soon as his head hit the bundle of grass that served as his pillow.

The noose lay forgotten on the floor.

As time passed, Edward became more and more engrossed in his trove of books. Each day, he finished his routine as fast as he could so he could immerse himself in another story.

He found a box of candles underneath the table, but when he got in the mind to save them, he would pick a nice spot in the surrounding forest until it got too dark. Other times, he spent so much time down in the cellar that he started to sleep on the sofa. He would simply either read until his eyes became too heavy or, on occasion, drink until he couldn't read the words on the page.

One day, when Edward was in search of his next book, he noticed a stack of thin, long books that were obviously part of a set. He opened the one on top and saw they were actually notebooks. Thin, cursive writing spattered the page, and Edward had to strain to read it. He was astonished to see that the first entry was marked as July 4th, 1936.

To whom it may concern,

The following pages have been dedicated to telling my story. I am neither proud of what I've done nor truly ashamed. I only did what I did because everything and everyone I have ever believed in turned its back on me.

My name is William Nell.

Growing up, I had always wanted to go into law enforcement. I lived in a neighborhood right next to Hell's Kitchen in New York. Crime was everywhere, and I was taught by my parents that the police existed to protect the people they served.

It wasn't until I was a street cop that I became aware that even the unimpeachable goodness of the police had been infiltrated by organized crime, and many officers were on the crime lords' payroll.

I remember the day my partner, who had saved my fanny numerous times, pulled me aside to show me something.

We had just grabbed some chow, and a burly man in an over-coat and fedora came up to talk to him. They had barely spoken a word to each other when the stranger pulled out a fat envelope. Once it changed hands, the man strode off as if lightning would strike him if he stayed in one place.

"What was that about?" I asked.

"Shush," my partner said and opened up the envelope to slide a huge wad of cash out and flip through the bills. They were all tens! He cut the stack in half and extended a portion toward me.

I asked him what it was for.

"Nothin'," he said. "And you get half for doin' nothin' too." He winked. I told him no thanks and for him to keep it.

He narrowed his eyes at me and said, "You're not gonna rat, are you?" I told him a man's business is his business, and he seemed to relax.

We never spoke of it again, but the damage was done. I only found out later it was all he could do to keep the people who'd paid that money from whacking me.

It was after that I decided something needed to be done. I'd heard of the stuff J. Edgar Hoover was doing to criminals who backed crooked cops like my old partner. I sought out the Bureau of Investigation and convinced them of my eagerness to take these people down.

I worked my way up the ranks until the day J. Edgar himself pulled me aside. He said he had a special assignment for me.

It was no secret that the man was obsessed with John Dillinger. He would do whatever it took to take him and the rest of his associates down. It was no surprise when he asked me to go undercover and infiltrate the Buggs McCann gang. McCann was considered a good friend of Dillinger, so naturally, the boss wanted to keep tabs.

I was to get in by "any means necessary" and was backed wholly by Uncle Sam. However, since he doesn't take too kindly to murder, it was agreed that I should enter his company as an earner instead of as muscle.

Prohibition was in full swing, and for those who knew where to wet their whistles, you couldn't go anywhere without running into a McCann import.

The bureau was cracking down on bootleggers, so the one thing that McCann was always in need of (and consequently what good ol' Uncle had confiscated plenty of) was hooch.

I made my play at a speakeasy known to be owned by the man himself. I let the barman know I had a contact from north of the border who was looking to move some product, if he knew anyone interested. He told me he would ask around and that I should come back in a day or two.

I did.

When I showed up, I damn near wet myself. Soon as I entered the bar, it cleared out. Next thing I know, I'm staring down the barrels of two Tommys.

"Who do you work for?" one of the men holding the guns demanded. I kept calm and told him it was none of their business.

Their reply was a nice punch, right in my kisser. My lights almost went out, and I saw stars.

"Look, I don't like repeatin' myself," he said, grinning from ear to ear. "So, I ain't goin' to. What I am gon' do is unload a whole lotta lead in you, then the gulls can have what's left."

I stared him right in the eye and told him that I didn't know how things were around this joint, but I don't reveal the names of my contacts; it's unprofessional. I also told them if they whacked me, all they'd get was a heap of trouble and no hooch to show for it. I knew they didn't want that—bad for business. What I had to move was some primo stuff. All I was asking was for them to take some to the boss and let him sample it.

The smile had never left, but somehow it seemed more genuine, and he said, "All right, lemme see what you got."

And that's how it started. For the next few years until prohibition ended, I was his go-to hooch runner. It didn't really bother me that we were letting this man break the law; the money I made went right back into funding the operation, and it was all a means to an end.

I guess that was my first sign that I should have taken a closer look at my life . . .

It went on and on for pages upon pages, notebook upon notebook. It slowly dawned on Edward that this was written by the cabin's former occupant.

The story continued for days as the stranger—who was slowly becoming more of a friend—described in detail his life among the McCann gang. Everything seemed to be going well for him. He'd help out the gang, then give the bureau vital information; each time, they would get closer to making their move.

So, why did this end with him sitting alone in a cabin with a bullet in his skull?

Through the handwritten pages, Edward found out that the cabin was a remnant of the booze-running days. Any time the heat was on, McCann would hide the stuff in one of the many places just like this one all over the country. Someone would have to be out there to watch over it. One person was all you needed, but it got lonely, and McCann wanted his men to be able to keep themselves occupied, so he got somebody to stock the places with tons of books.

Edward never thought he'd be thanking the Mafia for anything, but he found himself immensely grateful for everything here, especially the books.

According to the notebooks, after prohibition ended, the gang moved into more lucrative opportunities. This station, and hundreds of others like it, were abandoned with the intention of one day reclaiming the contents if the need arose.

One of the gang's newest activities was to smuggle or obtain gold to be used as financial backing.

McCann claimed that the price of gold was about to increase dramatically. He said that he had a contact in the US government that claimed they were working on something big surrounding a fort in Kentucky, and they were investing heavily in gold by buying it up in large quantities.

Edward was on the final notebook and tried to savor every bit. This was it, he realized; this was the final story of why the man had ended up here. His heart pounding, he read on.

My heart went cold at the mention that he had an informant. How could I be sure the guy wouldn't learn of the real reason behind my presence, and then what would stop him from letting slip the information to McCann?

One day, McCann himself summoned me to a meeting with all of his lieutenants. We sat around a huge table as he circled us like a shark. Everyone knew something was up.

"We got a rat." There wasn't anger, not in his voice anyway, but all the same, the room seemed to become dark and heavy. "Someone has been runnin' to Uncle Sam about every little goings on 'round here . . . One o' you."

My worst fears had come to fruition. My skin wanted to break out in a cold sweat, but to let it would be tantamount to signing my own death warrant. By this time, I had been used to keeping my cards close to the vest and had a serviceable poker face.

"I gathered you all here to first say how hurt I am that one among you would do this to me. Haven't I treated each and every one of you as if you were my own son?"

At this, he yanked his pistol from his side holster. He waved it around and pointed it at each one of us in turn, a mad glint in his eye.

"You're all here today so that you can see what happens when you stab me in the back. You look me in the face like a man, like I'm doing to all o' you now!"

My heart barely had time to skip a beat before he pulled the trigger. Over and over until all you could hear were the empty clicks. I think we all squeezed our eyes shut at the sounds. I expected to feel the pain of it any second, and yet, nothing.

I opened my eyes to see a man two chairs down from me now covered in blood, looking up blankly at the ceiling. It was

Montague. As far as seniority went in the room, he was at the very bottom, but I think it shook the boss up that a rat had gotten that far before being detected.

My mind started screaming questions: What about me? What if he finds out? If he found out about Montague, which I had no idea about, and the same guy probably signs our paychecks, what's to stop him from finding out about me? But I couldn't allow it. Not right then, anyway. I could have all the time to muse about it later. Now, it seemed, I had gotten a reprieve from the great governor in the sky. I had to do what I could to keep myself from being strapped back down to the chair.

When McCann finally calmed down enough, he said, "To the rest of you, now you know. If there is one thing I can't stand, it's a rat. Now beat it!"

We all got the hell out of there like the place was on fire.

This was a huge breach of etiquette. When you've been marked by your own people, you get walked into a room by your best friend, and you never come out unless wrapped in a rug. I decided that I had to look into the situation.

On the next scheduled bureau debrief, I figured I'd ask about this guy. When I did, they claimed that they had "no knowledge of him whatsoever."

That got me worried. It was these people's job to know everything they could about everything. To claim they didn't know anything was more than likely an outright lie. McCann wasn't the only one who smelled a rat.

I decided to take a page out of his book and reach out for a buddy of mine back at the office to do some digging. Meanwhile, on the front lines, everything was still uneasy. Something was still bothering the boss, but no one could figure out what it was. All anyone would tell me was that Montague had been caught copying the books they kept. They knew he was passing them on, but they didn't know to whom.

Finally, my buddy came through with the goods. Turns out Montague was not only an agent, but one of ours. He had been sent in under the same orders and apparently had no knowledge of me either. I understand having a second detail, but after he was killed, why not tell me about him? Why claim to have "no knowledge whatsoever"?

I was starting to get a bad feeling from both sides. So, rather than wait to end up like Montague and have them claim they had no knowledge of me whatsoever, I was going to do something about it.

I felt like, after risking my neck, my ass was going to be left hanging out in the breeze. I'll admit it; I was mad. That's when I got the idea of how to take a huge chunk out of both McCann and Sam at the same time while ensuring my retirement.

The following week, McCann was planning on moving a huge shipment of gold. He needed extra protection but still wanted to keep it quiet. All the better for me.

They would have a total of four guys protecting the best armored car money could buy. A driver, a lookout, and the other two would keep an eye on the cargo.

Through connections of my own, I was able to figure out who was assigned to the job. That morning, I bought the driver anything he wanted to drink. He was a coffee man, and I was more than happy to keep him swimming in the stuff. Afterward, I followed the car at a distance, waiting for the inevitable.

When they finally pulled over into a fairly empty gas station, the driver made his way to the toilets, and the passenger decided to light up a smoke. I snuck up behind him with a rag soaked in chloroform. He went down with barely a struggle.

Next, I reached in my pocket and pulled out a small explosive I had made specially; I didn't want to kill anyone, and I knew it wouldn't take much. I got in the cab of the truck and paused at the little window that communicated with the hold. I started the truck, lit the fuse, tossed the bomb in the back, and closed the little shutter.

"What the—" was all they had time to say before the bang shook the truck. I sat in the driver's seat waiting for it, and finally, I saw the door open and two men stumble out in a cloud of smoke. Both had their weapons drawn, and one started shooting randomly.

I took off as fast as I dared while the door was still open in back. I knew the gold was secured, but I couldn't take the chance.

I thought I had made it out scot-free when the driver, holding his undone pants in one hand and his gun in the other, popped into sight. He let his pants drop to use both hands and steady his aim.

His bare ass now hanging in the wind, he fired into the cab as I drove off. He missed but still saw who took the truck. I knew I was now a marked man—by both sides, because I wasn't going back to the bureau. Once they learned what I had done, they would confiscate the gold and either throw me in lockup or, more likely, suicide me.

Once far enough away, I pulled over to shut the back from prying eyes and carried on. I worked my way out to the woods where I knew of an old storage place. I decided to ride out the heat for a while and hope that in the meantime, the gang didn't need to move some liquor.

The means of my retirement have been acquired; all I have to do now is wait. Sit and wait until I can find a way to move it out of this godforsaken country and live out my life in the lap of luxury.

I believe I've earned it.

Edward turned the page, expecting to find more, but every page after was blank. Days of reading notebook after notebook of Nell's exciting tales only to reach this end was a letdown. So many questions left unanswered.

He closed the book and looked around as if expecting to see the gold somewhere in the room, like he'd just overlooked it every day until now.

Through the tales of Nell's adventures, Edward felt almost as if Nell had been speaking directly to him. A distant pen pal from the faraway land of the past. It was the closest thing he had to a companion, and to have this sudden stop in communication with so many things left unsaid seemed to Edward yet another crushing blow, almost as if Nell had abandoned Edward as well.

The thought manifested itself in Edward's loneliness, but when he recognized it for what it was, he felt silly.

Still, it was there.

What had happened to Nell to make him change his mind and give up the gold for death's embrace? Was it stripped from him and he was left with nothing, or was it still out there, just waiting for the right person to take possession of it?

Surely, someone had taken it from him. No one would kill themselves if they knew they could one day spend a fortune.

Then a pang of doubt rang through Edward. As someone who had contemplated suicide, he could sympathize with a man who was left to live all alone with only the hope that one day he *might* be able to make it out to spend the money. How long had he been here before he'd finally decided to give in?

Edward had felt a reprieve when he'd found the books downstairs, as if they'd given him a new reason to live, but Nell had all of this, perhaps more, yet had still come to the conclusion that life wasn't worth living. Was there still a clock above Edward's head with the numbers slowly winding down?

Chapter 7

ALL OR NOTHING

Weeks passed since Edward discovered the books, then months, and finally years. He went over each and every one of the books in the pile. Some were stories that spirited him away, other's were welcomed information, every once-in-a-while giving up a gold nugget about useful things like edible plants or hunting techniques. Once finished with the pile, he did it again. His life now consisted of self-maintenance and moving books from one pile to another and then back again, reading each as he went.

Edward lost himself in these realms. Rather than becoming bored, each time he restarted a book, it felt like he was seeing an old friend who'd come to visit. After a while, Edward could recite whole books by heart, but it didn't matter. He'd found solace in the escape they gave him.

One day, after reading all of Nell's notebooks for the umpteenth time, Edward flipped through the empty pages in the back, and something caught his eye. Two pages were stuck together.

A fresh pang of excitement caused his heart to thud as he pulled the pages apart gently. There, in the middle of the page, was written a single word: *chair*.

Chair, he thought. *What does that mean?*

The only chair he knew of was the thick wooden one upstairs. He went up to examine it, turning it over this way and that, but nothing caught his eye. He shook and twisted every part to see if anything came loose, but the chair was as sturdy as ever. He even knocked on pieces to see if any of them were hollow, but if there was a difference in sound, he couldn't tell.

For hours, he examined the chair, but try as he might, he couldn't see any mark of a secret.

That one word consumed his curiosity. He tried going about his normal routine but found his thoughts kept going back to the chair. Every time he saw it, it mocked him, and he would check again. Still, he found nothing.

Every time the chair proved solid, he got more agitated, until he got so angry that he picked it up and threw it down the stairs. He heard a satisfying crunch when it hit the bottom.

Edward immediately regretted this. He didn't have much, and now he'd destroyed one of his few possessions. He sighed and went down to inspect the damage. It was a lost cause, but still, Edward examined the pieces to try and think of a way to fix it. He picked up one of the legs, and a sudden movement startled him, like seeing a mouse bolt by when least expecting it. This was no mouse, however. A large piece of paper that had been rolled into a cylinder had slid out of the leg and onto the floor.

Edward looked at the leg still in his hand and turned it over to see the other end. There in the middle of the thick piece of wood was a hole the diameter of a dime drilled into the leg.

He dropped the leg and snatched up the piece of paper, unfurled it, and held it up to the light. It was a crudely drawn map that looked like it was of his beach, including a marker which he supposed represented his cabin, and followed up the river into the swamp, where a large, red *X* was placed. An arrow pointed from the *X* to a box in the corner displaying a drawing of the swamp and a tree with a heart and the initials *W* + *N* carved into its trunk. The tree looked like it was on the bank of land where its large, gnarled roots spilled into the pond fed by the river.

Edward examined the area of the beach more closely. It was weird to him that the map didn't have the cabin as the starting point. He looked over to the start and saw an arrow pointing off the page with two words written beneath it.

To Road.

Here was a curious thing indeed. He'd long since stopped looking for a way back to civilization, although along the way of his wanderings he'd see many marks, possibly left by die-hard hikers going down the entire length of the Appalachian Trail. He supposed that if he'd wanted to get out, he could have found a way on his own, but as time passed, he didn't exactly know what he'd wanted. Now he had something he didn't before: a clear way back to a main road—that was, if the map proved to be accurate.

He studied the map a bit more, and another realization clicked home. The little arrow that pointed to the road sat right on the cave. The cave where the incredibly large bear lived.

Welp, probably won't be using that one in a hurry.

The next day, curiosity got the better of him. Edward was certain that one end of the map led to the bear cave, but he wasn't sure what waited at the other end. Today, he would set out to see for himself.

When he got to the general area the map indicated, he looked around for the tree with the heart carved in it. He walked all around the pond until he finally saw the markings.

"Now what?" he croaked.

He sat down cross-legged in front of the tree and stared up at the initials carved into its bark. They were weathered with almost a hundred years of age, but they were there. He let his gaze slacken. In front of the initials was most likely the best place to start, but then his eyes picked up something else. One of the huge, gnarled roots of the tree drooped out and fell into the pond next to it.

He wasn't sure why, but it almost looked like a finger pointing down into the water. An idea so absurd came to him that he had to follow up on it.

He harvested a long branch a little taller than he was, then tied his stone knife to the end of the stick, walked over to where the root fell into the pond, and stabbed the knife into the water. Only about two feet of the makeshift spear submerged before it hit either the sand or clay that lined the large pond. He pulled out the knife and wrinkled his nose at clump of slimy green sludge looking back at him.

He aimed a little farther offshore and found about three feet of the stick became submerged.

Curiosity overrode caution, and he gingerly took the first step into the water. He entered right off the root and was knee-deep instantly. He continued until the water was up to his waist. He reached farther out, and more and more of the branch disappeared until the entire thing was underwater.

He took a step forward, found nothing, and instantly plunged underwater.

The suddenness of the drop caused him to choke on swamp water. When he was able to breathe again, he sucked in deep, grasped his spear tightly, and swam downward with the tip outstretched.

It seemed very odd that the ground would drop off so suddenly. He used his stick to feel the bottom, which wasn't too far from the surface, so he slowly blew out and used his spear to prod all around him. Sludge, sludge, and more sludge. It all felt like a big waste of time, and he needed to go up and get air. He needed to go home and get his chores done and stop this ridiculous treasure hunt.

With a great thrust, he plunged his spear down to push off and get to the surface, but when he thrust the tip down, he didn't feel the soft give of sludge. Instead, he felt and heard a hard *ping* that rang through the water as he went up.

A bolt of thrill shot through Edward, and he swam to the surface, gained his breath, and went under again.

Metallic, it was metallic! Something unnatural was down there. He had to go down again and investigate. He poked around with his spear at first, and when he felt that the metal was directly below him, he dove down into the murky depths.

He felt around and found large, rusted panels of metal, complete with huge bolts that made up the seams. He went up and down, up and down, trying to explore what he could. He opened his eyes to a world of green blurs. All he could really tell he was seeing was rusted metal covered in moss that crept up its sides. The metal had to be inches thick, and an image started manifesting in his head of an armored Studebaker at the bottom of the swamp. When he found what must've been the back doors, he tried the handle, but nothing would budge. If he wanted to crack this thing open, he would have to lay his hands on the proper tools.

He got out of the water and stared down at the spot where he knew the car was lying in wait. He didn't *know* that there was gold in there, but seeing as how there was what appeared to be an old, armored car lying at the bottom where the map said it would be . . . Well, it gave him many reasons to hope. He wanted to see what was in there. No, he *needed* to see.

If the map had been right about this end, shouldn't it be right about the other? And what if there really was gold down there? What would he do with it? Was he ready to finally go back? A tight knot formed in his stomach. There was a reason to get back, and if he could find a way of getting his hands on a truckful of gold, he would have the means to accomplish that reason.

Revenge. He'd often toyed with returning to the world, mostly to get back at those three. The sweet taste after beating that fox had been absolutely intoxicating, and it had led him to wonder what it would be like to get his *real* revenge.

Hell, if there was actually gold in the back of that truck, and if there was enough of it, nothing would stand in his way. He could come up with whatever scheme he wanted to get back at them, and no matter how exuberant, he would have the money to see it through.

His thoughts spiraled, and eventually, he returned to himself with a jerk. How long had he been standing here?

He shook his head and told himself that all of that was putting the cart before the horse. If he was to even have a chance to look inside the back of that truck, he'd have to leave his wooded sanctuary.

In the time he'd been out here, he had seen marks of humans scattered around. He was fairly confident he could find a way out if he really wanted to. Then again, if he *did* get lost, he could be wandering for miles, possibly thousands of miles.

His thoughts turned to the cave, and he tried to remember what he'd seen inside. He'd only been in there once, and it felt like a lifetime ago. He'd gone up to it and stared at the opening enough times, to be sure. Always keeping an eye on its black, yawning mouth, should its guardian make an appearance.

The cave and the trail of significantly younger trees would have definitely been wide enough to fit a car through, especially an old-timey one. It would make sense too; how else would they be able to get the "hooch" in and out of the place? The entrance must've been concealed by the road, and Nell must've taken the truck down the tunnel and somehow made it out to the swamp.

Edward stood looking toward the way that would lead him back to his camp. On the one hand, there was potentially a direct way to get out of this forest and back to the road. It was possibly suicidal, yes, but the alternatives would either be to try and find his own way back—which would take longer, and he might even get even more lost or die in the attempt—or stay here and wait for death, anyway.

He thought hard but made up his mind surprisingly fast. With the thought of revenge freshly on his mind, Edward wanted to leave the forest and settle the score.

The bear was just one more score to settle.

Once his mind was made up, he felt oddly light about it. Really, if he thought about it, what was trying to tackle the bear but one more game of Eddie Roulette? And, when he got right down to it, it was something else: *practice*.

As he walked back to his cabin, he pursued any and every thought that popped into his brain about dealing with the bear.

He devoted the next few days to fishing. He wanted to catch as much fish as he could lay his hands on to lure the bear out of the cave and observe it. The thought occurred to Edward that perhaps he could lead the bear off somewhere.

He took what he'd learned about bears—both pre-woods and what he had gotten from the books—and knew he couldn't count on outrunning or overpowering it. Bears could run up to thirty miles per hour if they had the room . . . if they had the room . . .

Suddenly, Edward pinched himself all over his body like a man trying to assure himself he wasn't dreaming. He had become thin, very thin, in his time out here, and there were tons of patches of woods where the trees grew so thick and close together that Edward could easily slip through the cracks, whereas the bear would be too big.

That still left the problem of disabling it long enough for him to get away. He had no idea how long that tunnel was, and the bear would have home field advantage. He absolutely could not let the bear pursue him into the cave. He either had to find a way of being able to distract it for long enough, or else ensure that it wouldn't be able to follow him.

The monumental task ahead of him seemed like it would take forever to accomplish.

So what if it did? He could spend weeks, maybe months, planning it. An insane laugh started internally and slowly grew until he couldn't keep it in.

"In fact," he said aloud, his words broken by hearty, maniacal laughter, "I've got all the time in the world!"

Edward spent weeks before finally settling on a plan, and he practiced it over and over until he felt he was ready.

To get started, he used whatever fish he could part with as bait to get the bear out of the cave. He placed the fish down at the base of a tree by the opening of the cave and retreated into the distance to wait.

The first day, he waited for at least an hour in the trees beyond the mouth of the cave. He grew weary of his task, and his head began to loll onto his shoulders. Then a growl, low at first, began to grow. Huffs and sniffs radiated from the darkness until his opponent stepped out.

The great mass of black hair paused at the mouth of the tunnel with its nose high in the air and sniffed all around. The meat of the fish was directly in front of him, but he seemed weary, as if already getting a whiff of the trap not yet laid for him.

This was the first time Edward had gotten a good enough look at the creature to notice anything beyond its size and the length of its teeth and claws. The face was made up of a long muzzle that ended in a short, almost piglike, rubbery nose and beady little eyes close together for looking straight forward with depth perception. The hair that surrounded the face was mostly a deep chocolate color with wisps of white dispersed throughout, giving the impression that it was a seasoned veteran.

Suddenly, the bear charged to the base of the tree where the fish waited. Just before it reached the fish, however, it gave a great swipe at the dirt with one of its forepaws, sending a cloud of dust into the air as it huffed and looked around.

Edward crouched behind his tree and made no movement, intently watching.

It was plain that the bear sensed something amiss, but seeing nothing come about, it bent its head down and began to eat. The bear stepped on the dead fish with its massive paws and lowered its jaws to tear meat away from the carcass.

Edward leaned forward to get a closer look around the tree, and a twig gave way with a loud crack.

Immediately, the bear rose up on its hind legs to defend its meal. It looked all around, still not sure where the sound had emanated from, and gave a loud roar before continuing to sniff. It wasn't long before the bear started to make its way into the tree line toward Edward.

Trying to make sense of the situation, Edward placed his nose beneath one arm and sniffed great whiffs of his body. He couldn't smell anything but was quite sure the bear could. He slowly started to back away, waiting for an opportune moment when the beast was looking off in the wrong direction.

The bear became frustrated, knowing that something was wrong, and sprinted straight up a tree with a speed that was almost too quick for Edward to keep track of.

Edward made a mental note that up a tree was not the way to go to escape. The bear's attention was more on climbing the tree at present, and it was now thirty feet above the forest floor. Edward took the opportunity to make a break toward the shoreline and zigzagged though the trees in order to get home.

He didn't dare look back for fear of what he might see. Once he made it inside the cabin, he lit a fresh torch, took it in the basement, closed the floor behind him, and waited.

Seconds passed with nothing but the crackle of the fire next to his ear. The seconds turned into minutes with no change, and Edward felt sure the animal hadn't pursued him.

He sat in the dim light of his torch on top of the stairs beneath the floorboards and went over all the events that had just taken place. He wanted to continue studying the bear, but doing so would be hardly worth the effort if it constantly smelled him out.

And then it came to him. When he had been poking around at the bottom of the swamp, his knife had found nothing but rancid green sludge lining the bottom of the water. What would happen if he covered himself with the sludge? The bear would be able to smell him for sure, perhaps even better than it ever had, but he wouldn't smell like himself. He would smell like dirty swamp water, right?

He shrugged his shoulders. What had he got to lose?

The next day, Edward gathered enough sludge from the swamp to cover every part of himself. He walked back to the cave to try again. He didn't dare put fish out this time in fear of transferring the swamp smell onto them, therefore defeating the whole purpose.

He waited for hours, but nothing happened. Not so much as a sniff or a huff. He took this for a good sign. If the bear was able to smell him, wouldn't it come out to investigate?

The next few days ran in much the same way. Edward came up with many different tests to coax the bear out of its den to see what would happen.

One important lesson came from setting fish next to a fire near the mouth of the cave. The bear came out to investigate but absolutely refused to get too close to the flames; in fact, it showed clears signs of aggression toward them.

The cogs began to turn, and a plan formed in Edward's head. The ideas he had would certainly be considered mad by anyone who wasn't desperate, but Edward was willing to try anything.

This wasn't like the fox; he knew he'd only get one shot. He was planning to go up against a humongous black bear that had years of experience in survival. It was fat and had no signs of living harshly. He remembered seeing those old television shows before he'd landed out here, usually titled things like *When Animals Attack* or *World's Most Dangerous*, any of which that concerned black bears either had testimony of those who'd barely survived and now bore the marks forever or else told the story of those who hadn't.

Even the accounts of bears in the books below the shelter didn't hold much hope. Many people who'd had working guns had tried to take on bears only to be killed and eaten. Edward had to take out what looked to be a full-grown male.

He spent the next few weeks preparing. He studied the lay of the forest, caught and stored as many fish as he could, cut down countless branches, whittled pounds of sawdust, collected huge mounds of dry leaves, and made at least a hundred spears. He hoped the last wouldn't be necessary, but he was playing for keeps—the bear certainly would be.

The plan was to set up a trail of fish to a large pile of them deeper in the thickest parts of the forest to keep it busy long enough for Edward to make his way through the cave. He would cover himself in the sludge to hopefully remain invisible to the bear and set a fire at the mouth of the cave to keep it from going back in as well as propel it forward *hopefully* towards the fish. The spears, as well as one final surprise, were set for the contingency of the bear going for him instead of the bait.

When the day of action finally arrived, Edward packed everything he could carry with him into a bag he'd made out of his blanket. He ate any food he wasn't going to use, and heartily. His struggles would be over today, one way or the other; at least if he died, it would not be of starvation, as he'd once thought.

Ironic, though, that I might end up as a meal.

His supplies had been laid throughout the trees, the bait had been set, and he now sat in wait to spring the trap.

Edward had laboriously chopped away at the base of a large tree that stood beside the mouth of the cave until he was certain that two or three more good whacks would send it hurtling to the ground, which had been laid with pounds of dry wood shavings and leaves. There at the base of the tree, keeping one eye on the bait and another on the mouth of the cave, he sat waiting, covered from head to foot with some of the worst-smelling sludge known to man.

He sat still as a statue. The only sign of life came from the bright whites of his eyes in the contrasting darkness, accented by the sharp, piercing blue circles. Next to him, flickering, stood his torch stuck in the dirt.

A long time passed. Still the first of the bait lay untouched, and not so much as a hint of movement came from the cave. Edward began to wonder if the bear was not there when finally, from the midst of the darkness, came a low sniffing sound.

Sniff. Sniff. Huuuuff.

Ever so slowly, the bear made its way out into the clearing at the mouth of the cave. Tentatively, it made its way to the fish.

Sniff. Sniff. Huuuuff.

It didn't begin to eat but instead raised a suspicious muzzle up into the air and swiveled its head around.

A shot of dread went through Edward. His heart leapt up into his throat, his stomach dropped in the polar opposite direction, and every fiber of muscle became tense.

He knows . . .

As if the bear could hear Edward's thought, it opened its mouth wide and bellowed a loud, challenging roar that seemed to shake the trees.

The roar awoke Edward from his stupor, and the entire reason for him sitting there came flooding back. He took the sharp, flat rock tied between two halves of a partially split branch that served as his ax and started wailing away hard at what was left of the tree.

A few strikes were all it took, and the long trunk crashed on the ground, causing the bear's attention to focus on it. Edward quickly lit the shavings and leaves that were directly in front of him, then threw the torch to the mouth of the cave. With an unearthly speed, all the dry tinder caught and lit the branches of the fallen tree, effectively blocking the mouth of the cave.

Rather than scaring the bear off towards the food, the bear let out a huge roar of anger and frantically searched all about for the cause of its distress.

The bear turned and locked eyes with Edward. It started towards him and Edward's eye's went wide.

"Shit!"

In that one word he felt the futility of at least half of all his planning. Edward ran, half panicked. The bear saw the movement, and a primal instinct took hold. The great bear gave chase.

Edward kept running as fast as he could, but he heard the thundering crashes of the bear's progress behind him. The power behind that charge was terrifying. When he turned to look, it was as if the trees were moving out of its way.

Edward made for the denser parts of the forest where both predator and prey had to move slower. He wasn't sure which side of the scale he was on.

He was hoping that he still might salvage his original plan, if he could only lure the bear to the pile of fish, maybe it would go for it instead of a moving target. He was just able to reach his invisible line where the trees began to restrict movement for the bear and found himself having to suck in his nonexistent gut to slip through. The bear, on the other hand, never took its eyes off him, instead pushing the trees until they bent enough for it to fit through. Edward stopped and stared, just for a half breath. In that short amount of time, he saw the huge face of the bear poking through the space between trees as it used its huge mass of muscle to make them give way.

He looked into its eyes, those beady, terrible, black eyes, but behind the black, he saw a flash of red and all at once knew that this was to be a fight to the death. There was something in that gaze that seemed supernatural and convinced Edward of the bear's intent. He knew he couldn't take on a bear strait on. But the small gaps between trees that Edward could fit through would slow the bear down. If he took enough bites out of it, he could weaken it enough for him to escape.

He tightened his grip on the ax as he waited for the bear to get close enough. Then he raised it high into the air and brought it crashing into the bear's skull. The rock that served as a blade exploded, a red gash opened in the fur, and a useless stick now lay in Edward's hands. The blow, far from subduing, enraged the bear further. It bellowed in anger, causing Edward's ears to ring with the force of it.

He dropped the handle and fled farther into the dense wood, all the while following his line to the shelter. The trees never stood a chance against the power of the massive claws that tore at them, but they did hamper the bear's progress.

Edward finally got to his first marker, picked up the spear that lay in wait, and stabbed with as much force as he could muster. The spear stuck just above the bear's left shoulder, and Edward backed away. As he turned, he saw the bear swat the stick protruding from its body with the ease of batting a fly.

Before getting far enough away and starting to his next marker, Edward felt a long road of pain bloom out from his flesh that started from his left shoulder and ended at the small of his back, just above his right hip. He shouted in pain from the swipe but knew his only chance was to keep moving forward.

Warm liquid dripped like candle wax down his back as he ran until, finally, he reached his next marker. He grabbed the spear and turned. The bear was so close to Edward that it didn't care its head was caught in the gap between two trees. It started swiping at Edward with both sets of razor-sharp claws, one already dripping red and dangling something. Edward could only pray it wasn't his flesh as he took the spear and gave another lunge forward.

This time, the spear lodged in the bear's armpit, and when it came loose, a large spurt of blood came with it, possibly from a nicked artery. Edward didn't stop to think; he turned and ran for his next marker.

The closer Edward came, the more he felt the pain spreading from the wound on his back, and exhaustion closed in. He could see his marker, though; he just had to reach it to get another chance of ending the chase.

Just as Edward's fingers tightened around the next spear, hot daggers plunged themselves into his upper right thigh. The bear had bitten down, but rather than taking a chunk out of him, the powerful jaws swooped him off his feet and threw him off to the side, into a tree.

The wind was knocked out of Edward, and he sat there, choking for breath. Hard gasps sucked in air, but no relief filled his lungs. His eyes watched as the bear turned to continue. It reared up on its hind legs and meant to come down with its full force on Edward.

The spear was still grasped tightly in Edward's hand, and he thrust it upward. The bear first came down, then stumbled back in surprise. Again, it batted away the nuisance now sticking out from its chest and returned its attention to Edward. This distraction had given Edward enough time to get back to his feet and make for the next spear. His upper leg and his entire back were on fire. He searched frantically for his next marker, and to his astonishment, he could see the shelter not far off in the distance.

The sight of the hut filled Edward with a new hope and gave him that extra push to keep going. He made it to the next marker with a spear and turned to look for his pursuer. He'd gained a little bit of ground, and his heart leaped at the thought that the beast was finally slowing down.

Slowing, but still coming.

He knew the surprise in the shelter still might not be enough. Instead of waiting for the bear to get close, Edward chucked the spear at the bear's face. It bounced off almost immediately but not before cutting one eye open, rendering it useless. Edward kept running between the trees as best he could, but his leg was making it hard to move. The gaps between the trees began widen as he got closer to the shelter, but still he heard the continuing thuds of paws on the ground and low huffs and growls. Once he reached the clearing, he gave a quick glance back. The bear was still coming and keeping its one good eye focused on Edward.

Edward hobbled his way into the cabin, making sure to give the closed cellar door a wide berth, and sat, legs splayed out on the floor with his back propped against the darkened stove, waiting for his pursuer, a knife grasped firmly in one hand. The cold metal felt good on his back as it drew the heat from it.

The bear emerged from the tree line, eye still locked on its next meal. It was moving slowly now, sluggish. Its dark fur was matted with blood, dirt, and leaves. It closed in on its prey, staring intently at Edward's head.

Groans emanated from the wood straining underneath the weight of the beast as it made its way into the cabin. Edward sat there, knife in hand, ready to die defending himself if it came to it. He glared into that one good eye. It was black and full of malice.

The devil is in that eye.

The bear was still huffing and grumbling, its mouth open, displaying a row of large lower teeth. The smelly, hot breath that emanated from it engulfed Edward. The bear finally came to the area right in front of Edward, and the basement door—whose supports were weakened by Edward in preparation for this very moment—instantly refused to hold such a heavy burden. The thin facades that remained of the wood burst out in great shards. The animal, caught totally unaware, fell downward, tumbling into the black abyss, its roars echoing throughout the cabin.

Edward crawled over to the large, yawning mouth of the hole. The furry mass lay helpless on the floor. The only movement came from the rapid rise and fall of small, shallow breaths.

Edward knew better than to go down there to either check or try to put it out of its misery; every animal was at its most fierce when close to death. Hadn't he just proved that? Instead, he hobbled out of the cabin and made his way down the path to the water, all the while keeping an eye and an ear out for signs that the bear had recovered.

None came.

Chapter 8

THE WAY BACK

Edward stayed in the cold water for a long time after it was over. He did what he could to clean up his wounds after washing all the sludge off, but he knew he was going to need medical attention. The adrenaline was gone, and the pain was beginning to come in earnest. It took him five attempts to fully leave the coolness of the water; each time, when the pain returned, he'd have to submerge himself again.

When he finally managed to get himself out, he drip-dried while grabbing the frayed piece of fabric that was once his undershirt.

His leg was still bleeding and felt very stiff. He had no idea what was going on with his back, but it felt rather soothing as the bright sun dried the water off it in waves, taking the heat with it.

He wrapped his leg in the fabric and tied his belt around the middle, not too tight, but enough to apply pressure. When he finished, he donned what used to be his pants and shirt, tying a piece of rope around his waist to keep his pants up.

Edward picked up the makeshift bag that contained the rest of his possessions and slung the strap over his shoulder. He did what he could to avoid the scratches, but touching them was inevitable. He gave a yelp of pain when the strap brought the full weight of the bag down on them.

Off in the distance, at the base of the steep hill, a large plume of smoke hung heavily around the tops of the trees that surrounded the cave entrance. He watched as the smoke moved upward, thinned out, and was carried off by the wind.

At the cave entrance, the remains of the tree that Edward had felled were still smoking. The leaves and small branches had all burnt to ash; the trunk itself was too moist to catch. A few of the branches were still smoldering. Edward found a dry one from the surrounding forest and lit it for his torch.

He took his first tentative steps inside the cave, on the lookout for any more bears that might've been hanging around. His biggest fear was to spot cubs that might now have been orphaned. He was pretty sure the bear had been male but hadn't exactly gotten a good look.

The first part of the cave looked how anyone would have expected: a large, enclosed cavern that seem to occur naturally within the rock. There were certainly bear tracks in the dirt floor, but at the far end of the cave was a large, uniform opening leading off in the opposite direction.

The manmade tunnel was big enough for a large vehicle to get through with plenty of room to spare. It led steadily upward with nothing but darkness beyond, but Edward pressed forward.

He'd been walking for at least twenty minutes before he saw a glimmer off in the distance. Steadily, the speck began to grow. When the bright archway was the same size as the rest of the tunnel, Edward dropped the remains of his torch and started running as much as he could with his injured leg. A large line stretched across the bottom portion of the opening with a square in the middle of it.

He stepped under the line and turned around. As his eyes adjusted to the light, he saw a plank of wood barring access to the tunnel with a faded sign:

WARNING
STAY OUT!

CONDEMNED

MINE SHAFT

An overgrown path lay before him, and he followed it around a large, bald rock that blocked it from the view of the road.

A long, black river of solid asphalt stretched out before Edward. He paused, shocked at the sight. He knew he'd find it here, but he still couldn't believe what he was seeing after so long. Here was the first tangible sign of the way back to the world he'd given up what felt like eons ago.

Edward stood for a few moments and looked in both directions. The thought of seeing his river for the first time sprang to mind. He had a choice: left or right. He had a fifty-fifty shot again. He chose to go right and hoped that this time, it was the right way to go. Either way should take him to civilization, but one direction might be significantly shorter than the other. A short time after getting started, he saw a mile marker on the side of the road with the number eighty-four on it.

Good! he thought. *Easier to be able to find this spot again.*

The day was swelteringly hot. Edward walked for what seemed like hours. Occasionally, he took a swig from his water bottle, but it would only give him so much relief. His back ached, and his leg was beginning to seize up. Exhaustion pushed on him with every step. The sun made agonizingly slow progress across the sky with no sign of a car in the horizon. When the sky finally started to turn red and orange, he found himself urging on the coolness of night.

He kept on going, not willing to give up yet. Each step was excruciating. He decided to look for a marker and vow to make it just to that point. A corner up ahead curved the road to an unknown destination.

He pushed himself to make it that far. And then he saw the headlights. A few of them. He stumbled his way toward three cars in a clearing off to the side of the road. Someone sat on the hood of one car, staring at the other three, who were bent underneath the open hood of another.

As he got closer, he noticed one of the cars was a Lamborghini Huracán. It wasn't any year he could recognize, but there was no mistaking that style.

"Whoa!" he shouted, unable to keep himself from doing so.

The four people by the cars had apparently been unaware of his approach in the dying light and now showed signs of apprehension.

Two of the three that stood in front of the open hood moved a hand behind their backs as if reaching for something. The third raised his hand up toward the other two in an attempt to calm them. Edward noticed all of this but forced himself to act as if he hadn't.

The third man, a muscular guy with curly, blond hair and a silk, short-sleeved button-up, smiled and said, "What's that?"

"Sorry, I was just admiring the Lambo you got there. Huracán, yeah?"

The smile on the stranger's face widened. "That's right."

Edward's eyes turned to one of the other cars. "And that's an Audi R8! I've only seen pictures of this car; never thought I'd see it in person."

"Right again, brother." The man was openly laughing now, but the other three still looked nervous.

Edward turned to the car with the hood popped. He didn't quite recognize it. It was a short car that sat low to the ground with gentle, luxurious curves.

"Is that a Ferrari?" he ventured.

"That's right, amigo; the F599. Gotta say, didn't expect such knowledge about cars from a wanderin' man such as yourself."

Edward paused for a moment, not sure what this could mean.

Then it came to him. He had to look like a homeless man walking the road with his dirty clothes and unkempt hair and beard. He only hoped he didn't smell too bad. He had a vague thought that his appearance might be why the others felt so nervous.

"Yeah, once upon a time, I was really into all things automotive," Edward said with a smile.

"What happened?"

"Went out for a walk one day and just kept walkin', I suppose."

The tension eased, not much, but a bit.

"I see you got some engine trouble. Mind if I take a look?"

All four laughed at this, and then the man said, "By all means." He gestured with a sweeping motion toward the car.

Edward bent under the hood and looked at the pristine engine block. "What year is it?" he asked.

"It's current," the man said.

Edward, having absolutely no idea what the year was, feigned deafness. "Pardon?"

"It's a '20, I said."

He froze while bent over the engine. Six years. He'd had a vague idea of how long he'd been away, but now it was cemented. He'd spent six long years in that forest. That must mean that he was around twenty-four years old.

Sweat sprouted on his forehead as his thoughts spiraled.

". . . wrong with it?"

Edward heard the last part of the question as if someone had finally turned up the volume on a TV.

"Nothing I can see, exactly. What happened to land you here?"

The other three seemed to become nervous again, but the man said, "I was just driving, and all of a sudden, the engine light came on, and then everything seemed to just quit on me. Lucky we were driving in a group, and I had these guys help me push it to a turnout."

"That is lucky," Edward said with a smile and a slight hint of a sardonic tone.

The man was no longer smiling, and through a much tighter face, he said, "What's that?"

"I was just saying that that *is* lucky! You could've lost control and ended up in a ditch or smashed into a tree or something." His own accident six years ago came back to him, and the last few words cost him great effort to get out, but the others seemed to relax a bit.

"Anyway, once I pulled over, we checked the codes it was giving, and it said a whole bunch of things were crapping out, but everything I checked that was coding looked like it was brand-spanking-new."

After studying William Nell's accounts over the years and unintentionally committing them to memory, Edward had his suspicions as to what was going on. The world may have changed in many ways over time, but what was the old saying? The more things change, the more they stay the same.

"So, any thoughts?" The man startled Edward out of the many he'd been lost in.

"One or two."

The day was hot, even as the sun was going down. Edward's face flushed, and he started to feel lightheaded. He shook his head and refocused.

A wild idea popped into his head from an article he read his last year at school. It was a hunch, but still he tried to locate where the electronic control unit was. After a few minutes of searching the engine bay, he lifted up the black plastic cover surrounding the edges.

"What are you looking for?" the man asked.

"I'll know when I see it." Edward's back was bent in an awkward position, and the scratches screamed in pain, but this was his one shot. He needed help, and to get it, he had to offer this group some in return. He began to feel faint, but he couldn't let things take their current course. The last thing he wanted was attention from any branch of law enforcement. If his hunch was right, they may already be on the way to this spot.

Then he saw it: a small, rectangular box with a stubby antenna poking up at the top, wired directly into the ECU.

"A knife!" He stuck his right hand out. "Someone give me a knife!"

A short pause filled the air as Edward stared at the little gadget. He supposed that they were deciding whether to give him one when he heard a flick and felt the handle of a large pocketknife thrust into his outstretched hand.

He brought it in and immediately went to work. He removed the little square and repaired the connection, hoping against hope that it would be enough. He was lucky enough for his theory to be correct given that he had a six-year gap in technology; maybe he'd be lucky again.

Once he felt it was good enough, he straightened up and took a few steps back. He swayed a little at the sudden rush of blood from his head, and the fire in his back quieted down to a painful throb.

"Give it a go now," he said, a bit out of breath.

One of the silent men crossed over. He was the tallest one with thick, brown, wavy hair pulled back into a ponytail. He wore boots that came to sharp toe-points with jeans and a T-shirt with the sleeves cut off. He crouched over low to stick his long legs into the cab. Edward would've marveled that the man could fit in it at all if he wasn't feeling so lousy.

Edward closed the knife and held it out while still looking at the man trying to position himself into the car. The woman of the group reached out and took it back.

Edward screamed silently in his head, asking the powers that be for this to work.

To everyone's astonishment, the engine roared to life, and the screaming, pleading voice in Edward's head became silent and eternally grateful.

"What did you do?" the blond man asked.

In answer, Edward held up the small black box for all to see, then tossed it to him.

"That's an ECU interrupter. I've only read about the concept of this device; when I learned about them, they said the tech was at least ten years away, I had no idea they'd be making them so soon. Someone must have spent quite a bit for this little gadget!

"It's a kind of trap, designed to mimic engine trouble so that not only does it stop the car from moving, but it also keeps the driver busy while a response team is set in motion. It's basically a disguised kill switch the owner can activate in case the car, uh, wanders off . . ." He broke off and tried as best he could not to sound judgmental.

Edward avoided looking anyone directly in the eyes. He worried about how they were going to take it.

The first man piped up again. "What are you trying to say?" He said it in such a way that Edward was unable to really judge the tone behind it, if there had been one at all.

"I'm saying that a man's business is *his* business. I don't know anything, and I don't need to know. Look at me; do I look like the kind of guy who can look down his nose at anyone?"

Edward paused for a moment. He was really starting to feel woozy, not from the position he was in but from the pain that seemed to have spread over his whole body.

"What I do need is a ride out of this godforsaken place and one hell of a strong drink if you got one." Edward was now struggling just to stay upright and conscious.

They all looked at him for a moment. The man who had first talked to Edward stared at him for a moment, sizing him up; then a small grin worked its way onto his face, and he nodded.

"All right. You ride with me."

He gestured to the Lamborghini. Then he gestured to himself and everyone else in turn. "I'm Jake. That tall drink of water over there is Lou. That's Erica, and that over there is Twitch."

Edward looked over to the last and saw immediately why he had that name. He was a close-cropped blond man of average height who also wore a button-up shirt, but he left his open to the wind, exposing a white wifebeater underneath. Twitch had a constant tic that reminded Edward of a horse trying to shake off a fly that would never really go away.

"Eddie," Edward said to the group at large, nodding in return.

"Well, Eddie"—Jake tossed the black box over his shoulder—"let's get the hell outta here."

"Thought you'd never ask." Edward limped his way to the car.

"Wait!" Jake said, going around to the back of the car and pulling something from the trunk. He walked over to the passenger side and placed a towel down on the seat. He looked at Edward and said, "Sorry, amigo; no offense."

"None taken, believe me. That actually makes me feel a lot better about getting in."

As Edward sank into the cushioned leather, the entirety of the day fell on him like a ton of bricks. He'd fought a bear; left all he'd known for six years behind by limping his way through a long, dark tunnel; walked for miles in the sweltering heat and right into a band of car thieves, only to become an accessory to the act in order to hitch a ride. He'd had a full day.

"Hey . . ." Weariness was overcoming him, and his words sounded slurred. "You got a guy you go to for medical attention?"

"Yeah, I noticed you were limping a bit back there. Anything serious?"

"I had a pretty nasty fall earlier; cut my back and leg up pretty good."

"No worries, man. I'll get you to him A-sap."

"Thanks." Edward felt himself slipping into sleep, but one thought popped into his head that he had to know. "Can I ask you something?"

"Shoot."

"How the hell'd you know there'd be a towel in the trunk?"

Jake let out a loud, booming laugh. "Man, nothin' gets by you." He paused, grinning broadly. "We *acquired* this car from a place that was in close proximity to a lake."

Edward smiled, and his eyelids, which seemed to weigh more than the car they were sitting in, sank.

When Edward finally awoke, he was in an unfamiliar place. It was clearly someone's bedroom, or possibly a guest room. It was completely dark save for a small decorative lamp that served as a night-light.

He tried to sit up but noticed he had tubes and wires sticking out of his arm. He lifted his coverings and saw he was naked but for a large bandage wrapped around his leg. He felt different. It was the first time he'd been in a real bed in six years, the first time he'd felt fresh linen on clean skin. Yes, that was it. He felt clean.

On the dresser from where the light emanated stood a large mirror. Edward wanted nothing more than to finally see himself in earnest but found he had to pluck up the courage to do so.

His bare toes felt the unfamiliar tickle of carpet beneath them. He trembled as he walked over to the mirror, clutching the cold stand that held his IV for support.

When he was right at the edge of viewing himself, he took a deep breath and stepped in front of the mirror.

In the glass, he saw the shadow of a man from the waist up. His body was completely unfamiliar: bony with a hint of muscle below the skin, which was stretched too thin across the framework and accentuated by the small, amber light. The face was pretty much nonexistent. A large, roundish ball of matted hair sat upon the stranger's shoulders with only a small patch of visible skin making up the nose and sunken eyes, nothing more than blackened pits in the darkness.

Edward looked to the left of the dresser, where the door stood. He reached over and flicked on the main light. Immediately, everything became a white blur, and he had to squint against it. Slowly, the room came into view. His eyes returned to the man in the mirror. He'd made things worse, if that was possible. A tanned skeleton with a fuzzy skull now stood before him. The only things there to remind Edward the man in the mirror was him were the piercing blue eyes he remembered from his childhood as they shone through the mess of tangled, black hair.

Edward looked around and saw a desk in the corner of the room with a chair in front of it. On the chair was a handsome, navy-blue robe. He crossed over and put it on except for his left arm, which was still attached to the IV, which he loosely covered with the front with the hand protruding in a reverse Napoleon fashion.

Once everything was situated, he went to the door and walked out of the room. The hallway it opened into was bright and inviting. The lights shone on the interior of a house that was much fancier than the one he'd grown up in. The hall had several other doors on either side as it led its way over to a staircase spilling downward. The window on the far wall showed that the world outside was dark. Slowly, he made his way down the stairs clutching his IV stand to support his sore leg.

He followed the savory scent of freshly brewed coffee into the kitchen, where a man he didn't recognize was poring over papers at a table. The man stirred when he sensed movement and looked over the rim of his glasses at Edward.

"It *is* alive." He stood up. "C'mon over here so I can have a look at you."

He was an older man with gray hair swept back from a wrinkled brow. He was wearing a white button-up beneath an open cardigan and shuffled over to pull out a chair for Edward.

"Sit with your face to the back of the chair." Edward was about to do so when the man said, "Hang on a sec; lemme make it a little easier on you." He closed the clip on the tube and took Edward's arm out of the front of the robe to remove the needle. "Now that you can eat and drink for yourself, you don't need this anymore."

Edward felt the pinch as the needle was pulled. "Thanks."

"No problem. Now, lean forward; I'm gonna have a look at your back."

Edward felt the painful tug of adhesive tape being pulled from his skin, and he sucked in air through a clenched jaw and winced.

"Sorry, young fella; had to be done." He poked and prodded at Edward's back and gave a low whistle. "Hell of a job you did back here. What happened?"

"I was walking through the forest, lost my footing on a hill, and got banged up pretty good on the way down." He wasn't exactly sure why he chose to lie, but he felt he wanted to keep actual particulars to himself.

The man gave a small smile, unseen by Edward, but he could hear it in his voice. "Must have been a hell of a fall to have symmetrical gashes all the way across. Perhaps you scraped along part of a rake. Then maybe that rake wrapped around your leg and impaled it."

Edward was at a loss but was determined to keep it out of his voice. "I think—"

"Spare me, sonny; I don't need to know. If you don't want to tell me, that's your business. I just need to ask if you think there might be a contamination of rabies."

Now it was Edward's turn to smile. "Definitely not."

"Definitely?"

He paused for a moment as a glaze of memory passed over his eyes. Then, with less conviction, "Ninety-nine percent sure."

The man raised his chin a bit and looked down at him through his spectacles. "Welp, that's good enough for me. 'Sides, if you're wrong, it'll be your problem." He crossed back over to his chair and sat down. "Name's Matthew Greenfield, MD. Retired."

Edward pulled the robe back up. "Eddie."

If the doctor was perturbed by Edward's unwillingness to share his last name, he didn't show it. He just picked up the paper he'd been reading, and his eyes started moving back and forth.

"So, Dr. Greenfield—"

Without looking up from his paper, he gave a great, singular "HA!" Then, "Call me Matt, Eddie; everyone always does. Haven't been Dr. Greenfield for almost twenty years now."

"All right, then, Matt." Edward was quite sure he liked him. "How'd I end up here?"

"You don't remember?" Matt looked concerned, as if this may have been a symptom he'd missed.

"I remember being in Jake's car and passing out."

Looking somewhat relieved, Matt said, "Well, that's about the long and short of it. Jake brought you over to me, and we got you inside and looked at. He's a good man, Jake. Says he found you by the side of the road, half-dead, seems like."

"How do you know Jake?"

"Oh, we go way back. Helped me out of a spot of trouble back in the day. Never lets me forget it, either." Despite also not wanting to go into particulars, his smile grew in remembrance.

"I don't mean anything by this statement, but . . . uh . . . I seem to have met Jake at the beginning of his new career."

The smile remained plastered on Matt's face. "Yeah, it's definitely a newer path. But I'll let him tell you about that. All I can say is I don't blame anyone for desperate acts nowadays. Not with everything going on in the world."

"How long was I out?"

"Two days. It's July fifteenth."

Edward's head was starting to spin a bit at the thought.

"I'll let Jake know you're up and about now, but he probably won't be awake for a couple of hours. It's only"—he checked his watch—"five fifteen. Why don't I give you something to sleep a little longer, and when you get up, the three of us can have a nice breakfast."

Edward wanted to say that he'd slept enough, but his head began to hurt, and the thought of waking up to a meal that wasn't caught and prepared by himself sounded amazing.

"That sounds like a great idea."

Matt got up and shuffled his way over to the pantry. He came back to the table with a prescription bottle and a glass of water. He pulled out a pill and handed it and the glass over. Edward placed the pill on his tongue and downed the entire glass.

"I have your bag of stuff over here on the counter," Matt said. "I hope you don't mind; I was trying to see if you had any allergy warnings on you, since I couldn't ask you myself."

"Oh, thanks! Don't worry about it. I'm just grateful for all you've done."

Matt fiddled with something and then came back with Edward's fur bag. "Took the liberty of charging your cell phone for you."

Edward's eyes went wide. "You did?"

"Yeah. Hell of an oldie you got there, but I can't complain. I still use a clamshell myself. I had a Nokia back in the day, and I can never bring myself to throw out a charger. I know the second I do, I'll need it for whatever reason. Got a whole drawer of tangled-up chargers all to themselves."

"Did it turn on?"

"Didn't try, but the little light on the top lit up, so I figured it was charging."

Edward didn't know what to say or think. He just stammered out, "Thanks again," as he limped his way back up to his bedroom.

When he reached the top of the stairs, he heard Matt's voice calling up, "I put a stack of clothes for you on the bathroom counter across the hall. They'll be a little big, but they should do."

"Thanks!" Edward called as he closed the door.

He crossed over to the bed and plopped down on it. With trembling fingers, his hand rummaged around in his bag for his phone. He felt the small brick, brought it out, and stared at it.

There was no way it would still work, not as a phone, anyway. Nevertheless, he turned it on and watched with rapt attention as the little screen went from a blank, empty green to a bright, active blue. Then the black letters of the home screen appeared. The little cell tower in the top corner had bars. One, then two, then three.

There's no way, he told himself. *There's just no freaking way.*

Then, incredibly, the phone began to buzz.

Over and over, the phone repeated its two-buzz notification. Each a ghost from the past.

After about a minute, the phone lay still in his hands. He looked down into the screen: twenty text messages and eleven voicemails.

He wasn't sure he was ready for this. His heart began to thump in his chest, but amazingly, he could also feel himself getting tired. The pill had started its work. Yet he couldn't look away. The train wreck of his life had been recorded as it all came to a screeching halt.

He started with the text messages. Most were from his father. Edward felt like he was reading someone else's journal, but everything was addressed to him.

Hey E! Hope you had fun. When ya coming home?

Where R U?

Call me!

Ur 3 is grass!

I'm sorry E, please call!

They went on like this, cycling through emotions.

Then he saw a bunch from Westley.

How'd it go?

Your Dad called, asking for you.

Where are you?

And so on.

Then, to his amazement and horror, he saw the next group of messages, labeled "Britt." He knew deep down that this was coming but was in no way ready for it.

Hey! I'm here. lmk whn Ur prkd.

You coming?

Hope ur alrite

Then came the voicemails. The ones from his father were pretty much the same as his texts, but hearing his voice after so long broke Edward's heart into a thousand shards with each pang of sadness or anger emanating from the speaker.

Then he heard the voice of his only true friend calling out to him from the deep recesses of the past:

"Hey, Eddie. Listen, could you give me a call as soon as you can? Your dad's *really* freakin' out, man. He's just trying to figure out where you are. He called to tell me he's already called the sheriff. Just call me, bro. Lemme know what's going on!"

Of all the voicemails he'd received, only one was from Brittany, yet this was the most unexpected and by far the hardest to listen to. Edward could tell that she'd been sobbing, and she was, in fact, still crying through the message.

Sniff. "Eddie? Listen . . . I know that you're probably never going to hear this, but I had to do something"—she laughed nervously—"or else I'm gonna go crazy . . ."

There was long pause filled with sniffs and wracking sobs. She couldn't stop her crying and decided to fight through it.

"I just wanted to say I'm sorry! I'm so sorry I got mad at you. I thought you stood me up. I didn't know that you were in a wreck. I just . . ." A big sniff and then, somewhat clearer, "I hope that, wherever you are, you're okay. I also wanted to tell you how much you meant to me. I've always . . . It sounds silly out loud, but ever since kindergarten . . . You were always so nice to me. I've always had a bit of a crush on you, you know? And when you didn't show up . . ." She started crying again. "I thought you were just being mean. I'm just so sorry. Please for—"

The message cut off.

Edward felt like someone had just scooped out his insides, yet he could feel the pill growing ever more insistent. His fading consciousness had time enough to grasp the huge mistake he'd made. Being alone for so long, starving and frustrated, had poisoned his mind to the point of forgetting that no matter how bad things got, he did have people that cared about him. It even tricked him into thinking that Brittany would never want to see him again. What else was he wrong about?

It seemed absurd to him that he would ever be able to sleep again after that, yet his eyes were growing heavier, and his muscles felt like they were loosening of their own accord. Edward fell back onto the pillows with the phone clutched in his hand. He had just enough will-power left to drag his feet onto the bed and under the covers. Then his eyes slammed shut, his grip relaxed, and the phone fell on the floor with a dead *thud*.

Edward stood in the shower, letting the warm water wash over him. *This might just be worth a return to civilization*, he thought when he toweled dry and finally donned the clothes set out for him. When he opened the door to let the warm, humid air out, a heavenly smell wafted in to take its place. It was a welcome, familiar smell that he hadn't known for years.

He inhaled deeply through his nose, tasting the smell on the air. "Bacon!"

He rushed down the stairs as the smell of brewing coffee mingled in. The smells gave him thoughts of a happier time and brought back mornings from his childhood.

Jake was already in the kitchen with a cup of coffee in hand, sitting at the table with Matt. They looked up as Edward entered.

"Mornin', Eddie! How you feeling?" Jake asked.

"Much better, thanks. Any chance I can grab some of that delicious grub?"

"'Course!" Matt said. "Been wondering when the smell would bring you down. It's all on the stove. Help yourself." He nodded his head toward the stovetop.

Edward fixed himself a plate of bacon and eggs and, for good measure, a cup of coffee with generous helpings of cream and sugar. The other two continued to talk as Edward lost himself in the first real meal he'd had in a long time. From the moment the first bite of food touched his mouth, he experienced pure bliss. Everything seemed to taste far better than he could remember.

He went back for seconds, then thirds. He shoveled great heaps of food into his mouth, and the other two looked at him admiringly. When he finally felt he could eat no more, he sat back comfortably in his chair, sighing in pleasure.

"Good?" Matt smiled.

"Clearly, he hated it," Jake said.

Edward just sat back with his eyes closed, nodding his head.

"Well, now that that's out of the way and you're on the mend, Eddie, what's next for you?" Jake asked.

Edward's eyes opened. "I don't know, exactly. I think what I'd really like is to go see a barber."

The other two laughed heartily, and Jake said, "I believe that can be arranged, but I was thinking more long-term, actually. I'm gonna go out on a limb here and say that you're probably in need of a job."

"Why; you offering?"

"Say I am. I get the feeling you already know what you'd be getting into, and I could always use someone who knows cars."

Edward pondered this for a moment. He would need a way to get the gold when the time came, and this opportunity might just offer him one. "I'd say I'm interested, but out of curiosity, how come you didn't know about the device? It seems to me that someone in your, uh, profession should've known about something like that."

Jake shrugged. "Well, you see, that's kinda what I need you for. We disabled the alarm and GPS systems, but I guess that wasn't enough. This hasn't been my profession for very long. Really, I'm a race and stunt driver. I used to drive the NASCAR circuit and did the occasional chase scene for some of the many movies and TV shows they film out here."

"Movies?"

Matt chimed in. "Oh yeah, they were filming a ton of stuff out here for a while. All the big shows on AMC, Netflix, and whatnot. Jake here was the go-to man for a lot of those companies. You've probably seen his work already; you just didn't know it at the time."

Jake smiled at the praise. "Then the whole Covid thing came along and swept everyone on their asses. Everything's postponed or canceled, and I can't book a single gig. Races aren't racing, and no one's filming. I've grown accustomed to my style of living, and I have to support it."

"Covid?" The word felt foreign on Edward's tongue. What had happened while he'd been lost in the wilderness?

"Yeah." Both men eyed him strangely, but Edward just sat there and waited with his own quizzical look on his face.

"You mean you don't know? How can you not? That shit's everywhere!" Jake gave a rushed version of the pandemic that was gripping the world, and Edward sat in amazement. When he finished, Jake asked, "How long were you wandering out there?"

Edward sighed deeply and said, "A long time."

"Well, I guess that would explain the hair, beard, and clothes, at any rate," Matt said. "I just figured you were a drifter."

"So I was. I just got lost in there." Edward offered a weak smile. Then the events that led up to getting lost and the sole reason he'd returned sped through his mind. "Will you teach me how to drive?"

"Wait, you mean you don't—"

"Like you, I mean. I want to learn to race, to do stunts. Can you show me?"

"If, as I take it, you're going to be lending me a hand, I think you'd better learn."

"Then what are we waiting for? Let's get started."

"'Kay," Jake said, "but first things first. We've *got* to take care of that bird's nest on your head."

"Better take him to see Debbie," Matt said. "I think the shops are still closed. She'll most likely do it out on the patio behind her house. Probably won't charge for Jake, so take a bottle of wine with you as thanks." He pointed off to a small rack of bottles on the counter.

Debbie greeted them both fondly when they arrived and took Edward to a chair out back.

When she finished, she told him that she'd saved as much hair as she could, but a lot of it had to go. She then trimmed down his beard significantly. She gave him a small handheld mirror that showed him a completely new face. It seemed to Edward that a new stranger had replaced the shaggy man from earlier. The face that stared back at him didn't hold a shadow of the face that had occupied his mirrors in the past. This one was handsome! His hair was just long enough to show the start of curls. The beard had been closely cropped with clean-cut lines.

"Whoa," was all he could get out.

"I know," she said in her light southern drawl. "Who knew there was such a good-looking guy under all that mess? If I wasn't married, I'd ask what you were doing for dinner tonight."

Edward blushed.

"C'mon now, let's go see Jakey and give him a thrill." She took his arm and wrapped it in both of hers.

When Jake first saw them walking into the den, he had a look of confusion on his face. It took Debbie saying, "Well, what do you think?" before he put two and two together.

"Whoa, I knew you were good, but I didn't know you could work miracles." He laughed.

"Hon, I didn't do nothing. This sheep's just been needing a shear for quite some time. Now, he's ready for the fair."

"I'll have to keep him away from Erica now; she might just leave me for this handsome devil."

The messages from his dad, Westley, and Britt still haunted Edward. But six years had already scarred that wound; possibly for everyone involved. Edward went back and fourth, he couldn't help but wonder if it was best to let them go on with their lives without him. He had a new life now, a new direction. Although he felt guilty for having turned his back on his loved ones, he knew it never would have happened in the first place if it weren't for Zack, Brent, and Corey.

Revenge was not something he wanted to drag the few people who had actually cared for him into. To them, he was dead. It was better that way. Every time he thought about going back to Peach Creek, he thought of Odysseus when he finally made it home to his island after twenty years abroad. Any other man would blindly rush home, but Odysseus sensed that there was danger lying in wait, so he took his time to think it through.

Danger or no, Edward wanted to keep the element of surprise on his side and started working toward his new goal of revenge. His mission, while slowly collecting the money for the supplies to go back for the gold, was to learn all he could from Jake and the others as well as any source of information he could gain access to.

Edward had avoided social media when he was younger. It hadn't taken long before he started getting cyberbullied on top of all he had to put up with at school. He'd had enough sense to delete his profile and never touch it again, but now social media seemed like the best way to get the info he wanted. Besides, who would cyberbully a ghost? Jake Did all he could to help Edward. He gave him his guest bedroom, even bought Edward his first smartphone. Edward used both and downloaded the Facebook app, then created a fake profile. Still, while revenge was his only intent, he couldn't help but type in his best friend's name when the search screen pulled up. He hadn't realized how many Westley Scotts there were, but it only took a moment of scrolling to see his old friend.

Westley still looked mostly the same in the profile picture—perhaps it was a few years old—and the smile was still its cheery self, with just a touch of sadness behind the eyes. He stood in front of a building with his arms outstretched above his head. The photo was taken at such an angle that it looked like he was holding up the black sign with the green lettering that read "Great Scott Deli" (the *c* and the *o* were made to look like goggles with bright white lines representing wispy hair perched above them) that had been fixed to the building. His smiling face was framed with familiar thick glasses perched on his nose.

Curiosity overcame caution, and Edward began to read all about what had happened with his friend over the years. It turned out that Westley had a wife and two kids now. When Edward clicked on a picture containing Westley's bride, he didn't recognize her and assumed they must have met after he went missing.

As was apparent from the picture, Westley was the owner of his own deli, and the address was right there in Peach Creek.

He smiled at the life his friend had made for himself. Then he took a deep breath and typed in *Brittany McLaren*.

Many profiles came up, but each one left him disappointed. He tried just googling the name and could find nothing relating to her. Perhaps she was married? That would mean a new last name, but without contacting anyone from his old life, he didn't have a clue of what it was, unless . . .

Sweat beaded on his forehead, and it felt like his heart was threatening to give way. It took him a few attempts before he was able to type in the name *Brittany Roe*, but this search ended with the same results as before, and Edward let out a huge sigh of relief.

He would in no way blame her for moving on, but the thought of her ending up with Zack was too much. He was just going to have to wait and keep an eye out for any information regarding her.

He found his hometown's news page and scrolled backward through the years. He didn't know what he was expecting to find, but he did come across an article that left him in tears.

Deep in his heart, he *might* have been expecting to see something like it, but to have it sprung on him through print was a terrible way to learn of his father's death. There were no details given, only that he was fifty-five when he turned his back on this world for good, which meant he lasted three years after Edward's disappearance before giving up. There was a small obituary, probably written by one of his friends. It was nice enough, but general and impersonal—that is, until the final line. That line struck at Edward's heart so hard that he could feel it shattering and was glad he hadn't been in town when he read it.

"I've missed you, son; I'm finally coming to see you."

It said he had written it on his wall. This detail left so many questions unanswered and picked at Edward's brain like a small splinter that he couldn't seem to get at; not enough to cause agonizing pain, but enough to constantly remind him it was there as it quietly festered. To keep his mind focused, he buried himself in learning all Jake had to teach.

Chapter 9

BEN GUNN'S TREASURE

Edward worked with the group for over a year before finally feeling he had all he needed to return to the forest for the gold. It hadn't taken him too long to track down the spot where his mile marker was. Every so often, his new job brought him close to that place, and he had to restrain himself from going to have a look.

He constantly reminded himself that without the proper tools, what would be the point? All it would do is risk someone following him and finding the spot.

Edward had been saving up all he could from his cut of all their little "odd jobs," as Jake called them. If the gold was still there, it wasn't likely to be going anywhere anytime soon.

In that year, he worked and learned, but he also planned how to go about retrieving his treasure. It was just like figuring out what to do about the bear, but this time, he had other things in his life that demanded his attention as well. It may have taken longer than he'd hoped, but time was on his side. Every conceivable complication was taken into account, and Edward was finally ready to make his next move.

He procured a four-door Jeep Wrangler and modified it to suit his off-road purposes; he even installed special concealed cubbyholes in which to place his findings. In the back, he placed scuba equipment as well as tools, provisions, and weapons he felt would be necessary.

The mile marker and the concealed tunnel beyond it were exactly as he remembered. Edward walked over to the plank with the sign on it, lifted it up, and, to his surprise, met no resistance other than the weight of the board itself. It was like lifting up one of those old-school door bars that served as locks way back when. He gently placed the sign off to the side of the tunnel and got back in the Jeep. With the flick of a switch, the light bars on the top and sides of the car turned on, and he could see everything around as far as the tunnel allowed.

Once at the other end of the cave, he parked the Jeep. He strapped a revolver to his hip, got out a chainsaw, and immediately went to work not only on the fallen trunk he'd used for his escape but also on the now-overgrown path. Edward was able to make quick work of widening it.

Once the way for his Jeep had been cleared, a new desire sprang to mind. It'd been a year since he'd seen his cabin, and he couldn't resist the temptation to check up on the place.

It looked almost as he had left it. The moss on top of the slanted roof was thriving, but the thick tangle of branches he'd placed all around had turned to dead twigs. The door was wide open, and he removed the gun from its holster.

Edward had left the door open in case the bear hadn't died from its wounds. He was sure that if it really wanted to, it could get through the door, but he still tried to make it a little easier. He was worried that the place might now be home to either the bear or something like it, and he wasn't going to take any chances.

No scent of death struck his nostrils, only old wood, dust, and now-disturbed debris that had moved in after Edward left. He glared down at the pieces of broken wood floor that looked like an open, jagged grin and walked over to them, gun first.

There were signs all around the place of animal habitation, but all small: mice, rabbits, or foxes. He pulled out his flashlight and pointed it along with his weapon down into the darkness below. The sphere of light followed the progress of the stairs one by one until it reached the bottom, where there still lay the bones of the large animal, now picked clean by time and nature.

So, it *had* died, then.

He looked down at the decay and nodded once in solidarity of a fight well fought before turning his back on the cabin. It was time to go to his treasure.

Edward backed the Jeep close to the water's edge, donned his scuba gear and tools, and jumped in. Even with the extra light from a waterproof headlight, it was hard to see more than a foot in front of his face. He surfaced and stayed above the water until he judged he was at the right distance from the tree, then made his way down into the murky depths.

Below him, the car finally began to take shape. Edward swam toward the seam that separated the two back doors. He banged the handle with the curved side of his pry bar, and inch by inch, it began to move, until it was at last perpendicular. He then turned the bar around and placed the long, flat end in the seam and pushed down.

The door moved.

A bolt of thrill rushed through him as the door begrudgingly opened. He shone his light inside, and from what he saw, it looked more like a hearse than a cargo transport. The sides of the back were empty aisles, and in the middle lay what looked like a large casket or sarcophagus. Everything was covered in algae and silt.

Edward brushed the debris away from the casket, and the freshly disturbed greenery dispersed all around the container, making it even more difficult to see. Edward had to wait until the debris settled enough to continue. When he started again, he used slow, controlled movements to keep the long-accumulated sediment from stirring too much. When he had enough of the underlying structure exposed, he saw it was made up of smaller rectangular trunks, each about two feet in length and width and one foot in height, all fastened together with cloth and secured to the floor. Edward grabbed his knife and cut the weathered piece of cloth so easily, it probably would have yielded to his hand.

He grabbed the handle of the top trunk directly in front of him. When he tugged, the trunk moved a fraction of an inch, but the handle threatened to give way in his hand. The box itself was made of metal, but the handle was some other, less sturdy material.

Edward jammed his pry bar underneath the first box and began to lever it. Even underwater, the box was a great, dead weight. Once it was lifted high enough, he slid a special recovery bag underneath it and slowly began to inflate it.

After struggling with the box, he finally finagled it completely over the bag, which flattened the middle until it looked a pie weight around rising dough. Gently, foot by foot, he and his load moved upward until they at last broke the surface.

Edward scrambled out and pulled the box onto dry land easily enough, but when it came time to lift it up to put it in the back of the Jeep, he found the burden even heavier than he imagined. Thick cords stood out on his neck, and a large vein emerged in the center of his forehead as his muscles strained to lift the box.

With great effort, he heaved it onto the back bumper, and the Jeep trembled with the impact. He gave the box a great shove to push it farther in and was suddenly very glad he had the foresight to back the Jeep so close to the water.

He looked down at the box on his tailgate and noticed a small lock on the hatch behind the disintegrating handle. He grabbed his claw hammer and gave it a few good whacks, and both the lock and what was left of the handle fell away.

His fingers moved forward on trembling hands.

This is it, he thought. *Everything that's happened since the day three bullies ran me off the road has come down to this.*

He took a deep breath and lifted the lid. There, packed snuggly into neat rows, were bright, roughly smelted bricks of pure gold. The light that slanted through the trees bounced off the gold's surface and sparkled brilliantly before Edward's eyes.

Here in this one small box was more money than he had ever dreamed of in his life; and this was just the first box. Back when it was first stolen, it would have added up to more money than he could have ever spent, and with the newfound price per ounce, he was looking at an unlimited supply of wealth to rival those of Jeff Bezos and Elon Musk.

All the things he'd mused of buying ever since he'd suspected the treasure had lain here whizzed through his brain. He'd get right on obtaining them. Money could never buy back the years, but it could buy the next best thing: retribution.

Edward dispersed the gold in what he now referred to as his "smuggler's holds." He knew he'd never fit the entirety in one go, nor did he wish to. He needed to turn the gold into cash a bit at a time, and it would not be wise to put all his eggs into one basket, as the saying went.

Edward went back down and retrieved as much gold as his Jeep could handle. It was growing dark as he finished packing up, made his way out of the forest, and started home, his Jeep now sitting significantly lower than when he'd set out.

Chapter 10

THE LONG WAY HOME

Over the next few weeks, Edward used his connections to start moving bricks. The person to whom he sold the first few didn't raise a single qualm at the transaction. Edward sold it to the man well below the actual value to avoid him looking too closely into the matter. Knowing how many more bars he had, he let the man get the better end of the deal.

Now that he had funds in hand, he felt it was finally time to make a trip back to Peach Creek. Over the past year, Edward had often thought about returning. The pull was strong, but going back would mean an end to all his plans unless he could master his emotions. Now, however, in order to move on with his plans, he needed information that only a trip back could supply, but strictly on *his* terms.

When he looked in the mirror, he found that most of his appearance would suit him well. He barely recognized himself and knew others wouldn't be able to either. He'd let his beard grow a bit to give extra security, and he let his curly hair hang down untidily when he set out. The one thing he made absolutely sure to do before going was get his hands on a few pairs of high-quality colored contacts.

Early one Saturday morning in the middle of August, a man no one knew walked down the streets of Peach Creek. He was dressed in long pants and rubber boots and was huddled underneath a hooded jacket, all to keep him dry from the rain that fell thickly down onto the sidewalks and roads.

He'd been gone for many years, yet it all seemed to have stayed the same. A few signs had faded, and the buildings that had been freshly painted when he was here last were now dark and cracked.

He wanted to see the town at his own pace and walked like a tourist, which is what the town took him for. Wandering slowly, Edward drank in all that had been a dream for so long.

Before he knew it, he was in the park. On the other side of the grass, he could see a tree with a wreath attached to it next to a cement running path. Beneath it were bunches of flowers, posters, and glass cylinders with pictures of saints and the Virgin Mary on them. Edward walked over to examine them more closely.

When he got nearer, he noticed the wreath was wilted, and the flowers were dry, flaky husks that flittered to the ground and disintegrated at the slightest touch. On the ground were candles that had been half used up, the wax soiled with ash and debris. There were remnants of chalk on the sidewalk, blurred and bleeding from time and the elements. He thought to himself that it was a miracle the rain hadn't washed it away completely.

Attached to some of the candles were old Mylar balloons that he supposed had once been bright and supple but now flattened and sagged next to the fading pictures of three young women who were immortalized in these small 4-x-8s, their smiles echoes of the happy lives they'd once lived.

"Terrible shame, ain't it?"

Edward turned around to look at the speaker. It was a man, slightly hunched with age, keeping warm and dry under a beige, zip-up raincoat and a worn, red baseball cap that had the words *Make America Great Again* embroidered on it. To Edward's astonishment, he recognized Mike Bryant, a man that most in the town referred to as "one of the old fellas at Crossin's Hardware," an elder of the town. Much like his counterparts in any of the thousands of small towns across America, he'd seen much of the history through his many years and wouldn't hesitate to talk your ear off about it if you let him.

Edward fought against showing any signs of recognition and instead turned his gaze back to the faded pictures. "What happened to them?"

"Sidewalk Strangler got 'em," he said, almost matter-of-factly, but it was evident that he enjoyed being able to relay his knowledge on the subject.

"Sidewalk Strangler?"

"Sorry, that's what folks here in town call 'em. Our town unknowingly played host to whoever it was that killed these girls. Their MO is thought to have stalked pretty, young girls then grab 'em, haul 'em off to some spot they had picked, and strangle 'em."

Edward looked back at the photos in disgust at the waste of life. "You're right. Terrible shame."

"What brings you into town, stranger?"

"The wind, maybe. Just kinda blew in and will probably blow right on out the same way."

"I hear you. Seems like that's the only way we see new faces 'round here. Stay safe, now. Don't go catching a cold; get outta this here rain as soon as you can."

Edward looked into Mike's smiling face. "Yes, sir. I sure will."

Mike turned and hobbled off. It'd probably been the highlight of his day to see a stranger walking around, and now he was sure to be off retelling the story all day to anyone who'd listen.

It was Edward's first test, and he'd passed, it seemed, with flying colors. He'd known Mike and let him talk his ear off on many occasions when his dad had brought him to the hardware store. Now, he was able to look Mike right in the eyes, and there hadn't been the slightest bit of recognition.

Edward walked around a bit more. The walk was not only to get a good look at the town but also to help get his courage up for the tasks ahead, the first of which was to visit his old house. He got in his car and drove to the old ranch-style home at the edge of town.

He wasn't sure he'd be prepared to see his old house in any condition. He suspected it would probably be occupied by a new family making their start in life. That would have been unnerving enough, so when he pulled up to the graffiti-encrusted shack that had once been his home, he was struck dumb.

All the windows had been smashed and boarded, the front door was gone, and a cheap sheet of OSB plywood leaned lazily over the entrance. Edward got out to inspect the carnage.

It was even worse on the inside. Crushed beer cans and broken bottles littered the floor. The air was moldy and dank, with the undertones of a fire that had barely been put out before taking down the shell of his old life.

Every room he passed was empty of furniture or possessions, but drug paraphernalia of many different types was strewn everywhere. Someone had been squatting in his old room. In the corner was an old, tattered thing that might have been a sleeping bag in a former life, and next to it was a stack of old skin magazines and an open ten pack of toddler boy's briefs. Fuzzy cartoon puppies smiled up at him with blank, unfeeling eyes, as if they had seen much more than they were meant to.

The thought of what may have happened here churned his stomach. It became hard for him to breathe, like the house was a weight crushing down upon him. He'd seen enough and needed to get out.

Edward ran back to his Jeep and wasn't able to calm down until he turned the corner and knew it was safe to look in his rearview mirror.

As lunchtime rolled around, Edward punched the address of Westley's deli into his phone's GPS and made his way over to the small shop tucked away in a strip mall. He approached the single glass door and looked in. The sign on the door reminded him of Lite-Brite pieces spelling the word *open*, although the place looked deserted. He pressed the little bar of aluminum, and the door swung inward as a low electric sound like a doorbell rang though the air and fell on emptiness.

He took a few steps before he saw movement in the back behind the counter display of freshly cut meats. A thrill struck Edward's heart as Westley came into view.

Fearing he would give something away, he turned his eyes up to the white plastic letters that spelled the names of entrees.

"Afternoon!" Westley said in a cheery voice.

Edward didn't shift his gaze, as if in contemplation. "Hey!" he answered warmly enough.

"What's your pleasure?" Westley's cheery voice continued. "Did you have something in mind, or would you like a recommendation?"

Edward was trying to read the sign overhead but couldn't retain any of it. When Westley's words finally registered, he cleared the obstruction in his throat. "What do you suggest?"

"Do you like pastrami?"

A real pang of hunger struck Edward's stomach at the question, and he seized it. "Don't know anyone on this planet who doesn't!"

Westley laughed. "Got that right! In that case, I recommend the Reuben. I make it hot and give you a good helping of my specially house-made Thousand Island, both on the sandwich and on the side for dipping."

"Specially made?"

"Yep, my own secret recipe. Won me first prize in the state fair last year." He nodded to something on the wall behind Edward.

Edward turned to look and saw that a newspaper article, complete with a picture of Westley holding a trophy, had been framed and hung for all the world to see.

Edward smiled. "I'll have that, then."

"Coming right up!" Westley said as he punched it in his register.

He went straight to work, whistling the entire time. Edward found a seat closest to the counter and sat down to examine the place. Along with the article showing off Westley's award were other frames containing many different things: old pictures of the town, people with happy faces digging into one of Westley's concoctions, baseball banners, posters, cards, and a great smattering here and there of film memorabilia surrounding the *Back to the Future* franchise, to which the name of the deli nodded.

"Interesting place you got here," Edward said loudly enough to carry to the work area.

"Yeah, my wife and I love *Back to the Future*, but it's kind of lost on the people who live here. We added all the other stuff to try and keep everybody's attention."

A few minutes passed with nothing but the sounds of Westley working. All of a sudden, the smell of his creation wafted out into the dining area, and Edward's pang of hunger grew into a ravenous need for whatever was producing that delicious scent.

Just as Edward completed the thought, Westley made his way out and placed a red, plastic basket with checkered paper down in front of him.

"Enjoy!" Westley said.

Edward took a bite, and a wondrous explosion of flavor spread over his taste buds. It was a struggle not to wolf the whole thing down in a few bites. The sandwich was delicious, but the sauce was divine. He dipped not only his sandwich in the amount served on the side but also the seasoned french fries that came with it.

When Edward finished devouring everything in the basket, he sat back, contented.

Westley leaned over to check his progress. "Guess you didn't like it, huh?"

"Absolutely hated it," Edward said with a grin.

Westley smiled and began to walk off when Edward spoke up.

"You mind if I ask you something?"

"By all means."

"That may have been the best sandwich I've ever had!"

"Thanks!"

"No, thank *you*!" Edward looked around at the place for effect. "So why is this place so dead?"

Westley's cheery disposition dampened slightly. "Well, when we first opened a little over a year ago, the place was a big hit. Still is, I guess, if you ask any of the townsfolk. But I s'pose the novelty kinda wore off. We still get enough business, to be sure, but Wally World put in a Subway a few months back."

"Why should that matter?" Edward asked, knowing the answer perfectly well.

"Folks around here, if given the choice, will go with what's easy and cheap rather than go out of their way to spend more money. Luckily, the flavor of my joint occupies a place in enough of their hearts to pop up as a hankering time and again that none but my food can satisfy."

Edward paused for a moment. He was so happy to see his old friend making a go of it but couldn't stand the thought of him floundering, especially not after the food he'd just had.

"Ever thought of making your own franchise?"

"Sure have. That's the dream, isn't it? But that's for luckier folks. I only make enough to keep the doors open; even then it's a struggle." He gave a small laugh. "Maybe I'd do better in a bigger location, but I have my hands full just paying for this place."

"Couldn't you find investors?"

Westley gave another laugh, but this one was small and bitter. "My father helped me to get this place—he was so happy that I wanted to start my own business—but even with his help, this shoebox was the best we could do. The only people in this town that really could invest have either grown up and out or are just too busy to be bothered. I've tried to get the man who owns the local brewery to invest a few times, but he never seems interested." Then, under his breath, "Probably better off anyway."

"Who owns it?"

"Brent Wheaton, an old classmate of mine, actually. Inherited it from his father. Now there's a lucky man." Westley wasn't quite able to keep the bitterness out of his voice.

Edward cringed at the thought of Westley having to grovel to Brent for help, but one of the many lessons he'd learned over the past six years was that life was hard, and sometimes you had to do things you'd once called unthinkable. But he'd finally gotten Westley onto a topic that could give way to some information he needed. He had to press further.

"Why do you say that?"

"'Cause he got to ride the coattails of his father without really doing anything for himself. He already had a great product that his family has sold locally for generations. Word through the grapevine is that he tried to get his father to export the stuff to really start raking in the dough, but the man was content with the life he was living. Wasn't until that life came to an end that Brent got his wish. Now, our local brew can be found at any grocery store in the state."

"Must be some beer," Edward said, despite the fact that anything coming from Brent made him want to spit.

"Hang on a sec; I'll get you some." Westley walked off, then returned with a bottle of beer in hand and presented it to Edward. On the label, there was a man sitting on a cask and looking up at a mug of frothing beer, either to examine it or raise a toast. Beneath, the lettering said "Ol' Creek," the name of the company.

Edward took the bottle and drank, more for his friend's hospitality than to support Brent's company. The spark of recognition was undeniable. The beer was the exact same recipe as the beer in the cellar of the hideout. He'd drunk too much of the stuff not to make the connection. Edward stared at the bottle, puzzling over what this new information could mean.

"Good, ain't it?"

"Can't argue with you there," he admitted, still wondering over the bottle.

"Some guys just have all the luck."

"Why's that?"

Westley started as if brought out of his thoughts. "What's that?" Westley asked, stalling for time.

Edward could tell by the look in Westley's eyes that he was right on the edge of getting to the heart of things. All Westley needed was a little push.

"You said some guys have all the luck. I was just wondering why you thought that."

Westley sighed heavily. "I don't know; it just seems that life is really unfair sometimes."

"Brother," Edward interjected, "you're preaching to the choir."

Westley laughed, but sadness clearly crept behind his eyes like it had in his pictures. "It just seems to me that life rewards those who don't deserve it. Like I said, I knew Brent growing up. Biggest spoiled brat you'd ever see. He and his friends are now all well off. They were little hell-raisers growing up, and now it seems they have more money than God. When I think that arrogant little prick's now trying to get into politics—" Westley must have remembered he was talking to a customer and looked ashamed. "Sorry about the language; it just really grinds my gears every time I think about it. Then you have their other friend now gallivanting around Hollywood; lately, it feels like there's always some tabloid or another with his picture plastered all over it."

"Wow, you know an awful lot about the people here."

"That's just how it is, I guess. Everybody knows everybody."

Edward finally saw his opportunity and seized it. "I wonder if you could help me, then."

"Can't promise anything, but I'd be more than happy to offer what I can."

"The reason I'm in town is that I'm trying to track down an old friend of the family. Maybe you know him; Steve Dalton."

The smile that had lit up Westley's face at the prospect of helping immediately fell away, and something visibly dark passed behind his eyes. "Yeah, I knew him, and I'm sorry to be the one to have to tell you."

"You mean . . ." Edward piped in, feigning ignorance.

"Yeah, few years back, I'm sorry to say."

"What happened?"

"Well, Steve's son Eddie was my best friend growing up. One night, he seemed to up and vanish. Steve didn't have much in the way of finances, but what he did have, and even beyond that, he sunk into finding him. Steve borrowed everything he could, maxed out every card trying to find him. After a few months, the state called off the search, and Eddie was presumed dead. Steve never gave up hope entirely and did all he could to keep trying. In doing so, he spent the rest of his life trying to get out from underneath the debt he'd accumulated. One day, it just became too much for him, I guess, and he . . . uh . . ."

"Please, I need to know." Edward tried not to appear frantic, but he'd waited for this truth for far too long.

Westley eyed him, then relented. "He hung himself in his bedroom."

The shock that passed over Edward was real and pitiable. He wasn't sure what he'd been prepared for, if anything. Maybe that he'd gotten really sick or even stopped caring for himself and wasted away, but this? He'd been cornered, in his mind, and forced to take his own life. Hanging, of all ways to go.

It was all Edward could do not to cry, but a shudder ran down his spine at the thought of his father going through with the plan he himself had toyed with on a nightly basis not so long ago.

"Yeah, real sorry I had to be the one to tell you. But maybe it was better it came from me, since I was also a friend of the family. He even mentioned me in his will."

Edward looked up, startled. "His will?"

"Yeah. He didn't really have anything to bequeath, but in the reading of his will, he asked a favor of me."

Edward's mind was still reeling, and he struggled to understand. "What was that?"

"Even in his dying moments, I guess he still hadn't given up on Eddie. He gave me all the information and paperwork needed for Eddie's cell plan. He said with everything that happened, that was the one bill he made sure was always paid in case Eddie needed it to find his way back. He asked me to keep it going for him."

"And you did."

"How could I not? The last wish of a dying man." Westley stared off to the side, and his eyes lost their focus as his words fell off until they were a whisper.

"I get it, and I'm sure Steve's grateful," Edward said. Then after some thought, he added, "If Eddie *is* out there, I'm sure he's grateful too." They sat in silence for a moment before Edward asked, "Do you think he's still out there?"

Westley paused for a moment. Edward felt his gaze and was suddenly afraid he'd tipped his hand. He looked up into that stare and was grateful to find it went past him in thought.

"Hard to say, really. Eddie disappeared just when he'd started talking to this girl he'd had a crush on for a while."

Edward's stomach tightened around his lunch in anticipation of what might come next. "So you think it wasn't an accident that he went missing?"

"Well, *accident* is the word, isn't it? They found Eddie's car wrecked out in the middle of nowhere down south of here. There was no reason for him to have been out that way."

Edward—who knew he'd been lost in the north—finally understood why no one had come for him in the forest.

"Then this guy, Zack, starts smiling at me and the girl Eddie was supposed to go out with every time he looked at us. Smuggest damned look I'd ever seen. Brittany couldn't handle it, I guess. Got out of town as soon as she could."

"So, you think this Zack guy did something to him?" Edward's stomach flipped.

"All I'm saying is that if ever there was a person I've met in my lifetime I'd say was capable of murder, it would be him."

The conversation was spinning faster and faster; it was all Edward could do to think of the right questions to ask.

"And the girl? What did she think?"

"Same. Neither one of us came out and said it, but we're pretty sure he did it *because* of her."

Edward felt his face drain of color but saw Westley's had reddened as he relived the past.

"Why?"

Westley's voice grew louder. "Because he started moving in on her as soon as Eddie was out of the picture. She would always tell me how creepy he made her feel every time he'd make up an excuse to talk to her."

"Do you guys still keep in touch?"

The anger that filled Westley's face dispersed. "No. We were great friends for a few years. She even introduced me to her cousin Ashton, who's now my wife."

"That's great!" Despite everything, Edward couldn't help but feel joy that Westley had married into Brittany's family. But something didn't make sense. "But wait, then why don't you still talk?"

"Zack."

That one word was all Edward needed.

Westley continued. "That guy has a lot of trouble with the word *no*. Brittany would always talk to me about it when she still lived here. It got so bad that she took out a restraining order. But that just made things worse. Apparently, once he started getting higher-up connections, he started making her *real* nervous. And for that woman to show it, you knew things were bad. I don't know what he did, but she decided to get out of here and cut all ties just to get away from him. Haven't heard from her since."

Edward felt himself getting angry at the thought. Suddenly, he had to get out, had to start working on a plan. Most importantly, he had to calm down before he made a careless mistake.

He took a deep, steadying breath. "I'm sorry I brought up such hard memories. I'll get out of your hair."

"Not a problem, Sir. Not a day goes by I don't think about that stuff. Sorry I had to be the one to give you the bad news."

"Had to hear it." It cost him, but a small, genuine smile touched Edward's face. "Like you say, I'm glad it was from a friend." He stepped out of the shop, and Westley waved him off good-naturedly.

Chapter 11

A FINAL FAREWELL

A few days after the stranger had blown through town, a man dressed to the nines in an expensive three-piece suit and a haircut that looked like it cost even more strode into the Great Scott Deli.

Westley eyed the man wearily from the kitchen, assuming this was yet another one of the collectors that seemed to circle the restaurant like the vultures they were.

The man stood in front of the counter with a pleasant look on his face, so Westley drummed up a smile to match.

"Hello, there. What can I get you?"

"Actually," said the man, "I'm looking for a Mr. Westley Scott?"

Westley's smile wanted to falter as his fears seemed to be realized. "That's me."

"Mr. Scott, my name is Fred Thomson. I represent an investment firm and am here today because my client was here not too long ago and exclaimed that he had the best sandwich he'd ever had in his life. He expressed he saw a lot of potential in you and feels that your business could do very well if it got off the ground.

"My client has bid me make an offer to you in the sum of three hundred thousand to do what you need in order to make this business boom, in return for a good share of stock, of course. If the sum is agreeable to you, I can have the money wired into your account by the end of the day . . . Mr. Scott?"

Westley's eyes had gone wide, and he couldn't process what he was hearing. Then, finally, he felt he had a handle on what was really going on.

"Man, you had me going for a second there. I think it's the suit that did it; very convincing."

Thomson raised an eyebrow. "I'm not sure I follow."

"I see what's going on here. You walk in here like the infamous Nigerian Prince and want me to give you my bank account so you can wire me a ton of money. Maybe if you hadn't gone with such a classic, you'd've gotten me."

Thomson smiled good-naturedly, finally understanding the situation. He produced a flat billfold from the inner pocket of his coat and pulled a business card from it. He handed the card over and said, "I assure you, Mr. Scott, this offer is quite legitimate."

Westley took the card, examined it, and said, "Nice job on the card too! Must have cost a pretty penny."

"Oh, it did. As I say, the offer is completely legitimate. By all means, call around and check for yourself. I assure you, you'll be most satisfied." Thomson's grin grew even larger. "*When* you're satisfied, you have my number. I can even accompany you to your bank if you wish. Until then, I hope you have a wonderful day." With that, he exited the store.

Westley thought to himself that this was complete lunacy. He examined the card once more. It really was a nice card. It claimed the name of the company was JPMorgan Chase. Well, *that* should be easy enough to check.

He called the firm and made inquiries about a Mr. Fred Thomson. The phone slid out of his grip and would have smashed on the counter if not for the case in which it was secured.

He snatched it back up and fumbled to dial the number on the card.

After hearing his friend had received the contribution, Edward sat in his Jeep as he looked down at his old cell phone. He lounged across the driver's seat, his right arm propping him up by the elbow on the center console, his left leg dangling causally out into the night air through the open door.

He sat there in the dark of the evening with only the familiar bright blue light projecting from his old phone screen, his thumb resting on the send button. He sat completely still, no sign of movement or life.

He was lost in thought, reflecting over all the information he'd gotten with his trip into town. He couldn't help but feel at least partially—if not wholly—responsible for what happened to his father and Brittany. Zack was the reason it had all taken place, but if he had only tried a little harder to get back . . .

But that isn't certain either. Yeah, I might have made it, but I might have died in the attempt, or it might have taken so long that it wouldn't have mattered.

The venomous voice he hadn't heard since leaving the forest spoke up.

And now you'll never know. You chose to turn your back on them.

I was sick. I was overwhelmed with all that had happened and my mind couldn't cope. I even tried to kill myself.

And yet, you lived.

That was the kicker, wasn't it? He was alive and his father wasn't. And who knows what type of life Brittany was forced to live.

What should he do next, there was nothing he could do to erase the damage his absence had caused, but maybe . . . just *maybe* . . . in continuing with his plans, he could help make up for at least some of the pain it had caused.

An eye for an eye . . .

Suddenly, the silence broke with a deep intake of breath that seemed to suck the life back into him. He pressed down hard on the button. The soft tone the phone gave to let the user know a button had been pressed clanged through the air like a church bell.

Sitting on the seat next to Edward was a shiny, new, steel drilling hammer he had dubbed "Thor," purchased specifically for this purpose. Edward got out of the car and placed his old phone gingerly, almost lovingly, on the pavement. He then reached in and took Thor from off its throne.

Staring at the phone, he raised the hammer high in the air, reminiscent of the demigod for whom it had been named, and brought it down with all the force he could muster. The phone, which had survived so much throughout the years, gave a huge crunch as the outer casing gave way. Then the hammer came down again, and pieces flew off in all directions like a flock of birds, and finally, one more strike for good measure.

What was left was a small pile of electronic entrails, and he swept them away with his shoe.

Edward got back into his Jeep and drove away.

Miles away, while staring at his phone with his wife, still wondering if the many zeroes his bank account showed were really there, a message notification plopped down from the top of the screen, showing it was from a number not in Westley's contacts.

There was something familiar about that number, though. He clicked on the notification, and the screen changed to reveal only two words.

Thank You

"Who's that from?" his wife asked.

"I have no idea," he said distantly.

A thought occurred to him, and he went to the file cabinet beside his desk where his wife kept all the bills before they became old enough to throw out. He quickly riffled through until he found the one he was looking for.

He unfolded the sheet of paper, then held it up to the phone to compare the numbers. Ashton watched this entire scene play out with mild curiosity, still stunned at the good fortune they'd received. But when she saw the color drop out of Westley so quickly, as if he had been bled white, she got up and went to him, expecting to have to catch him.

When she reached him, he was still standing but looked like he was made of marble. The paper in his right hand was trembling as his eyes bore down onto it.

"Wes?"

Nothing.

"Wes?" she said again with a change up in melody.

Nothing.

Finally, she called out loud enough to wake the kids upstairs: "WES!"

Startled movement, eyes that searched all around until they met hers, then finally recognition. He was still colorless as he launched into his explanation, after which the house hung in wondering silence.

As Edward stared at the long road ahead. He knew that if he was going to do this, he was going to give it everything he had. But he wouldn't be able to do it on his own. He needed help. There was one man he knew he could trust beyond all others, so he picked up his smartphone and texted Jake.

Hey Brotha, you up?

Almost immediately, the three dancing dots popped up on the screen, then the reply.

Yep, just about to hit the sack when you caught me, why?

I need your help, it's important.

Immediately, Edward's phone began to vibrate, showing Jake's picture. Edward hit the green button.

Before Edward could so much as utter a hello, Jake was spouting off in his ear.

"What's up, brother? You hurt? Something happen? What's wrong?"

Edward smiled, now sure he'd made the right choice in confidants. "Everything's okay; I just have something important I need to talk to you about. I'm on my way home, mind staying up for a bit so we can talk?"

"Fine by me, but it's, like"—a pause came as he checked—"almost midnight. You sure?"

"I'm sure."

"Then I'll be waiting. What's the matter? Did somebody hurt you? All I need is a picture and a name."

Edward could tell he was saying it as a joke, but a chill crept into his voice as he said, "That . . . is not as far off as you might think, my friend."

When Edward pulled up to Jake's house, he was already outside waiting for him with two open bottles of beer. He went straight up to Edward to coax him inside, but Edward stopped him.

"Get in."

Jake looked at the two bottles in his hand for a moment, shrugged, and got in the passenger side. "That bad, huh?" He handed over a bottle.

Edward grabbed it and took a long pull. "Brother, you don't know the half of it."

"So tell me."

Edward did. He laid every last detail bare before Jake. It was hard to get started, but as he relived all of his traumas, it felt like he was relieving some of a great pressure that was building up critically inside him, and the words came flooding out.

They hadn't moved from Jake's front yard, and as Edward told his story, he stared out the windshield as if in a trance. When he finally felt he'd told Jake everything, he looked down at the clock. Two hours had gone by. Edward had been pulling from his own bottle, more to keep his throat wet than anything else, but it was now staring up at them, long since empty. Jake's was completely untouched.

Throughout the story, Jake hadn't said a word. Edward finally looked up to see his reaction. Jake just stared at him, mouth slightly ajar.

Edward gestured to Jake's untouched beer. "You gonna finish that?"

It was such a bizarre shift that Jake couldn't help but laugh. "Help yourself, amigo."

"Thanks." Edward drank long and deep, then let out a huge belch.

Jake was staring at him in amazement. "Yeah, I feel you. I just can't believe it." He looked at Edward's face and quickly went on. "I mean, I do, don't get me wrong, but holy cow!"

"Oh, you don't have to tell me. I was there!" He took another swig of what was left in the bottle. "Any questions?"

"Just the obvious one. What are we gonna do about it?"

Edward's heart soared at his use of *we*. "That's what I want to discuss with you. I want to get back at them, all three, and money, obviously, is no object!"

"Well, should we start with Zack? He's the one who deserves it most, yeah? Maybe we go up to the office he's working at and—"

"No! I'm not gonna rush this. I want them all together again one last time, like they were when they ran me off the road. It started three against one; I'm gonna end it three against one."

"What about this Westley? Why don't you want to let him in on it? Seems to me he could use some retribution."

"And he'll get it! But after it takes place. He's made a life for himself, a wife, kids; I don't want any of them to be caught in the crossfire."

Jake looked into Edward's eyes. "Well, this could take time. I mean, two of them have already moved out of there yeah?"

"I don't care how long it takes; I want it to be brutal! I want everyone to look at them and shun them like they did to me. I want them to have to live out the rest of their lives dwelling on all they did to land them there. I will leave them in *anguish*!" He didn't think this would make up for all he had gone through, but he felt like he would get a piece of the life they had stolen from him back. Finally, he would be the one to look at them and laugh, as they had done to him for so many years.

They both sat in silence for a moment, thinking it over. Finally, Edward spoke again.

"Do you know of any lawyers you can trust?"

Jake laughed. "I know a couple. Why?"

"Get in contact with them; we need to get a think tank together. The best way to go about this is to get any and all information about those three as we can, by any means necessary."

"Eddie, I mean, sure, I will, but that kind of thing and all the money you're going to be throwing around is going to lead to questions. Not to mention that in order to get the right circumstances to get them all together without spooking them, it may take years to not only get all the necessary information but use it all at the precise time to get the kind of revenge you want. If you're gonna do all this, you're gonna have to come up with some legit means as to how and why you're spending that kind of dough."

"Well, the years I got, so let's think of what I can do for the legit means."

Jake considered for a moment, then a curious smile grew on his face. "I'll tell you what you need to do. Pick up your life where you left off—" Edward opened his mouth to protest, but Jake cut him off. "I don't mean exactly. I mean, let's create a whole new life for you and have it continue your old one. Like you said, money is no object. Pick whatever college you want to go to, study anything and everything you want. Get some interests, some hobbies. Get a life! Try and enjoy yourself. After all you've been through, I think you deserve it. Leave all the details to me. You tell me what you want, and I'll figure out a way to make it happen."

"What's going to make it legit?"

"The same way all shady dealings in this country are. You, my friend, are gonna start a company."

Chapter 12

THE PLAYERS

Ten years passed since the day Edward limped out of the woods. Ten years in which he meticulously positioned his pieces before moving to strike. He threw off any ties to his past life and, with a little help from Jake, was able to acquire an entirely new identity, driver's license, social security card, passport, the works. Edward Dalton was now Henry Picaud to the world at large, and he planned to remain that way for as long as he needed to. For all intents and purposes, Edward was dead, and Picaud would remain until he was no longer needed.

Picaud was able to liquefy more of his assets. After purchasing a new abode, he made three more trips to the swamp to remove what was left of the gold. Most of it was stored in a secure vault that only he could access, but he transformed plenty into the electronic currency that the world set its store by.

He sent that money out into the world, investing it in several different areas and businesses suggested by his financial advisers. Henry Picaud was an octopus, slowly extending his reach into many different facets of society.

He applied and got into Johns Hopkins University on the first try. The prestigious college had no qualms about admitting a student with an apparent lack of scholastic background after a generous contribution was made in his name. Talks were in the works of a new medical lab being built with the name Picaud Hall.

He learned anything and everything he took a fancy to. He studied medicine, biology, chemistry, and engineering and graduated top of his class with a doctoral degree.

After leaving school, he started his own company that specialized in creating and producing state-of-the-art medical equipment. Although he hired the best of the best for his think tank, his own ideas were the brightest and set them at the peak in the race for medical advancement.

The company grew so large and fast that no one could believe it. Henry Picaud was quickly becoming one of the most influential men in the world. Yet he kept a surprisingly low profile unless giving some interview, press release, or presentation.

Nevertheless, his clean, close-cut hair; the professional, stubbled look of his beard; and his spectacled, hazel eyes—contacts so convincing that he paid a small fortune for them—were all over magazines and tabloids: *Time*, *People*, and *Rolling Stone*, just to name a few.

He also bought anything he had a fancy for. He found new hobbies that held his interest, the newest one, sailing, being his favorite among them. No matter how he chose to spend his time, his overall schemes were fresh in his mind, knowing that three debts were out in the world, waiting to be collected.

All the while, he and Jake kept their eyes open and their ears to the ground, searching for any and all information they could gather on the three, no matter how seemingly insignificant. It was a long time before they found the facts that would serve Picaud's purposes. After that, all the dots that had no correlation at first finally started coming together. As more time passed, the well of information swelled greatly and rapidly, ensuring the moment he had dreamed of for so long would be coming to a head soon.

With all his growing connections, he still couldn't find the piece of information he most sought for. The location and fate of Brittany remained a mystery. He knew that even if he found her, he would want to attend to his other business first. She never fully left his mind, however, and he was constantly keeping an ear to the ground for some news of her, but she apparently didn't want to be found.

When it was finally time to start closing in, his mouth began to moisten in preparation for the sweet taste of revenge, sixteen years on ice.

Senator Roe was hosting a fund-raiser for his next campaign. He was up for reelection soon, and now that he had a taste of this life, he was set on keeping the seat. He made his usual smiles and waves to the necessary people. It had worked for this long, but he was beginning to set his sights a little higher.

Although he hadn't really done much with his office in the short time he'd had it, he saw himself as a representative of the people. That is, as long as their wants coincided with his. He had a snappy slogan that had won the community over: "Life is a great sea, and the only way through is to Roe." The people had eaten it up. Now that he was looking to keep his position, the slogan had turned into "Keep Roe-ing Along." God, people were stupid. Sheep, nothing but mindless sheep.

Being a senator had its perks, but Zack hungered for more. He wanted power, and if he had to kiss certain, well-chosen asses to get it, then so be it.

All these thoughts floated through his mind as he tried to keep up the song and dance of a gracious host. He just needed to find the right ass to kiss. Which is why when one of his assistants waddled over in a hurry to tell him that Dr. Henry Picaud was in attendance, he was all ears.

"Picaud?! What's he doing here?" Zack asked.

"Word on the floor is he's the guest of the NRA rep. Apparently, Picaud is a huge backer."

"Really? A gun nut, huh?" Zack was already trying to figure out just how to act toward Picaud to gain favor.

"That's not what I hear, sir. Apparently, he's got his fingers in a lot of pies: guns, hospitals, military; the list goes on about a mile. He gives a ton of money to a bunch of different charities, etc."

Well, well, well, just what the doctor ordered. "Thanks, Hank. Go and make sure the kitchen has everything in hand, will you?" He would've loved to add *and don't eat anything in there while you're at it* but managed to restrain himself. He'd always hated fat people. Every time he had to look at one, it felt like an assault on his eyes. Still, it was nice to have him around on the occasions when he could make a few choice comments about his weight.

Zack crossed the floor, weaving around the hundreds of people taking advantage of the free food and alcohol. Each time he'd manage to get away from someone trying to hold his attention, someone else would step in to distract him.

Finally, he was close enough to see Picaud talking directly to Frank Walsh, the lobbyist said to have brought him. Picaud was surrounded by many guests either trying to engage him in conversation or else just trying to get a glimpse of one of the richest and most powerful men in the world. Zack's mouth watered at the thought. Picaud was rarely seen out in social settings. Zack saw all the people looking at him in wonder and knew that word of Picaud's appearance at *his* gala was sure to cause a huge stir.

He worked his way over to the NRA rep.

"Frank!" he said in a well-practiced fabrication of pleasantness. "How are you, you old salt?"

Frank's face lit up in a smile. "Zack! I was wondering when you'd make your way over. I figured I wouldn't have to wait too long with my friend here." Frank gestured to Picaud. "Zack, I'd like you to meet one of the NRA's best contributors and a good friend of mine, Dr. Henry Picaud. Dr. Picaud, this is Senator Zackary Roe."

Zack extended his hand toward Picaud. "Nice to meet you!"

Picaud gave just the slightest hesitation before extending his hand. Zack was unsure of how to interpret the feeling that passed between them but found the shake to be sturdy and firm. An art that has been lost on all the people of today's world. Handshakes had only recently come back into fashion, but people had forgotten how the old gesture was supposed to be.

A smile that didn't touch the cold hazel eyes boring into his spread across Picaud's face as he said, "Pleasure to meet you, Senator. I've been watching your political career closely."

"Well, don't worry. I'm sure it's not as bad as the media makes it seem. And please, call me Zack."

"Very well, Zack. Nothing to be ashamed of, from what I hear. You must have been doing things right to gather this much attention for reelection." He gestured to the room at large with its crowd of guests still staring at them.

"Seems like only yesterday I got the job."

"Glad to see we'll keep Roe-ing along."

At this last remark, everyone watching laughed heartily and genuinely. Zack manufactured to match.

"So, to what do I owe the pleasure of seeing you, Dr. Picaud? I've always had the impression you avoid gatherings like this."

"Usually, yes. Honestly, I wouldn't be here if it weren't for our friend Frank; he insisted I accompany him."

Frank looked pleased with himself for bringing Picaud to the party. "Damn near had to beg him." He laughed.

"He said he really wanted to attend but didn't want to come alone. I expressed my feelings on such parties, as you so astutely noticed, but I owed him a favor, so here we are." Picaud's eyes never left Zack, as if he was assessing him, and Zack wondered at the possibilities of having this man in his pocket.

"Must have been one hell of a favor." Zack wanted to know what favor he would need to do to catch a fish this big.

Frank chuckled. "All I did was connect him with a few people that would help him in a new business venture. I hardly think it was worth anything, especially after all of his generosity."

"Nevertheless," Picaud said, cutting Frank off before he could say more, "I take favors very seriously, and if you've done me a service, I consider myself in your debt. I might still owe him a favor after this. I have to admit, I'm actually enjoying myself. Perhaps I should do it more often."

Zack, always sharp to spot an opportunity, said, "Well, in that case, I'm throwing a little party at my house next week. It's my wife's birthday, and I'd love for you to meet her."

"Won't I be intruding?"

Zack felt the thrill of the hunt that he had been missing for some time. "Oh, no, Dr. Picaud. I use the term *little* rather loosely. There are going to be plenty of business acquaintances there, both mine and hers. Frank, I'd love to have you there as well. Besides, Dr. Picaud, my wife is a big fan of yours. She buys all of your latest fitness equipment."

"In that case, I'd love to meet her. I even have the perfect birthday present. My company is about to release something very new and exciting. Your wife will be one of the first to try it out."

Roe's eyes sparkled with greed. "Really? Can I ask what it is?"

"Let's not spoil the surprise. Rest assured, she'll be very happy. What day next week?"

"Tuesday."

Picaud's face fell. "Of course you'd have to have it on my busiest day." His eyes looked up to the sky as if riffling through the notes in his brain. "But I think I might be able to shift some things around." Picaud gave a small wink as he reached into a pocket and pulled out a business card. "Here, have someone in your staff call this number and give the details as soon as you can."

"Absolutely," Zack said, taking the card. "I'll take care of this right away. Please enjoy the party."

Zack gestured to the room, and Picaud made his way through a mass of people, each of whom would sell their soul to have as much conversation with him as the senator just had.

Zack looked over to his right, where Hank was standing a few feet away, and gestured to him to come over.

"Here," Zack said, handing over the card. "Call and make the necessary arrangements."

"Sure!" Hank was already waddling away when he stopped and turned back. "Would you mind if I kept the card afterwards?"

"Why?" Zack asked with narrowed eyes. "You planning on selling it?"

"I'd probably get a lot for it if I did, but I actually just want it as proof."

"Proof? Proof of what?"

"That I met him."

An all-too-familiar flash of anger went through Zack, and it was hard to restrain himself. "You *didn't* meet him. Look, just go do your job." Zack's hand itched to be let loose on the tub of lard before it was out of reach.

Hank scuttled off as fast as he was able.

Zack looked around and was relieved to see that no one had been watching that little scene. All eyes were on the mysterious doctor. If Zack could befriend this man, his eventual presidential campaign would be in the bag.

Zack laughed out loud, thinking of what Hank had said. Zack was sure he was right, too. What people wouldn't do for a shred of evidence that they'd seen Picaud in the flesh.

⚊⚊⚊⚊⚊

It was already six o'clock on the night of Lydia Roe's party, a full hour after the designated starting time. Zack had been greeting the guests with the same manufactured warmth as on previous occasions. He smiled and talked to anyone who wanted his attention; still, he couldn't help but look over the heads of all who had gathered to see if *he* had arrived yet. It was fashionable to be late to parties, of course, but a full hour usually meant they weren't coming.

Hank had assured him Picaud would make it, and Zack had gone straight home to tell Lydia, who'd nearly fainted at the news. She was indeed a huge fan of the products Picaud's company produced, but it was more than that. Like those who had spread the news that Henry Picaud had been at her husband's fund-raiser, everyone would talk about how Henry Picaud had been at *her* birthday party.

When told she'd be one of the first people in the world to get a new product of his, she'd screamed like a preteen girl. She'd pressed and pressed her husband until she was certain that he didn't know any more about it.

Now, she came toward Zack, all smiles and pleasantries until she was directly in front of him. Her back to the crowd, the award-winning smile was immediately wiped off her face.

"Where is he, Zack? You said he'd be here. You promised!" she whispered through clenched teeth.

Equally quiet, though a head taller than his wife so he had to keep his smile, he said, "Relax, Liddy; I'm sure he will be. Frank says he's never gone back on his word."

"Well, I hope so, for your sake."

"Why? What'd I do?"

He could sense her onset of panic. "I told everyone that he'd be here, and if he doesn't show, do you know what a laughingstock we'll become?"

"And that's my fault? Geez, I thought you'd be happy. I didn't tell you to go blabbing to everyone on the planet about it. Hell, I'm sure even the pool boy knows."

"Zackary!" she said indignantly.

"Don't 'Zackary' me! Look, don't get your panties in a twist. Just relax and try to at least pretend to have fun. Maybe you'll actually have some by accident."

She looked at him with as much contempt as he was certain she could muster. Zack paid no attention and stared across the large back lawn, through the guests and strung lights, where he saw one of the hired help was escorting none other than the man himself out of the back door and into the thick of things.

"Well, there you are, dear. Shall we say hello?"

It was hard not to notice the state that seeing Picaud's arrival put her in. She took out a compact and began fussing with her hair, teeth, and breasts.

Zack rolled his eyes. "Ready?"

"Ready," she said, giving no recognition to his sarcasm.

They weaved their way around the many guests until they reached Picaud, who was waiting on a drink at the bar, staring at his phone.

"Dr. Picaud!" Zack said in his most winning tone. "So glad you could make it. May I present to you the lady of the evening." He swept his wife forward with his left arm. "Dr. Picaud, my wife, Lydia Roe."

Lydia, completely flustered, extended a hand. Picaud took it gently, grasping below the middle knuckles and bringing it up as if to kiss her hand, but instead, he looked over it into her eyes and said, "It's a pleasure to meet you, Mrs. Roe, and a very happy birthday."

Her cheeks went bright red, and Zack thought she might faint at the gaze. "Oh, thank you. The pleasure is mine!"

Zack rolled his eyes again at his wife's reaction but was graceful enough to keep it out of his voice. "Your timing is impeccable, Dr. Picaud. Your ears must have been burning as you pulled up."

"Ah, yes, sorry about that. I've recently come under the microscope for a piece of land I acquired. Apparently, the FBI says it'd been a crime scene not too long ago and wanted to question me about it. The first interview landed earlier this afternoon, and it ran a tad longer than I anticipated."

"Nothing serious, I hope," Lydia said, slowly coming back to her normal color.

"Oh, no, they know I had nothing to do with what 'may or may not have taken place there,' but they wanted to question me about my interest in the property all the same. Waste of time, if you ask me. For one, as I told them, I have yet to even see it, so I wouldn't be able to tell them anything. For another, as it turns out, I spent the whole time talking to the local authorities, and I've been requested to return when the FBI agent assigned can come down to talk to me personally."

Zack was taken aback. "You've never seen the property and you bought it? That's a bit reckless, don't you think?"

"Well, I have a person who buys properties for me. *Usually*, he does his research. He didn't say anything about its sinister past but assured me it was a lovely chunk of land that I'd be really happy to have."

"Well, let's hope for his sake, he's right." Lydia laughed.

"He has yet to be wrong in such matters, so I have faith."

Lydia nudged Zack in the ribs and gave him an urging look.

"I'm sorry to say, Dr. Picaud, I sort of ruined the surprise and told my wife that you were bringing her a gift."

"Oh, yes!" Picaud said, spinning on the spot and turning back at once with a beautiful leather box that looked like it would contain a jeweled necklace. "Here you are, madame; hope you like it." A large grin crossed his face and showed off a set of perfect teeth.

Lydia took the box and immediately raised the lid. Inside looked something like an Apple watch. It had a little metal screen for the face and was connected to a black, rubber band but was surrounded by an array of other tasteful bands that could be easily changed out for the user's preference. Lydia took the watch out and noted how extraordinarily thin the screen was. She touched it and found it was flexible.

Picaud watched her inspecting the gift. "This little gizmo is of my own invention and is the latest bit of tech coming out of Picaud Industries. It's going to be the biggest game changer in the medical field since they started video-call doctor visits."

Lydia looked up at him, puzzled.

"What you hold in your hand is the world's first handheld diagnostic device. That little watch connects with your phone or tablet, scans your body each day to check for any changes, and shows you all the results in an easy-to-understand display on your screen. It has all the normal functions you'd see on any smart watch, but with all it can do beyond, it will be the biggest leap forward in catching cancer—or any other disease, for that matter—in the earliest stages. For instance, if you ever feel under the weather in any way, it can tell you instantly what the matter is and give you recommendations on how to treat it. We're currently banging out the details with all the doctors we can, but you *should* be able to register your device with a doctor of your choosing, and if your scans show anything serious, they can prescribe medication or treatment without you ever having to enter their office."

"Wow," said Zack, feeling flabbergasted. This man really was a godsend.

"But wait, there's more," Picaud said in his best infomercial voice. "This little beauty not only monitors your body's health but will give you suggestions on how to improve it, whether it be through certain foods your body needs or exercises that will help wherever your body needs improvement."

Zack marveled. "So, what you're saying is that not only is this a handheld doctor but a personal trainer and nutritionist?"

"Yes, but I'm actually saying it's better. With all of those professions, there is a lot of trial and error. This device knows exactly what your body will and won't respond to, effectively taking out all of the guesswork."

Zack thought for a moment. "Won't the constant scanning cause some health issues?"

"I'm not at liberty to go into details because we are still in the middle of procuring the patent, but we found a way of scanning that leaves almost no traces of radiation. We've done tons of studies and can effectively show the FDA that you get more radiation carrying around your cell phone than using this watch." Picaud shrugged with a smile. "And if it somehow did start to give you health issues, at least it would catch it right away."

"Well, that certainly is amazing," said Lydia. "Thank you so much. I think this will probably be the best birthday gift of the evening."

"I must apologize to your husband, then; I never meant to outshine him." They all laughed, and Zack couldn't help but admit that Picaud could have his wife's attention all he wanted if it meant a fat check toward his campaign at the end of the day.

The lady of the evening took great pleasure in showing Picaud off to her guests. She delighted in each stare of incomprehension and jealousy. She would be the talk of the town, and she loved it, which was exactly the in Picaud needed.

He patiently went with her, smiling and making all the right pleasantries, until finally he found his second reason for being at this party. A large, bald man with a neck as thick as a trunk and a suit that was at least two sizes two small made his way toward Picaud and his hostess. When he got close enough to hear them, Lydia said, "This is Mr. Brent Wheaton, a friend of the family."

"How's it going?" Brent said as he smiled underneath a curling black mustache and extended a large paw of a hand.

Picaud met it, this time without even the shudder of hesitation he'd had when he first took Zack's hand. His composure was getting better, and he reveled in being able to match Brent's firm grasp pound for pound. A curious look passed over Brent's face, and it was clear he was not expecting the strength that came from a man that looked roughly half his weight.

Brent continued talking. "No need to tell me who you are, of course. I see you on the news or in some story almost every day."

"Please don't believe everything you read." Picaud smiled, but his eyes seemed to never leave Brent's. They were fixed as if homing in on a target.

"Guess I can't now, can I? After all, you have been called a shut-in by pretty much every hack with a word processor, yet here you are."

"Trying something new." Picaud still stared unblinkingly. He recalled every whack, kick, and punch Brent had ever released on him when he was Edward, and he took this moment to contemplate just how sweet his revenge was going to be.

Brent either didn't notice or didn't care, for which Picaud was grateful; he worried his hatred might shine through those ridiculously expensive contacts and ruin everything.

"Well," Brent said, grinning stupidly, "I'm glad it was us you chose to include in your little social experiment. We're flattered."

"So am I," Picaud said with an air of *you have no idea.*

"Look at what Dr. Picaud has given me for my birthday." Lydia extended the wrist that held the little band and gave a brief description of what it did.

Brent gave a long, low whistle. "That's some fancy piece of hardware. Bet it costs a pretty penny."

Picaud shrugged this off; every penny had been worth it to get him to this moment. "People pay twice as much for the newest iPhone."

Brent laughed. "Amen to that! So, I'm curious. I happen to not be so shallow in the pockets myself, but it can't be anywhere close to you. What does a true billionaire do with all that money?"

Lydia at least had the decency to give Brent a look to reprimand him for such a tactless question. Picaud almost felt bad that she was caught in this storm, but anyone who had not seen past Zack's evil couldn't be given extra thought. Brent, the greedy bastard he'd become, just smiled at Picaud, completely unabashed.

"To tell you the truth, I give most of it away: charity, scholarship programs, investing in small businesses, local shelters."

"Yes, I heard you are the number one contributor for local women's shelters!" Lydia said.

A small smile touched Picaud's face. "Am I? Well, I certainly do all I can to help the women who visit those shelters get back on their feet. I even employ some of them. But that's just one of the many charities I try to—"

Brent waved his hand as if trying to disperse a bad smell. "Yes, and that's all very noble of you, I'm sure. But what do you do for fun? What gets your blood pumping?"

Lydia gave another of her outraged looks that seemed to go unnoticed, but Picaud politely continued. "Well, I do like my hobbies. I have grown a taste for many different things over the years and am always on the lookout for the next."

"Like what?" Brent asked.

"Anything I take a fancy to, really. I've recently gotten into real estate investing."

"Really?" Brent's face lit up. "I'm in that game occasionally myself. I've been thinking of buying this plot of land that has an abandoned theme park on it, just outside Atlanta."

"Ooh, spooky," Lydia said. "Which theme park is it?"

"It's called The White City. It was modeled after the Chicago world's fair. It opened twice, first in 1907 and refurbished in 2017. For whatever reason, it just couldn't stay afloat."

"What's keeping you from buying it?" Picaud asked.

"The price! They're asking a lot for a broken-down old theme park."

"Yes, it *is* an expensive hobby. But even that pales in comparison to the price I pay for my obsession with cars. That's one hobby I would not recommend."

"Oh, believe me, I know," Brent said. "Probably a little too well. I wish someone had told my wife that. Her current baby is a '26 Pagani Zonda R. It's easily the most expensive thing we own. That's one bug you two have in common, I guess. Perhaps I can introduce you, and the two of you can plot the next step in my financial ruination."

Picaud laughed heartily. "I would be delighted to talk to any fellow car nut. I have quite an extensive collection, if I do say so myself. Perhaps you two would like to see it sometime."

"You kidding? She'd die! . . . When can you tell her?"

Picaud laughed at the thought. Thankfully, Lydia chimed in before the hate in his eyes gave him away.

"I would also like to see this wondrous collection," she said. "Any chance I might crash the party?"

Picaud turned to her. "Absolutely. You should bring your husband as well. The five of us will make a day of it. How does two weeks from today sound?"

"Two weeks?" Brent sounded put out, which pleased Picaud.

"Yes," he said somberly. "Unfortunately, I'm booked solid until then. Busy, busy, busy, you know. My staff keeps me moving so often that I'm beginning to wonder if my time is my own at all."

"Completely understandable," said Lydia. "Two weeks from today it is."

"Can't wait," Picaud said, his perfect smile returning.

Picaud *was* a very busy man, but more so of his own doing than his staff's. He'd set the date two weeks in advance for multiple reasons. First and foremost was that he wanted to make them wait, let the feeling he knew he'd left them with have time to grow vines and tighten its grip. The next reason was to make absolute certain he had enough time to accomplish what he wanted before then. Most pressing was to settle the business around his newly acquired property. It was the keystone of his master plan, and he needed to make sure everything was settled.

The house that stood on the property was said to have been the home base for a serial killer at one point, the same one his hometown referred to as the Sidewalk Strangler.

The house and property had been up for sale for some time, but no one wanted anything with such a dark past. The FBI had apparently kept an eye on it, and when Picaud purchased the property, the brow over that eye raised.

When they'd requested to talk to Picaud, they had been pleasant enough and just wanted to know his interest in it. They'd asked if he wouldn't mind letting them come around if any new evidence was brought to light.

It'd been ground into him ever since he'd met Jake and the others never to trust the cops no matter what they said. Law enforcement uses the "throw everything at the wall and see what sticks" method. They'd proved on many occasions that, guilty or not, they would always try to form a case around anyone until they'd made one strong enough to present to a district attorney.

Truth be told, Picaud wanted the property *because* of its dark past and was going to use its stigma to his own ends. He sure as hell wasn't going to tell anyone this, let alone the authorities, so he thought about telling them it was none of their business. The property had been obtained legally, after all, and it was his right as an American citizen to claim his privacy. But when they were explaining the details surrounding the case, Picaud was nearly floored when they mentioned the FBI agent who was heading the case.

He had to meet this man. When they'd arranged the first meeting, he'd agreed to be there promptly—along with his lawyer, of course. He'd arrived only to find that the agent wouldn't be there. Though Picaud had been irked, the pull of the name was too strong not to return. They'd asked for a second interview, and after being assured that Agent Nell would, in fact, be there, he'd cordially accepted.

Agent Bill Nell was tired of coming to this podunk part of Georgia. He'd been here many times over the years ever since he'd been charged with finding this asshole. It'd been years since the last body surrounding the case had turned up, and the trail was ice cold.

Back when the crime scene was processed, Bill had a nagging thought that he'd missed something, but protocol demanded the release of the property. He begrudgingly let it go.

When it got swooped up for the asking price, the buyer not even bothering to try and get it cheaper after it had been on the market for so long, Bill's gut started churning. He was desperate for any new lead, so he decided to get in contact with the purchaser.

Turned out the guy who bought it, this Jacob Withers, didn't even buy it for himself. He was part of some rich guy's company and bought it to add to a long list of properties around the area the company was buying up.

When Bill found out just *who* the rich guy was, he was thrown through another loop. This case was getting stranger by the second, and damned if he couldn't smell something fishy. He was going to figure out what was going on, even if it meant going back to the sticks.

Bill knew who Henry Picaud was. Who in this century didn't? To him, as to many Americans, Picaud was the physical representation of "the dream." A man so rich he could do anything his heart desired.

That was another reason Bill wanted to talk to him. A lot of these rich-and-famous types often considered themselves above the law. He was sure that the man waiting for him in the local sheriff's office was no different. They all thought they could do whatever they wanted and get away with it just because they had money, which would certainly fit the profile of the psycho who'd committed these murders.

Bill walked into the sheriff's department twenty minutes late for the appointment. Scruffy and disheveled after the long red-eye flight and the following drive to get all the way out here, clutching an abused cup of Starbucks, he walked up to the front desk.

"Go on back, Bill; he's in there waiting for you." The receptionist gestured to the side with her head.

Bill grunted. "Thanks, Alice." He walked toward the interrogation room, which in this backwater office was also the briefing room.

Bill was a young man around the age of thirty-five, although you wouldn't guess it in his current state. His shiny black hair, normally combed back, had stray strands hanging down in front of his face. The black stubble of his chin had just a few flecks of salt, giving the impression he was older than he really was. He'd always been the ambitious type, constantly on the lookout to prove himself. When this case was transferred to him eight years ago, he'd seen it as a way to gain the recognition he felt he deserved. The case, already complicated, quickly spiraled out of control in the few years after his appointment. Then it all up and stopped out of nowhere. He was worried that the perp was either in jail or dead.

The man waiting to see him was clearly at his ease, spread out on one chair next to the long table with his feet up on another, as if he didn't have a care in the world. After a few seconds, Bill could see why. Sitting achingly upright on the opposite end of the table was a very clean-cut, very high-priced suit. Bill could practically smell the six-hundred-dollar cologne from the hall.

Great, he thought and opened the glass-paneled door while the loosely opened blinds bounced from side to side.

Picaud looked exactly like he did in the press. That was the first thing Bill noticed. The second was the look Picaud gave him as soon as he stepped in. His eyes seemed to swim over Bill's face, taking in every pore, every wrinkle, and then he smiled at Bill like he was an old friend he hadn't seen in years.

Bill had seen a lot in his time, but he had to admit, this was a first. He was used to people lawyering up at the first mention of law enforcement—the smart ones, anyway—but this man seemed to brighten at the sight of him rather than immediately go on the defensive.

"Dr. Picaud, my name is Bill Nell. I'm the lead investigator for the case surrounding your new property."

"Catchy name," Picaud said, still smiling.

"Thanks." Bill tried to brush it off. "Sorry to have to disturb you like this; I know you must be a very busy man. I just have a couple of questions for you." Bill looked over at the suit at the corner of the table, expecting him to interject, but he sat there, going over papers in front of his opened briefcase as if he was alone.

Bill forged on. "First and foremost, how did you end up purchasing this property?"

"Well, to be honest, *I* didn't purchase it. Real estate is something of a hobby of mine. I like to buy up property, perhaps flip it. My staff saw the plot and snatched it like any other property around the area."

"And you had no idea about the murders that took place on it?"

"Not until after the money had changed hands, but I was told that the property was up for grabs in spite of it, so I figured what was done was done."

Bill drank in this statement. It seemed real enough, but there was just the tiniest bell that rang in the back of his mind. Like most of it was true, but not all of it. That was the best way to tell a lie, wasn't it? Mix in as much truth as possible so it goes down easier. He'd expected something like this, but what part was Picaud lying about? More importantly, why?

"I assume Bill is short for William, yes?" Picaud asked him.

Bill was thrown off-kilter just the slightest bit by the question. "Yes, it is. What plans did you have for the property?"

As if his question and Bill's answer didn't exist, Picaud went on. "Hadn't decided on it yet. Originally, I think we were going to turn it into a hunting lodge. It's in a prime location out in a beautiful acreage of woods." Then, just as swiftly shifting back, he smiled. "William Nell . . . William Nell . . . There's something very familiar about that name. I think I've read it someplace before."

Bill's cheeks flushed the tiniest bit. "Perhaps you've read it in the papers surrounding the press clippings on this case." He floated it out there, hoping that he might catch Picaud in a lie of knowing more about the case than he claimed, but Bill knew that even in the papers, they called him Bill. He always insisted on it.

"You know, that was my first thought too, but that's not it. For some reason, the thought brings up bootlegging." Picaud visibly shook the thought off. "Ah, it's gone. But I'll think of it!"

The tiny red buds on Bill's cheeks opened to full bloom. Picaud saw it, and Bill saw he saw it. Bill saw something in Picaud's face in return; was it victory? Certainly the aha moment he himself wanted. He hoped one would come from this meeting, but never in a million years did he imagine the person of interest would have it.

Bill felt he'd lost control of the interview and quickly tried to change the subject. "Look, Dr. Picaud, my main reason for asking you here, other than if you had any information surrounding the investigation, was to ask for your help."

Picaud's smile widened. It wasn't a sneer; it was surprisingly warm, which made Bill even more nervous, because it was yet another curveball, and he had no idea how to swing at it. Bill's immediate thought was that this guy was a greaseball trying to get his rocks off, but his gut didn't agree.

"My help?" said Picaud.

"If there's any new evidence surrounding the property, or if, for instance, you find anything of interest, will you allow us access to check it out?"

Movement finally came from the man behind the briefcase as he shot two looks, the first to Bill and the second to his client. Bill found this comforting because it was finally something familiar.

Picaud looked at his lawyer, then back at Bill. "If I find anything, I will certainly turn it over to you, and if you ever need to see the property, all you have to do is contact Mr. Scutti over there to go over what you want, and we'll be more than happy to accommodate. Within reason, of course."

"Of course," Bill said.

"Anything else, Mr. Nell?"

Something was clearly off about this situation, but damned if he knew what. He needed time to process this. "Not at the moment, but I do want to thank you for taking the time to meet with me."

"Not at all; it was my pleasure."

Bill whipped out a business card. "If you have anything you'd like to share, call that number at any time."

"Of course." Picaud took the card and left.

Bill watched him go, lawyer close behind, and continued to wonder at this man. Picaud was worth billions of dollars, yet he'd showed up himself, and after Bill was late and the interview so brief, he'd made no comment of inconvenience. Anyone in his position would have asked why it was necessary to meet in person when a phone call could answer the questions Bill asked.

He knew, Bill thought to himself. He knew that the answers weren't what mattered, but his reaction to them. And Bill *had* gotten a reaction, he was sure of it, but Picaud had gotten a reaction too. Crazy slipup that Bill attributed to how tired he was; still, it was stupid, like being caught with his pants down.

Picaud knew something more that he wasn't telling. But what was behind it? Guilt? Bill actually shook his head at this. Picaud was hiding something, but that wasn't it.

And what was all that about his name? Picaud almost certainly knew about Bill's great-grandfather. He'd even mentioned bootlegging. Did he really not remember, or was he just toying with him? Probably the latter.

Bill wouldn't be surprised if Picaud knew of dear Great-Granddad Nell. It's not like the man's story wasn't public. His family bore the shame of his treason and passed it down the line. A black spot on one of the country's most patriotic families.

Ever since Bill was old enough to remember, he'd heard the stories of William Nell I. A man who had brought himself up from nothing and become one of the biggest players in the creation of the FBI, and then had turned on them like a rabid dog and made off with a ton of stolen money. Since then, every firstborn male had been named after him, each doing his own service to try and bring back the good his name possessed until the very end.

This Picaud must've used money, and the connections that always seem to come with it, to do his research, just like every other upstanding citizen with a silver spoon up his ass. Except there was something else about this one. Picaud seemed all right, like in another world they could've gotten along.

"Agh!" Bill said aloud, shaking everything off. If something was there, it was only a matter of time before he'd find it.

Later that evening, Jake was called to Edward's—no, Picaud's— office. God, it had been how long, and he still hadn't gotten used to it?

Jake knew why Picaud wanted the property but was puzzled at what he was going to do with it. Picaud didn't always reveal the whole motive behind a move before he made it. He liked to keep things close to the vest. Jake knew better than to question him, though. Because when his hunches were right, and they usually were, the little piece that they had earned from each lead made the overall puzzle that much more interesting.

When Picaud had told Jake to purchase this most recent property, it'd seemed like a pretty straightforward job. Jake had gone with instructions to purchase the property for whatever price they wanted for it.

The place was a good chunk of woods with a nice, spacious cabin on it. What they were asking for it seemed low, but after talking with the realtor, Jake had gotten the impression that he could have dropped an offer for less, and the woman would've snatched at it. But that wasn't his business. He'd offered her the money up front, and she had been more than happy to take it.

That wasn't the weird part, though. What was weird was getting a call from the local sheriff the very next day asking what his interests in buying the property were. Jake told them it was none of their business and asked if they didn't have anything better to do. But they wouldn't let it go.

Eventually, Picaud got involved, and when he took the phone from Jake, the weirdest thing happened. Picaud started off agitated at the person on the phone, but after a few moments, the agitation was gone; it was like someone flipped a switch in his head, and he pulled a one-eighty. When he hung up the phone, he'd been smiling.

When Jake got to the office after Picaud supposedly had the most recent appointment, Picaud was at his desk, and when he looked up to see Jake, his face lit up in a smile.

"Ah, there you are. How's your day been?"

"Pretty good, actually. How was the interview? The guy show up this time?"

"He did. And I believe he's exactly who I thought he was. Do we have anyone who can dig into his background?"

A sly smile crept onto Jake's face. "Don't I always?"

"My friend, there is no one on this planet that I have more faith in, which is why I want you to see to it."

Jake nodded. "Speaking of which, the women's shelter is sending over another looking for a job. Erica is supposed to interview her next week; says this one might be another you need to add to your personal staff."

"Another one? That's the third this month! Man, that guy gets around, doesn't he?"

"Just more ammo for you to use against him, and all the sweeter when you bring him down."

A genuine smile crossed Picaud's face. "Amen to that. It also means we need to get a move on. What do the lawyers say?"

Jake knew his face fell a little. "Same as always, unfortunately. They can definitely bring the case before a judge, but with the man's connections and resources, it's not a sure thing."

Picaud clenched his fists. "Well, what do they suggest?"

"That when we make our move, not only do we have to make it airtight, but it should come from a legitimate source."

A curious look passed behind Picaud's eyes, and the smile came back. "I think I have just the man." He shook his head. "But that's putting the cart before the horse. I'll be gone for the next week. Is the house out there ready?"

"It is. I'm actually very proud of this one. I got you the coolest house right on the beach. The place has been furnished to your taste, and the paint should just barely be dry when you get there. When you're done with it, if you don't want it anymore, I'd like to just remind you that my birthday's coming up, so, you know, wink-wink."

Picaud laughed loudly and heartily. "When I'm done, you can have your absolute pick of the litter. Not like you're left wanting now, though, is it?"

"Can't argue there."

"Listen, while I'm gone, I want you to prepare for our visitors. Make sure everything is ready. The motor pool has to be spotless. Make sure you keep one of the main stages clear for our next acquisition."

"Are you going to be back in time? The race is scheduled for Saturday."

"I'll be there, come hell or high water. You just make sure she's entering."

"I have double- and triple-checked; so far, she's still on the roster. I'll keep an eye out and let you know if it changes."

"Good; you're not getting out of the bet *that* easy!"

"Wouldn't want it any other way. Even if I lose"—Jake shrugged his shoulders—"I win."

"All right, my flight is set to leave in about two hours. You got everything?"

"Get outta here. And enjoy yourself, please."

Picaud smiled. "Wouldn't want it any other way."

Jesse Tovin walked eagerly to what awaited him in the upstairs bathroom. Although he wasn't considered an A-lister, he'd been in enough supporting roles that he was a household name and, therefore, had no problem getting into any upscale party in LA. There seemed to be at least one a day, if not more. Jesse had his pick.

Movie stars were abundant. It was funny, really. Everywhere you went at one of these parties, you could always tell where someone famous was. The entire place consisted of each celebrity on an island of people with small channels of walking space between. Of course, the two biggest islands weren't surrounding people but rather the bar or catering. Every once in a while, you'd catch a smattering of people off on their own, but usually this was because they were occupied in activities that didn't need a crowd.

Jesse's second-favorite aspect of these parties was getting to see how the person who owned the place spent their money. A lot of parties were in high-end spaces, but a lot more took place at someone's house—well, one of their houses, anyway.

Some people had the normal stuff, just expensive versions of it. You'd see a dining room with a long table carved from a single redwood or a rec room with a gorgeous pool table and giant screens surrounded by overstuffed leather sofas. But every so often, you'd come across someone who got creative with their money, and you could really tell what they valued.

One house had a full-on arcade with every modern video game known to the public and even a few that had only been released to a select elite. Bowling alleys, movie theaters, shooting ranges, the list went on. One guy even had his own Irish pub right there next to his kitchen, like his own private restaurant.

The house he was in now was this huge, modern, three-story job right on the beach in Santa Monica. It looked like an architect's wet dream with its whimsically slanting walls and jutting balconies.

Jesse's favorite reason to go to these parties was all the blow he could ever want, and it was absolutely free. Not that he was short on cash, but there was just something about never having to pay for his own. It made it seem less like it would develop into a problem.

That's what awaited him upstairs. He'd asked around to see if there was anyone he could score off of. The guy that owned the place didn't want to provide anything recreational beyond the full bar.

Finally, he found someone who'd brought their own, but they had to go somewhere out of view to make sure they didn't either get thrown out or attract the attention of others who wanted to join.

It was a job getting away from the masses, being the center of one of those islands himself, but eventually, Jesse was able to go off on his own and follow his new best friend. The guy seemed all right. He was well dressed and, more importantly, seemed to know the layout pretty well.

He showed Jesse into an enormous bathroom absolutely covered in marble. White marble tile for the floor and walls, with black for everything else. It kind of reminded him of a suite he'd stayed at in Vegas.

The man didn't speak, and that was okay by Jesse. He just got to work pulling out the bag of white powder, placing it on the counter, and arranging it in neat little rows with a black credit card, then pulled out a hundo to roll up for the straw. Jesse watched, the picture of Franklin winking at him before disappearing into the roll.

The man bent down in front of the coke with his back to Jesse, gave a loud snort, jerked his head back, and cleared his throat. Once finished, he turned and gestured for Jesse to take the straw. Jesse was more than happy to oblige.

He too leaned down to the neat lines and made short work of them. The familiar feeling closed over him like a warm blanket. He didn't think of himself as addicted to the stuff, but he had definitely been jonesing for a fix. He let his head droop back, relishing the high that enveloped him.

But this time, something didn't feel right. His head was swimming, but not in a good way. The warm, comforting blanket had turned on him, now constricting him like a hungry serpent. A cold sweat broke out all over his skin. He felt pain start to spread rapidly through his body, and suddenly, there was a hard pounding in his left arm. All at once, he knew he was going to lose consciousness.

The other man watched all this, saw the rapid change from high as a kite to rigid as a corpse.

"Hey, man, you okay?"

Jesse had enough sense to back up against a wall, and the other man watched as he slowly slid down it.

"Shit," Jesse heard him say with no real conviction as he yanked out a cell phone, and that was all he knew.

Jesse began to stir after what seemed like hours but may have only been minutes. There had been a loud clicking, first next to his ears, then in front of his eyes.

"Hey." More snapping. "Hello in there. You all right? C'mon back to us."

Jesse opened his eyes. At first, he had no idea where he was or any recollection of how he'd gotten there. Then, slowly, it started coming back. A man, not the same one he'd followed up to the bathroom, was staring at him.

Seeing Jesse's eyes wander all over and start to come around, the new man said, "Ah, there he is. Almost thought I'd lost you there."

Jesse looked at his surroundings to find he was no longer on the floor or even in the bathroom. "Where am I?" he asked in a croaked voice.

"Still at my place. You really hit the jackpot today. If this had happened anywhere else, you would've almost certainly died. Now you know why I don't want drugs when a friend borrows my house to throw a party." The man sounded reprimanding, but jovial too, like a father who had stood by and watched as his three-year-old put a fork into a wall outlet only to laugh when he knew they were okay.

"What happened?" Jesse asked.

"You snorted some bad stuff and had a reaction. Drugs are getting more and more dangerous these days. Dealers are starting to use strange substances to make or cut them with. Your body overreacted. Manny had the sense to call me and let me know what happened. Lucky for you, I happen to be a doctor. Many would say a good one at that. We tracked down what the coke was laced with and gave you the antidote." The man had an odd smile on his face. "You're that actor who played Jonas in *The Magic 8*, aren't you?"

It took Jesse a few moments before he realized what the man was talking about. "Oh, yeah. That was me. Jesse Tovin, at your service, I guess." He ended with a feeble chuckle. *The Magic 8* was a movie he'd worked on over ten years ago, back when he'd first started out. It wasn't exactly a big role, but people did seem to remember the plucky comic relief.

"I knew it."

"You did?" Jesse paused to consider the man. "You look really familiar too, but I guess the coke's still messing with me. I know that I know you, but I can't seem to place it."

"Dr. Henry Picaud." The man gave a small bow. "Quite literally at *your* service."

The name struck a chord, then finally registered. "The guy who makes all that fitness stuff!"

"Among other things, yes. You have indeed heard of me. Don't believe all of it; I'm sure I can't be that bad." The doc laughed.

Jesse had seen dozens of reports on his rescuer, but they all seemed to come up short when it came to Picaud's personal life. He was somewhat of a legend when it came to mystique, and Jesse did all he could to mimic him in order to show the public only what he wanted them to see. He was particularly proud of the fact that he was able to keep his drug indulgences out of the public eye. Not that that was anything new when it came to celebrities.

Crazily enough, it was a lot easier for people to accept and forgive that than other, seemingly less dangerous things. Having a drug problem would normally mean a public apology followed by a short trip through the revolving door of a nearby rehab clinic. It wouldn't ruin your career like when an actor accidentally lets something slip that goes against current political correctness, the rules of which were constantly changing. What was funny and normal to poke fun at one day became a deliberate act of prejudice the next. It was either make sure you kept completely up-to-date with all said rules or be absolutely shunned by the world at large. It was therefore more hazardous to be caught with bad PC than bad PCP.

"I *knew* that was you," Picaud said again. "The only reason I had to stoop to asking was that when I tried to find out who your doctor was to tell them what was going on and get a copy of your medical history, I couldn't seem to find any of your records."

"What?" Jesse thought for a moment. "Oh, you were looking for records that were for Jesse Tovin. Those wouldn't be mine."

"I noticed that. Why not?" Picaud asked.

"That's a stupid stage name my agent had me assume when he first started looking for work for me. Guess my real name just wasn't snappy enough."

"What name will it be under, then?"

"Cory Mar," Jesse said.

The grin that had slackened on Picaud's face during the chewing of the fat came back in full force and brighter than ever.

Picaud looked up to the man in the corner of the room, presumably his assistant, and nodded. The man immediately went out the door and closed it behind him.

"He's going to go get your records for me; should only take a few minutes. I just want to make sure I didn't miss anything, and you can go rejoin the party if you like."

"Thanks."

"No problem! So, Mr. Movie Star, you working on anything currently?"

"Unfortunately, no, but my agent's working on something big, so I'm keeping my fingers crossed."

"What is it?"

"They're making a film adaptation of the Malcolm Phoenix series."

"Really? I love those books. I've been wondering why they haven't turned them into movies yet."

"They're going to make the first one, and if it does well, they'll finish out the rest. I'm pretty sure it will. Rumor has it that they managed to get the writer and creator of the series to sign on. My agent says I'm a shoo-in for Phoenix."

Jesse made a good living off the things he did, but this would be his ticket to the next league. He wasn't old, but he wasn't getting younger, either. Thankfully, he always remarked, he was male. Women in Hollywood were held to a much more biased scrutiny. For them, if you hadn't made it to "the bigs" by the time you were thirty, it was unlikely you ever would. Men had a lot more leeway. It was unfair, but hey: that's Hollywood.

The novels had done extremely well on their own, and Jesse was sure that the movies would follow suit. If he could land this part, he would not only be an A-lister, but he would also be completely set until the series finished; even then, it would be much easier to land bigger parts in the future.

"Well," said Picaud, "I'll certainly keep my fingers crossed for you as well!"

The man came back into the room, holding a stack of papers. Picaud took the papers and perused through them. He seemed to just be skimming, but they must have made sense to him.

"Well, I think I have all I need. And that, as they say, is that. Please go and enjoy yourself." He gestured toward the door.

"Thanks, Doc; what do I owe you?"

Picaud smiled again. "Nothing, nothing. Just try to be more careful, please. I think you should know that Manny is no longer in my service, and I'd just be grateful if you didn't try to sue me."

"Are you kidding? Like you said, if it didn't happen here, it probably would've happened somewhere else. Trust me, I'll never forget this. You saved my life."

"Then don't gamble with it in the future. I'm not judging you. I know many people who use recreational drugs, but I think you would do better to kick the habit. Mark my words: It *will* be the end of you."

"This will probably be my wake-up call, Doc. I'll definitely do my best." Jesse knew the words would fall flat on Picaud, but he would do all he could to stop using.

Jesse had promised himself years ago, before he had even booked his first major gig, that he wouldn't be one of those guys that ended up on the news, strung out or overdosed.

Picaud had not only saved his life but had also kept completely quiet over the whole affair, and it stayed out of the public eye.

Jesse was eternally grateful.

When he got home, *she* was waiting for him.

It had been many years since they'd embarked on this little indiscretion, but he still melted at the sight of her.

She immediately wrapped him in her arms and kissed him deeply. When they finally came up for air, she said, "Well, you were certainly out late; should I be jealous?"

Jesse blushed at the thought. "You never have a reason to be jealous." Then he launched into the explanation of what had happened and who, of all people, had saved his life.

"Wow, not every day you have your life saved by a mysterious billionaire. Did you know it was his house?"

Jesse's mind thought this over. "No, actually. Carl texted me about the party. I'll have to ask him if he knows Picaud. Maybe he can help me get to know him."

"Well, before you do, I've had a craving of my own that you've left me alone with all day. I think you owe me an apology." She reached forward.

Jesse immediately rose to the occasion, lifting her up and wrapping her legs around him to carry her into their bedroom. What they were doing was so wrong, but it always felt so right. He had thought many times over the years of the possibility of putting an end to it, but he knew he couldn't. She was his true addiction.

Just before midnight on a deserted stretch of road, the location only known by those with an invitation, hundreds of wealthy car owners gathered and prepared for the night's festivities.

Invitations to Garmen Brothers races were only given to a select few who proved to have the most high-end cars around. Street-legal was encouraged but not enforced. Each owner who received an invitation had the option of either driving themselves or designating a driver in their stead.

Lucy Wheaton always drove.

She'd been part of GB races for years now and had cleaned out the competition many times. Her gorgeous Zonda was the envy of all who saw it. There was no shortage of money being thrown into each car in these races, but Lucy's car was endowed with the most generous helping of good, old-fashioned TLC. That extra heap of love made the Zonda the belle of the ball.

At first, when she'd started this circuit, the others had refused to take her seriously as a competitor, not only for the fact that she was a woman but also because she was her own driver. Many would normally just throw money at their car and hope it would work with a more experienced driver.

Lucy may have grown up with a sliver spoon in her mouth, but she was no stranger to overcoming bias. She worked her way to each new underground circuit by winning race after race until invited to the next step up, and the process would start all over again. That was fine as long as their money was good, and it always was.

At a quarter to two in the morning, her second race was scheduled to begin. She made her way to the stoplight that served as the starting line. She'd won her first race of the night and was growing more confident by the minute.

Her competitor had been a rich investment broker named Arnold Zarakus. He'd spent a lot of money, to be sure, but even his driver, when he'd pulled the Lotus Evora up next to Lucy's car, had known the race was already over.

It was therefore no surprise to anyone except Arnold when the Zonda took an early lead, which started in feet and grew rapidly to many yards. The driver, quite literally, was left in Lucy's dust.

Money exchanged hands, but few were brave or stupid enough to take that bet. Arnold, who'd just lost thousands of dollars to Lucy, was now throwing a huge temper tantrum, which was frowned upon by even the WASP community of investors.

Lucy didn't care. The money was added to the pot of her winnings, and she'd collect at the end. She'd won many races over the years, and since dearest hubby didn't know what she was up to during these late evenings (not that he would ever notice her gone; the man was usually either out or bombed out of his mind), she saw no reason to let him in on the proceeds. She had her own offshore banking account that was growing steadily, waiting for that proverbial rainy day.

She looked up at the large board listing the races to see whom her final would be against. It was a name she didn't recognize, which was uncommon but certainly not unheard of. Every time this happened, she'd only think to herself, *Fresh meat!*

The name listed was Luigi Roma. He was probably a foreigner, but that was nothing new. Most of the pool was made up of Americans, but there would be the occasional owner that had traveled from across the pond. Even members of the notorious Japanese Mafia, the Yakuza, made an appearance from time to time.

Lucy was standing by her car, waiting until it was time to head over, when a short man with buzzed, blond hair approached her. He looked like he belonged at *a* race, but not necessarily this one. He was dressed in cheap clothes: an off-the-rack cotton button-up with blue and red flames up the sides, regular slacks, and a Nike visor hat with the brim pulled to one side. When he got close enough, she noticed that he had a nervous tic, like he was trying to shoo a fly. Her first thought was *junkie*.

"Hello, ma'am," he said.

Well, he talks nice enough. "Hello," she said in kind, but not as kindly.

"I work for the man you're racing next. He sent me over to give you his regards."

This was almost as irksome as the fly he couldn't shoo. "Why didn't he want to tell me himself?"

"Well, he wanted me to ask you something he feared might upset you."

Oh, great; here we go. "And what's that?"

"Luigi wants to know if you'd be interested in sweetening the pot—if you want to play Bourbon Rules."

Luigi was right. This did upset her. With these races, normally the owners of the cars in the race would put a fixed amount of money into the pot. The winner of the race would win the pot—minus 20 percent for the house, of course.

Occasionally, owners would play Bourbon Rules, which was similar to racing for pinks but with a twist.

It boiled down to the winner getting the loser's car, but in return, in a show of gratitude, the winner would present the loser with a bottle of bourbon, the quality of which represented the respect the winner had for the competition.

This form of racing was rarely done, not only because most people didn't want to part with their cars but also because, adding insult to injury, it unintentionally said your car was now only worth a bottle of bourbon. Still, it became somewhat of a tradition for racers in these parts to always carry a bottle in the trunk. More of a good-luck charm than anything else.

"Why does this Luigi want this?" Lucy asked.

"Well, he has a friend who collects cars. Luigi is in his debt and knows he doesn't own a Zonda. He thinks it would make a perfect addition to the man's collection."

Lucy's immediate thought was to tell the visor man to inform his boss to go fuck himself. After the initial burst of indignation, however, she looked over to the car she would win if she played.

Lucy had a weakness for cars, and Luigi had a nice one, but not nice enough to beat hers. She hadn't seen it until now. Must've arrived late, because it stood out, and she'd have noticed. Not many people drove a Koenigsegg Agera. None that she'd raced with, anyway. Even more, it looked like it was one of the brand-new models. It was almost as good-looking as hers . . . almost.

After going back and forth in her mind, she looked up. "Fine; if he's that eager to lose his car, I'll be more than happy to take it."

The man smiled and walked away to inform his boss.

We'll see whose car's worth a bottle.

When the announcement sounded that the next two combatants were playing Bourbon, the surrounding crowd whistled, cheered, and whooped. It was always a sure bet that these races put on a show.

She looked over to the man driving the other vehicle. Most of his face was covered in a black helmet with the visor up, she assumed because the visor was tinted. Her own bright white helmet had the clear visor already down. Staring over at her through the open slit was the most astonishing pair of bright blue eyes. But then a black-gloved hand came up and pulled the visor down. Maybe this *was* going to be as easy as she thought.

A bell sounded, signaling that the next green was the start, and her attention snapped immediately forward. The thought of the bottle of Weller's Special Reserve sitting nestled in the back, where it had lain dormant for years, put a smile on her face.

Today's the day you and I part, old friend.

The light turned, and they were off.

Lucy immediately took the lead as the cloud of smoke from the tires cleared and revealed the racers off in the distance. Once they were out of sight, the spectators shifted their glances to the giant monitor showing the live feed of dash cams and drones to keep everyone in the loop.

Luigi's car was right at Lucy's back tire and would not be shaken. The first turn came, and both cars made it effortlessly.

As the race went on, she held her lead, but her confidence began to shrink along with the distance as the Agera inched closer.

Up ahead came the track's sharpest turn. Lucy, being on the outside of the turn, gripped the wheel tighter and steeled herself. She needed to pay close attention not only to the road but also to how tight the Agera hugged the curve. She meant to take every inch the opposing vehicle gave her. She was astonished to see a large gap immediately open up as the Agera hugged the turn within a few inches of the rock wall. She did what she could to close the gap but couldn't manage to take all.

She prepared herself for the inevitable loss of the lead, since he'd outperformed her and was able to gain the straightaway first, but it didn't happen. A cold sweat formed as the thought that the man was toying with her reared its ugly head.

Up in the distance, the final traffic light marking the finish shone bright green among the surrounding amber of streetlights.

This was what the other driver had been waiting for. He pulled ahead with a speed Lucy had not thought possible. Luckily, she had one more trick up her sleeve.

She needed a burst of speed and decided to use a special move she usually saved for just such an occasion. She dropped her gear from sixth down to fifth and floored the gas pedal. Immediately, the car lurched forward as the RPMs skyrocketed.

The gap the Agera had gained began to shrink. Three feet, two feet, one foot, mere inches. When it looked as if she'd finally retaken the lead with the finish line yards away, she began to celebrate in her head.

But then a similar rev-explosion took place in the car next to her, and like Lucy's Zonda, the Agera shot forward, leaving Lucy in the same dust she'd left so many others in. The Agera reached the finish line with time to spare, and Lucy's heart sank as the cars slowed and prepared to turn around for the drive back.

For the winner, it was a victory lap; for the loser, a walk of shame.

On her way back, Lucy looked around at every aspect of her car—the rich Corinthian leather, the sleek dashboard with the custom heads-up display—and silently said her goodbyes to it all.

She pulled down the vanity mirror to look at the eyes staring back through her visor. They were brimming with tears.

To add insult to injury, she watched as the winning car didn't bother to stop but drove off into the distance. She knew this wasn't a reprieve. She was expected to surrender her car and hitch a ride or order a Lyft. Any hopes she had of Luigi changing his mind vanished when she saw the visor man walking toward her as she parked. He was carrying a good-sized, shiny box, most likely her newly acquired bottle of bourbon.

She grabbed the ignition fob and got out to face him. He smiled. Her immediate thought was to throw the fob off in the distance and storm off, but she didn't want to give anyone watching the satisfaction. She had built a reputation, and she wasn't going to let one show of bad losing mess up years of hard work.

"Mr. Roma would like to express his deepest apologies for not accepting in person. He's a very busy man and has an appointment elsewhere he had to leave immediately for."

She said nothing but wondered what meeting could possibly take place this early in the morning. Not to mention the arrogance this showed, positive he was going to win beforehand. The man was smearing mud into her fresh and gaping wounds.

"He told me that if he won, to accept the winnings myself and present you with this." He handed over the box, and she handed the fob in return.

The box was made of rosewood and polished to a bright, glossy shine. She opened it to see a long-necked, rectangular bottle with an ornate stopper and two glasses snugly enveloped in red satin. The label identified it as "Pappy Van Winkle's Family Reserve."

She thanked the visor man as graciously as she could and walked off to the bleachers. She used an app on her phone to call for a ride. While she waited, she decided to look up the brand of bourbon.

Her own bottle of Weller's Special Reserve was worth around eighty bucks. Enough to show that she didn't devalue her opponents too much and to ensure a good amount of luck, but not needlessly spending on a bottle she thought she'd never use.

The bottle she received, along with the glassware and handmade box, ran for more than three thousand dollars. Small consolation for losing a car roughly worth three million after all the work she'd put into it, but the gesture meant he held the competition in respect, was very superstitious, or was just a frivolous spender.

No matter what she decided to take from it, there was one terrible fact she'd have to face: She'd lost her most prized possession. What would she tell her husband?

Chapter 13

THE PICAUD ESTATE

The evening agreed upon had arrived. The guests rode in a single stretch limousine for two reasons. The first was that the two couples lived somewhat close to each other, and Picaud's estate was out in the middle of nowhere; the man liked his privacy. The second—and probably more dominant—reason was that this allowed the four to engage in a little social drinking on the way.

The first thing Brent Wheaton was struck by was the long drive between the front gate and the main house. Once they passed the surrounding trees, the lawn was neatly manicured and occasionally marked with old, ornate statues. When the guests got out in front of the mansion, they were greeted by the butler, a short, skinny little man with wispy gray hair that stood out every which way, by the name of Gene. He welcomed and toured them through the large mansion.

Picaud, Gene explained, was a great student of history that some said bordered on obsessive, and therefore, each room contained an antique or a preserved relic from a significant period in history.

One thing that immediately stood out to the guests was Picaud's aquarium. It was massive and so full of a great many colorful and rare fish swimming among bright corals that it would make professional aquariums jealous. Gene told the guests it had been added to the house when Picaud developed a taste for diving.

It was implied that Picaud used this tank as his own personal diving spot, but Brent looked over to see Zack pointing at something. He followed the line of sight and saw what looked like a glass igloo at the bottom of the tank. Inside was a grand suite.

Gene must have noticed the pointing. "Yes, Dr. Picaud loves to get creative with his guest bedrooms, and here you can see one of his less favorable ones."

Astonished, Zack said, "If that's one of his least favorites, what's one of his most favorites?"

"Allow me to show you, if you'll all just walk this way."

They were lead down a hall until they reached an ornate set of wooden doors with gilded trim around the frame.

Gene paused with his hand on one of the doorhandles. "In here, we have the doctor's favorite room in the house: the main dining area."

He swung the doors and gestured for the party to enter. At first, everyone was confused because it just seemed like a small, white, wooden room with a bit of lattice work. They walked in and found that the far wall was just to block the sight line of the dining area from its main entrance. The openings on either side were dark.

More confusion spread when they emerged into what appeared to be an outdoor patio at night, lit only by paper lanterns. As their eyes adjusted, sounds of croaking frogs and chirping crickets and grasshoppers filled the air.

Brent looked down at his watch and it saw it was only five o'clock in the afternoon. So why was it so dark? They looked around and saw that a dining table, set with fine cloth and china, appeared to be on an outdoor patio of a southern plantation on the edge of a swamp. Something about this place seemed awfully familiar, but none of them could place it until Gene resumed his speech.

"What you see around you is based off the Blue Bayou restaurant in Disneyland, which is located at the beginning of the *Pirates of the Caribbean* ride. Dr. Picaud is particularly fond of that restaurant and took painstaking steps to replicate its design for this dining area and guest bedroom for him."

Yes, of course. That was why it looked familiar. Hadn't they all eaten at the very restaurant, ridden the very ride it was molded from countless times? The only difference was there weren't large boats floating through the swamp to usher patrons underground and see the pirates.

Lydia piped up. "Excuse me; did you say *and* guest bedroom?"

Gene looked exceedingly delighted at their puzzled faces. "Yes, I did. Look around. Dr. Picaud has a little running contest for his visitors. If anyone can spot the guest suite, they win one of his prized cars residing in the hangar."

"The hangar?" Lucy asked excitedly.

Brent rolled his eyes at his wife's obsession but quickly joined everyone else in their search. If Picaud was eccentric enough to build this in his house, he might actually give away one of his prized cars. The car itself was enough incentive, but the real prize would be the ability to tell everyone, *Oh, yes, you see my Porsche over there? I won it from Dr. Henry Picaud. Yes, the eccentric billionaire. It's from his personal collection.*

"I should warn you, though," Gene continued. "No one has yet claimed a prize."

All four were on the hunt. They looked everywhere, from the high windows and rooftop of the plantation facade to off in the distance, where a perfect, moonlit sky illuminated the lush trees that ascended from the waters below and fireflies frolicked playfully. The obvious choice was behind part of the house's facade. But when Lucy guessed it, she was informed that it actually led to the kitchens.

Zack pointed to a boat that looked like the one from the *Jungle Cruise* ride. "Maybe that's just the top of the room and you have to go beneath it to get in." No one agreed, since it left about twenty feet of watery distance in order to get to it.

When they all had either guessed or given in, Gene took them over to the kitchen door entrance and showed them a little box with three buttons on it. He informed them that in order to get to the guest bedroom, they would actually have to use the boat.

The three buttons were labeled "Room," "Stop," and "Patio." He pressed the one that said "Patio," and they watched as the boat made its way over to them. It pulled all the way up to a small dock on the edge of the patio. Gene opened the gate and helped everyone board.

In the front where the helmsman would stand, there was an old-fashioned lever that had pie wedges from left to right that displayed the same labels as the buttons. Gene moved the lever to the wedge that said "Room," and the boat reversed its movement into the swamp. He demonstrated that you could control the speed of the boat by how far away from the "Stop" wedge you positioned the lever. He stopped the boat at the halfway point and revealed that the structure in the middle, which looked like a steam engine that powered the boat, was just a cleverly disguised dining table. At the press of a button, the structure popped open, the occupants were able to pull out chairs, and the top of the barrel lifted to reveal a set dining area.

"When desired, one can eat their meal right out here in the calm waters of the swamp."

Brent, of course, noticed the absence of food. "So, I'm guessing you probably preload it before taking off, yeah? But what happens if you find you're missing something? You'd have to take the boat all the way back, right? That's gotta be annoying."

Gene smiled. "I'm glad you asked that. If you'll all look to the starboard side."

They did, and Lucy, who was sitting on the right side of the boat, gave out a loud shriek.

The boat had a deep setting for its passengers and consequently sat approximately one foot above the water line. A huge alligator had apparently snuck up and swam toward them.

When the passengers turned to look, it was only about two feet away. Lucy jumped away in terror, but the creature didn't seem fazed. It continued swimming until it got right next to the boat, then opened its mouth wide and froze, like someone had just pressed pause on a horror movie.

It was clear that Gene was enjoying himself; he had the smarts to not openly laugh but still couldn't repress a smile. The four guests stared at the open mouth of the creature.

"Press down on its tongue," said Gene.

They looked at him and then at one another as if confirming the man was crazy. No one wanted to volunteer, but Gene just stood there, vainly trying to repress a grin.

Eventually, Lucy came to her senses and said, "Fine, I'll do it." Brent wasn't sure if he should stop her or cheer her on. With a face that looked like she was smelling something awful, she reached out and touched the lifelike alligator with its slimy tongue and razor-sharp teeth.

The others watched in trepidation. A loud scream of pain came from Lucy, and everyone looked shocked before rushing forward to her rescue.

But as soon as they got there, she pulled up her unmarked hand.

"Gotcha!" she said, laughing.

Only Gene found this deliciously funny. Brent scowled at her while the other two just let out a collective sigh of relief. Lucy pressed down on the tongue, and the top jaw drew up even farther, taking the gator's back with it and producing a tray of food. Beneath the tray was a cooler with different assorted drinks.

Once Gene stopped laughing, he explained, "Betty here is a direct line to the kitchen. You can take anything you want from her, and if there is something else you require, you simply call the kitchen on the radio over there by the lever, and Betty will swim up with it in no time."

"Betty?" Zack asked.

"Have you ever seen the first movie of the *Lake Placid* franchise? It's kind of the crocodile version of *Jaws*. The movie has a notable cameo of Betty White. Of course, here in the bayou, we used an alligator to make it more authentic."

Zack nodded as if this made perfect sense, but Brent couldn't help but think this was all a little crazy. Luckily, Gene got his attention by offering one of his favorite activities—food.

"Go ahead and help yourself to a refreshment." Gene gestured to the alligator.

While they nibbled on a few gifts from Betty, the boat pressed on. When they got closer to the skyline, they saw that the carefully crafted trees partially concealed a wall that'd been expertly painted and lit to mimic a foggy night sky. Toward the bottom where the wall met the water, there was the illusion that the swamp went on and disappeared into the mist. They came up on a small shack that mimicked the one from the *Pirates* ride. Although the boat's passengers could still hear the faint music of a banjo playing in the distance, the rocker that sat on the porch was empty.

When the boat stopped alongside the porch in front of a rickety-looking ladder, more faces of confusion arose.

"Here we are!" Gene gestured for everyone to climb up.

Surely, this was a joke. The little shack was maybe five feet by five feet. No one would want to stay in a room so small. Still, Picaud's palace had not disappointed thus far, so they all made their way up and squeezed onto the porch. Brent plopped down in the rocker and began a back-and-forth motion, looking out at the hanging paper lanterns beautifully illuminating the dining area.

Gene pulled out a key and unlocked the rusty-looking padlock on the door, which looked as if it were made from driftwood.

"For show," he said, pointing at the ancient lock.

He pressed the door inward, and a light popped on, revealing a pristine, dark-brown door in a soft amber glow. He pressed down on the black metal handle and swung the second door inward.

They entered a large, lavishly furnished suite. A lofty seating area was staged in front of a huge television screen that could be retracted until it disappeared entirely. Behind the screen was a window giving a wonderful, elevated view of the swamp and plantation house.

The entire tour took over an hour. This was due to a combination of the grandeur of the estate and at least one of the guests dawdling at some aspect along the way. Everyone was thoroughly impressed.

At last, they arrived at a large hangar to the side of the main house.

"This is Dr. Picaud's motor pool. The doctor is inside waiting for you, so let's not keep him waiting any longer."

Inside sat row upon row of brand-new, well-preserved, and well-restored vehicles. The sheer magnitude was enough for all four guests to go silent.

Brent wasn't entirely sure, but he could've sworn he saw his wife wiping drool from the corner of her mouth.

Oh, great. She didn't need any more excuses to spend more of his money.

But Lucy's eyes bulged at the sight before her. A 2017 Ford Mustang, a 70s Nissan 240z, a VW Sand Rail, even an Ariel Atom. All mechanical marvels, and the list just kept growing.

"Well, what do you think?" asked a voice that boomed all around them through the acoustics of the hangar.

They looked around until they saw a loft above them, where two smiling men looked down at them. Picaud walked down the stairs to meet them, and the other man followed close behind.

"Glad to see you all made it. This is my friend, Jacob Withers." Picaud indicated the man following him.

"Jake, if you please," the man said, smiling while he shook the hands of the men and kissed the hands of the women.

The others still speechless, Lucy was the first to chime in. "This. Is. Amazing!"

"Thank you."

"Was that a De Tomaso Pantera I saw back there?"

Picaud smiled. "You must be Lucy; your husband did not oversell you. You certainly know your cars."

"My husband"—she turned and gave a somewhat snide look—"seems to have undersold you. He told me you had an affinity for cars, but he neglected to say that you had such great taste."

"Coming from you, I'll take that as a wonderful compliment. But I don't think I gave him any indication of my collection here, merely that I had one. Would you like to see more?"

The group moved about the rows of cars, Picaud and Jake in the lead. Every so often, someone would break off to inspect one more closely.

They passed many noteworthies: an '01 BMW Z3, an '06 Hawkeye, a Cobra 427. Even a pristine 1971 silver-gray Chevy Corvette. Something pawed at the back of Brent's mind at the sight of this car, but it stayed just out of reach and was soon gone entirely. The car's long hood had been propped open to show a shiny, chrome-plated engine. Lucy stuck her head under the hood to get a closer look but almost immediately moved on.

Toward the far side of the building were revolving display stages where Dr. Picaud presented a few of his favorites. Beyond these was a large, elegant, wooden bar surrounded by retired road signs and sheet metal. A smiling Gene was already behind it.

"If anyone would care for a drink, please make yourselves at home," Picaud said, motioning to the bar. "Gene will be more than happy to make anything you'd like. I assure you, he is an expert mixologist."

Brent, Zack, and Lydia made their way toward the bar, but Lucy stayed where she was, her mouth agape as she looked at the stage farthest from them. It only took Brent a second before he realized what had grabbed his wife's attention.

There, showing off its magnificence as the stage slowly turned on its axis, was Lucy's 2026 Pagani Zonda R.

There was no mistaking it. This was *her* car. Lucy's mind whirled to try and make sense of it. How did Picaud get her car? Why did he have it? What would her husband say?

She remembered the visor man saying that Luigi owed someone a car. Could Picaud be that someone? If so, he also had some shady dealings.

As for her husband, could it be possible he might not notice? She thought that unlikely with how much attention she'd given the car—so much that he often asked why she didn't give him as much. She'd told him it had been stolen; he'd even filed a police report and everything. He'd insisted because there was no way he wasn't going to place an insurance claim.

"What the . . ." she heard him say. It was too late. "Hey! Isn't that your car?"

He'd almost yelled it, so much so that his voice was carried by the hangar, and everyone came over to get a good look.

Picaud made his way over to the stage. "What's that?" he asked, surprised.

Lucy stammered, "No, I don't think it could pos—"

"That car!" Brent said, still yelling. "That's Lucy's car! Someone stole it just the other night!"

"Really? Are you sure?" Picaud asked.

"Why would she lie?" Brent asked, more to himself than Picaud.

"No; I mean are you sure it's hers?"

"Without a doubt. I've seen it often enough."

"I had no idea. This car was a gift to me by a very dear friend. He gave it to me just yesterday. I wanted to show my gratitude, so I displayed it among my favorites."

"Who is he? What's his name? I'll—"

"Mr. Wheaton, I am sorry. I have certain friends that have somewhat less-than-reputable pasts, but I assure you, the man who gave me this car would never do such a thing as steal."

Lucy watched as Jake left briefly and then came back with a folder in his hands. He riffled through, pulled out a piece of paper, and handed it to Picaud. Lucy's stomach clenched.

Picaud examined the paper and showed it to Brent. "There, you see? He had the pink slip and everything."

Brent's bald head began to turn red, and his black, curled mustache quivered. Lucy was sure this was the end for her. What was she going to say to him?

"How?" he asked.

"I assure you, I will look deeply into this matter myself. In the meantime, why don't we all enjoy our drinks?" Picaud ushered everyone back to the bar, and Lucy was grateful for Picaud's dismissal of her husband's question. She knew there was no way to get around questions, but at least now she had time to figure this out. For now, she just downed drink after drink in an effort to forget the future inevitable argument.

After the excitement died down, Picaud said, "So, would anyone like to give one of these babies a test drive?"

Zack chuckled nervously. "I don't think it would be safe."

"I quite agree, but I'm sure Jake here would be more than happy to drive you around for a lap. I have a track just outside."

"In that case," said Brent, not quite able to keep the slur out of his voice, "I would love a go in that one over there."

They all looked to the combination of dune buggy and dragster he was referring to.

Lucy looked at her husband in surprise but was at least glad he had not pointed at the Zonda.

"The Atom? Good choice. Perhaps I'll go after," she said.

"Certainly! Jake, what do you say?" Picaud asked.

"As the great Samuel L. Jackson once said, 'Hold on to your butts!'" Jake grinned and ushered Brent toward the vehicle.

The others, who were still sitting at the bar, stood up to follow, but Picaud held up a hand.

"Gene, if you please."

"Yes, sir. Everyone, hold on to something."

Looking back and forth at each other, they did what they were told this time without question. Once they'd all gripped the bar, Gene reached over to the beer taps and grabbed the flat gray one on the end. He pulled, and the entire bar began to move. It did a complete 180-degree turn until the bar was now outside under a waiting cabana, facing out on the track. They watched the car make its way to the starting line.

Even from this side of the track, Lucy could hear her husband yell to Jake, "Give her all she's got!"

On command, Jake made the wheels screech in place for a moment, then the car took off like it'd been shot out of a gun. Those at the bar watched as the car expertly gripped each corner. There was a turn into the middle of the outer ring of the track leading to the obstacle course, and Jake threaded through with dizzying speed.

Throughout the whole run, all Lucy could hear was the engine revving and shifting, but when the car got closer, another sound came wafting in on the breeze. It was a high-pitched wailing. She realized that Brent was screaming in terror.

When Jake pulled up to the bar, Brent clutched at his chest as if he was having a heart attack. He got out of the vehicle still clutching, made it three steps away from the car, and promptly doubled over and heaved all that was in his stomach.

"Jake, what did you do to him?" Picaud asked reproachfully.

"He told me to give her all she's got, so I did."

Despite the clear distress Brent was feeling, Lucy laughed with the rest of them, but when Jake asked, "Who's up next?" she was not the first to volunteer.

The late afternoon progressed into the evening as the four guests all spent the remainder of their visit watching the sun set and getting progressively drunker.

Picaud, who still nursed the first bottle of beer he'd been given, watched as Zack moved closer to him so that they now formed what evidently was meant to be a private conversation. Zack was clearly intoxicated, but Picaud felt that Zack was able to conduct himself remarkably well considering how much he'd seen him consume.

In the past few weeks, Picaud had only had to have direct contact with the people he despised a handful of times. With each experience, it didn't get any easier to smile in their faces and pretend to like them, but he was becoming more confident in his poker face and acting abilities.

He was inspired by his detailed knowledge of William Nell I's accounts that he'd studied many times. Nell had gone undercover with one of the most notorious gangs of the time and was able to keep his cool knowing that his very life was at stake.

Picaud in no way felt in danger, but he needed to lull Zack and Brent into a false sense of security in order to lead them by the nose to spring his trap. In order to get them to do what he wanted, they had to believe him a friend.

To this end, he made the first move to strike up the private conversation.

"So, how's the political life?"

Zack smiled through glassy eyes. "Wonderful. I love my work. Being able to represent the common man and make a difference for them; it's such an honor to have been chosen to do so." He held his delicate fluted glass up as if in toast.

What a load. "That's wonderful, and so very noble. I know I always try—" Picaud was going to add more but was cut off and smiled at the interruption.

"Thank you. You know, I knew that I was destined to be a politician ever since I was a kid."

Picaud's throat tightened. "I can imagine."

"Yep, ever since I can remember, people would always look to me to take the lead. I found I had a great liking for it, so I took it and ran."

Completely inaudible to anyone but himself, Picaud said, "I'm sure you did." Then, louder, "And now you're a senator. That is impressive."

"Yes, but you know, I think I can do even better than that."

"What do you mean?"

Zack looked at him for a moment as if appraising him. "We're getting to be friends, yeah?"

Picaud said nothing but smiled broadly, hoping the nausea he felt was hidden behind his facade.

"Keep it to yourself," Zack went on, as was to be expected—too caught up in himself to notice anyhow, "but I'm thinking I might throw my hat into the ring during a presidential race someday, maybe even someday soon."

The thought of this man sitting at the nation's helm was infuriating, but Picaud calmed himself knowing he'd never get there, not with what Picaud had in store.

"Is that so?"

"Mm-hmm. I've started asking around, and everyone seems to think it's a good idea. I'm already in talks with the leaders of the Georgia Republican Party. They think I have what it takes to get a nomination; I just need to convince the rest of the nation's party leaders."

"How do you do that?"

"Unfortunately, it all boils down to one word: money. Spend a bunch of it here, get people to donate some there, help get a few bills passed to save some for somebody else. The world revolves around digits on a screen, but what can you do? One can try to gain the nomination with their own money, but those people are usually just pandering to the masses."

"Isn't that the goal? Aren't you elected by those masses?" He knew Zack didn't give two shits for the people he claimed to represent, but was Zack actually drunk enough to say it out loud?

Zack laughed as if Picaud had said something incredibly funny. "You're serious?"

Picaud continued looking confused.

"Sure, that's what it's supposed to be in theory, but that's certainly not how it works, particularly to get a main party nominee in a presidential race. Yes, it is everyone's right to vote for who they want. But the leaders of political parties choose whom they want to back and make sure that *their* man wins the party's nomination. Since the party is a private organization, it's entirely legal for them to do so. And that's why each of the two main party candidates are not usually backed by most of their constituents.

"Take those idiots who run the Democratic Party. Back in President Trump's first presidential campaign, the majority of Democrats wanted Senator Sanders to win the nomination. Sanders, however, didn't play ball with the leaders of that party, so they chose to back Hillary instead. It was all over social media at the time. Sanders would pack entire stadiums full to bursting with supporters, while Clinton would only have a fraction of the size. But the powers that be tried to cover all of that up in order to sway the vote, presenting it as though Hill-Dog was winning. But they botched the job, and everyone knew it. I don't know exactly what they ended up saying to Sanders, but they eventually got him to drop out. After that, they thought Clinton was sure to be the next president because even Sanders knew that if they split the vote, Trump was sure to win."

"But he did win," Picaud said, noting a flaw in the story.

"Yes, but that's not the important part. The Democratic leaders basically told their constituents that they had no choice in the matter and *had* to vote for Hillary. Furthermore, they knew that they had to vote for her, or else Trump would become president, because it's a two-party system."

Picaud gave a cynical laugh. "No wonder people feel like their vote doesn't matter."

"It's sad but true. And until they're changed, you have to play by the rules that are given. But is it really so bad? I mean, the only reason that Hillary lost that election was because the party stopped lying to their constituents."

"Really?"

"Yes! That's the American voter right there. They have absolutely no idea what they want, and they prefer being lied to, just not to find out about it. They want to be able to think that there is someone out there to represent their best interests, because most have no interest in politics at all. They don't care what happens just so long as they're able to keep their version of the American Dream alive. As long as they get to live their life the way *they* want, they don't give a shit about anything else. Didn't the Founding Fathers say as much when they came up with the whole concept of the Electoral College? Governmental policy is dangerous in the hands of the common man."

Zack grinned smugly and wickedly. Picaud wanted to punch him so badly he could taste it, but Zack went on, giving him time to regain his composure.

"I plan to give them exactly what they want. All I have to do is get the attention of the rest of the leaders of the Republican Party; if I have their backing, I'll be sure to get the nomination."

Picaud had been expecting something like this, but it still made his insides crawl. Here was the same old Zack, doing whatever he had to in order to manipulate circumstances in his favor. That was always his most prominent quality. It's how he'd been able to get away with everything from bullying Picaud—back when he was still Edward—and turning people against him to running him off the road and Brittany out of town.

"How do you plan on obtaining the nomination?"

"Campaign. That's first and foremost. Make sure my stances are in line with theirs and go out and get public attention with it. That's the most crucial step."

"Sounds like you're well on your way, then," Picaud said.

"Thanks, but I could always use more help in finding campaign contributors or powerful connections." He paused, as if steeling himself to say what he really wanted to. "Dr. Picaud, have you ever given any thought to getting a hand in politics?"

Picaud had listened to these drunken rantings as if indulging a child. Every sentence that spewed out of Zack's mouth proved that he was the same bully, just with a bigger playground. While Picaud listened, he'd savored his thought of *Oh, what I'm going to do to you.*

But here was something so cosmically absurd that even Picaud hadn't seen it coming: Zack was about to ask *him* for help. Picaud was sure he could think of a way to use this to his advantage.

"Me?"

"Yes. You are one of the wealthiest and most powerful men of this great nation's elite. Surely, you want to protect your interests."

"I'm afraid I choose to keep my political influence to a simple vote for my choice of policy or person. I make it a rule never to spend a dime on politics. I feel that that is how it was meant to be fundamentally. It's supposed to be a 'free' country, after all."

They both laughed, but Picaud could see in Zack's eyes he knew he had just been rebuked. Picaud tried not to enjoy the disappointed look too much.

"I do, however, know plenty of people who would like a candidate like you. Perhaps I'll let them know that you'd like to run someday."

Zack's face lit up. "Would you? That would be great!"

"I won't promise you anything beyond that. I will simply tell them *of* you. I absolutely refuse to endorse anyone politically."

"That's more than enough; thank you very much." The gleam in Zack's eye turned green. Picaud saw it and knew it was only a matter of time before he'd wipe that look clean off. This time, it was easy to smile at the senator.

Chapter 14

THE OPPOSING PIECES

The morning after her visit to Dr. Picaud's estate, Lucy Wheaton awoke to an unexpected visitor.

When she opened her front door, she was alarmed to see the visor man standing there. She moved outside and hastily closed the door behind her.

He looked up to his right, screwed up his face in remembrance, and, almost as if he were reading off a card, said, "Excuse me, ma'am. I have been sent here by Dr. Picaud with both your vehicle and a most sincere apology. Mr. Roma would like to express his regrets not only that he could not be here in person but also that he engaged in such a presumptuous act that resulted in acquiring your vehicle in the first place. He was reproached heavily for this by Dr. Picaud and would like to make amends. He therefore includes not only your car but also another case of Pappy Van Winkle's Family Reserve and hopes that you keep and enjoy the previous one as well. If he or I can help you in any way, please do not hesitate to ask.

"Once again, I would like to reiterate all three of our most sincere apologies and hope that we will speak no more of this matter and consider it closed."

After the whole thing was recited, the young man relaxed his face and gave a sigh of relief. He sat there waiting for a response, looking proud he was able to remember all of it.

Lucy looked beyond him and gasped at the sight of her prized Zonda in the carport, looking better and shinier than she could ever remember seeing it before. She ran to it as if reunited with a lost child and turned to thank the visor man, but he was already gone.

Lucy's husband had been furious at the loss of her three-million-dollar car and planned on making full inquiries after seeing it in Picaud's motor pool. These inquiries would surely have led to him discovering not only the events that had gone on last Saturday but also what she'd been doing for many years right under his nose.

Now, not only did she have her car back, but it also seemed like everyone who'd been involved wanted to keep the event just as quiet as she did. To add to that, she now had two three-thousand-dollar bottles of bourbon. She could keep one entirely for herself and do whatever she pleased with the other—not to mention the third, less-expensive bottle sure to still be in her car. She figured she'd probably share it with her husband, sauce enthusiast that he was. He'd be so happy over it being such a grand bottle acquired for free that, coupled with the return of the car, maybe he wouldn't ask questions.

This also put her into great debt with Picaud. She was both incredibly grateful and curious as to why he would want to keep everything so hush-hush. Obviously, he didn't want it to get out that he had friends who would engage in illegal street racing, which begged the question, what else did he have to hide?

The thought made her feel better about the doctor rather than put off. After seeing what an eccentric man he was, no matter how many millions of dollars he gave to charity and how much he presented both himself and his company as nothing less than philanthropic, the man had secrets, and he wanted to keep them. He was just like everyone else.

She grabbed one of the bottles and went inside to tell her husband the good news.

After not being able to find him, she figured he was in his man-cave basement. She walked over to the door that guarded the staircase, and sure enough, the little red light above it was on. He was down there and didn't want to be disturbed.

Lucy knew she was the reason for the red light, but she was still puzzled at it years after its installation. He'd installed it shortly after she had gone down to tell him her mother was in the hospital and that she needed to fly out to her. She'd walked down the stairs, calling his name the entire way. She'd found him passed out on the leather couch next to an empty liquor bottle and walked over, meaning to shake him awake.

His pants were unzipped, and he was partially exposed. That's when she noticed the items on the coffee table in front of him: a box of tissues and a pump-action bottle of lotion.

Men, she thought with a roll of her eyes.

But then the large blue binder snatched her attention, and she found herself drawn to it, completely sure of what she'd find. Her father had been the same way. Luckily, she'd never caught him like this, but she had found his collection of *Playboy*s.

When she opened up the folder, she paused and frowned. It wasn't a stack of *Playboy*s, or even porn at all. It was just a bunch of pictures of women that were completely ordinary, all clothed and smiling. It reminded her of an old makeup class she'd had in college; the students had been assigned to assemble random pictures that could inspire the reader in whatever project they were doing. It could've been any number of things. Good examples of beauty makeup had been a big part, but there had been different sections of the book that they'd needed to add as well. Things like fantasy, special effects, and gore. The students had assembled these collages into one big binder that was called a *morgue*.

What on earth he had one for, or why he'd been looking at it while pleasuring himself, she had no idea. She was just thinking it over in her mind when she was startled out of her thoughts by a tug on her leg.

Not completely sober yet, Brent yelled, "What the hell are you doing? Who told you could come down here? You have no right!"

"Calm down; I just came to tell you—"

"I don't care! Whatever it is can wait; get the hell out of here!"

"Okay, all right, I'm going."

Lucy started up the stairs, and he called after her, "Don't ever come down here without my permission again."

"Oh, you don't have to worry about that." She slammed the door at the top of the stairs.

So, that's a pretty normal reaction, huh? Okay, she'd caught him jerking off, but she was his wife, so what did it matter? Still, he'd installed the light the very next day and told her never to bother him when it was on.

Now, years later, she looked at the burning red light, then down to the amber-colored liquid that had waited so many years for someone to come along and taste it.

Oh well, she thought with no real regret, *more for me*. And she walked off to put her own sanctuary back in her garage.

A whole month passed after his brush with death before Jesse began using again. He was very proud he'd been able to go so long, but this was a special occasion. He'd gotten to know Henry Picaud over the past few weeks. Jesse knew he'd be mad, but surely he wouldn't begrudge him a little celebration, right?

Jesse had gone over to the beach house at least four times a week since the incident. Picaud had actually been there only a handful of times but had told Jesse he was always welcome to come and go as he pleased. The staff had been given special orders to let him in and wait on him if he were to come by, even if the doctor was away.

Jesse liked it over there. He enjoyed his own house, to be sure, but Picaud's place was his own private getaway. Not to mention the thrill he got whenever he had the pleasure of telling a friend that he had the use of the illusive billionaire's beach house.

Even his agent was impressed, and Tom was never impressed by anything. Maybe Tom thought that if he helped the friend of such a person, the man would help him in return, either directly or indirectly.

Whatever the case, Tom worked damn hard to make sure Jesse was put in front of the D'alos. The smash-hit husband-and-wife team had signed on to direct the first movie and reserved the rights to be brought on for any sequels. When Jesse had walked in, it was like he was in a dream. There he was, in front of two of the biggest directors in Hollywood, about to be seriously considered for the role of a lifetime.

When news had reached him that he'd been chosen, his friends had been so happy that they absolutely had to throw him a party. He'd never felt more exhilarated in his life. He was living the dream. He'd thought over all he'd had to do to get to this point in life, and when Carl had offered to "take him skiing," he'd thought, *Why not; I earned it.*

Nothing happened this time, and he felt that he was not only on top of the world but also invincible. He was confident that if he was careful, he could keep his using out of the public eye. Even if he didn't, after this movie was made, he'd be so set that he'd be able to get away with murder. Hell, in a way, it was almost expected of him to either do drugs or kill somebody—or both. As long as they couldn't prove it was intentional.

He just had to be careful about that *other* thing. There were only a few things that meant career suicide once you reached A-list status. He was sure that *it* was one of them, but he'd be damned if anyone would find out.

Zack looked out at the lawn surrounding his large estate from the huge second-floor window of his home office. This was his favorite time of day because the sun was slowly lowering below the western horizon, and the rays of dying light among the scene, with the deep hues of purple and blue, were slowly consuming the sky from off in the distance. It was always a beautiful sight. He leaned up against the window frame on one elbow while his hand dangled above him. It was a fine sun that was setting on a fine time in his life.

He still felt a little rebuffed at Picaud's refusal to help outright, but he had given Zack the card of a publicist who had wanted to work for Picaud for years. Picaud had said he'd never really met the woman but was told she had done great things.

When Zack had looked up her name—Maxine Calswell—he'd found that she had plenty of work in the public eye. She'd first worked in Hollywood and had helped make some of the biggest names, but she was tired of pandering to moviegoers and couch surfers. She wanted to make a difference, and what better way than to help the people who influence how our great nation conducts itself?

Max, it turned out, was everything Zack had ever needed. She was an attractive young woman with straight, dark hair and glasses, always in a well-fitted pencil-skirt suit. She knew not only tons of famous people with deep pockets—usually celebrities who wanted to take a more active approach in politics; they all seemed to feel it was their duty to do so these days just because they had a following—but also other wealthy and famous individuals who had nothing to do with the silver screen.

Her biggest strength was the fact that whenever she didn't know about something, she made damn sure she learned everything there was to know about it, and quickly. Namely, the priceless currency of secrets.

It was a perfect symbiotic relationship: Max got to make her difference, and through her, Zack met everyone he needed to rub shoulders with. She had increased his fan base to outside his local constituents, making sure he took the right stances on all the hot issues. All he had to do was smile and wave to the camera.

Once put in touch with the people that could help him eventually win the nomination, Zack just had to know the right buttons to push, and he'd be in.

A knock on his office door awakened him from his musings. The best part of his now almost-daily routine was ready.

Zack made sure all of his files were locked away and his computer was turned off before making his way down to the little spa room that'd been built for him when he moved in. He stepped into the white-tiled room and quickly undressed. The routine never varied: First, he would enjoy a steam for ten to fifteen minutes; then he would towel off and climb naked, facedown, under a small towel on the massage bed.

There was a knock on the door.

"I'm ready for you." He drew out the last word to show his excitement.

The door opened, and a young, blonde girl, hardly fourteen years old, stepped in. He looked up to see she had been making use of his pool while she waited. She was in a skintight red bikini.

He smiled at the thought of what was under it, and her own smile fell away as if the life had been sucked out of it.

The girl's eyes went wide, and she turned for the door.

"I think I'd better be—" she started to say, but she cut off when she turned the knob and found it locked.

Zack's smile grew at the look on her face. "Relax; it's just a massage. You'll be out of here in no time." He lay facedown and waited.

After a moment's hesitation, tentative, tiny hands began to rub his back. Ah, this was the life.

His taste for this sort of thing hadn't made an appearance until he'd really started getting into politics. Zack had always known the value of secrets. They were the blood that kept the political heart beating. When he had first decided that he'd have to get in bed with the powers that be, so to speak, he'd had an inclination that the old saying might have to be literal in order to get where he wanted. This was not only an understatement but also just the tip of a penetrative iceberg.

He had been quick to find out the secret that was poorly kept among almost everyone in a power seat but that was always guarded viciously from the public eye. There were only a few things left to the world that were considered forbidden fruit, and this was by far the most intoxicating.

It was the biggest secret society in the world. Oh, sure, he met tons of Freemasons, Knights Templars, even a few claiming to be Illuminati, but all were at the parties of this secret society that was so large and notorious, no one dared name it.

The girls were sent as gifts from one member to another. It was expected of members to both give and receive in order to hold their ranks within the society. Those who not only gave but also procured were the ones held in the highest regard.

Zack never procured, but he was more than happy to receive untouched fruit, then ship the little lady off to the next person and pay it forward. When that person sent one back, he would have his fun, then send her to another benefactor. This system not only allowed members to indulge in this sweetest of delicacies but also formed a tight-knit bond between them through the medium of mutual flesh—young flesh that'd been plucked just before ripening.

Now that Zack was growing in his ambition to occupy the nation's biggest seat, the web of members grew to an astonishing size and went far beyond the realm of politics. Every position of power in the country had at least one who held membership. Movie stars, wealthy businessmen, law enforcement officials of all different rankings; the list was endless. The number of gifts grew respectively. Once, a congressman from New York sent him triplets along with a card wishing him a happy birthday. And oh, how it was.

The reluctant hands started to relax and grow confident. After a few minutes, she asked, "Can . . . can I go now?"

And then he turned over.

Chapter 15

THRILLS AND CHILLS

Whenever the month of October rolled around, the staff knew Picaud's favorite holiday was coming and would delight in setting out the decorations. It always seemed to put a smile on his face when he saw them.

This year, he had something special planned for Halloween. He was to host a "Spooktacular" on one of his properties, and it was expected to be the event of the season by all who heard of it, promised by the man himself to hold many thrills and chills.

Jake handled all the arrangements, of course. He was the one who'd acquired the property in the first place, and after everything he'd found out, he was eager to have a hand in the festivities.

On October twenty-seventh, many people were surprised to find an elegant, black, glossy card with gold trim in the day's mail, inviting them to a special Halloween party. Every single person who found themselves lucky enough to receive an invitation, although very short notice, had RSVPed immediately. Any other plans intended for the evening were scattered to the winds for the first real party the famous Dr. Picaud had ever been known to throw.

Picaud and Jake worked nonstop to make sure everything was ready for the event. Many notable figures were placed on the guest list, the main focuses of Picaud's among them. Early in the morning on the day of the party, he held a special meeting with a few choice members of his staff.

"Let me first start by saying that I trust each and every one of you in here, which is why I've chosen you for this event. Before I release you to get on with your preparations, I'm going to speak to each of you in turn about what's going on tonight. I want you to think hard about participating before you answer. I'll be in my office, and Jake will send you in."

Murmurs spread among the staff as Picaud stepped into his office.

The first one up was a pretty brunette, about twenty years old, named Rachel. A quizzical look was plastered on her face, and Picaud felt apprehension at what he was about to ask of her. The one solace he had in proceeding was that it would be her choice.

"Rachel, do you enjoy working here?"

A look of astonishment flooded her face. "Are you kidding? Of course! I was in such a bad place when the shelter sent me over. I'd been carrying around this heavy weight for years; I didn't know how long I could go on. Then I came here and found my true family. The others that I've met here have given me so much love and support. I'm beyond grateful."

The blood rushed to Picaud's face, and it was hard for him to keep it under control. "You don't know how glad I am to hear you say that." He took a deep breath. "The reason I'm talking to all of you is that the persons that have caused the pain that have sent all of you to me will be here tonight."

Rachel's face drained of its color as if she'd been bled white. "You mean . . . he . . . the man who . . . He'll be here tonight?"

Picaud found it hard to keep eye contact but knew she had a right to it if he were to ask this of her. "In your case, yes, the man I believe to have done those deplorable acts to you will be at the party tonight."

Rachel looked like she had been slapped, then anger flared up in her eyes. "Why? Why would you do this? The man takes advantage of me, and now you want me to serve him?"

"Yes and no. There are two reason I want you to go through this tonight. I need to know it is him, without any doubt, and"—Picaud looked up at her now to let her see that he was fully on her side—"I want you to unnerve him."

Her face softened a fraction. "What . . . what do you mean?"

"I'm going to make sure that he is brought to justice, but I don't think that's enough. I think that we—that is to say, all of us—deserve more payback on the side. Before we try and take him down for good, we need to get in his head, have him make mistakes, psych him out so he'll be ruined when the final blow comes. What do you say? You interested in getting a little payback?"

The shadow of a smile came out. "What do you want me to do?"

"Nothing too crazy. If we're going to do this right, we can't move too fast. I plan on having each and every one of you who want to be at his trial have your chance to pound your own nail into his coffin, but tonight, just be as rude as you see fit. Talk back to him, refuse him service, that kind of stuff."

"Can I spit in his food?" Her smile broadened, making Picaud relieved his inclinations were right. There were others who needed revenge as badly as he did.

A small laugh burst from him. "If you wish, but I do ask that you don't let anyone see. Although there are some nasty people coming tonight, the vast majority are innocent bystanders. If you choose not to participate tonight, I assure you that I completely understand, and no matter what, you will be compensated all of tonight's wages."

Rachel stared off, lost in thought.

"What do you say, Rachel?"

She looked up at him, and the smile finished making its way over her face.

The rest of the meetings were the same. Although a fair few were told they were to come up against their rapist, others would see their former employer who had wronged them in some way or whom they had seen doing something terrible. A small portion chose to take the night off, but most wanted to join in the fun, and Picaud knew that power resided in their numbers.

When Picaud had acquired this infamous property, it had consisted of a mountain cabin and a lot of greenery. Since then, he had cleared a huge portion of the trees away from the cabin but had kept enough still within walking distance. When Picaud had given Jake the plans for what he wanted done, he had made sure it was absolutely clear the cabin and the forest immediately surrounding it were to remain untouched.

On the cleared area, Picaud had erected a village dedicated to his favorite holiday. Each structure served a purpose, whether it be to serve food, drinks, or scares.

When hatching his plans, he'd brought in many well-known architectural designers that had studied under the great minds behind buildings in all of the best theme parks.

Like with everything Picaud did, money had been no object.

The result was a Halloween village completely dedicated to spooks and scares with practical effects and secret passages.

"Elegantly scary" was the term coined. The food was top-notch, and the drinks were top–shelf. In the middle of the village was a large, whimsical gazebo that lit up a band dressed as zombies and skeletons playing raucous hits that all enjoyed. It was the party of the year.

The area was large enough that the crowd was able to thin and congregate as it pleased without ever feeling bunched in. In short, if one wanted to avoid another guest, it was easily done. This proved to be important, because along with the intended thrills of the evening, many of the attendees had internal moments of horror as well. Although Picaud lived up to his obligations as the elegant host, he kept a close eye on those who concerned him most. Each of them behaved exactly as he'd hoped.

Lucy walked around, trying to keep her husband leashed and away from a familiar man that kept popping up in their sights. Picaud had made sure Twitch knew just the right times to put himself in view of Lucy. Picaud waited until Zack and Lydia had joined them before he had Gene, who'd been showing another guest around and introducing him, make his way over.

Gene announced to the Wheatons and the Roes that this man was Hollywood's own Jesse Tovin. He'd made a name for himself in the film industry and was just announced as the lead role in an upcoming movie franchise. All four seemed impressed by the news and even admitted to Tovin that they'd seen a few of his movies, but they otherwise gave no indication of knowing him. However, when Gene went on with his appointed task, Zack and Brent exchanged a passing, but meaningful, look that appeased Picaud's curiosity.

As the night wore on, Picaud saw that Lydia began to notice that whenever they went to collect food or get a drink from the bar, the person who was attending the station would freeze at the sight of her husband before taking their order. Some were very rude to them, and one actually walked off and out of sight. Lydia was obviously trying to shrug it off, but here again, Picaud had placed just the smallest seeds of unnerving in her mind.

At nine o'clock, Picaud got up on the stage and announced he had a special treat that would make tonight unforgettable.

When Bill Nell received the black invitation to a party being thrown by the rich a-hole, his immediate response had been to toss it. He had been just about to crumple the card when he caught sight of the address where the party was being held: none other than the property that had brought this Picaud character into his line of sight in the first place.

Something lit in his belly, and he knew he couldn't turn the opportunity down. Here was his chance to see firsthand what Picaud wanted the property for.

He had to admit, what Picaud had done to the place was pretty cool. He'd gotten glimpses into how the one percent lived their lives before, but nothing like this.

A pang went through him as he thought of the old family tale. It was widely known through the family that Great-Granddad stole a bunch of money from a notorious gangster, but nobody knew where he went. He just up and disappeared, leaving the wife and kids to fend for themselves. Did he escape with all that dough and live equivalent to this?

The thought made him sick.

Bill supposed that not all rich folk came by their fortunes under such circumstances, but every one he knew of had a shady story to tell. He'd tried to look into Picaud's past, but the man seemed to be squeaky clean. Bill didn't buy it, of course—how could he when his gut was screaming that there was something there—but without any actual evidence to back it up, what could he do?

Bill decided that since he was here, why not enjoy the food available, but he absolutely refused point-blank to let any alcohol pass his lips. Although he wasn't strictly on duty, he had taken this as a work trip and wanted to keep a clear head. There was a lot to take in, of course, but nothing that pertained to the case. That was, until Picaud announced his little surprise.

"Ladies and gentlemen, may I have your attention, please. This property, although now home to many fake attributes of the occult, was once the base of operations for a notorious serial killer who was never caught and is believed to be still abroad, perhaps still lurking near these very woods!" Picaud manifested a maniacal laugh that seemed all too real, and a shudder went through the crowd.

"You have all been presorted into smaller groups and given a tour guide. If you walk over to the tower"—Picaud gestured off to a structure at the edge of the village that looked like the Grimm fairy tale version of Rapunzel's tower—"a staff member will let you know what time your group is scheduled. When it's your allotted time, wait by the sign next to the pathway in front of the tower."

Immediately, guests started making their way toward the tower. Bill was surprised at how fast the staff was able to keep the line moving; apparently, they had drilled like a freaking ballet to get through this evening.

Bill made his way over and saw that he was one of the first groups scheduled. When the time came to gather at the sign, he saw that many were already patiently waiting for the tour to start. There were about fifteen people in his group, and he knew they were all people who held rank within society. There was even a senator and another guy he'd seen in a movie not too long ago.

Bill felt a little out of place, not only for not knowing anyone but also because one glance around told him he was the only one here who worked for a living. He didn't let this bother him, of course, but he couldn't help but wonder why he'd been invited. What was Picaud up to?

Bill saw Picaud making his way over, and before he could take his place in front to address the group, Bill saw a small commotion. Apparently, a man had a little bit too much to drink, and his wife was trying to help him up from a tumble. She stood there, mopping his bald head with a handkerchief. After Picaud made sure the bald man was all right, he told them all to follow him. This was one of the few groups to be led by the man himself.

Ain't we the fancy ones.

Although Bill had been on this property many times, nothing looked familiar, but as they walked on the path leading away from the party, he began to get his bearings. This path, he knew, would take them straight up to the cabin. After seeing all the practical scares provided in the village, he started to wonder what was waiting for them there. Did Picaud rig it as well, or turn it into one of those haunted mazes that were everywhere this time of year? One of those cheesy thrills that allowed college kids to earn a few bucks and keep themselves supplied with ramen and pizza for a few weeks?

When they got to the cabin, Bill didn't find cheap thrills waiting. In fact, nothing had been changed at all. Hell, even the crime scene tape had been left up; or at least re-placed.

"Ladies and gentlemen, up until this point, you've enjoyed cheap imitations of scares dreamt up by some of the brightest minds the entertainment industry has to offer. However, through this doorway, we leave the realm of fantasy behind and explore just how terrifying reality can be.

"We are about to enter the base camp of what most say is the worst serial killer the state of Georgia has ever seen. As we go from room to room, I will reveal to you the research dug up on this individual and the acts that have been perpetrated in this very house. What you are about to see is real."

Bill was expecting Picaud to go on and say something like, "Those who are prone to weakness or have heart conditions may want to leave now," but the option for anyone to leave hadn't been offered. He supposed having your tour guide be one of the most famous medical doctors in the world would probably help shield his estate from death or lawsuit.

The cabin was a simple three-story job—two floors and a basement. The paint on top of the wooden paneling was probably once a vibrant red but had deteriorated into a chipped, flaky maroon that sprung out of the two-foot rock-wall base extending down to the lowest level. The place itself was entirely unremarkable. Any random person might have either lived there or, more likely, used it as a hunting cabin or weekend getaway.

Picaud climbed the stone steps to the porch and main entrance first. He removed one side of the tape that roped off the entrance and bid the group enter. Bill held back, wanting to keep an eye on everything. The others seemed reluctant but curious about going in. The bald man who'd fallen earlier was having a bit of trouble going up the steps. He clutched at the handrail for dear life. Bill was grateful he hadn't taken part in the drinks.

Stepping inside, the first thing to hit him was the smell. It wasn't the decay of flesh but that of disrepair. The air was moldy and stale. The cabin itself was dimly lit by the bulbs that hung either from the ceiling in metal chandeliers or from the lamps plugged into the outlets.

The main entrance led into a foyer that mainly consisted of a staircase leading upstairs with branch banisters. To the left led to the lounge; to the right, the kitchen. The place had been stripped of its furnishings. Any lighting fixture that hadn't been secured to the cabin itself was the one aspect added since Bill was here last.

Picaud led them to the kitchen first. There in front of the stove was a tape outline, marking where investigators had found the first body after learning of the cabin's existence.

"Here, as is indicated, is where a body was found that turned this property into a crime scene. It was actually that of a local detective said to have been following up on a lead. He hadn't been heard from in several hours, so reinforcements were sent looking. Officials theorize that he surprised the killer, who unfortunately gained the upper hand, and this was the result. His was the only male body found."

Everyone looked grotesquely intrigued. Many pulled out their phones and started to take pictures and videos of the place. Picaud motioned them to follow him into the next room. It'd once been the lounge but was now just a big, empty room with a fireplace. When Bill had first found it, it'd had plenty of furniture and even a bearskin rug; now, it was just bare wood floors.

"Psychological profilers say that the killer likely seduced some of the female victims early on in his career, taking the so-called wooing phase that all serial killers experience at a literal level. Where you stand now is likely where the date led up, then went horribly wrong. Later on, when stolen vehicles related to this case were found, it was surmised that he no longer bothered enticing his victims here but found it more efficient to incapacitate them and carry on with his evil deeds."

How did he know all this stuff? Bill supposed that he was probably well connected all around, but if he'd invited Bill here to make himself look innocent, he was doing a piss-poor job of it.

Next, Picaud led the group to a small door that might have been a closet at first glance. He opened it and showed the staircase down to the cellar. He went first, and everyone followed gingerly after. Once again, Bill took up the rear.

There was one fixture in the entire basement that provided light: a single bulb with a pull string dangling down in the middle of the room. Although it cast enough light to see, support beams broke up the light and cast long, black shadows across the floor toward the guests.

Picaud told everyone to stay close to the staircase, and Bill felt he knew why. All over the room, giant holes had been dug out of the floor; each empty socket represented where a body had once lain.

"Here is what makes experts theorize that this cabin was a mark of the early stages of his career. As you see in front of you, there are ten holes representing the ten bodies that once lay here. When the killer had had his fun, he'd drag the corpse down the stairs and bury her.

"It's common that killers of this nature find pleasure in living close to the bodies of their victims or else collect trophies in order to relive the act in their minds whenever they wish. The ten bodies that once rested here are only a third of the victims found on the property. When the killer ran out of room down here, the surrounding woods were the next logical site."

Bill had known what they would find down here, but he noticed the faces of the other guests as they glowed in the soft yellow light, either staring with horror toward the open graves or whispering to one another. Bill watched and listened closely.

"Oh, my God . . ."

"How could someone do such a thing?"

"There's just something about seeing those open graves. They're like open mouths, just waiting . . ."

There was a moment of shocked stillness, then out came the phones again, flashlights jerking around every which way. Some people were actually Snapchatting and talking to the camera about where they were and what they were seeing. Bill could only look on in disgust.

One person in the crowd hadn't pulled out his phone. Bill supposed that the bald man was just focused on staying upright, but that didn't seem right. The man looked dead sober now, as if someone had dunked his head into a bucket of ice water. He walked around like the rest of the group, but unlike the rest, he didn't seem to care one way or the other.

He just looked like a man who was killing time until he could once again go back to drinking. Something about this scratched at the back of Bill's mind. He didn't like it.

Picaud showed the rest of the house and escorted the guests, who were chattering excitedly, back to the main party. All except Agent Nell, who mentally seemed a million miles away. Picaud watched him, wondering if the wheels were turning just as he had hoped.

The guests stayed for a few more hours, enjoying everything the party had to offer. The one thing that was on everyone's lips was the story of the killer they'd learned about in the hours before. As he looked at the faces of his guests when they prepared to leave, Picaud smiled to himself. The party had gone off without a hitch.

Chapter 16

NO HONOR AMONG THIEVES

Zack was in a difficult situation. He went back and forth about what to do about it. Last night had started out fun and exciting, but out of nowhere, a face from the past had felt like a slap to him. He and Brent had been talking privately among themselves when who should come to be introduced to them but Cory.

The last time either he or Brent had spoken to Cory was heatedly and many years ago. It never sat well with Cory what they did in high school, but they all knew nothing could be done about it. Cory had decided to go his separate way and pretend like he had no knowledge of the other two, who returned the favor.

Seeing Cory was a shock, but then, right before they had been about to take their tour, Brent had started to act funny. He had been all for everything that evening, but all of a sudden, something had changed. He had gone as pale as a sheet, then said he wasn't feeling well and wanted to leave.

Zack hadn't wanted to go yet; he and Lydia were having a blast. Brent and Lucy had ridden to the venue with them, and if they left, they'd all have to. Brent had even fainted momentarily while they stood waiting for their tour to begin, but he had quickly recovered and said he was feeling much better.

At first, Zack had decided to shrug it off, thinking the poor guy probably had too much to drink, but his heart had sunk when he'd realized that both he and Brent had been there before. On the walk to the cabin, he'd started to feel a sense almost like déjà vu. When they'd reached the cabin, he'd recognized it. Hadn't Brent invited him all those times years ago?

After that, it hadn't been hard to put two and two together. The question now was what to do about it.

He finally decided to ask Max. He obviously couldn't afford to be associated with someone suspected of such things if he was to have any chance at becoming president. She paused to think, but only for a moment.

"This could actually be a blessing in disguise."

Zack had never felt so confused. "How do you figure?"

"What better way to show that you're a defender of the people than lending a hand in taking down a notorious serial killer? The public eats that stuff up."

"You don't understand. The man has been considered a close personal friend of my family for years. How's that going to look? Having such a brutal killer so close to me?"

The fact that Zack was friends with a murderer didn't seem to faze her. "What's one of the most chilling facts about almost every notorious serial killer in history?" She paused to let him consider. "Ted Bundy, Jeffrey Dahmer, John Wayne Gacy, Michelle A Ross—they all have one thing in common. When people were interviewed about them, they all said the same things: They didn't look like a serial killer; they looked harmless; they looked just like everyone else. Hell, Bundy and Dahmer were considered attractive. The fact that you were taken in means that you're just as human as everyone else, but even better because if you act to get him caught, you were brave in the face of danger and made sure that even a friend didn't escape justice. It's a win-win. They'll be sympathetic knowing you're just as regular as they are and inspired by your actions to put the man behind bars, not to mention grateful for taking out a threat that has plagued Georgia for years."

Zack soaked it all up. The way she put it, if he did it right, he'd not only avoid a scandal but would also come out of this mess looking like a hero. The more he thought about it, the more he liked it. When he left her office, he went straight over to Picaud's estate. It was already going on ten in the evening, and he hoped that this would qualify as an emergency.

His car pulled up to the main gate and his driver announced who it was into the little speaker box, and Zack was pleased when the gate immediately swung open. Even more, he was surprised to see that when he pulled up, Picaud himself had come down to the main entrance to greet him.

"Senator! To what do I owe this wonderful surprise?"

"Well, unfortunately, I come with some disturbing news and wanted to ask you for help."

Picaud's expression immediately fell to one of concern. "Anything. Come on inside. We'll get you warmed up; it's freezing out here."

Picaud lead Zack into his home office and offered him a seat. For a moment, the two sat in silence.

"Can I get you something? Food, drink, anything?"

"I wouldn't mind a stiff drink if you've got it," Zack said with a nervous chuckle.

"Easiest thing in the world. You see that globe over there?" Picaud pointed to a sepia-toned globe on a pedestal standing next to a large bookcase. "The top lifts up to reveal a mini bar."

Zack got up and staggered toward it. He lifted the top, which swung on a hinge. Inside was a selection of bottles and glasses and a small ice bucket. He mused at this last point because there was actually ice in it. Was he already working in here tonight? Did he drink in here on a regular basis? Or were the staff under orders to constantly check and refill it? He selected an elegant-looking bourbon, poured three fingers, took a sip, considered, downed the glass, and refilled.

Picaud, who was watching this entire scene, raised an eyebrow. "That bad, huh?"

Zack gave a small huff of laughter that turned into a cough and tried to smile. "Yeah, I guess so."

"Well, no rush. When you feel ready, tell me all about it."

After a few moments, Zack finally regained his seat and stared down into the glass he clutched in his hands. The liquid swirled dizzyingly. "First off, I want to thank you for inviting us to your party yesterday. My wife and I, we had a lot of . . . fun."

"Not at all; believe me when I say it was my pleasure." Picaud paused, seeming to know this couldn't be the reason for Zack's acting so erratic.

"Well, I know your intention in showing off that cabin last night was to give us all a good thrill, and I guess you succeeded." Zack gave a little, nervous laugh again. "But I guess it thrilled me a little too much."

Picaud waited for him to continue.

"At first, I was intrigued when you announced that you were going to show us all a real murder scene. Imagine my surprise when I started to recognize the place."

"Recognize it?" Picaud asked.

"Yes; once we were there, I realized just who it had belonged to."

"You mean you know—"

Zack cut him off. "I don't *know*; that's the thing. At this point, I only know the person who at least owned the property at one point. That's not an indication of guilt, is it?"

Picaud pondered for a second and stared at him. "No, I suppose not, but you don't think it's just a coincidence." It was not a question.

"What makes you say that?"

"Would you be here if you did?"

"No. No, I suppose not."

"What is it that you'd like me to do to help?" Picaud asked.

"Well, I want to tell someone." He looked up into Picaud's face and unconsciously let all nervousness fall away. "Someone official, I mean. I thought that since you knew so much about the property and what happened there that you might know somebody I could talk to."

"As it happens, I do." Picaud opened his desk drawer and pulled out a little black box, opened it, and riffled through it. Then he pulled out a business card and handed it to Zack. "Here; this is the agent that is working the case. I'm sure he'll be more than happy to hear what you have to say."

Zack took the card and glanced down at the name, title, and number of the man. He looked up at Picaud and ran one edge of the card across the knuckles of his right hand, making a flapping sound like a playing card against the spokes of a bicycle.

"Thanks! You really don't know how much this means to me!"

Picaud stared unblinkingly into Zack's eyes. "I think I can imagine. Is there anything else I can help you with?"

"No, I don't think so. I'm just . . . kind of shaken up a bit, that's all."

"Completely understandable." Picaud rose to place a hand on Zack's shoulder. All Zack could register was how cold the hand was. "I know how hard this must be for you."

Zack finished his drink and got up. Picaud walked him out to where his car was waiting, thanked him for coming to him and trusting him with such matters, and reminded him to come back if ever he needed anything else.

Zack thanked Picaud and told him he would. On his way out, as he was being driven down the long driveway, he took out the card and thought about his next move.

Bill Nell stared at the clock in agitation.

12:30 a.m.

Whoever had woken him up by calling his cell had better have a damn good reason. He looked down at the unknown number displayed on his screen while trying to clear the remains of sleep from his eyes. He pressed the little green button and lifted the phone to his ear.

Trying to keep the agitation out of his voice, he said, "Bill Nell."

"Hi, Mr. Nell. This is Senator Roe. Sorry to call you so late, but I was given your number and told you were the one to speak to in regard to a certain murder investigation. I think I might have some pertinent information for your case."

What sleepiness was left vanished immediately. "Yes, sir; any and all information you could provide would be greatly appreciated. To which case are you referring?"

Bill knew there could be only one case that he'd be referring to but wanted to make sure it wasn't a hoax.

"Well, I think it has to do with that serial killer that's been running rampant in Georgia."

That didn't narrow it down enough, but it still piqued his interest. "Would you like to talk over the phone, Senator, or would you prefer to talk to me in person?"

"In person, if you don't mind. Would you mind coming to my office?"

That was strange. Normally, snitches didn't want Bill anywhere near their home turf in fear of being seen. Oh well, no skin off his nose.

"Absolutely. When would you like me to do so?"

Bill was getting ready for the man to say right away; that would explain both him wanting Bill to come to his office and calling at this late hour.

"Is it possible for you to get here tomorrow?"

Tomorrow? Something was definitely weird. "Sure; as luck would have it, I'm already in Georgia."

"That *is* lucky!" Senator Roe said.

"It is indeed," Bill said musingly. He did not believe in luck. "What time were you thinking?"

"Let's aim for noon. I'll order some lunch for us and have it waiting. You like sandwiches?"

Bill was thoroughly confused. In want of anything real to say, he replied, "Sounds great." He took down the address, thanked the senator, and ended the call.

Something definitely felt hinky. Usually, people wanted to remain anonymous in situations like these, but this guy seemed to be going out of his way to make himself known. He gave his name *and* title, asked Bill to come to his office, and chose a time in the middle of the day. He just hoped that in any case, he'd finally get some answers. Not to mention the fact that this was the senator he'd recognized at the party the night before. Bill wondered if the senator knew he'd been there.

Bill arrived a half hour early the next day. He thought he'd have to wait, but although the office was teeming with people, he was sent straight in. He walked into the spacious office and saw the senator sitting behind a large wooden desk, which looked like it was worth more than a year of Bill's salary.

The senator got up immediately. "Mr. Nell, so glad you were able to make it here on such short notice."

"Yes, I guess it was a real stroke of luck that I was invited to the party." He said it straight off to see if it got a reaction. He was not disappointed. The smile was immediately wiped off the senator's face, and he went instantly pale.

"You were there?"

"Yes, Picaud invited me." Bill didn't know if the senator realized that he'd even been in the same tour group, but he wasn't going to reveal that little tidbit if he hadn't.

"Why would he do that?" Zack asked.

"A joke, I think. When he first bought the property, I decided to, uh, introduce myself. I guess he hadn't forgotten."

"Dr. Picaud does seem to have a peculiar sense of humor, doesn't he?"

"I guess so." Bill shrugged.

"So, then you know why I haven't come forward about this until now."

"I don't *know* anything, except that you may have information regarding a case."

Senator Roe nodded. "Yes, about the case that concerns the cabin on the property the other night." He motioned for Bill to take a seat. "You're a bit early; I'm afraid lunch hasn't arrived yet."

Bill was starting to get annoyed. He couldn't quite put his finger on why, but he got the feeling the senator was either stalling or making a show of something. He bit back his annoyance before it could escape with his words but wasn't entirely able to keep it out.

"That's all right, Senator. What is it that you have to tell me?"

"Well, I'd like to state for the record that I had no idea the cabin had been a crime scene until the other night." He paused to see if Bill had anything to put in. He didn't. "I don't know if he had anything to do with the murders, but a friend of mine actually used to own that property. He invited me to it many times, years ago."

This caught Bill's attention. He sat forward in his chair and waited eagerly.

"A friend of mine, Brent Wheaton—you might have seen him the other night—at one point owned that cabin."

Bill thought it over. He'd researched the ownership of the land going back the past fifty-some-odd years. Wheaton was not a name that had come up.

"Who was he? At the party, I mean." Bill asked this knowing fully well what he was about to hear.

"Big, burly guy, totally bald. He has a bushy mustache that he likes to curl."

Bill wasn't surprised. The man had caught his attention, but it didn't make sense to him until now.

Roe went on. "He was acting really strange right before we got to the cabin."

"Strange how?"

"Well, he was enjoying himself up until the point when he seemed to realize just where we were, then claimed he felt ill and wanted to leave."

"Is that all?" Bill's annoyance once more began to rise.

"He seemed to regain his composure after that but got really quiet, and if you know the man, that's not normal."

Bill scrutinized Roe's face for a moment. "I see. And neither of you knew where you were going beforehand?"

"I can't speak for him, but I certainly didn't recognize the address. We all carpooled in a limo, so it wasn't as if we were paying attention to the road."

"No attention to where you were going?"

Roe paused and looked a little embarrassed. "Well, we, the four of us, were kinda pregaming on the way. Like I say, I can't speak for him. Maybe he knew all along but didn't think that anything would come of it."

Bill thought about that for a moment. It was true that the longer killers like this got away with their crimes, the more arrogant and fool-hardy they became. Maybe he saw this invitation as one last time to revisit his deeds there.

"Was there any time before the other night when he seemed to act out of the ordinary? Maybe like he would suddenly disappear for long stretches of time?"

Roe wiped his brow, but Bill could see it was dry. "No, that's one of the reasons I called you. If he *does* have anything to do with your case, it's very disturbing that such a close friend could be able to do so without me getting a whiff of it."

Bill agreed, but only because he found it hard to believe it was possible if they had been as close as the senator said.

"Any hint of criminal activity at all in the past?"

Roe paused for a moment as if to think it over, but Bill felt that hinky feeling again, as if Roe was just stalling for time.

Roe cleared his throat, looked him dead in the eye, and said, "No. Not that I know of, anyway."

He was hiding something, but what? Then again, what politician didn't have something to hide? Bill felt he had enough to go on and got up. He plastered on the smile he always used while talking to a witness.

"Thank you for coming forward with this, Senator; you've been very helpful."

Right before he reached the door, it swung open, and a very chubby assistant walked in carrying a large plastic bag.

Roe stood up. "Oh, Mr. Nell, at least take a sandwich with you. I guarantee it's the best in the state."

Bill took it more to be polite than anything else. He held up the foil-wrapped cylinder in salute. "Thanks."

It wasn't until he got back in his car and sat with the ignition off, going over the conversation in his head, when a sudden rumble began in his stomach. It coincided with the smell of the hot sandwich permeating the air with its savory scent. He looked at the foil cylinder shape sitting in the passenger seat. He grabbed the sandwich and unwrapped it. It had already been cut in half, and when Bill pulled off the first section of the hot Italian sub, he noticed the logo printed on the paper side within. It looked like a pair of goggles with tufts of white hair above them. Bill took a bite and found it delicious.

Later, when Bill got back to his hotel room, he pulled out a tablet and looked up the senator on Instagram. He was riffling through the list of accounts the senator followed until he saw a familiar bald head grinning up at him. He clicked on the profile. It was private.

Bill went back to the previous list and discovered a profile with the same last name. He clicked on this to find thousands of pictures of who could only be the bald man's wife. There were tons of the obligatory selfies, followed by a large portion of car pics.

Bill scanned through the account to find quite a few pictures of the party. He looked through but didn't see anything special. Down in the captions was the hashtag #PicaudParty. He held his breath as he tapped on it. Could it really be that easy?

The page for the hashtag popped up. At the top, it claimed to have 502 posts. Apparently, many of the people who had taken pictures that night had posted them here using the same hashtag.

Bill went through the pictures, and any time he saw a bald head or the cabin interior, he clicked on and saved it. Once he was certain he had captured all of the pictures and videos, he scrolled through them and took a closer look.

He wasn't really sure what he was looking for but figured he'd know when he saw it. When the video popped up, he nearly dropped his tablet in his excitement. It was just a glimpse, but it was there. Someone had been taking a video on their way up the stairs from the basement. The video was of that famous actor guy talking about his experience down in the cellar with the graves shown off in the background, then the angle shifted as he began going up.

Thank God for the many advancements in technology, because although the video was mostly in the dark, it clearly showed Wheaton pulling out one of the stones from the rock wall, ducking his head down a little as if to check something within, and hurriedly putting it back as the camera swept him out of frame.

Bill immediately picked up his phone to call Picaud.

Brent Wheaton sat naked on his couch in the basement, clutching his blue binder. He had just added a few more Polaroids, and he was reminded of the ecstasy that had come with each new acquisition when he was still active. These weren't new—they'd been waiting for him all along in his old basement—but he felt the warm sensation he always got when adding to the binder.

He clutched the plastic to the flesh of his chest, cradling it as he rocked his whole body back and forth. It'd been years since he'd added the last pictures to his binder and thought he had finally kicked the habit for good. He didn't *want* to stop, exactly, but he'd heard plenty of stories of career killers. They all grew too long in the tooth and eventually got themselves caught. So-called experts would always say that they'd gotten cocky in the end and slipped up, but he knew better.

Careers were methodical. Everything right down to the last detail was always meticulously planned in advance. It was part of the thrill, the appetizer before the main course. Did the experts really think that these individuals, who had their processes ingrained into the very fiber of their beings, would just forget something? Not only *something*, but something so big that it would lead to their capture?

No. They *wanted* to be caught. Hubris was their real enemy. They were performing their own masterful opera for themselves and decided that it wasn't fun anymore without a proper audience.

He never felt that way. He enjoyed doing it and in no way wanted to get caught. The reason careers got this way was that they stayed in too long, and the need developed over time. Isn't it the same with everything sexual? When you're young, you're able to masturbate with just the pictures in your head, but then suddenly, that's not enough. You graduate to using real pictures, clothed at first until you to take the next step, then the next step and the next, until you finally get to the real act. Even that sours over time, and you have to search for ways to take the next step and spice it up a bit. Killing is possibly the most sexual experience life has to offer. Where is there to go from there? What better way to avoid that final step than by getting out before the experience lost its flavor?

Brent hadn't known he was going back to the cabin. He'd nearly kicked himself when he started to figure it out. Why hadn't he paid more attention to where he was going? But really, who did nowadays? When was the last time he'd driven himself anywhere? That was the point of going to parties—take care of all the details beforehand so that you can let loose and enjoy yourself. The Roes had offered their driver and limo, so there was no point in checking where it was going to take them.

Once he'd gotten in the car, Mr. Daniels had been the center of his attention. He'd drunk the whole way there, just like the rest of them. When they'd arrived, the place didn't look remotely like it had back then. Picaud had changed everything—except for the cabin.

And what was he doing with it, anyway? Brent had taken scrupulous steps to ensure the property wouldn't be traced back to him, just in case someone stumbled upon it like that cop had. Christ, what a screwup that'd been. But that was exactly how careful he'd stayed to keep himself out of prison, so that even when he *did* make mistakes, he was still ten steps ahead.

It was all because of that redheaded cheerleader. He'd watched her for weeks after he'd seen her at the Starbucks all those years ago. When he saw that face, he'd known she was the one. Well, the next one, anyway.

When he'd finally gotten her back to the cabin, he had been bursting with anticipation. He was going to take his time. He had just been starting the cat and mouse when he heard a knock coming from the front door upstairs. He quickly gagged her and went to see who it was.

As soon as Brent looked through the peephole, he knew it was a cop. He wasn't in any kind of uniform, but they always seemed to dress the same. Hell, you could practically smell it on them. The cop introduced himself and wondered if he could ask a few questions. Brent answered him as casually as anyone, but when the cop asked to have a look around, Brent politely declined. If he was going to search the place, he'd have to get a warrant.

That's when the bitch got her gag off, or at least partly. She made a kind of screaming noise, not loud, but enough.

The cop pulled out his gun and told Brent to take him to wherever it'd come from. Brent cooperated. When they got to the kitchen, the cop's focus was on the cellar door. Brent seized his chance, and the gun, knocking it to one side as he stuck a knife in the cop's neck. The cop managed to squeeze one off into Brent's shoulder, but Brent reversed the gun, and the cop went quiet.

The first thing to do was take care of the wound, of course. Make sure to stop the bleeding and clean up whatever residue was left. He kept the bullet in for the time being but cauterized the wound; he'd dig it out later. The next step was to clean up.

Next was to deal with the bitch in the basement. He felt cheated and had to make a quick job of it. It was like wolfing down a perfectly aged filet mignon. He tried to enjoy it, but the moment had passed, and now it was more like work than anything else. Next, he cleaned up any traces of anyone, except for the two bodies. Thank God for bleach spray cans.

That had taken too long. Once he was satisfied, he felt he needed to get the hell out of there. There weren't any other houses close by, but there had been gunshots, and that sound travels. He didn't need any more unannounced visitors.

The other night at the party, when he finally realized that he was back at the cabin after so long, it'd all hit at once. He hadn't been prepared, and it'd knocked his wind out. After so many years, not only was he back, but he was there with his wife, his friends, and a shit ton of other people. Being loaded with alcohol sure as hell didn't help. He damn near passed out.

After the initial shock wore off, however, he felt cool and collected again. It was like driving drunk and immediately sobering up when you saw a patrol car. He took the tour just like everyone else. It wasn't until he was back in the basement that he thought about the Polaroids.

He'd left them there all those years before, completely forgetting they existed with the rush he'd been in. They were hidden, of course. Was it possible they were still there? He waited until he was sure everyone was looking the other way when his well-practiced hand removed the rock, grabbed the bundle inside, jammed it in his pocket, and replaced the rock, quick as a flash. He got out and even joined in the chatter about the place with everyone else. It was impossible not to; no one would talk of anything else.

Being there, remembering all that took place in his little nest, having the pictures and fawning over them like they were lost artifacts—it had brought everything back. The monster inside had awakened and was yowling for attention. Brent went through his notebook religiously but knew it was only a matter of time before that wouldn't be enough.

He'd have to shake off the rust, and soon, or else he'd pop. If ever there was a surefire way to make a mistake, it was popping.

He already started turning the cogs in his brain. Planning the how and where. The only thing left, of course, was to find the who.

Chapter 17

MOVE TO STRIKE

A few days after Jesse got back to Hollywood from the party, he heard Picaud had made his way out as well. Jesse went over to Picaud's house to thank him not only for inviting him but also for letting him use one of his private jets to get to and from and even setting him up in a nice hotel close to where the party was held. But the doc wasn't home.

One of the staff said he was at a harbor down the road and told Jesse he could find him there. On his way to the harbor, Jesse started thinking about the party. It'd been loads of fun, and for the doc's first party of his own, he'd certainly pulled out all the stops. Interesting theme, especially the part of exploring a real murder scene, but what about that other thing? He supposed it wasn't too out of the ordinary; everyone who was anyone was there, and Zack was a senator. He knew that Brent was still seeing a lot of him too, but still, he didn't like it.

It had been over fifteen years now since he'd gone his separate way. Those two seemed like two completely different people after what they'd done, and they had agreed to pretend like they never knew him. The moment he'd left, he'd felt like a giant weight had lifted, but not entirely. At the party, he could tell by their faces they hadn't been expecting to see him either; that was the one thing that had calmed him. Perhaps it'd all just been one huge coincidence.

He pulled into the parking lot of the harbor before even realizing it. The car basically drove itself once he plugged in the address.

He parked the car, got out, and walked to where the pathway down to the ships was blocked off by a large gate. There was a booth with a young guard in it, plowing his way through a novel. Jesse approached the booth and knocked on the window to grab the guard's attention.

The guard looked up with a cocked eyebrow but said nothing.

"Hi, I'm looking for a friend of mine. I was told I could find him here. Dr. Picaud?"

The guard looked down onto a sheet of paper and traced a finger down a list. "Name?"

"Jesse Tovin."

The guard's finger stopped abruptly. He looked up and squinted at Jesse's face. "Wait, aren't you that guy who just landed the Phoenix role?"

Jesse smiled. "That's the rumor."

"Nice! Don't screw it up, 'kay? I friggin' love those books."

Jesse rolled his eyes. "I'll try not to."

The guard picked up a phone and called someone, told them Jesse was at the front gate, then hung up.

"Someone will be out in a minute," he said, then immediately went back to his book.

Jesse wasn't sorry for the excuse to not chat it up with the man and waited silently for the someone to come get him. To his surprise, a few minutes later he saw Picaud himself making his way down the plank walkway.

"Jesse! What a surprise. Come on back; you're just in time to see my new yacht."

"Yacht?" Jesse said, surprised.

"Yes, I had it custom made. It took them a lot longer than I hoped, but I'm happy with the result. Come check it out."

Jesse followed the doc through a maze of different buildings leading away from the actual harbor. The two of them reached a large building that resembled a soundstage on the back lot, and Jesse was just about to ask why they weren't going to the harbor when he saw it.

Through the large open door, a ship on stilts, completely out of the water but facing another set of open doors that had a large ramp leading down to the harbor, waited to be launched.

"We're just going over some of the finer details now before we let her loose."

The bright sun bounced off the water, blinding Jesse as he made his way to the building, and he could only see the outline of the ship. When he stepped inside and his eyes adjusted, his jaw fell.

In true Picaud fashion, this yacht wasn't just a yacht. It looked like a brand-new version of an old pirate ship.

Picaud, noticing Jesse's expression, said, "Magnificent, isn't she? Had her designed using models of famous pirate ships, but I wanted it to be my own, so we threw in some new influences until we settled on this." He gestured with both hands to the large ship. "C'mon, I'll show you around."

The ship was huge, at least to Jesse, who had no real knowledge of ships. It was sixty feet long and outfitted with every technical advantage available. Picaud pointed out that although the ship had two powerful engines, it could sail, if so desired, with a simple press of a button. That was another thing, Picaud explained; it would normally take a crew of at least four men, but due to the ship's automation, one was all that was needed.

"According to the design engineers, it can boast the same as the *Titanic* did before it set sail, but out of respect and not wanting to tempt fate, I refuse to say it out loud."

He was referring to the claim that the ship was unsinkable. Supposedly, no matter what was done to this boat, it would not sink. Even if fully capsized and taking on water, the material the boat was made from would keep everything afloat and immediately send out a distress call.

The ship had everything you could ask for. Large, tall staterooms, a gorgeous galley, and a main cabin that had all the modern conveniences but kept the look of a captain's quarters. There was even an armory where museum-quality pirate relics were on display. Rich, dark mahogany color ran throughout. While walking on the main deck, Picaud pointed up into the ship's rigging to a crow's nest high above them, perched on the mainmast.

In an awed voice, Jesse asked, "So, why? I mean, is there a reason behind having a pirate ship?"

Picaud laughed at the directness of the question. "Well, I've recently picked up sailing as a hobby. I like it so much that I plan to retire and sail the world one day. As far as the pirate theme goes, I don't know if you've noticed this, but I like my stuff to be out of the ordinary. I think regular things, however expensive, are boring. If you're going to spend the money, why not do it with your own personal flair? That way, you know you'll always be happy with it. I happen to be a history nerd and have always found pirates fascinating, so why not?"

Jesse laughed. "I think that's your theme."

"What?"

"'Why not?'"

Picaud smiled. "I like it: 'Why not?'"

The foreman came up to them standing on the deck and addressed Picaud. "Doctor, if you've finished your final inspection and are happy with everything, I think we're just about ready to cut her loose."

"Excellent! Thank you, Dustin." Picaud turned to Jesse. "So, what do you say, Mr. Tovin? Wanna go for a ride?"

"Like, ride the ship as it slides down into the water?" Jesse asked the foreman.

Dustin smiled with pleasure. "Yeah, hell of a ride, if you're up for it!"

Jesse looked at Picaud and smiled. "Hell yeah!"

Picaud nodded to Dustin, who promptly scuttled over to the far railing and said, "Send her out, Charlie!"

Picaud turned to Jesse. "I'm glad you came by. They have to take me out for the first trip to show me how everything works, and I'd just as soon have someone I know come along."

Maybe it was the thought of pirates, but a pang of unease went through Jesse. "You think they might . . . what? Try something?"

"Oh, no, but you can never be too careful." Jesse felt Picaud's eyes scurry over him. "You should remember that."

A lump caught in Jesse's throat, and he had a hard time swallowing it. "I will."

"Hold on to something," Dustin called, and the two grabbed the railing.

The ship began to move, slowly at first, but it soon picked up speed. Air started blowing through their hair as they went through the far open door to the ramp.

Jesse looked over the side and watched as they went down the coolest slide he'd ever gone down in his life. The ramp itself was over a hundred feet long, and the farther they went, the faster the ship traveled.

The water was starting to come up at an alarming rate, and Dustin yelled, "Hang on!"

Jesse knew the sudden deceleration was coming, and fear crept in. He looked at Picaud, who was grinning from ear to ear at the rising water. There was something mad in that grin.

Jesse gripped the rail so tightly that his fingers began to ache with the strain, until finally, the bow hit the water. Everything gave one huge lurch forward and then slowed with the gentle flow of the water.

A huge hum, like something powering up, flicked on from below, and Dustin started making his way up the stairs to the upper deck where the helm was located, waving for Jesse and Picaud to follow.

When they were clear of the no-wake zone, Dustin called out, "We're going to let her out and show you how much of a punch she's got!"

Hardly any time passed before the ship began to pick up more and more speed. The ship seemed to be flying rather than sailing as it cut through the water like a knife. The workmen put the ship through her paces, showing what the vessel was capable of, until Picaud seemed satisfied.

Then Dustin called down, "We're switching to the sheets!"

The engines quieted as invisible hands unfurled the sails, and just like that, the ship was gliding along with the wind, turning the yacht into a pleasure cruise.

As Dustin showed Picaud how to work everything, Jesse looked out past the ship to the scene beyond and thought that Picaud was definitely onto something.

Jesse began to think about what he spent all of his money on. He had a nice house, car, what have you. Everything that was supposed to represent the American Dream, but the most creative he'd gotten was buying expensive things. They were considered by all who looked on them to be very nice, but they brought him little joy, if any.

And, if he was really honest about it, *she* spent most of his money, anyway. He had also begun paying for his own coke. It seemed to be in short supply recently, and he had to jump through a bunch of hoops just to get a dime bag. Even *that* was expensive. Vaguely, Jesse wondered if this was the celebrity equivalent to a smoking habit for the rest of the population.

But all of that was about to change, anyway. The *Malcolm Phoenix* movie was going to begin filming in just a few weeks, and the first round of paychecks was in the mail. After seeing the doc's ship, he decided that once he got his check, he was going to get creative with his money and spend it more like the doc.

Picaud saw Jesse staring out at the open ocean. "Beautiful, isn't she? I could spend hours just doing that: looking out, reflecting on whatever the waves decide to send my way. The adrenaline of the open sea, absolute and total freedom. It's like a drug to me, my own addiction."

Jesse's stomach dropped, and he wondered if Picaud knew he was using again or was just referencing the time they met.

Quickly, he changed the subject. "I want to thank you, Doc."

"Thank me?" Picaud sounded amused. "For what?"

"Everything. You've been really kind to me, always allowing me to stay at your house, inviting me to a party on the other side of the country, and flying me out in such style."

"Psh, that's nothing. Just treating others the way I'd like to be treated." Then the doc lightly said something under his breath that Jesse couldn't quite make out, but it sounded like, "Or have been treated."

"I also wanted to thank you for helping me land the Phoenix role."

This seemed to genuinely confuse him. "How'd you work that one out? I had nothing to do with it."

"When I was auditioning for the D'alos, they said they'd heard I've been spending a lot of time in your presence. I think they were impressed."

Comprehension flooded Picaud's eyes. "Ah, well, I certainly can't take credit for that. It's not my fault that you're a celebrity, and people can't help but talk. They probably follow you wherever you go. That's the price of fame, I suppose."

This made Jesse pause. "How do you do it?"

"Hmm?"

Jesse looked into Picaud's eyes. His bright, hazel eyes that seemed to be glowing from the sun. "You're famous. How do you keep your personal life out of the tabs?"

Picaud paused for a moment, as if wondering how much to tell him. Then, finally, he said, "My dear Mr. Tovin, if there is one unfortunate truth in life, it's this: It's not what you know, but who you know. The right connections open the doors you want and close the ones you don't. And money certainly helps."

Jesse pondered this. Did he mean he knew the people who ran those stories and paid them extra to keep him out of print? This made Jesse think he might also be keeping legitimate stuff out of the public eye, and he again wondered what Picaud might have to hide.

⌐══━━

When Jake heard the movie star had come by unexpectedly, he decided to make himself scarce, but he had made sure to keep Jesse and Picaud in sight. He was certain Jesse wouldn't recognize him, only having been introduced at the party, but Jake knew it was essential to not spook him. Not this late in the game.

Jake had watched Picaud talking to Jesse the whole time. He couldn't help but admire Picaud for being able to put up such a great front. Jake had to admit that if he were in his friend's place, he probably would've just beaten them all within an inch of their lives and called it a day. Picaud's plan was much more savory, but it required a lot more patience, of which Jake had little. Just looking at these people, knowing what they had done, were *still* doing. It made him sick.

They were all out on the water for a good half an hour before they put the yacht in Picaud's new private slip and let Jesse off. Picaud saw him down to the gangway and sent him cheerily on.

Jake grabbed a couple beers from the ice box, went to his friend, and fully expected to see the look that now resided on his face.

"How you doing?"

Picaud stared at Jesse as he disappeared from sight. "Like I swallowed glass for the past half hour."

"I've heard of worse excuses to drink. Here, wash it down." Jake handed a bottle over.

"Gladly." He grabbed it and drank deeply.

Jake wanted to get Picaud's mind on better sights. "So, you got the contact for me?"

"Yeah," Picaud said, reaching down into his pocket to grab his cell. He riffled through for a second and air-dropped a digital contact over to Jake.

Jake pulled his own phone out after feeling the buzz and opened up the screen. "Got it."

"Good. Once you have the pictures, make sure you contact him. He'll take it from there."

"Do you think he'll publish them immediately?" Jake asked.

"Probably not. He may be a 'razzi leech, but he's thorough. I think he's just been sued too many times."

Jake looked at his phone for a moment. "Is Tovin *really* doing that?"

"Oh, absolutely. And you've gotta remember that I've known them since they were kids. I wish I could say I hadn't seen it with my own eyes, but I'm afraid that image has been burned into the back of my retinas."

"You gonna be hangin' around?" Jake asked.

"For a little while, but I can't stay too long. Nell checked out the hidey-hole yesterday. It'll only take him a few days before he puts his case together and makes his move."

"Did he find anything? When I checked after the party, it looked like Wheaton took all the pics."

Picaud smiled at him. "Well, wouldn't you know it, seems he left one behind."

"Man, you think of everything. How do you do that?"

Picaud thought about it for a long moment, and a dark shadow seemed to pass over his face. "You familiar with the old saying 'outfox the fox'?"

"Sure."

"Well, in my case, it started literally. Back when I was first lost in the forest, I'd almost starved to death for the umpteenth time, this time because a fox had discovered my rabbit traps. The first day, I decided to forgive and forget. But the next time, the same thing happened; every rabbit I snared was taken. It got to the point where I stopped resetting the traps because the fox was walking my trap line before I could even get to it."

"So what'd you do?"

"At first, I decided just to give up and hope that he would leave once I stopped catching rabbits for him."

"I'm guessing he didn't leave?"

"On the contrary! Little bastard started breaking into my cabin and stealing what I had when I wasn't looking. Probably wouldn't leave on his own until I dropped dead and he picked *me* clean.

"At that point, I knew I had two choices: try and live my life completely hand-to-mouth, continuously watching over what food I had until it was consumed, or kill the fox.

"I chose the latter. I say 'chose,' but really, he didn't leave me with a choice. Once he started taking what I had, it became clear that he'd given up trying to find his own means of survival. Why bother when you can take from somebody else who'd done the work? Going into it, I knew it was going to be difficult, but I was in no way prepared for *how* difficult it really was. No matter what I bizarre trap I thought of, he found a way to get past me and take the bait without a scratch."

Jake sucked in through his teeth. "That's gotta be frustrating!"

"Brother, you don't know the half of it. Over and over, I'd try and figure out how he was getting around the trap and figure out how to counter it. All the while, he would not only take my bait, but he would still take any food that I tried to save. As the days wore on, it became harder to think."

"So, how'd you end up killing it?" Jake asked.

"I got just enough food in me to clear my mind, and something inside me just clicked. Why was I bothering with the trap if I knew he'd come to me? Once he knew he could get away with taking from me, he was just going to keep coming until he couldn't anymore. So I made one more trap inside my cabin. I looked at it from every possible angle until I was satisfied that there was only one way for the fox to proceed: my way. Before he knew what hit him, he was dangling in the air, caught in my net. It may have been because I was starving, but I don't think I have ever tasted anything as good as that fox, before or since.

"This is no different. These people got away with something once, and they're going to continue to press their luck until they find themselves hanging from the ceiling—my ceiling."

"I'll drink to that!" Jake held out the long neck of his beer, and Picaud clinked his own bottle against it.

"Godspeed, my friend. Take care."

"Oh, don't worry; if he's getting as high as you say, he's not going to notice anything but what's right in front of him, disgusting as that prospect is."

As Jake turned to leave, he saw Picaud lift his phone to his ear. "Hey Erica, what's u—" The smile instantly wiped off his face. "All right, keep an eye on him. I'll head to the airport right now. Do what you have to do; take him down yourself if need be. We need to make sure she's safe!"

Jake felt the tension growing as he watched Picaud shove the phone in his pocket and start down the gangway. Jake followed close behind.

"Bad news?"

"Wheaton's trying to come out of retirement earlier than expected. They're keeping an eye on him, but I have to hurry back to make sure everything is done properly."

Jake turned pale at the prospect. "You mean he's already chosen his next victim?"

"Apparently so. We need to take him down as quick as possible; I'll never forgive myself if he takes another Polaroid."

When Picaud landed, he was surprised to see Erica waiting for him. Something about her manner as she hurried up to him said she didn't come with good news.

"What's wrong?"

"We've got problems. We've lost track of Wheaton."

"What do you mean, 'lost track'?"

"I mean we saw him go into a diner and didn't see him come out."

"Well, he couldn't have gone far. Let's go. What car you driving?"

"The Ferrari."

"Mind if I drive?"

She scoffed. "I thought you said you wanted to get there in a hurry. I'll get us there."

"Fine." He didn't have it in him to argue. He needed to stop Brent at all costs. He should have stopped him the minute he realized he was the Sidewalk Strangler, but Brent had been lying low for so long, Picaud thought he had time to play the game. His mistake sickened him.

They rushed to her car and sped off, leaving two long tracks and a cloud of smoke behind.

Picaud pulled out his phone. "Where's the diner?"

"In a town not too far outside Atlanta. We should be able to get there in about twenty minutes."

"Make it fifteen, and you can pick any car out of the hangar."

"You got yourself a deal. There's a Bugatti I've had my eye on for a while."

Erica drove at breakneck speed while Picaud popped the location in his cell and watched their progress. He stared at the map with a little prickle scratching at the back of his mind. There was something he knew about where they were headed, but he wasn't sure what it was.

They would have made it back to the diner in another minute or so, but just outside of town, Picaud saw a turnoff onto a disused road. Far off in the distance, he saw a large dome popping out of the trees, glowing white in the moonlight. Something clicked in Picaud's brain. It was so loud he wouldn't have been surprised if Erica heard it.

"Stop!"

Erica slammed on the brakes. Picaud's body wanted to leap forward, but the seat belt tightened to an uncomfortable grip as the car skidded to a halt.

"What?" Fire burned behind her eyes.

"Flip a bitch."

"Wha—"

"Flip a bitch right now! Take that road back there."

Erica swerved over the double yellow to make the U-turn; luckily, there was no one around to see—or unluckily, depending on how you looked at the situation.

As they made their way to the turnoff and down the road, Picaud said a silent prayer of thanks that he had followed up on the property after Brent had mentioned it. The dome became larger, and they pulled up to the old, abandoned amusement park.

A rusted, battered sign read "The White City." They parked next to it and got out of the car.

Once out, Picaud looked around, and his heart leaped at what he thought he saw in the gravel. He turned his phone's flashlight on and illuminated the tire tracks pulling into the old theme park.

Picaud turned to Erica. "You packing?"

"Am I ever not?" She made her way to the trunk.

While Erica busied herself getting her handgun out of the back, Picaud doused the light and made a call.

"Gene?" he whispered into the phone. "I'm going to send you my location. I want you to use the secure line to call Nell and give him an anonymous tip that will lead him here, okay? Tell him that there's a piece of evidence waiting for him inside the park." Picaud ended the call. "Hopefully she'll still be alive . . ."

She will be; she will! his mind and heart demanded.

A click replaced the silence as Erica placed a magazine in the gun and loaded the chamber. "What's the plan?"

"Follow the tracks inside; he probably took her into a building. Our first priority is the girl, but maybe we can put an end to this tonight."

"God willing."

They made their way along, trying not to see the ghosts of merriment that had once taken place there. The Ferris wheel, roller coasters, empty concession stands, all were standing corpses, posed morbidly, hulking over them in the moonlight. As they passed the merry-go-round, they saw the shapes of dolphins that happy children used to ride around and around, now slowly decaying.

Picaud whispered, "How much you wanna bet there's a fun house?"

The thought brought a little huff of laughter from Erica, but when they saw the dark shape of a car parked next to a building that said "City Hall" in bold letters, and beneath that, in smaller print, "of Mirrors," the fun went out of the joke.

As they approached the entrance, making sure to stay out of view of the dimly lit windows that gazed out into the park, they started to hear scuffling noises and tiny whimpers floating out of the open double-hung glass and into the night air.

Picaud let out a silent sigh of relief, sure the young girl was still alive. Now, he just had to keep her that way.

He started to formulate a plan in his head. He was just turning to talk to Erica about it when he realized she wasn't there.

Picaud knew how personally Erica took Brent's deeds. She must have already started making her move. Woe is he that got in that woman's crosshairs.

Christ, he thought, *I hope she doesn't kill him. Death is too good.*

He rose slowly and carefully to the bottom corner of the window he was under. He needed to see what was going on in the room. A picture started revealing itself as he got farther into view. At first, a pair of stiletto-heeled boots tied together, then long legs clad in tight-fitting pants. The knees were drawn up; she was in the fetal position, except her arms were tied behind her back. He continued letting his eyes drift and saw the young brunette girl with a ripped button-up blouse. She was facing toward him and had been gagged with a piece of cloth; her eyes were bulging and shiny, reflecting the moonlight in her tears.

Picaud moved his head a little farther and saw the back of a large man. His head was covered by a beanie, but Picaud was sure it was Brent. He was messing with something in his hands; Picaud couldn't see what. Picaud saw sudden movement to the side of Brent, and he realized that the girl had seen him and was trying to call for help. Picaud immediately dropped out of sight, knowing that Brent would have noticed her sudden change.

He paused and waited.

He could hear footsteps. They came closer to the window, and Picaud snuck farther away, sucking up against the wall. He waited, hoping he'd suddenly see a head or a hand pop out of the window. He locked his fingers together to make one big fist and raised it up high. As soon as he saw something make an appearance, he would bring down the hammer.

Nothing came.

Suddenly, he heard a scuffle, two sets of grunts. Erica had made her move. Picaud was just moving back toward the window again when Brent's head smashed through both sets of glass on the upper half of the window, then pulled back.

Picaud scrambled to the opening, swept the shards aside, and climbed in. Erica had used the distraction of Brent going to the window to climb in through another and come up from behind.

Apparently, Brent had had enough time to knock the gun from Erica's hands, because Picaud saw it lying useless on the floor. He was just in time to see Erica deliver a well-placed kick to Brent's head, now bloodied from going through the window. Brent staggered back and ducked through the doorway leading into the rest of the building.

Picaud grabbed the gun and went over to Erica. "Stay here."

"Wha—"

"Stay here!" Picaud knew she wouldn't like that, especially if he got a few licks in, so he continued. "Nell's on his way. Stay with her and make sure she's safe. When she calms down, make sure you tell her his name so she can give it to Nell. Once you know she's safe, get the hell out of here and come find me."

She looked at him distastefully but nodded. "Right."

Picaud moved toward the doorway. He only had to take one look at the long, mirror-lined hallway leading into the maze beyond to know why he'd been right that there would be a fun house.

Sure, you'd see that kind of stuff in movies all the time. The killer would go through the mirror maze to add more suspense to the scene, right? Well, although this was true, it had a more practical reason. Brent had chosen this place, had taken long pains to make sure he knew every square inch so he would not only be able to move through with speed but would also disorient any pursuers who were unfamiliar with the terrain. Either he was going to make a break for the exit, knowing that any followers would get caught up, or he was waiting in some concealed corner, ready to pounce on an unsuspecting victim.

Picaud took the first two tentative steps into the hall. It was pitch black, so he grabbed his cell and turned the flashlight on again. The small, bright light bounced off all the different mirrors and bathed the hallway in light. He moved slowly, methodically. He was facing the fox in its den, and he didn't like it.

He got to the end of the hall and stepped into the maze. The walls were a combination of mirrors and clear panels. The light bounced off everything, leaving an empty space in the middle and making the way clear with walls of light on either side. In the mirrors, he saw bits of himself above and below the bright light; beyond that, darkness.

Picaud made his way slowly through the path, gun in one hand, phone in the other. At one point, he saw a flash of what could only have been eyes staring at him through the darkness. He pointed the gun and tried to move closer but found only mirror as the eyes disappeared once more.

The silence pressed in upon his ears; it gave him the feeling that the walls were starting to close in. Then a loud crack reverberated off the walls, and Picaud knew Brent had just made a break for it. The sound must've been from an emergency exit or trap door.

The floor was hard paneling painted a deep purple that had faded behind layers of caked-on dust. He looked down and saw many sets of footprints from all the times Brent had mapped the place out. Picaud followed the floor along until he finally saw it.

A large square had been cut into the floor with a metal triangle recessed into it. The triangle looked like a wind-up key from an antique toy. Picaud placed his fingers into the two holes of the key, twisted, and pulled up,. The door swung up and revealed an opening to the crawl space under the building.

Picaud dropped down through the hole and saw the moonlight revealing an opening at the edge of the building. He could just make out boots lifting up and disappearing. He heard the slam of a car door, then an engine firing into life, and the car that had been waiting outside sped off.

Picaud crawled as quickly as he could to get out from underneath, then ran for his own car; already knowing where the other would go.

Brent's time was up, and he had to know it. He had left a living witness that could ID him if he were brought in, and that was only a matter of time. He *had* to make a run for it. He had probably planned for just such an occasion and would likely make one stop before disappearing forever. Picaud drove as fast as he could to get there first.

When Picaud pulled up to Brent's home, it looked as if he'd beaten Brent back. He knew of the man cave from a maid Brent had let go for going down and cleaning it.

"I was just doing my job, but he came in and started screaming at me. I had no idea why. Okay . . . There was obviously something about that blue binder he had. He swooped in like a hawk and snatched it up before rounding on me and yelling. It wasn't as if I had, or would, look in it. I've been a maid for one household or another for thirty-five years, so I know better. Still, he fired me that very day."

When Picaud had learned what Brent really was, he'd been sick. He'd studied all he could surrounding the pathology of known serial killers, so when the maid had told him about the little blue binder, he'd known instantly what it was.

Picaud and Jesse had a lot more time than the authorities to tare the cabin apart. When they found the bundle in the secret hiding place, Picaud finally knew what was in Brent's binder. Murderers like Brent often kept trophies of the people they'd killed. For some, it was articles of clothing or jewelry; for others, it was body parts; for Brent, it was pictures.

Brent's behavior when he'd suddenly found himself back in his old killing grounds showed just how reckless he would be in retrieving the pictures. It was doubtful that he would carry the binder with him to each kill, so it was a safe bet that it was still in his basement.

Picaud walked around until he found a window leading down. He tried it but found it locked. He took Erica's gun from his pocket, smashed a panel out, reached in to unlock the catch, and swung the window open. He squeezed his way inside and proceeded to close the window after him. When he did, he noticed a sensor with a wire leading from it off into a wall.

Shit! He had just tripped a silent alarm. Right that moment, cops were probably scrambling to head over. It was a stupid mistake, one that you make when you're hyper-focused on one thing and could cause you to lose control of the situation. *Better make this quick.*

Picaud went over to the door leading to the staircase and waited. He waited and waited. He started to wonder about the sensor on the window. The thought crossed his mind that it had sent an alert directly to Brent's phone, warning him there'd been a breach. Just when he started coming to this conclusion, he saw headlights float in through the window, swerve across the wall, and come to a stop.

Picaud looked across the room at the glass-paneled door leading outside and figured that was where Brent would likely make his entrance. Picaud watched as the light that spilled through the glass suddenly blackened in shadow. The sound of a key scratched its way into the lock and turned until the bolt slid home, then the door swung in.

The form of a man entered hurriedly, leaving the door wide open and crossing straight past everything to get to the desk on the opposite wall. He slid open a drawer, paused, riffled through its contents, and slammed it shut. In quick, frustrated movements, he looked through each drawer in turn, finding them all wanting.

He paused for a moment, running both hands up his forehead and removing the beanie in one motion as if to mimic running fingers through hair.

The exposed skin of Brent's bald head caught and reflected the surrounding light, and Picaud saw the many tiny bandages that had recently been added. This was probably why it had taken him so long to get here. Brent continued his search, frantically checking every nook and cranny in the darkened room.

"It's over, Brent," Picaud said, walking into view.

Brent nearly jumped out of his skin and spun about as he pulled a large knife from his jacket and faced Picaud.

He squinted at him in the darkness. "Dr. Picaud?"

A low, grumbling laugh escaped Picaud as he walked closer. "Oh, much worse." The moment he had been working toward was coming. He could feel it building in the air, and he let it wash over him.

Brent stood there, trying to work it all out in his head. "So you were the one that snuck up on me at The White City?"

A grin of pearly white teeth shone through a face covered in shadow.

"No; I think it would interest you to know that *that* was a young woman, much like the ones you target."

Brent looked as if he'd been slapped but recovered into a snarl. "Where is it?"

Picaud said nothing.

Brent lifted up the long, shiny blade and pointed it toward Picaud. "Where is it?!"

Picaud ignored the knife and drew closer, still encased in shadow. "What does it matter? Where will you go? It's *over*." He said the last word slowly, savoring it.

"How did you find me?"

"I've been keeping an extra-close eye on you, *Brent*." He laid as much contempt on the name as he could. "You've been very naughty. You developed a taste for killing at a young age, and after the thrill of the first, you had to do it again, and again, and again . . ."

Brent looked bewildered at him. "I . . . I can't help it. I'm sick . . . I know I am. You're my friend, Dr. Picaud; please help me." He shuffled closer in supplication.

A dark, booming bark of a laugh exploded from Picaud and resounded through the silence. "Nice try."

Brent shrugged his shoulders. "Eh, worth a shot." He burst forward and thrust his knife toward Picaud's gut.

Picaud saw the clumsy attempt and spun to the side while grabbing Brent's wrist and bicep. In a swift motion, he brought Brent's arm down over his knee as one would snap a branch. Brent's elbow bent in the opposite direction, and a loud crack sounded as the tendons let go, the blade fell to the floor, and Brent cried out in pain. Once Picaud released his viselike grip, Brent retrieved his arm and cradled it to his chest with the other.

"Sixteen years ago, you chased down an innocent kid and left him for dead. Do you remember?"

Brent was breathing loudly and heavily, trying to think amid the excruciating pain.

"I don't . . . I don't know what you're talking about."

"Yes, you do; you and two others ran down a *kid!* A kid that did nothing to you. You tried to kill him. Why?"

Brent clutched at his arm, and through gasps of pain, he managed to get out, "I don't know what you're talking about. Where's my binder?!"

The words *I don't have it* were on the verge of leaving Picaud's lips when another voice, although soft and light, cut through the basement.

"*I* have it," Lucy said, walking slowly closer, the blue mass in her hands.

Brent gazed at his would-be savior. "Luce, help. I—"

"Cram it!" It wasn't loud, but there was no mistaking the authority in her voice. "I always knew something was up with you." Her words were frigid and steady. "After I got back from the Halloween party, I googled what happened there. You know what came up?"

Picaud could only watch as the scene played out in front of him; he was beginning to think that his plan had worked better than he could ever have dreamed. Brent stared at the binder clasped in his wife's left hand. She held it close to her body like she was hugging it, but her right hand was squished between the binder and her chest.

"Pictures and names of the victims that had been released. I saw one that looked familiar somehow. 'Well, how could that be?' I asked myself. I thought maybe I'd seen her face on the news before or something, but my brain kept yelling at me that wasn't it. Then it came. I had seen that same picture in your binder."

"Lu—" Brent tried.

With a sudden jerk of her right hand, Lucy freed the revolver she'd been hiding and pointed it at Brent. "Shut up!" She was shouting now. "Shut your God . . . damned . . . mouth!" She continued to point the gun at him, but a quake warbled into her voice, and tears began falling down her face.

"How could you? How could you do that? You did all those things to the women in here." She shook the binder. "And then you had the nerve to come home to me? To smile in my face? Share my bed?"

Another sound drifted into the basement from far off in the distance: It was sirens. The police were coming.

Picaud felt what Lucy was about to do. He reached out to stop it but was too late. The report of the lone shot blasted through the basement, temporarily blocking out the sirens.

Brent dropped his limp right arm and clutched at his gut with his left. His knees gave out from under him and dropped to the floor. He fell back, eyes wide in surprise.

Picaud finished his grab for Lucy, took both of her shoulders in his hands, and spun her toward him. The binder slid from her grasp, and like her husband, it hit the floor with a dead *thump*.

The blank look of disbelief showed on her face, and Picaud was so angry at having his moment, the one he'd dreamt about for sixteen years, ripped from his grasp when it was so close. It felt as if the fires of hell bloomed behind his eyes. He shook her and forced her to gaze into those flames.

Picaud's body trembled with rage. Lucy looked as if electricity was shooting into her through his grip. All he could say to her was, "What have you done?!"

The sirens were steadily growing louder. She continued to stare blankly up into his face. "This." The word was unnervingly simple.

The sound of the second shot took Picaud completely by surprise. He flinched, then pulled her in tight as if embracing her. He felt warmth start to spread around his midsection. He touched it and brought his hand up to the light. Crimson liquid shone on his fingers. A queer smile touched Lucy's lips for a moment as she stared at it, then her eyes rolled up and her lids closed. Her body went limp and fell to the floor.

Picaud stared at the blood on his hand for a moment until the growing sound of sirens snapped him back to the task at hand. He wiped the blood off on his clothes, then ran over to check on Brent. He was still alive, but judging by what Picaud saw, he didn't have long.

Picaud grabbed him by the front of his shirt and heaved him up off the floor a little. Moonlight bathed the two from the open door. With cloth clenched firmly in both hands, he shouted, "Look at me!"

The command in his voice seemed to revive Brent a little, as if he was called back from the dead. He looked up into Picaud's eyes. His piercing, blue eyes.

Picaud saw the dawning comprehension in the man's face. His expression went from pain to wonder and, finally, pure terror.

Trembling, Brent tried to speak. Blood bubbled in his throat.

In the same commanding tone, Picaud shouted, "Say my name!"

Eyes still wide in horror, Brent said in a small, gurgling voice, "Edward Dalton?"

For the second time that evening, Picaud felt the body opposite him slacken. The eyes glossed over, the look of his last terror still etched on their surface, but only nothingness beneath. Picaud let Brent slump to the floor.

The sirens continued to grow. Picaud fished for something out of his pocket. He pulled out a small white card covered in plastic that he had made specially for this moment and had been carrying like a talisman for years. He removed the plastic, used it as a buffer between his skin and the surface of the card, and placed the card in Brent's pocket.

He took a deep breath, let out a long, slow sigh, leaped to his feet, and dashed to his car, getting out of sight just as the flashing blue and red lights began to come into view of the house.

Chapter 18

HAIR OF THE DOG

Bill Nell pulled up to the Wheatons' manor house in the first rays of sunrise. He was stunned to see that the place was already swarming with the local PD.

It'd already been a crazy night, what with getting that cryptic phone call telling him to go to that creepy abandoned theme park, where he'd found a young girl who claimed to have been rescued from a man planning to kill her.

The girl had told him the name of her kidnapper was Brent Wheaton, the very man he was planning to arrest. Bill had asked how she knew the man's name, and she'd said that the woman told her. When he'd asked where this woman was, the girl had simply shaken her head and said she didn't know.

Now, things are going to get a lot weirder, he thought, and knowing that whatever had happened here was already over, his belly and head ached for coffee's sweet embrace.

Bill parked and got out of his car only to be stopped by one of the officers. Bill held up his badge, and the man apologized.

"What happened here?" Bill asked as they began to walk to the crime scene.

"Looks like domestic homicide. All I know is what they've told me. An officer responded to a break-in set off by the house's alarm. When the officer arrived, he stumbled upon two dead bodies in the basement and called for backup. Apparently, the wife caught her husband looking at pictures of other women, shot him, then herself."

"That seems a bit thin," Bill said.

"Well, you know these rich housewives: crazy bitches, every one of 'em."

Bill gave a small *humph*.

The officer gave Bill a once-over. "What brings the Feds out to this part of nowhere?"

"I believe that the male owner of this house had a role to play in a case I'm working."

"Well, shit. I hope you didn't need to question him."

Bill sighed. "So, the male body is Brent Wheaton?"

"That's what his ID says, anyway."

Shit! Bill thought.

The officer led him around the back of the building to the open door. Along the way, he pointed out the broken glass window that had summoned them here.

When the two of them walked in, the room was brightly lit with officers everywhere, logging the scene. Flashes from cameras filled the room in every direction as the officers behind them clicked away. There had been low talking, but when Bill entered, everything came to a screeching halt.

Bill said nothing as he surveyed the room. The officers looked first to him, then to the officer who'd let him in. The officer mouthed the word *Fed*, and the others understood and watched.

Bill paid them no heed. He was looking at the result of the scene that had played out earlier. Brent Wheaton lay on his back in a pool of blood directly across from the open door. Not too far from him, a woman, presumably his wife, lay in a crumpled heap in a pool of her own. He knelt and examined each body in turn.

When he went to examine the woman, he saw three yellow cards with numbers on them. The first was over the woman's head, and the other two had nothing, suggesting the evidence had been photographed and moved.

"Still waiting on the coroner?" Bill asked the room at large.

He looked up to see a brown-haired man with a mustache and with a gold badge hooked in the belt of his khaki suit.

"Yeah, he's over dealing with a homicide in Atlanta; should be here within the hour," the man said. "You wanna tell me what this is all about?"

"Where's the gun?" Bill asked.

A young woman in a patrol uniform held up the revolver in a bag. "Here."

"Now, just a minute—" The detective began but was cut off by Bill.

"What else was found here?"

"I need to see some identification."

Bill held up his badge for the man to see. "What else was here?"

The detective tongued his cheek for a second. "A binder. Just has pictures of a bunch of girls in it."

"Porn?" Bill asked.

"No, just regular pictures, like a photo album."

Bill couldn't keep the excitement he felt from creeping into his voice. "Let me see."

The detective handed over a pair of rubber gloves and brought him to where the binder was lying open on a desk. Bill flipped through the pages, almost drunk on happiness at knowing the case was now all but closed. He recognized what it was and who these women were.

"So what?" The detective started. "Feds get called down for domestic disputes now?"

Bill looked up and smiled. "They do when one of them is a serial killer."

The detective looked awestruck. "No kidding?"

Bill held up the binder. "What we have here is a smoking gun."

He told the detective whom he believed Wheaton to be. He concluded that after Wheaton had been chased away from his last victim, he'd come back here to grab his binder and go on the lam. Only, his wife had gotten to it first, must have figured out what he'd been doing, killed him, then turned the gun on herself.

"One thing doesn't fit, though."

"What's that?" the detective asked.

"The window. Wheaton didn't do that; he most likely came in through the door. The wife was probably home and came down the stairs. So why was the window broken?"

The detective stroked his mustache in thought for a moment. "Maybe he forgot his keys and had to sneak in. He could've been on his way out when the wife caught up to him."

"Maybe. Did you check to see if he had them?"

"Not yet." He turned to one of the uniformed officers. "Murph, check his pockets."

Murph crossed to Wheaton with his camera in hand. With each item that was pulled out, Murph would take a picture, move to the next object, and repeat. When he finished, Murph took the keys and tried each one in the door lock until one was able to trigger the bolt. Murph looked up at the detective and shook his head.

"No go," Bill said. "Must've been a third person."

"Must have," the detective agreed.

"Maybe they were the shooter?" Bill thought out loud.

"Well, we ain't gonna know till the lab work gets done, but at least from the way we found them, it looks like she was the one that did the shooting."

"But why would she shoot herself in the chest? Why not the head, like most suicides?" Bill paused for a moment. "Lemme see some of the pictures you took of the scene before you processed."

Murph got up, cycled back to the beginning of the photos, and handed the camera over. Bill scrolled through. He saw angles of the scene as it had first appeared to the officers. Everything seemed to support the theory that the woman was the shooter. The gun was found gripped in her hands; it was possible that it had been planted, but there was only one way to tell, and that could take weeks. The labs always took forever. At least, Bill was certain, the serial killer had been stopped.

Bill had already finished making the case against him and was going to the District Attorney's office in the morning for the arrest warrant. He'd still get the credit for the collar.

He continued scrolling through the camera. He knew he was coming to the end when he started seeing objects lying next to Wheaton's pants. These were the pictures he had seen being taken of the pocket contents. He got to one and froze.

He turned to Murph, showed him the screen, and said, "Get me this right now!"

Murph went off and came back with a plastic baggie with a small white business card in it. Bill looked at the front, turned it over to inspect the back, then turned it back once again. Bill knew instantly that this was important but would still have to wait for the lab to analyze it.

The card was completely blank except for a large, bold number: **1**

⚔️

Fans across the nation who relished the latest bit of celebrity gossip tuned into their favorite source: the show known as Television & Movie Info-tainment, or else TMI.

The host stood among his team and said, "Morning, everyone. What have you got for me today?"

A few people started, each thinking that their bit of celeb gossip was the juiciest, but a man stood and held his hands up to silence his coworkers.

"Hang on, everybody; I have the best story possibly ever to make it onto this show. And I guarantee that we're the first to catch it."

"Well, don't keep me drooling," the host said. "Tell me."

"Jesse Tovin, well-known supporting actor, recently signed on as the starring role in the film adaptation of the Malcom Phoenix novels, appears to have a love interest."

The man clicked a button to show pictures of the well-known movie star in intimate poses with a auburn–haired woman. They were shown to be kissing very deeply and getting progressively intimate until the pictures got "too hot for television."

"Well, that's great!" the host said. "Good for him! You're right. I think that's the first time he's shown interest in anyone. Good work!" He smiled and was about to move on when the man stopped him.

"Wait! That's not all of it."

"Oh? What is?"

A smile crossed the man's face that showed how pleased he was with himself and that he knew he was holding a prime steak above a pack of very hungry wolves. "The source that gave me these pics told me to dig into this girl's background. You'll never believe who she is."

"Geez, would you just tell us already?"

"The woman you see pictured here goes by the name of Sara Mar."

"Never heard of her."

The man's smile just kept widening. "I suppose you've never heard the name Cory Mar either, then, huh?"

"It rings a bell," he admitted with the glazed look of someone going through the filing cabinet of their mind.

"Cory Mar is Jesse Tovin's real name."

There was a pause as the room at large started putting two and two together.

The voice of another reporter chimed in. "What? Are they already married or something?"

"Nope. She's his fraternal twin."

An invisible bomb exploded, setting off a chain of events. The story snowballed as the pictures went viral, covering all social media. By that evening, it was all over the main news.

Jesse remained blissfully unaware. As the news spread, he prepared for another one of his favorite parties.

When the time came to depart for his social outing, Jesse decided to do a little pregame skiing. Sara had been there to partake, and when he got up to go out, she put a hand on his arm, turned him to face her, and wiped off a spare bit of powder that hadn't made it into Jesse's nose.

"Thanks, babe," he said and looked into her wonderfully bright eyes.

She always drove him crazy with that look, and this time was no different. He was late for the party; otherwise, the passionate kiss he drew from her just before leaving might have led to something more.

He was feeling great. He sped through town, barely paying attention to the road, let alone anything else. Subsequently, when he arrived at yet another fancy Los Angeles home, he hadn't noticed the funny looks he was getting.

It took him a moment to realize that he'd been here before. It was the house with the Irish pub in it. He found the drugs immediately and renewed his high, not noticing that he was now a reverse island. At every party until now, he had been surrounded by a mass of people; now, it seemed no one wanted to go anywhere near him.

He needed to use the restroom. On the way to the nearest one, he caught a piece of someone else's conversation.

"Beats me. If I were him, I'd definitely be laying low right now. The last thing I'd want is attention."

"Yeah, but talk about a career killer. He'll be lucky to get out of this with a job flippin' burgers."

The words registered, and Jesse couldn't help but wonder who they were talking about. He gave it a couple seconds' thought, then let it melt from his mind.

He was washing his hands when the door swung violently open and a voice Jesse recognized started to bark.

"Jesse! I couldn't believe it when they said you were here. Don't you think you should be home right now? With all the rumors going around, it'd probably be best if you stayed out of the public eye."

Jesse's mind was still in the blissful rush from the coke. "Hey, Carl! What's goin' on?" He laughed lightly.

"Jesse, did you hear me?"

Jesse tried to sober up a little with a quick sniff and a shake of his head. "What?"

"You shouldn't be here, man! You need to go home right now. Hell, I could end up on the shit list just for talking to you."

Jesse was beginning to sense something amiss, and his good feeling soured into dread. "What are you talking about?"

"That thing on TMI the thing about you and your sister. Is it true? Never mind; not my business, and I don't want to know. Point is you need to get out of here."

"I still don't—"

"Don't you watch TV? Use Twitter, Facebook, anything? You're all over it. They're saying you're boinking your sister!"

Jesse's heart sank and chilled about thirty degrees. "Who's saying that?"

But Carl was already looking up the snippet on YouTube. He pressed play and gave the screen to Jesse.

Jesse watched in horror as life as he knew it started to come down around him. Jesus, they had pictures. The first few were a little blurry, and the focus had been on Sara. Maybe he'd be able to deny the whole thing. The next few, however, shifted focus, and the high definition depicted the same face seen so many times on the silver screen.

Jesse'd had enough. He jabbed the phone back to Carl. Everything was spinning, and he felt like he couldn't breathe. It was lucky this scene had played out in a bathroom because it was all Jesse could do to turn and reach the toilet in time to lose everything. When Jesse finished dry heaving, he rose, meaning to talk to Carl and see if he could help Jesse leave. Carl was gone. No word, no help, just gone.

Jesse splashed water on his face, still trying to sober up, but it was no use. His mood had spun, and the drugs were making it worse. He stabilized himself on the counter and took deep breaths. Once he'd gained enough control, he went out to try and leave as quietly as he could. When he reached the party, however, the silence smashed against his ears, and all eyes were on him. Each pair judging him, accusing him, *hating* him.

He tried to stagger his way out, but he heard someone spit and felt something warm and wet hit the back of his neck.

He turned around, and a man he'd never seen before broke away from the rest of the crowd, making no attempt to conceal that he was the culprit, wanting Jesse to know it was him.

"You make me sick! Why don't you crawl back to the hillbilly cesspool you came from?"

Another person yelled, "Hey, how was Jesse Tovin circumcised? Someone kicked his sister in the chin!"

The crowd laughed. Jesse's heart, already going a mile a minute, pumped liquid fire through his veins, and a cold sweat started to bead up and roll down his skin. Without thinking, he went over to the spitter and looked him dead in the eye, then clocked him in the nose. The man went down instantly.

This was not enough for Jesse, however, and he continued landing punch after punch on the motionless form on the floor. Hands grabbed him and forced him up and back. Jesse shook them off, prepared to fight, but the hands that lifted him off belonged to men who just wanted to keep him from killing the guy.

Jesse's eyes roved around the surrounding crowd, and in a drug-fueled rage, he shouted, "What the hell is wrong with you people?! Look at you, all just looking for someone to hate. That's all anyone wants nowadays, isn't it? That's the future in entertainment. No one wants to see people succeed. They see that, and all they want to do is bring them down. You see someone building a life for themselves, and you people can't stand it. But what do you do, huh? You don't aspire to better yourselves. Instead of using your efforts to raise the bar, you scheme and connive to bring it down to your level. You want to see anyone who's doing better than you fail because you're too lazy to go and try and raise yourself up. Well, you're all a bunch of hypocrites. Only in America is lazy ruthlessness a trait to be rewarded."

He took one more look around the room and fled at what he saw. Everyone had their phones out and on him.

⌦⟶

When Jesse was gone, Jake checked the man who was now lying on the floor, picked him up, and took him to the nearest hospital. While in the waiting room, he laughed while staring at his phone. It may have been only an hour since it'd been recorded, but Jesse's little episode had already gone viral.

Chapter 19
A TRAIL OF BREADCRUMBS

Jesse awoke feeling groggy. When his vision came into focus in the bright light, he looked around at the dull gray walls with hard blue lines and realized he had no idea where he was. He was disoriented, but when he saw he was closed in on one side by bars, he started to panic.

What had he done?

Try as he might, he couldn't remember anything from the night before. He couldn't remember much of anything, really. He tried to lock down the last thing he could actually remember doing.

He thought about the party just days before. His secret was out, and it seemed the whole world knew. He'd taken Carl's advice and gone straight home. Sara had been there waiting for him. The first thing she'd done was show him the video of him yelling at everyone in a coke-fueled rant.

"What the hell is this?"

"Did you hear what everyone's been saying about us? About the pictures that've been going around?"

"So *this* was your answer? Jesus, you might as well have just told everyone that it's true."

He'd looked behind her and noticed she had a roller suitcase standing at attention. "Going somewhere?"

"You can't think I can stay here. Not after all that. Frankly, I'm surprised the house isn't surrounded by paparazzi or something already. We can't keep doing this. I've . . . I've gotta get out of here."

Jesse reached out and grabbed her wrist. She shook it loose with one swift jerk and walked to her car in a huff, never once looking back.

He'd been abandoned.

His head felt like it weighed a ton; it drooped down to his chest as he walked in the door and slammed it shut behind him. He took just enough time to think about what Sara had said before diving nose-deep into his stockpile. There weren't any paparazzi or reporters of any kind. Not at the party, on the drive, or even waiting when he'd gotten home. That little scene with Sara would've been a juicy one. Maybe if he'd stayed sober, he would've come to the truth of the matter himself. He'd committed a faux pas so colossal, no one wanted to come anywhere near him, as if mere association would cause them to fall into the growing sinkhole that was Jesse Tovin. He had been cast off to the leper colony of the entertainment world. Untouchable.

He got a call the next day saying he'd been dropped from his upcoming movie contract. Not long after, his agent said he could no longer represent him.

Rats, he'd thought. *Rats deserting a sinking ship.*

There was nothing he could do. He'd crossed that invisible line. The kicker was no one cared *that* he'd done it; everyone in the entertainment industry did something to cross it at one time or another. He'd even been offered a "membership" to a club where they would supply him with fresh underage girls whenever he wanted. He'd respectfully declined, but inside, he'd felt he wanted to puke because such a thing was taking place.

No, the real problem was that he'd been *seen* crossing the line. Once the public saw it, you were absolutely, undeniably, and irrevocably untouchable. How many people did he know of that could be in his very shoes right now, or worse, if they had the misfortune of getting caught? Hundreds? Thousands?

This world was sick. His only source of comfort throughout the years had been boiled down to two things. One had beat it out the door the night before, suitcase in tow. That left the sweet embrace of the clean white powder hidden away throughout his house.

He'd hit the stuff pretty hard, but what else was there to do? No work, no family—they'd probably disowned both him and Sara by now. Life had become a continuous string of highs and lows. The only thing that mattered was the next fix.

At some point, he remembered going to the doc's place. He remembered wanting to ask him for some advice, maybe a little help to get him back on his feet. But when he'd gotten there, the staff had told him that Picaud was away, but Jesse was welcome to come in and make himself comfortable. So he did.

That was the last time he'd really felt sober; he was sure of it. He'd thought the change of scenery, even some company, would do him good. The only downside was that he'd had no way to get high. It was just as well, really. He didn't have anything left at the house and could only pull so much cash out of his bank at a time. He'd paid no attention to his dwindling resources. Just figured that with Picaud's help, he'd be able to book another gig. Picaud could fix anything. Jesse just had to stay sober.

But when the doc showed up two days later, it didn't go as planned.

"Jesse!" he said in a cheery voice. "How have you been holding up? I've been hearing some pretty nasty rumors."

"Actually, that's kinda why I'm here. Is there anything you can do to help me? They ripped up my contract for the movie gig. If you could just get it back, I know this whole mess can be swept under the rug. You can do that, can't you? All you probably gotta do is make a phone call, right?"

As Jesse plead his case, he watched the doc's face cool by degrees with each sentence.

Picaud waited patiently for him to finish. "I'm sorry, Jesse, but I don't think that there's anything I can do for you. In your current state, I couldn't get you a minimum-wage job washing dishes, let alone get a multimillion-dollar role back. Besides, think about it. You said to me once that you thought you got the role because the directors respected me, yes?"

"That's right, so if you were to call them up, I know that they'd take me back."

But the whole time Jesse was speaking, Picaud was shaking his head.

"Think about it, Jesse. If they *had* respected me before for taking an interest in you, don't you think that by *your* actions alone, you've ruined my credibility with them since? You know how this world works. The D'alos might be two of the hottest directors Hollywood has right now, but if they were to use you, instead of bringing your head back above water, you'd pull them under with you. Three promising careers snuffed out instead of one. You have to face facts: Your time in that world is over." Picaud crossed over and started straightening Jesse up, as if trying to physically put him back together. "And if you don't stop using, your time in *any* world will be over."

Jesse stared into his face, and all he could think was *Pontius Pilate*. This man had the power to save his career, his life. Instead, he had washed his hands of him. Without another word, Jesse stormed out of the place. God, he needed a fix. He just needed enough to get his head on straight, that was all. Not enough to reach the clouds; just enough to clear his mind and stop the shakes.

He went to the nearest ATM, pulled out as much cash as he could, and called his plug. When he got there, the man demanded three times as much as he normally did. Said if he was seen dealing to Jesse, some-one would narc on him.

Jesse had reluctantly handed over the money with a threat that he would never come to him again. The man had seemed relieved rather than hurt. He'd shoved the money in his pocket as if wanting to rid his fingers of the feel of it and left Jesse with all he'd had on him.

Something had been different about that batch, like there was something different the night he'd met Picaud, but this time, he hadn't woken up in a bed; he'd woken up on the cold steel sheet that served as a bed in a drunk tank.

Jesse looked down and saw that he was wearing the blue, smock-like shirt and pants of a prison uniform. Where were his clothes? How long had he been in here? He had only minutes to wonder before a loud, harsh buzzer sounded and the door of his cage opened.

A tired-looking man stood in the doorway, looking down at him. The man looked familiar, Jesse knew it, but he couldn't place where from.

The man just stared down at Jesse as if waiting for something.

"Well?" the man finally said.

Jesse, feeling more confused as time went by, just answered, "Well what?"

"Why am I here?"

"I don't know. Hell, I don't even know why I'm here. Why *are* you here? Forgive me, but you don't look like you're my lawyer."

The man laughed. "Damn right, I'm not. I hate those bloodsucking bastards!" He paused and looked at Jesse as if sizing him up. "You really don't know why you're here?"

"Mister, I just woke up with absolutely no idea where *here* is, let alone why. I'm starving and I have one hell of a headache. Then you come in here looking for answers instead of giving them; cut me some slack."

The man considered Jesse's response for a moment. "Mr. Tovin, my name is Bill Nell. I'm an agent for the FBI, and I've been called into this little investigation going on here. I'm currently trying to tie up a few loose ends surrounding a multiple-homicide investigation that you *seem* to be a part of."

Jesse's face must have shown panic again, and he'd just opened his mouth to protest when Nell held up a hand to forestall him. "I already checked into you; all the records indicate that you were thousands of miles away when the crimes took place, which is why I'm confused. But," Nell said with particular emphasis, "you *are* wrapped up in the investigation all the same. I just have to figure out why."

"Well, when you do, let me know. I'd love to help, but in case you haven't noticed, I got my own little mystery on my hands. Any chance you can help me with that?"

Bill thought for a moment, then relented. "You're in the LAPD North Hollywood Jail. From what I gather, you're in isolation until whatever you had in your system clears out. Probably doesn't hurt that you're a celebrity."

"What am I in for?" Jesse asked.

"Couple of things." Bill pulled out a small notepad and looked at it. "Most prominent is aggravated assault with a deadly weapon. You beat the shit out of some drug dealer, I guess; he's in an ICU. You better hope he gets better, or you're looking at a charge of at least manslaughter, if not murder."

A brief image flashed in Jesse's head: that of a bloody face with hands raised in supplication. Then looking down at the dirty pipe smeared with red. The image was too much, and Jesse felt sick. All he could think to do was put his head between his knees. That felt insufficient, so Jesse grabbed on to the back of his neck and started rocking back and forth.

After a few minutes, Jesse seemed to regain control of himself. Head still cradled in his hands and facing down toward the floor, he asked, "So, what brought you into this?"

Jesse heard the rustle of plastic and looked up to see Nell holding a crumpled evidence bag with something small inside.

"This was found on your person when you were brought in. They called me up and sent me a picture. I made it a priority to come out here to ask you about it."

After looking at both sides of the small piece of evidence, Jesse said he could honestly say he'd never seen it before.

He held the bag with the little white card out to Bill. On one side of the card was written *Agent Bill Nell, FBI*. On the other was just a large, bold number: **2**

LAX was always crowded. Today was absolutely no exception. Still, Bill was able to find a secluded corner in a currently vacant gate as he awaited his flight home. Finding this little slice of privacy was a pain, but it was crucial anytime he was to use his agency laptop. It wasn't exactly the most cutting-edge piece of equipment, but it did have the unique ability to view highly classified government documents. After this little excursion, he needed to do some digging. He'd always thought that after he figured out who'd been behind the murders, things would get clearer. Instead, the further he went down this road, the foggier things got.

For instance, what the hell did this Tovin character have to do with it? Sure, he beat that drug dealer pretty good and may have gotten it on with his sister, but that had nothing to do with the case.

The guy had been in Hollywood when Wheaton's murder took place. But there was no denying he was connected somehow. Those cards didn't just magically appear on both people. So what did they have in common?

There was one obvious thing they had in common: Wheaton and Tovin were both at the party on Halloween. But so was Bill. Picaud may have invited the other two, but he'd also invited him, so if Picaud was involved in this, he'd have to be pretty stupid to think he could get those two arrested and not implicate himself. Something connected the three of them, but what? Bill had to dig deeper.

Before the murders had even started taking place, Tovin had moved out here and changed his name. Bill looked up the info of Cory Mar. A picture of a young Tovin came up. He'd gotten in a few small skirmishes when he was a kid, but nothing major. Then Bill noticed the town he'd grown up in, and suddenly, his head was filled with the sound of warning bells and visions of red flags.

Peach Creek. He knew it was familiar. It only took a second, and when he brought up Wheaton's dossier, he confirmed the connection.

He pulled up Picaud's info as well, sure he would find he'd at least lived there at some point in his life, but the file said that he'd been born and raised in New York. There was nothing on Picaud's record, which, if accurate, meant he was the first rich man in history who was squeaky clean. Bill wasn't buying it.

Bill went to the nearest flight kiosk to change his travel arrangements. He may not be able to figure out where Picaud fit into all of this, but he did have the very real connection of Peach Creek between the other two. Perhaps he could find out more there.

Hours later, his flight landed in Atlanta, and he drove a rental car to Peach Creek. There was nothing special about the place. Just another small town you'd never know was there unless you had business in it. It took him a few moments to realize he'd been here before. A few of the people Wheaton was suspected of killing had been here.

Bill decided his first stop would be the local law, but that was no help. When he got there, he was informed that the sheriff when Wheaton was growing up had been dead for five years. Cancer, the new sheriff said.

When Bill looked in the two records, he didn't find anything of consequence. When he asked if the sheriff knew who Picaud was, he said, "That rich fella? Yeah, I see him on the TV every now and again. What's he got to do with the other two?"

"That was what I was hoping to find out."

Bill left the office feeling down, but not defeated. He decided to drive around for a bit to see if anything could spark some interest. Nothing did.

He was getting low on gas and pulled into a little station across the street from the local high school. He looked down at his watch and saw that it was now twelve thirty in the afternoon. All the kids would be in class. None of the students would know anything, but perhaps the faculty might remember Wheaton and Mar.

When he pulled up to the gas pump, he saw that the credit card slot had been blocked with masking tape that, by the color of it, looked like it'd been there a while. It read "See clerk."

He walked inside to put some money toward his tank and saw that the clerk, a wizened man who looked older than God, was in conversation with another, less old gentleman with bright white tufts of hair. The two stopped talking immediately after he walked in.

"Help you?" the thin, raspy-voiced older man behind the counter said.

"Yeah, can I get sixty on three?" Bill handed over his card.

The man punched a few buttons, swiped the card, and said, "Receipt?"

"Yes, please."

The man grumbled and went to it. Probably been a while since someone actually needed one, but Bill wanted to be reimbursed.

The man handed over the receipt with a shaking hand that was gnarled with arthritis. Bill took it and was suddenly sparked with inspiration.

"How long you been working here, if you don't mind me asking?"

"All my life, seems like," the man said bitterly.

One look at the man was enough to tell Bill that that was long enough for him to be around when Wheaton and Mar had gone to the school adjacent.

"Get a lot of students in here?" Bill asked, jerking his head in the school's direction.

"Every day, Sonny, like clockwork."

"You remember a couple of kids named Brent Wheaton and Cory Mar?"

"What business is it of yours?"

Bill pulled out his badge. "I'm looking into a case that may have involved the two of them. Remember anything about them when they were growing up?"

"Hell," the voice of the other white-haired man chimed in. "Everyone who was around long enough knows those two."

The older man gave his friend a sour look. "There you go again, Mike, running your mouth off to every stranger you meet. Can't seem to ever shut your trap, now, can you?"

"Oh, hush, Abe; he's already shown he's part of the law."

"Like that makes a difference to you," Abe spat.

Ignoring Abe, Bill asked Mike, "Why's that?"

"Well, first off, the Wheatons have always been big 'round here, long as the town can remember. They've owned the local brewery since way back in prohibition days. Ever since his father passed, Brent took over and expanded it. He and that other fella you mentioned left this town and got super rich. Wish I'd done the same when I was their age."

Bill pulled out his notebook and pen. "So, you all knew that Jesse Tovin was really Cory Mar?"

"Oh yeah. Can't ever forget a face in this town, even if you wanted to," Mike said with a laugh.

"Can you tell me anything more about those two? Did they know each other growing up?"

"Course they did. Those two always hung around together, along with that Roe kid. Thick as thieves, they were."

A bolt of electricity went through Bill. "Roe? As in Senator Roe?"

"Yup, that'd be the one. There's another smart fella that went out into the world to make something of himself."

"Were any of them in trouble a lot while they were growing up?"

Mike seemed to be thinking it over; all the while, Abe glared at him. Finally, Mike answered, "Nothing serious. Not really. You know how boys can be growing up. Getting into a few fights now and again. They even chased two kids in here that one day, didn't they, Abe?"

Abe looked, if possible, even angrier at Mike for pulling him back into the gossip. Bill couldn't have cared less.

"What two kids?" Bill asked.

Mike looked at Abe, not worried about his expression in the least. "It was Westley and that Dalton kid before he passed, wasn't it? I'm almost certain it was."

Abe's lips pursed tighter. "I don't remember."

"Sure, you do. You said it was that big fat kid that always took his bike in here and messed up your floors? He and Westley were always together. Must've been them."

Information seemed to be flinging itself at Bill, and it was all his pen could do to keep up. "Wait, how did this other kid die?"

"Went missing back in '14. Found his car wrecked by a sharp turn in the road." Then in a loud whisper, "Most think texting and driving."

Another red flag popped up in Bill's head; apparently, there was yet another death mixed up in all of this.

"Can I talk to this Westley?"

"Sure, if you can get ahold of him. He owns a chain of sandwich shops. They do so well, he never really has to go in 'em anymore. He owns a huge place on the edge of town. Can you pull up the GPS on your phone?"

Bill did, and Mike dropped a pin on the general area where the house was located.

As Bill approached the part on the map the old man had marked for him, he saw a long wall that ran off in all directions. It looked relatively new. The road led to a large, ornate wrought-iron gate. As Bill pulled up to it, he saw a small metal box with a pin pad and a speaker. He pressed the call button.

After a few moments, a harried voice came on the speaker. "Yeah?"

"Hi, my name is Bill Nell. I'm an agent for the Federal Bureau of Investigation."

"I've already filed my taxes this year. You're not getting another dime."

Bill rolled his eyes. "Sir, that's the Internal Revenue Service."

"Oh, right. Well, what do you want?"

"I just have a few questions for you about a couple of old school-mates of yours. A Mr. Brent Wheaton and a Mr. Cory Mar."

A pause, then, "Why; they in trouble?" The voice was brightening up.

"I should say so. One's dead; the other's in jail."

In answer, the large double gate swung inward, and Bill heard a high-pitched voice in his head say, *Well, that's a horse of a different color . . .*

Bill followed the lane toward the large main house in the distance. Along the way, he saw a small ranch house just inside the gate that would be typical for the town, not so much to be some rich guy's estate, and he figured it must be a guest house.

Bill followed the road to the main house, where a tall, skinny man in thick-framed glasses was waiting for him in the open door.

"Come in, Mr. Nell," he said excitedly. "Come in."

Bill extended a hand to the thin man, who shook it fervently.

"Westley Scott; pleased to meet you!" Westley led him inside to a large sitting area and asked, "Can I get you anything?"

"No, thank you."

A smile lit up Westley's face. "First things first, then. Who's dead, and who's in jail?"

Bill eyed him. "You seem to be pretty happy to hear about the misfortune that has befallen your old pals."

"Ha!" Westley said bitterly. "They were no pals of mine. All they did was give me a bunch of hell. Pretty sure they even killed my best friend, but I could never prove it."

"That's kind of why I wanted to talk to you. I'm working a case that primarily involves Mr. Wheaton, the deceased."

"Brent died? Figures. I would've heard about the showboat dying even after he'd been disowned for fucking his sister." Westley looked a little abashed. "Pardon my French. How?"

"He appears to have been shot by his wife."

Westley punched one hand into the open palm of the other. "Serves him right. Can't believe anyone would've married that guy in the first place."

Bill twirled his finger in a "move on" gesture. "About your friend, Mr. Scott."

"Westley. And you mean Eddie?"

Checking his notes, Bill nodded. "Edward Dalton, yes."

"That's right. That was his house out there. I bought it along with all the surrounding land when my business took off. It was abandoned, and it didn't seem right to just leave it like that. So, I had it remodeled at the same time I had this house built. Did you already look him up?"

"Just what they had on file."

"Then you know what happened to him."

"I know about the car crash, but it seems that a lot of people that surround Mr. Wheaton end up dead, and I'm trying to figure out where Mar fits in. This might be the one death they have in common."

Westley's smile faltered a little. "I don't know what good it'll do. They used to pick on me and Eddie. When I heard about Eddie losing control of his car and going missing, something felt really odd about it. I mean, he was supposed to go out on his first-ever date with a girl he'd had a crush on for years. What was he doing out in the middle of nowhere?"

"Cold feet?"

"I suppose it's possible, but it doesn't sound like Eddie. Then the next day at school, the three of those guys—"

Bill raised his notes again. "The third being Zackary Roe, yes?"

"Someone did his homework. Yeah, all three of them started bullying me and bugging the girl Eddie was set to go out with, worse than usual. They never outright said that they did anything, but they were always making snide comments about Eddie going missing, then smiling at each other like it was some big damned inside joke."

"Why didn't you tell the sheriff about this?"

"I did. But that old windbag just said it would be just like their sick sense of humor to taunt me like that, and it didn't count as real evidence."

Bill thought for a moment. "And Senator Roe, in your opinion, was in on this?"

"In on it? He was their leader. Neither one of those other idiots could wipe their ass without Zack's say-so. Pardon my French."

Not caring the slightest for Westley's vernacular, Bill went on. "Was there a fourth member of this gang?"

"No, not that I remember. Maybe Sara, Cory's sister; you know, the one he just got caught . . ." Westley made a grimace and a crude gesture involving his right forefinger and his left forefinger and thumb in the shape of an *O*.

Bill nodded. "Have you ever met a man by the name of Henry Picaud?"

"The billionaire doctor? I wish. I got a couple ideas I think he could market. What's he got to do with this?"

Bill stood. "Thank you, Westley. I think that's all I need."

"You sure? I don't think I really told you anything."

"Oh, believe me, I have quite enough to be going on. In fact, you might say I have my work cut out for me." He shook Westley's hand.

Westley saw him out the door, and on the way to his car, Bill spotted the lone ranch house by the front gate again. He turned back toward Westley and squinted through the bright sunlight to see him.

"Can I ask you a personal question?"

"Sure," Westley said.

"I was just wondering why exactly you chose to keep your friend's house."

Westley paused. "Honestly? Well, I'll tell you, but you're gonna think I'm crazy."

"Try me," Bill said, still smiling.

"I don't think Eddie's really dead."

"Why's that?"

"I don't know, exactly." Westley paused as if remembering something. "It's just, this really weird thing happened some years back."

Bill's finger was itching for his pen again. "Yeah? What's that?"

"This weird, homeless-looking dude showed up in my shop. He asked about all this same stuff. Then, out of nowhere, I get this offer saying that that homeless guy was really a wealthy investor and wanted to back me. I took the money, and business has been booming ever since."

"And you think that guy might have been Eddie?"

Westley shrugged. "It's just that as soon as I cashed the check, I got a text from Eddie's old phone. And you gotta remember that this was six years after Eddie went missing."

Bill stood stock-still. "What did it say?"

"Just 'thank you.' But the timing and the fact that it had been from *his* number. I told the old sheriff, but nothing came from it."

Bill thanked Westley and drove back into town to find a hotel to hole up in while he figured all this out. As soon as one question seemed like it was answered, twelve more would pop up. If the numbers found on Wheaton and Mar were any indication, there was probably at least one more left on the list. Bill had a feeling that other person just so happened to be the good senator.

So what? Roe convinces his two buddies to kill this Edward Dalton, and Wheaton gets a taste for killing? Did the senator know about it? When Bill had talked to him, he hadn't gotten the feeling that he did. And if Senator Roe had killed this Dalton, and he, Mar, and Wheaton were connected to it, it was a ballsy move to implicate Wheaton, even *if* it was just to shed light on the serial murders. This Dalton was the one that seemed to connect all three of these people. But where did Picaud fit in? Did he know what they did to Dalton and was now trying to get payback for him?

Bill could feel that there was something there, but it was one of those things that sat right at the edge of conscious thought and just got further out of reach the more he grabbed at it. The one concrete thought he had to go on was to see just what Picaud had to say about all this.

Chapter 20

THE BEST-LAID TRAPS

Bill spent the next few days trying to fit it all together. Picaud was the link, and Bill was sure he was behind Wheaton and Mar coming to justice, but why? That was the missing piece. Bill collected all the data he could about Picaud, but the man was extraordinarily clean. Normally, at the very least, the companies that these rich guys owned were involved in some shady deals. But whenever Bill ferreted out something that looked like it would fit that description, everyone attested that it was unintentional and that Picaud not only insisted on transparency but also always dealt swiftly and harshly with those who tried to ally his company in such underhanded ways.

The only thing that was truly hinky about Picaud Industries was that it was, if anything, too clean. All the t's were crossed; all i's dotted. So what did that leave? At least on paper, the man was an upstanding individual. If he was doing anything outside the law, Bill was going to have to catch him the old-fashioned way: with his own two eyes.

What Bill needed was a stakeout. He got to Picaud's estate just after noon, parked well outside the property line, and hoofed it the rest of the way. Picaud owned not only the huge property the house sat on but also the surrounding forest that reached as far as the eye could see. Bill chose to park as close as he could to the house without being seen.

It was a beautiful little hike to get from his car to where he stationed himself. Although it was a bright, sunny day, there was an unmistakable chill in the air, broadcasting the fact that winter was pressing in upon them. Bill stayed just beyond the tree line and pulled out a pair of binoculars to survey the scene. As far as he could see, there were two main structures on this part of the land: a house with a large swimming pool that looked like a small lake with its own waterfall and a huge metal structure that looked like it was meant to keep aircraft in.

Bill methodically worked his way through the tree line that bordered the clearing. When he got a little closer to the metal structure, he saw what looked like a driving track right behind it. He worked his way around until he could see inside the structure through the enormous open door. The place was full of cars—rows and rows of bright, clean cars.

Bill was about to bring his binoculars up for a closer look when something caught his eye. Light was bouncing off an envelope taped to a tree about five feet away from where he had stationed himself.

Cautiously, he made his way over and saw the two handwritten words on the front: *Agent Nell.*

Bill snatched the envelope and tore it open.

Dear Agent Nell,

 I'm so happy that you have finally found time to pay me a visit. I'd hoped you would feel comfortable enough to come straight to the front door, but I know that I haven't yet proved myself a friend. All answers await you inside, and it is my hope that by the time you leave my estate, I will have earned that title.

The staff are waiting and will show you in whenever you're ready. Feel free to make yourself at home.
Sincerely,
Dr. Henry Picaud

Bill read the note twice before trying to figure out what it meant. Had Picaud really known he was coming? The note seemed to prove as much. How long had he been expecting him?

Bill was starting to get the feeling that he was being led by the nose, and he didn't like it. More questions were sprouting by the second. Bill came to get answers, and by God, he was going to get them. He marched his way through the estate and straight up to the front door. Before he could get within ten feet, a wild-haired man in a suit opened the door.

"Good afternoon, Agent Nell. I don't know if you remember me from the party, but my name is Gene. It's my pleasure to get you anything you'd like to make you more comfortable. May I offer you some refreshment? Perhaps a stiff drink? It does seem to be getting rather cold out nowadays."

Bill stared at the man with one raised eyebrow. It took him a moment before he could say anything.

"Nothing, thank you. I would like to speak to Dr. Picaud. Is he in?"

Gene's smile widened. "Right to the point; that's why he likes you. As you well know, he *is* in and eagerly awaiting your company. Follow me."

Gene led him through the house into what he said was the main dining area, but when Bill went inside, he did a double take. He was in a room that looked like a swamp in the evening. He looked at the hanging lanterns and the facade of the plantation house, and memories of old family reunions came to mind.

Bill walked over to a small dock looking out to the water and marveled at the attention to detail that had been given to everything. Lost in his thoughts, lulled there by the ambient noise of frogs and crickets and by the buzz of the fireflies twinkling in front of him, all he could do was sigh in a moment of pure relaxation like he hadn't felt in months.

"I know what you mean," a voice said, jerking him back to reality. Bill turned to see Picaud walking toward him. He walked past Bill to the edge of the dock and sat down, dangling his feet mere inches above the water. "I often come here and just get lost in my thoughts. I find this room to be so peaceful."

Bill stared down at him, somewhat unnerved that Picaud even seemed to know what was going on in his mind. "How long have you known I was here?"

Picaud kept staring out across the swamp. "Since you arrived. We have the whole place wired to let us know of anyone drops by unannounced."

"Does that happen often?"

Picaud turned his head. His face glowed softly in the low lighting, and a bright smile lit up his face further. "One can never be too careful."

Bill held up the letter. "How'd you know the exact place I'd end up?" An edge crept into his voice.

Picaud tried in vain to keep the chuckle out of his words. "We actually printed a few and placed them in all the spots we figured you might get to." One look at Bill's stern face as he thought it over was enough to send Picaud into a rolling laughter. "I know. Dramatic, right? You should've seen your face!"

Bill felt the seed of a laugh plant deep in his gut, but he refused to let it grow. "Why were you expecting me?"

"We both know the answer to that." He gestured for Bill to sit. "Join me, won't you?"

Bill didn't like it, but he wanted to keep Picaud talking, so he sat. "So, you *are* responsible for Brent Wheaton, then?"

A flash of anger was so palpable that it conducted into Bill as if Picaud was a Tesla coil.

"That man is responsible for his own actions. He got much less than he deserved."

Bill felt his color rise. "So, you knew what he was doing? Then why the whole song and dance? Why not just come to me and tell me how you knew? Why wait until Wheaton picked another victim?"

"*That* was an unfortunate accident. I'd been keeping an eye on him for a while. I wanted him to be punished for the horrible things he'd done, but I certainly didn't want to put anyone's life at risk. As soon as I caught wind of what was happening, I called you."

"Why didn't you say something sooner?"

"Why couldn't *you* work faster? I had no idea what kind of man you were. I sure as hell wasn't going to just trust you. I did, however, basically lay everything out in front of you. You were supposed to be able to bring him down with your own investigating."

Bill said nothing. He didn't enjoy feeling like a pawn someone was using to their own ends.

Picaud must've picked up on what Bill was feeling, because he said, "Don't give me that. You know better than anyone how the law works. If I had just come to you outright, all of the evidence given would be seen as eyewitness testimony, and you know how shitty that is in court. This way, you collected all the evidence yourself, and even though we didn't mean for that girl to end up in the middle of this, you now have a survivor that can attest to what Wheaton tried to do."

"And how does him being dead work for this little scheme of yours?"

"To quote Al Pacino, 'Free will, it is a bitch.' That's the key to everything we're wrapped up in here, isn't it? Free will? We can plan for the actions of others all we want, but in the end, no matter what, it's still their decision. Take our unfortunate Hollywood friend. Even though

I knew all he was doing, I gave him a choice. I warned him off drugs and told him that they'd be the end of him. He agreed, and for the short time he was clean, everything was going great for him, and if he would've stayed away from drugs, he would've been set for the rest of his life. It wasn't until he started using again that his little secret slipped out. Even then, I did all I could to make it hard for him to get his hands any more drugs. But he still found a way. Everyone makes their own choices. People may influence each other, but no matter how heavily they do, each person is still responsible for their own actions."

"So, by that logic, Manson should've been let off."

"Of course not! His actions lead to the killing of those people, even if he hadn't touched a single one of them. It's the same reason why the people who actually committed those crimes were still convicted. They chose to listen to that psycho; they chose to get their hands dirty."

Bill scoffed. "So, what makes you any better? You seem to be pulling all the strings. What's to stop me from bringing you in?"

"I haven't done anything. I didn't tell anyone to do any of these things. I simply brought matters to light."

Bill thought this over for a moment. His head was telling him to bring this guy in, but his gut was screaming that it was the wrong thing to do. Maybe he could change its opinion.

"How long have you known what Wheaton was doing?"

"I found out a couple years ago—"

"A couple *years*?"

Picaud held up a hand. "By then, he'd already stopped killing. I had tons of people in place to make sure he didn't start again, and I had other things that needed doing. I figured he'd waited this long; as long as he wasn't hurting anyone else, he could wait a little longer for me to get all my affairs in order. I wanted to take care of everything in one fell swoop."

Bills eyes widened. "That's why you bought the property; you *knew* it was his. That whole party was a setup to put my focus on him?"

Picaud turned and smiled again. "Among other things, yes. That was the domino I set up to knock all the rest down. People may have free will, but that doesn't stop them from being incredibly predictable."

"So what? Am I supposed to just let you go on doing what you're doing?"

Picaud's eyes bored into him. "Am I doing anything against the law?"

"I don't really know for sure, do I? I suppose if I wanted, I could arrest you for interfering with a federal investigation."

Picaud let out a loud, short laugh. "But you know my lawyers would have a field day with that, and you'd be going blind with paperwork."

Bill sighed at the thought. "Yeah."

"Look. You're not going to stop me. I've waited too long and worked too hard. But I *would* like your help. The people I'm going after, in case you hadn't noticed, are very bad guys. There's just one more to go, and he's the biggest fish of the three."

Bill thought about it. So far, an incestual drug abuser with a budding taste for assault and a notorious serial killer had been neutralized. He figured he could at least hear the man out.

"And Senator Roe is the last?"

Picaud's eyes sparkled in admiration. "Somebody really did his homework."

Bill paused slightly at Picaud's choice of phrase, remembering Westley. "No, somebody did his job. Strictly speaking, that job requires me to bring you in for being at the scene of a murder, among other things."

Still smiling, Picaud said, "*If* I was there, I don't think you can prove it, which is why you haven't brought me in. But think; if you play your cards right, you'll not only be known for unmasking one of America's most notorious serial killers, but immediately afterwards, taking down one *very* corrupt senator, possibly even more. But the thing is, we *have* to do this right. The whole Wheaton thing got botched, but at least his victims have their retribution, and their families have closure. The senator's victims are still very much alive. They deserve true justice. If we do this right, we can save hundreds, possibly thousands, from suffering what they suffered. We've looked at it every which way, and the best chance we have is if someone official brings it into the light of day."

Bill thought it over for a moment. "*If* I do decide to help you, it would be on two conditions. The first is that if I catch wind of you doing *anything* illegal, I'm taking you down with no impartiality."

Picaud held his hands up as if at gunpoint. "I would expect nothing less."

"The second, and most important, is that I want you to look at me full in the face and tell me you had nothing to do with Wheaton's murder."

Picaud's eyes seemed to gloss over and stare at something that wasn't there. "Well, I can't deny that my actions ended up leading to the man's death. But I can promise you that not only did I take no part in killing him, but I also feel cheated by his death." The distance between Picaud and Bill seemed to widen. "I wanted you to catch him. I wanted him to suffer for the rest of his natural life." Then, in barely above a whisper, he added, "The way I suffered."

The final piece slammed into place. Bill couldn't help but believe him and actually felt his heart soften.

He looked at the man now staring out with blank eyes at the artificial sanctuary he'd made for himself.

"So, tell me," Bill said. "I want to hear the whole story, Edward."

After finally reaching his hotel, Bill sat on the edge of his bed, staring down at the large manila folder. The only light in the room came from the fixed lamp on the nightstand. The sound of rain gently tapped on his window. He had to process all the information from the last few hours. Picaud had told him what the three had done to him and what he'd had to do to survive. That was a crazy story in and of itself. After thinking about it, Bill would have done the same—probably worse.

But that other thing . . . He'd sat and listened in horrified amazement to all Picaud had to say about Senator Roe. He didn't think he would have believed it if Picaud had not handed over a huge file for him to go through. Inside was a mountain of evidence that would bury Roe for the rest of his life.

Bill had weighed the heft of the file in his hands and looked up in wonder.

"How do get all of your information?"

Picaud laughed. "Ever read The Adventures of Sherlock Holmes? Well, my way is kind of similar. I find people who've had contact with anyone surrounding these three and entice them to tell me all they know—usually disgruntled employees. Most are all too ready and willing to help."

Bill looked at the file in his hand. "Is there anything I need to give you? Surely, there's a price for all this."

"You taking him down will be payment enough for me, really, but if you felt so inclined, there *is* one thing I think you could get for me."

Bill felt a little sturdier after that. He was about to really find out who this guy was. But what Picaud had asked for in return was so simple that Bill could only laugh. It would be entirely worth that price, but what about all the other costs that came with something this big?

If what Picaud was telling him was accurate, much more power-ful players than a single senator would be implicated, and there was a number of possibilities that could stop one or all of them from being prosecuted. There would be legal hurdles. Lawyers would put Bill under a microscope and try and tear his credibility apart or try to find a way of stopping him altogether by turning his life into a living hell.

A buddy of Bill's had been charged with the task of looking into possible illegal and cultish activities surrounding survivors who'd claimed they were kidnapped and brainwashed. The case happened to surround a certain well-known "church," and when this church had caught wind of the investigation and witness testimony, they'd hit from all sides. Their lawyers tried any means necessary to get the case thrown out while a team of private investigators straddled the legal line of stalking by constantly harassing and digging up dirt on all who were moving against them. The agent had made it through and brought the case to trial, but not before someone found his home and had him constantly followed wherever he went. No death threats had officially been made, but the intent was there.

That was only one powerful faction; Bill was about to be facing dozens. He had to decide if this was a hill he wanted to die on. But then he thought about all the women Picaud said had come forward and were willing to testify. Those were just the ones brave enough to stand and fight. How many nameless others were there, too frightened to say anything? Worse, if Bill didn't help put a stop to this, how many more innocents would be sacrificed to these human traffickers?

Bill had joined up with the agency because he believed in doing what was right. His family had always instilled that in him. Even Great-Grandad was said to have believed in it before he disappeared. If Bill didn't stand up and fight for these girls, who would?

Later, in his room, Bill opened the file and began to read. With each page he managed to get through, although he told himself there couldn't be anything more disgusting, the horror on the following page would make him change his mind. He read through the night, which was just as well; he would have trouble sleeping for many nights to come. When he finished all that was in the file, although repulsed, he was filled with hope. The work was basically done for him; all he had to do was verify it. Everything lined up, and the small flame that had lit inside him when he'd decided to take Roe down grew immeasurably.

The girls had grown close to each other when they'd found out that the same man had caused them so much pain. They'd even started their own support group. Bill was emboldened by the strength these women were able to draw from one another. After many days of checking and rechecking facts, testimonies, and allegations, Bill felt that this was an ironclad case that would push down the first of hopefully many dominoes. With a feeling of triumph, he handed in the case file to his superiors.

When he was called in to speak with them the following day, he suspected it was to place a "job well done" on him, followed by the old "go get the bastard." He was therefore astonished when his superiors looked him dead in the face and told him they didn't want to pursue it. They claimed it was a no-win situation and would be a waste of taxpayer money and dismissed him without a second thought.

He couldn't say he was completely surprised. This may have been a black, infected tree, but its roots grew deep. To try and press further would just cause unnecessary trouble for him, if it hadn't already. But who do you go to if the very people who are supposed to put an end to American corruption have been corrupted themselves?

Bill didn't know, but he knew where he was going to start.

The very minute he left the bureau, he called Picaud. He needed help if he was going to move forward. The conversation was short, but meaningful.

"Picaud? It's Bill. I need to talk to you in person."

"What's your nearest airport?"

"DCA."

"A private jet will be waiting there for you in one hour. I'll leave instructions with them to let you on and bring you straight to me."

The phone clicked off, and Bill checked to make sure his travel bag was in the trunk. He drove to Ronald Reagan Washington National Airport, and in an hour and a half, he was in the air on his way back to Georgia.

Bill was surprised to find Picaud waiting in a limo for him.

"So, tell me," Picaud said. "I want to hear the whole story, Bill."

Bill spouted off all that'd happened in the past few hours. Picaud listened intently but gave no indication as to whether the news troubled him or not.

After Bill finished, he paused to hear what Picaud had to say. When ten seconds passed in silence, he asked, "Well?"

"A few old sayings come to mind, Bill. The first is 'There are no problems, only obstacles to overcome.'"

God, this man was frustrating. Bill clenched his teeth. "The second?"

"Ever been a Boy Scout?"

"I'm an Eagle Scout, actually, but why do I get the feeling you already knew that?"

Picaud smiled. "Always be prepared."

Chapter 21

NOT WITHOUT A FIGHT

Zack stared off into the distance of his empty office. He'd been acting funny recently; at least, that's how Hank put it. He was constantly on edge and jumped at the slightest sound. A lot of strange things had been happening lately.

It all seemed to have started at that stupid Halloween party. First Cory showed up, then Brent started acting weird, and look what that turned into. Zack had done exactly what Max had told him to do. As soon as the press got ahold of who Brent was and what had happened to him, it didn't take long for them to come asking questions.

Zack felt that he'd mastered the situation beautifully. He kept his mouth shut until the press wanted explanations. Then he'd told them he'd only recently become aware of Mr. Wheaton's unsavory activities, and as soon as he caught wind, he went straight to law officials and gave any information he could. A quick look into the security footage the day Bill Nell showed up, along with the testimony of the people who'd seen him there, was enough to satisfy even before they got ahold of Nell himself to attest to it.

Still, even though he'd handled himself well, the taint of being friends with Brent, and then the stuff with Cory and the mess he'd become, weighed on Zack. It didn't look good. Those two had really messed up, and he couldn't shake the bad feeling that had been steadily growing.

As he nursed his whiskey, he looked out the window to his parking space and felt a small stroke of comfort. It was his own personal talisman that made him feel secure. Nine times out of ten, Zack would be driven to and from work, but ever since he'd started feeling weird, he'd decided it might be prudent to have the means for a quick getaway.

Looking down at his bold Challenger Hellcat made him feel safe and calm despite its fiery, cherry-red color with the two thick black stripes stretching from hood to tail. Seeing the soft morning light glint off her brightly polished paint relaxed him. Nowadays, it was the only thing that could. But today, the sun also bounced off something to the right in the distance, and it hurt his eyes. His brain had just enough time to pop up an image of a silver bullet in his head before a knock on his office door jarred him out of his thoughts.

"Senator Roe?" came the muffled voice of Hank through the closed door.

Zack remained standing in front of the window. Maybe if he ignored him, he'd go away. To his annoyance, the knocking turned to pounding.

"Senator, the press have been calling nonstop. They want a statement."

Zack gave a great huff of exasperation and walked over to the door, setting down his glass along the way. He opened the door to see the harried face of his hefty assistant staring wide-eyed at him.

"They want to hear what you have to say about the allegations against you."

Zack's mind reeled, and sweat beaded on his forehead.

"Allegations? Of what?"

"Didn't you see the paper I put on your desk this morning? The one with the giant printed note that said *read immediately?*"

Without a word, Zack slammed the door and walked over to his desk. He had set his whiskey right down on it, too distracted to notice. As he picked up the paper, he was surprised to see a large photo of himself staring back on the front page. His stomach dropped into his feet as he began to read.

Allegations of Sex Trafficking Made Against Georgia Senator

A recent article has been circulating throughout the worlds of print and cyberspace about Georgia State Senator Zackary Roe, claiming him to have allegedly taken an active part in human trafficking. Investigations have started into the validity of these statements. No comment has yet been made by Senator Roe. *Copy of said article on page 53.

With trembling fingers, he turned the pages until he found the article.

"And Then He Turned Over"
The Secret Side of Senator Roe

Georgia Senator Zackary Roe has charmed many of this state's constituents, seemingly whether they wanted him to or not.

Recent evidence has been presented that the senator frequently spends his evenings in the company of underage girls, all of whom claim was against their will. In an interview with a few of his alleged victims, most claiming to be from ages ten to fifteen at the time, they state to have engaged in sexual activity with the senator while in fear for their lives. The age of consent in Georgia being sixteen, none were of legal age to give consent in any case.

When interviewing the staggering number of women and girls that have come forward to make claims against the senator, it quickly became apparent that each story was strikingly similar and had one sentence in common: "And then he turned over."

Zack dropped the article to the floor. There was no need to read more.

Shit!

For the next twenty minutes, that was the only thing to go through his mind. When his brain eventually began to work again, he went to his little black book and made a few calls.

Yes, his situation had been made aware of, but countermeasures were already employed; go about business as usual, but above all, stay calm.

Stay calm? That was easy for them to say; it wasn't their asses hanging out in the fire. He looked down at the small black book, turning it over in his hands. At least, not yet.

When he was first welcomed into their ranks, it was like becoming a made man in the Mafia. He was taken into a dark room where the only light was from candles, each elder member's face softly reflecting the flickering yellows and oranges from the source in his hands.

When the initiation began, the book was placed in Zack's hands, and he was told to pledge that he would die a horrible, gruesome death before allowing it to part from him without first burning it to ashes.

Like the Mafia, their ability to continue existing depended on everyone's silence, *his* silence. He would go along with their advice and pretend that all was normal. But Zack had grown quite attached to living, and if he felt for any moment that his life was in danger, he sure as hell would use his get-out-of-jail-free card.

⚔

Bill was poised and ready to take the next step. When he found out Picaud owned one of the top-rated news platforms in the country, he knew what his plan was and couldn't help but feel hopeful about bringing justice to Roe for all those women who deserved their chance to see him locked up. He wanted them to be able to tell their story for a judge and all the world to hear in hopes of moving toward a tomorrow where this kind of thing would never happen again.

When the article and the news coverage came out, it was comical how fast the powers that be changed their minds and told him to bring the son of a bitch in. People turned on Roe with surprising speed. The public became a mob and demanded that this man be brought to face them. Because he was such a high-ranking official, public outcry immediately came to the federal authorities whose job it was to deal with such matters. Since Roe had so much evidence and testimony as proof against him, the powers that be had no alternative but to arrest him and hide their blushing faces for being caught with their proverbial pants down.

It took a single day after the news hit the stands for Bill to receive the call. He was all too happy to oblige. He wanted to tell Picaud, but his gut told him it'd be best to do so after Roe was in custody.

He drove to Roe's office and arrived moments before the local police were sent in as backup. He walked proudly into the building, relishing the moment he lived for. He flung open the double doors and walked to the receptionist's desk to ask where Roe was. The receptionist motioned to Roe's office. Bill strode up and knocked on the door.

"Senator Roe, this is Agent Nell. I have a warrant for your arrest. Open up."

Bill paused to listen. No sound or sign of movement had been made. He tried again, pounding on the door this time. When again he received no answer, he gave a nod to the supporting officers who were prepared for just such an occasion. They set upon the senator's door with a battering ram that burst it inward after a few powerful blows.

Bill drew his sidearm and entered, thoughts whizzing by about what awaited him, doing his best to both pay attention to them and ignore them at the same time. He advanced into the room to find it empty.

One of the windows was broken. A small bit of blood shone bright red in the morning light off the broken glass.

He turned to the policemen. "Find out what kind of car the senator uses and put out an APB. Have a team seal off and search the building. No one gets in or out without a badge. Got it?"

In answer, the uniformed officers ran off to do his bidding while Bill made his way back to his rental. He didn't know what he'd do, but he had a feeling Picaud would have an idea. Whipping out his phone, Bill called the one person he was beginning to trust in all of this mess.

No answer.

One of the officers came out of the building and sprinted across the lot to catch him.

"Agent Nell, you're gonna want to hear this." He handed over his radio.

⚔

When Picaud woke up the day the article was published, he knew he'd have to keep a close eye on the slimy politician. This was the last real play of the game, and he wouldn't return to his house until it was finished.

He got ready that morning with a delightful sense of anticipation of what lay ahead. When he deemed himself ready, he walked out to the hangar. It wasn't the exact same as the one he'd had before, but in front of him sat his spotless '71 Corvette. He'd bought it years ago as a promise to himself that he would not let those three get away with what they did.

Although the same in essence as that fateful day, both driver and vehicle were vastly different. He was hardened by years and experience. Like an expert marksman trains with his weapon until it is as much a part of him as his own arm, so had Picaud done with his cars. The

Corvette had been intensely upgraded from the original factory make of its predecessor. Both man and machine separately would be hard to go up against, but together, they were a force to be reckoned with.

He climbed into the driver's seat and turned the key. The engine roared to life, and he let the sound fill and reverberate within him.

It could be hours or days, but Picaud was ready to watch and wait. Zack was the last piece in the game, and he would not get away.

When Picaud saw Zack park and walk toward the building, he couldn't help but notice how he shifted left, then right, and looked over his shoulder constantly.

Unlike Zack's usual clean-shaven, sleekly combed, and impeccably dressed manner, today he seemed hurried and disheveled. Beard stubble darkened his chin, and strands of hair broke loose and hung down before his eyes. His tie was slackened as if he already felt the noose and was trying in vain to loosen its grip.

Good, Picaud thought. *He's worried. He should be.*

When Zack left that evening, Picaud followed, wondering if he would make a break for it, but he went home as if nothing had happened, and Picaud again watched and waited.

The following morning, he repeated the process, keeping a close eye on his old bully, knowing it was only a matter of time. Zack barely had time to get into his office before Picaud heard chatter on his special radio tuned to police frequencies. Forces were mobilizing, moving in, and going to arrest him immediately. Zack either had his own way of listening in on their conversation or was tipped off, because minutes later, Picaud watched chair legs punch their way through the window.

Immediately after the shards settled, Zack made his way down to the roof of the office below, then to the ground and into his car.

Picaud gave a moment's thought to just driving over and blocking his escape until the police came, but something stopped him. The other two had been taken down so easily and quickly that Picaud couldn't savor the flavor. He planned to play with Zack. He wanted him to suffer. *Appetizers*, he thought. *Just appetizers.* Here before him was the main course, and he intended to relish it.

Picaud allowed Zack to get to his car, even gave him a few seconds' head start before turning on the ignition and taking off in pursuit. He kept a large buffer zone between himself and the cherry-red Hellcat. The intention was not to spook his prey until the streets grew less clogged.

Zack must've noticed he had a tail because he threw caution to the wind. With no regard for the people he once claimed to represent, he weaved his Challenger around cars moving much too slow for him. If Picaud wanted to follow, he had no choice but to do the same.

Up ahead, a line of vehicles blocked every lane in front of a stoplight as they waited patiently for it to turn green. The Challenger climbed onto the sidewalk, its bumper screeching as it scraped along, and two pedestrians were just able to avoid getting smashed. Zack pulled into traffic coming from his side that squealed and swerved as their drivers tried to avoid crashing into him. Picaud gave no inch but followed until Zack would have no more human shields to throw in his way. The air became choked with the sounds of screaming and the roaring of the two engines as their drivers put them through their paces.

Finally, Zack started moving toward more rural areas, and the playing field opened up. At first, Zack put his faith in how well his car was able to grip the road, making last-minute decisions to turn left or right. But the silver Corvette stuck to him like glue. Picaud couldn't help it. He was having fun despite everything. Dimly, off in the back of his mind, he wondered where Zack was trying to go. It took a moment to realize that he was going toward Picaud's house. He must think, like Cory, that his salvation lay in Picaud's hands.

Picaud felt the delicious irony spread through his body and squeezed his hands against the wheel as if snuffing out that profane hope.

Once the roads began to empty, Zack put on the gas. His high-quality horsepower, chomping at the bit, was more than happy to have the rein let out. But no matter how far he pushed, the Corvette kept close behind, and he realized with horror that it was toying with him. One thought kept repeating in his mind: *Dr. Picaud will know what to do.* He just had to get to him.

Desperate and trapped, he lashed out in any way he could. He allowed the Challenger to slow and the Corvette to get nearer, but when the Corvette's nose crept alongside and he turned the wheel to swerve into it, the Corvette would suddenly break and get behind him once more, and Zack had to fight to regain control.

The other driver was after him, and Zack was certain he intended to kill him, but why? Who was this madman? He felt his car give a sudden lurch forward and did all he could to keep it on the road. The Corvette kept contact with him for at least ten seconds before he finally felt it break away.

The road began to twist, and Zack had to split his attention between it and the other car. He didn't want to decrease his speed but knew that he had no choice if he didn't want to end up a crumpled heap on the side of the road. He had no more time to complete this thought when the Corvette started nudging him again. This time, it had gone for one of the rear corners and pushed when it hit. The Challenger began to swerve, and then, to Zack's great surprise, the other car backed off. When the Challenger once again came under control, the Corvette attacked the rear corner again, like a cattle dog nipping at his heels.

The Corvette stopped clipping the bumper, but Zack didn't loosen his grip on the wheel. His body was stiff, and sweat drained from him in sheets. When the other car started coming up on his driver's side, he found himself paralyzed with fear. The car stayed neck and neck with him. Zack finally plucked up the courage to look over, but he was disappointed to find that he couldn't see through the Corvette's tinted windows.

Zack inched his car closer. If he was going to die, he would at least know who had the balls to take him out. His tormentor must have read his mind, because ever so slowly, the tinted window rolled down. As the glass drained away, a face began to swim into recognition. A sick knot formed in his stomach. The other driver was Dr. Picaud, the man who'd been helping him these last few weeks, the man who, just a few seconds before, was the one person on earth he'd wanted to see.

Picaud was playing with his prey. He wanted to fully enjoy his food before he swallowed. Off in the distance, he saw a tractor, and his opportunity to utterly mindfuck his opponent came to be. He boxed the man in. Zack couldn't go to either side without meeting with the Corvette or with trees. He could go faster or slower, but no matter what he chose, Picaud would match. He made sure his passenger window was flush with the driver of the Challenger, then rolled it down.

The face he saw looking back at him was one Picaud would remember and relish for the rest of his life. Zack went from terrified to the spark of recognition to utter betrayal, but as the two cars approached the tractor, his face went suddenly blank. As if his mind had already started the process of shutting down in preparation for death.

Like hell! Picaud thought. *You're not getting off that easy.*

Picaud slammed on the brakes. Once the Corvette's nose was on the same plane as the tail of the Challenger, he pressed hard to the right, taking Zack's back end out from behind him. The Challenger spun off to the left, away from the tractor, and Picaud sped up to get between Zack and the tractor.

The Challenger slid to a halt, facing the opposite direction. Picaud pulled up next to it, anticipation swirling in his mind. This moment was the one he'd waited for, imagined, planned. He parked his car and opened his door to get out.

Picaud stood above Zack, whose car door was open enough that Picaud could see the blood that pooled on his lips, that trickled from a broken nose. If there was one word that described what he saw when he looked at Zack, it was pain. He smiled. Good. Zack deserved all the pain he could get.

Zack coughed, and blood splattered across the deployed airbag. He tried to remove his seatbelt, but his arm was twisted in an unnatural, grotesque position. He turned his eyes to Picaud in question.

"Why?" he managed to sputter out.

Picaud looked down on him. This was exactly the scene he had imagined, and Zack's question allowed him to provide the answer he'd waited so long to give.

"You exist."

Picaud tended to Zack's wounds enough to ensure the best chance of living, then called Bill to let him know where they were.

"Picaud? Why the hell are people calling in about a couple of cars weaving their way around them and almost killing the whole population?"

"It's not my fault you guys let him slip through. Look, he's banged up over here. He'll make it, but he needs medical attention. You gonna come get him, or am I going to have to do all the work?"

It only took a few minutes before Picaud heard the sirens. He didn't want to leave the unconscious man alone, but he couldn't stay. The longer the name Picaud could be kept out of this, the better.

He wasn't worried about Zack getting away—the man wasn't going to go anywhere—but chances were that some of the big names had already started to move against him.

Before leaving, he searched the wreckage and Zack himself, hoping that he would have it on him. When he found the little black book, he took as many pictures as possible with his phone and placed it back in Zack's inner breast pocket.

He knew Bill would find it, but it never hurt to have a little extra insurance. The machinery would take over, but his job wasn't done yet.

Chapter 22

THE FINAL PLAY

The courtroom, despite the case being so early in the process, was packed full of spectators. Normally, it could take days for a suspect to see a judge, but with this being such a high-profile case, the judge was called in immediately to start the arraignment.

Bill sat in astonishment at the hate that boiled over from the people who, most likely, had at some point voted for the man. They stayed calm in compliance with the judge, but only just. As Bill looked around, the one face he expected to see wasn't there.

Where was Picaud? Maybe he was afraid that his presence would raise too many eyebrows, but Bill's gut told him that wasn't it, which troubled him further. Still, there were plenty of others to watch the man burn.

After the ruckus Roe had caused (first through the news media, then the streets), Bill could definitely understand why so many wanted to get a glimpse of what was going on, but the most exciting thing that would happen today was finding out whether or not the judge would allow him bail.

Bill was grateful so many people wanted to be there today. The judge was moved by the masses, and along with the file Bill had submitted and the witnesses that were signed up and ready to give testimony, the judge could only come to the conclusion that not only was Roe a flight risk, but he also would probably be safer in police custody.

Pedophiles and other sex offenders were never kept in the general population but were placed in a separate containment among those with similar offenses. Roe, both being accused of such matters and being a high-profile prisoner, was kept in complete isolation. Bill was *very* happy about this but couldn't shake the feeling that it wasn't enough. He saw hate in the eyes of each spectator and felt that the man's life was in danger.

There was also the matter of that little black book he'd taken from Roe upon arrest. He looked up the first few contacts and found that they were wealthy and powerful people. If the people in this book felt that they could be implicated by Roe, then he was a dead man walking.

As little affection he had for the man, he couldn't let that happen. Roe was the monkey wrench Bill planned on throwing in the machinery of this so-called secret society. If Roe died, all the work Picaud had done would have been for nothing. Yes, the evidence that tied these people to what Roe was doing would still exist, but lawyers are slimy and have an uncanny knack for slithering through loopholes, no matter how tight the squeeze. Roe's testimony would go a lot further.

When the judge finished and everyone rose, Bill made his way over to Roe.

The bailiff was checking the cuffs when Bill reached him.

"I'm going with you to take him to processing."

The tired-looking bailiff had no objection and seemed glad for the extra help. Bill saw a few of the arresting officers.

"Hey, come give us a hand here, would you?" They didn't complain, but Bill could read their lack of enthusiasm.

Something was growing, as if this whole situation had found itself over a powder keg and the match was on its way. He looked over at Roe, still battered and bloody in the clothes he'd worn to the office earlier that morning, and felt a little better when one of the officers started fixing a Kevlar vest over Roe's torso.

In order for them to get Roe to processing, they had to take him outside and walk to the jail facility next door. He'd be exposed but surrounded by Bill and the other officers.

Once the courtroom emptied, the prison party made their way through the little door at the back and down the hallway leading to a set of double doors. The officers pushed them open and were temporarily blinded by the late afternoon sky and setting sun. Their eyes adjusted, and they moved into the chain-link passageway with two layers of fences, both topped with razor wire. Outside, people congregated to shout at the senator as he walked by. Bill looked around and recognized some of them. He'd interviewed them himself before making his move.

Pockmarked throughout the crowd were some of Roe's victims. Some were banging on the outer fence walls; others were holding up signs:

I survived Senator Roe

Stop Government-Sanctioned Sex Trafficking

#METOO

Roe Needs the Needle!

This man had clearly made many enemies even before today. Bill understood their need to be here. It was a way of taking power back from the man who'd left them so defenseless. In Bill's experience, it was always hard for a woman to come forward in cases like this. He couldn't blame them.

These women were already victimized and violated by a predator, and by coming forward, they opened themselves up to the rest of the world. Their story would have to be told over and over. On top of all that, the defense attorney wouldn't be doing their job if he didn't try every nasty trick in the book in order to present these victims as less credible. No, Bill would never blame a woman who didn't want to go forward; to be thrown into this world by no fault of their own and have to deal with the consequences of their rapist's actions would take *unfair* to soaring new heights.

If ever there was a surefire way to get a victim to come forward, it was to show them they were not alone. Bill smiled at that. It's what Picaud had done. He had not only encouraged the victims to want to speak out against their attackers but had also gathered them together to draw strength from one another. That was like a snowball effect. First, it would be small, but as it rolled along, more and more mass and momentum would add to it, and—

Suddenly, movement caught the right side of Bill's eye. He snapped his head over to look and saw figures struggling at the top of a building not too far in the distance. It was like watching the reverse of a fire, with dark flames dancing in front of the bright orange and yellow backdrop of the setting sun.

Bill looked forward at the back of Roe and saw something he hadn't before. He lunged forward to check it. There were two frayed holes in the back of the vest. Kevlar vests were great at stopping bullets—once. They were like motorcycle helmets; after the first impact, they were useless. Likewise with the vest, after one shot, they were just expensive weighted vests.

Everything became crystal clear in Bill's mind. He pushed the senator to the ground, knowing what was about to happen. Just as Roe began to fall forward, Bill felt an enormous pain light up his right shoulder, and his arm stopped responding as the report of a loud gunshot finally made its way over, telling Bill what his shoulder already knew.

Bill's left hand fumbled to get his sidearm out of its holster. He had to wrench his wrist awkwardly, slowing him down. As he looked up, he saw the police officer who'd placed the vest on Roe look down at the Roe, then at Bill.

Bill could see in that glance that the man had been aware of what was going to happen and was now in shock that it had all gone awry; the wrong man was shot.

Bill's eyes bored into the cop, knowing what was about to happen. "Don't do it! Don't you dare!"

He watched as the officer pulled out his own sidearm and started it toward Roe. Bill raised his own gun toward the officer and let two rounds fly, catching the cop in his arm and upper hip as the sound of even more shots rang off in the distance. The place had turned into a damned war zone, complete with tons of civilians in the line of fire. Most had the sense to drop immediately when they'd heard the first shot. Others ran away in a screaming panic.

Bill managed to get to his feet, gun in one hand and his right arm dangling uselessly. He bent down and told Roe, "Get up."

Roe was shaking stiffly on the ground, refusing to move.

"Get up!"

Roe remained rigid on the ground, making sobbing noises into the pavement.

Finally, Bill placed the barrel to the back of Roe's head. "Get up or I'll shoot you myself!"

That did it.

Roe made his way to his feet, and Bill pushed hard in his back to get him to start running. He got Roe inside to processing without another shot. Only when he was certain the senator was safe did he allow him out of his sight.

As he watched them leading Roe off to his isolation chamber, he heard a soft voice in his ear.

"Sir? Sir?"

It took Bill a moment to realize the voice was speaking to him. He turned to see a female guard trying to get his attention.

"Sir, let me get you to the infirmary. You're losing a lot of blood."

"What?"

The woman pointed. "Your arm, sir. We need to get that looked at."

Bill looked down, and that's all it took. Suddenly, his shoulder was on fire again, and all the pain he had pushed aside swept back in full force. He couldn't stop himself from letting out a loud groan of pain.

"Yeah," he managed to get out, "let's do that."

She walked him to the prison's medical facility, and he began to feel faint as soon as he walked in. They gave him what treatment they could, but once the prison was secured, an ambulance was let in to take him to an emergency room.

Later that evening, as Bill tried his hardest to fill out all the medical paperwork with the wrong hand, one of the local officers walked into the lobby.

"Agent Nell."

Bill looked over at the officer who had addressed him. The little golden tag on his chest read "Evans."

"Yeah?"

"I was sent to get an update as well as give you one in return. How are you?"

Bill held up the pen in his left hand, then shifted the arm in the sling. "Frustrated to hell, but I'll live." Then he gave a silent prayer of thanks to the inventor of opioid painkillers.

"That's good, sir."

"There's mine. Now what's yours?"

"Thought you might like to know that the officer you shot is going to pull through."

Bill could detect a bit of resentment in Evans's voice.

"Did he say *why* he was trying to shoot a restrained, unarmed prisoner?"

Evans looked like he'd been slapped. "No, sir; hasn't said much of anything yet. Still talking to his lawyer."

Bill eyed Evans for a moment. "Lemme guess; real high-priced suit, yeah? Leaves you wondering how he could afford such an attorney on his salary?" Bill expected to see another hurt look in Evans's eyes, but something passed by them, as if Bill had said the very thing that had been on Evans's mind.

Evans was a young officer and had probably been around long enough to build up the brotherhood between officers but not to see actual corruption. Bill remembered the first time he'd seen it with his own eyes. He'd been prepared for it all his life through the stories his family told. He didn't know if that made it easier or harder to see the real thing; all he knew was that it made him sick.

Bill's voice softened. "I'm sure he's a good man. Even cops who lose their way around money matters tend to still be good cops at heart, but he knows something, and unless you want this whole thing to continue, we need to find out what."

Bill finished filling out his paperwork and turned to go. Evans reached out to stop him, grabbing his right shoulder above the sling.

"Wait!"

It was too much for his meds to handle. Bill let out a yelp of pain and turned ready to slug the kid, but Evans had already began to stumble out apologies.

Bill waved them off. "What?"

"We also found the shooter from the rooftop."

"Where?"

"That's what's odd, sir. He was still up there. Apparently, he'd been knocked unconscious, tied up, and left there for us to find."

Picaud, Bill thought immediately. "Any ID?"

"His name is Konnor Stevens. The rumor going around is that he's a well-financed hit man. I gotta say, looking at the guy, you'd never guess it."

"Which is probably the point. He wasn't supposed to be caught; guess he just got sloppy."

"Maybe we have a guardian angel or something."

A sardonic smile just touched the sides of Bill's lips. "Maybe, Evans. Maybe."

After making a generous donation to the facilities in which Zack was being held, Picaud was ushered out of the warden's office so that he might be able to see his "old friend." The visitor center was at a corner of the building, still separated from the fence line, but the shouts of the returning protesters made themselves known. As Picaud was escorted to the visitation room, the cries grew louder and more distinct, even through the heavy concrete walls.

The guard who escorted him called for the door to be unlocked. A loud, buzzing blast alerted the halls that the door was opening as it mechanically swung forward on its own. Picaud looked into the mostly empty concrete box with the rubber-coated, mesh-metal tables—reminiscent of the ones used in schoolyards—equidistant across the floor. The room, not usually occupied during non-visiting hours, was dimly lit by one lamp hanging from the middle of the ceiling. At the table beneath the lamp, Zack was cuffed and slouching over, looking at the cuffs as if not yet able to perceive why they were there.

He was no longer bloody but was still disheveled in his bright yellow prison shirt and pants. Picaud walked over to the table and heard the door slam closed behind him. At the sound of the door locks finding their way home, Zack looked up with the wild eyes of a trapped animal. Then the reality of his situation took him, and he slouched back over his restraints, not bothering to look at Picaud.

"That color suits you."

At the sound of Picaud's voice, Zack looked up, startled. His eyes quickly narrowed.

"Picaud?"

"Yes, it's me."

Zack retreated into himself, possibly reliving the events from earlier that morning.

Picaud smiled. "Hope you like your new surroundings; they or another just like it are all you're going to know for the rest of your life."

A smirk that would surprise any man other than Picaud crept its way onto Zack's face.

"What's so funny?" Picaud asked, as if indulging a child.

The smirk wiped itself off. "Nothing. You're absolutely right. I imagine this *will* be all I see for the rest of my life."

"You just don't see that being very long."

Zack turned red. "Of course not. The cops have my book. How long before the people in it find out? After what happened, I'd say they already do or are at least moving forward on the assumption. What would *you* do if you were one of them? These people run this country; they'll do what they have to in order to make sure that this gets buried."

Picaud gave a low growl of a chuckle. "Same old Zack."

"What?"

"You never think things through, not unless you're forced to; no imagination."

"What do you—"

"You're right; evidence without context is generally useless. After all, what is that book but a list of names and phone numbers? Even with the testimony of some of the victims yelling outside, how can we nail those bastards for the justice you are about to reap?"

"That's right. All I have to do is die, then all of this stops with me."

"And you're okay with that?"

"Hell no! But I'm a realist. That's just what's going to happen."

Picaud drank in the look of desperation on Zack's face and smiled. "You may not be as close to death as you think. After all, I was able to keep you alive all through today, wasn't I? You thought you were going to die this morning; I didn't let you." Zack looked like he just had the wind knocked out of him. "They tried to shoot you earlier. I didn't let them."

The look of desperation and confusion grew. "Why, though? Why put me through all of these things and not let me die?"

Every time Zack asked why was the sweetest music Picaud had ever known. He relished and replayed the question again and again in his mind, savoring it. Meanwhile, the sound of the yelling protestors outside crept in on the symphony in Picaud's mind with a delicious underscore.

His eyes returned to Zack. "How can you stand it? Knowing that the entire world hates you? And I can assure you they do. I have the luxury of the proof *you* never had."

Zack looked up at him as if trying to figure out his meaning. There was a faint bell of recall Picaud could see behind the eyes that had once haunted his very existence.

"You've been completely abandoned. Your wife, I'm told, took everything she could and skipped town; seems she wants nothing more to do with you now that the world sees you for what you really are. Your political supporters turned on you like rabid dogs. When the world got wind of what you'd been up to, they immediately demanded your head on a pike. Your so-called allies only want to beat them to the punch in order to save their own skins."

Anger seemed to be mounting in Zack.

Makes sense, thought Picaud with an inward roll of his eyes. *Nothing is ever his fault.*

Zack said, "And they are the reason I'm not safe—anywhere. No matter what I do, no matter where I go, they will find me and ensure that I don't bring the spotlight on them. Remember what happened with Epstein? Those same people are after me. They knew no one would buy the story of him killing himself, yet they did it anyway. Even the medical examiner gave his opinion that it wasn't suicide, yet it was still classified that way. *That's* who we're dealing with. You think they give two shits about anything you do? These people don't care about the law—or anything, for that matter. In their minds, they *are* the law. I'm dead—my body just hasn't caught on yet."

"As dirty as it makes me feel, I cannot change the fact that you have been to my house. You've seen my collections. Do you know why I study history?"

Zack sat and stared.

"The old axiom is right: Those who cannot learn from history are doomed to repeat it. But those who study the past can move forward. I've examined the Epstein case closely, and I have already taken steps to prevent you from meeting the same end."

A faint glimmer of hope rose in Zack's eyes. "How?"

Picaud saw that hope and was ready to seize and twist it. "With another shameful truth of the world that can fix damned near anything: money. You see, I've set up an entire firm at my company just for you. Are you flattered? I bet you are. You always loved the attention, even when we were kids."

Picaud saw that this confused Zack further but could also see the gears beginning to turn, and he kept on before Zack could interrupt. "It's amazing what one can do when money is no object. People who are in the like tend to be one of the damned whose name appears in your book, but I've chosen to use my means to stop them. For instance, I've just had a wonderful little chat with your warden. The law firm I set up is instructed to pay a large sum to not only the facility itself but also to every employee therein. As long as you are alive, conscious, and in custody of the law, they—and any other parties, should you be moved to another facility— will be paid the same generous sum every year you meet those conditions. As a matter of self-interest, they will be most attentive to make sure that no attempt on your life be made by yourself or an outside party.

"They're also instructed to not let you have any special privileges beyond that. No creature comforts; no using your money for extra benefits. You get the full prisoner experience, except for the knowledge that you will *probably* not be killed. After all, some things are worth more than money."

Zack looked like he felt the noose around his neck tighten another notch. Enough to cause suffering, but not to kill. In a numb voice, he asked, "Why?"

Picaud's eyes rolled up in ecstasy at the utterance. Then he quickly controlled himself.

"Because I want you to suffer. You deserve every bit of what you are about to get and more. Listen to that." Picaud paused so that they could listen to the angry cries of the people outside, crushing their way in. "You're going to have a long, miserable life, thinking again and again about all the souls you've desecrated over the years. Each of the women brave enough to come forward deserves the right to look you in the face and watch as they add to the large weight of evidence dragging you down into the abyss.

"But there's another purpose. I'm going to give you a chance that even *I* don't think you deserve. A chance of slight redemption. If you give testimony against the others who are involved in this little club, it won't be a get-out-of-jail-free card, but it *will* be your one chance to repent and try to make good on your sick deeds. It's entirely up to you, but if there is even a shred of decency left, you should do it."

"What good would it do?"

"From society's standpoint, it would do a great deal. They will see you trying to bring down the others that have done the very thing you're being tried for. I imagine that you don't like being used as a scapegoat. This is your chance to take them all down with you." Picaud saw that he'd struck a nerve, and he went on. "Society will be rid of that much corruption, and you will get the attention you crave so much. That book will burn, but in the fiery pits of hell. On earth, it will be put on display for all the world to see. Those people keep to working in shadows because they must. If not, they wouldn't care who knew what they were capable of. The truth is that any form of power less than divine has to pacify the people who, as a whole, have the power to consume them. No amount of money can save you once the public sees what you really are."

Zack gazed at him, open-mouthed. "Who are you, really? What was that about when we were kids? What do you get out of this? Why is it you who's been chosen to be the spearhead?"

"I get to see you suffer. Over the years, that's all I ever wanted. Not money, not fame. I wanted to take everything from you. I saw you make your own noose, just as you made me make mine, and now I'm going to watch as it tightens. No matter what happens, it *will* tighten."

"But why? What have I ever done to you?"

Picaud brought the thumb and middle finger of his right hand up to his eyes in a gesture that he had done thousands of times over the years, then flung his hand down in a fluid motion toward the table.

The two colored contacts stared up like dead, disembodied eyes. Then Picaud leaned forward, grabbed Zack's collar, yanked him up out of his seat, and forced him to look into his face.

As Zack stared up into those brilliant, piercing blues, his look of disgust changed rapidly to that of comprehension.

"Eddie?" Zack asked in confusion.

Back from the dead, Edward grinned widely as Zack began to scream.

Chapter 23

REDEMPTION

In the days that followed, Edward was pleased at how well his planning had worked. Something was wrong, however, and he couldn't quite put his finger on it. He had finally gotten the thig he'd wanted most for so long. The feeling in the moment was the most intoxicating thing he'd ever known, but now that it was over, he felt an overwhelming sense of hollowness and shame. He needed answers and decided to go to where he had always found them.

The chill of a December morning was in the air as Edward got out of his Jeep on the beach in front of his old cabin. It'd been many years since the last time he'd been here to pick up the remainder of the gold. He looked at the sky reflected in the glasslike lake and was reminded of the beauty this place held. He breathed it all in, knowing today would be the last time.

The trail he'd cut down in order to get his Jeep through was still there, but nature had already begun the process of reclaiming it. He walked around the land he'd claimed all those years ago.

When he entered the cabin, it looked much the same as when he'd first happened upon the little shack. The bed had fallen into disrepair; dust and dead leaves were scattered over the floor and table. The one thing that had never changed was the black hulk of a stove in the middle of the far wall.

Edward took in all he could as he approached the hole in the floor where the bear had gone through. Everything was exactly how he had left it. The dusty barrels of whiskey and beer off to one side, covered in a thick layer of dust and dirt. In one corner, a large leather couch, dulled under the grime, and in another, a large pile of books. He had work to do.

He backed the Jeep up to the entrance and took great care as he loaded every book into it. There were so many that they filled up the entire back from carpet to ceiling. The most important ones had yet to be loaded, so Edward took out the three fire extinguishers from his front passenger side and placed the stack of journals lovingly into the seat.

Once all was secured, he drove the Jeep back onto the beach and walked to the cabin. He cleared everything in the direct vicinity so all that surrounded the structure was damp earth. Edward took some dead branches and threw them down into the cellar. He kindled a fire in the stove and waited for a proper-sized log to catch.

He took the unburned end and pulled the flaming log from the stove, gazed into the swaying oranges and yellows with just a glimpse of crimson in them, and tossed it down onto the pile of branches.

They caught quickly, and Edward was reminded of the beginning of the fight with the bear. He backed out of the cabin and watched as the flames licked, tasted, and consumed his old sanctuary. He watched with an extinguisher in hand, ready to make a move if the fire tried to expand beyond its boundaries, but it never did.

Staring into the funeral pyre of his old life, he sat in contemplation. Why didn't it feel over?

Why do I feel like this?

As he dug through his mind for answers, he thought of all those lives that had been put at risk through the years because he had failed to act quickly enough. He could feel the poisoned presence that he thought had lain buried for years trying to claw its way to the surface.

Was it worth it?

It took a few hours, but Edward waited until the only thing left was a hole in the ground, lined with ashes and a large metal stove. Once sure that the fire would not rekindle, he headed home, the question repeating in his mind.

Bill Nell walked around Wheaton's old cabin. He knew why it had to be here, but he was somewhat irked that it had to be so close to Christmas. His wife and two little girls were back home in Virginia waiting for him. For anyone else, he wouldn't have come, but he supposed Picaud had earned it.

"So, what's going to happen to this place?" Bill asked.

"Jake's going to turn it into a bit of a tourist attraction. Based on all the feedback we received after the party, people seemed to really enjoy it and have already requested to book parties and get-togethers here. We've even had a request to use it as a wedding venue. Don't ask me why; people are weird. The money earned will go into a fund to help support the families of all of Wheaton's victims."

"Even with such a dark past, it can still do some good. I like that. His binder shed some light on a lot of the families he hurt. Hopefully, they can get closure now that he's out of the picture."

"That's the hope, anyway. How's our senator friend?"

"You should see him. I think he's adjusting to prison life beautifully, even has some new ink. When I asked why he got the number three tattooed to the inside of his left wrist, he said he'd woken up with it one day. You wouldn't know anything about that, would you?" He paused and looked at Picaud, who was trying not to smile. "Well, he's alive at any rate, and really, that's something to be grateful for. I don't even think Epstein lasted this long."

Facetiousness crept into Picaud's voice. "Told you I took care of it."

"But you can't tell me how?"

Picaud let out a long sigh as he gathered his thoughts. "Actually, that's one of the things I wanted to talk to you about. I set up an entire firm that was dedicated to taking Zack down. Now, we've expanded the project to try and get every one of his associates we can. In a world where money is power, you have to fight money with money. Shameful that it holds sway over so much, but what can you do?"

Bill could taste how disgusting the prospect was, but he shrugged. "I suppose you're right."

"Jake, of course, will be the man in charge of my company and how that money gets spent, but we need someone with the know-how to take charge of the operation. I was hoping *you* might want the job."

Bill thought about it for a moment. There were a lot of names in that book. He was always honest with himself, and he knew that he'd want to see it through till the end.

"I'll have to talk it over with my wife, but I'm pretty sure I know what she'll say."

Picaud looked like he was about to open the best Christmas gift anyone could ask for. "So, you'll do it?"

It was hard to look at him this way, to see the hopeful child he must've been before this whole business, and keep a poker face. So Bill looked off into the trees while trying to suppress a smile. "Yeah, I guess." Then he paused for a moment. "You really think that he'll testify against the others?"

"As long as we keep him safe, yes. Don't get me wrong, I don't think it will be out of any remorse a decent human being would possess, but Zack always had at least two vices throughout his life: being in the spotlight and pride of his own existence. Now is no different; he craves attention, and he *will* get it. I think that he knows now how much his so-called friends are literally gunning for his life. His pride can't handle being the loser or the fall guy. He'll try to take as many of those people down with him as he can."

Bill smiled. It made sense. For the first time since he'd taken on this case, he allowed himself to hope they might take out more than just one cog.

"So, now that the three main focuses of your life are finally stopped, what's left for you?"

Picaud looked out at the trees for a long moment. "I've been think-ing about that a lot, actually." Picaud fumbled over his words and Bill could see tears brimming in his eyes. "I never really did leave that forest, did I? I'm incredibly glad that all those people who'd been caught in the wake have their justice, but I'd be a liar if I said I did it solely for them.

"I often wonder how many of those could have been saved if I had tried to come back earlier. If I hadn't chosen to stay out there so long, or even if I had made my moves faster, I could've nipped a lot of thorns in the bud. I let revenge run rampant in my mind and I honestly can't tell if I'm the hero or the villain of this story."

Bill saw where this was going and inwardly agreed that it all could have been prevented with the proverbial *if only*, but that's not how life worked. "Did you rape and murder?"

"No. But—"

"Did you run that poor girl out of town?"

"No, bu—"

"Did you make them chase you down and into the forest?"

Almost whispering, he answered, "No."

"I seem to remember you telling me that everyone is responsible for their own actions. Could all of this have been prevented by different actions? Possibly, but who knows? You will never know what *could* have happened, only what did happen. Hindsight is always twenty-twenty, and I think you're being a little too hard on a young man who'd been bullied throughout his life and spent six years alone in the wilderness. Hell, I know if I spent more than a few weeks like that, my mind would've done some funny things too!"

Perhaps remembering Ben Gunn, Picaud gave a small huff, and the corner of his mouth started to raise. "I guess."

"I can see that you're dragging a huge boulder behind you, and you'll never get anywhere until you drop it. You've got to move on and keep the past where it belongs." He gave Picaud a moment to consider, then said, "So, what are you going to do now?"

After a while, Picaud said, "I guess that depends. Did you get that thing I asked for?"

Bill's smile widened as he reached into his coat, underneath his sling, where he'd been keeping a manila envelope close to his chest. He pulled it out and handed it over. "Everything we know is in there."

Bill went back to looking at the snow-covered trees as Picaud pored over the file. Bill chanced a glance and saw that his face lit up.

"Well?"

Picaud held up the file. "Looks like I still have a couple things to do, then it's off to Hawaii! You're right; it's time for Picaud to be put aside. I need to get on with life and put the past behind me. Perhaps with that, and maybe a whole lot of therapy, I can be Eddie again."

"Merry Christmas to all, and to all a good night, huh?"

Picaud gave a short bark of a laugh. "Something like that, I suppose. Speaking of which"—he waved the file in his hand—"thank you for my present. I got you a little something as well."

Bill's eyes narrowed in suspicion. "It's not a check or something, is it?"

"Oh, please. Do you think I'd insult you like that?"

"Then what?"

"I had it shipped to your house. It should be there by now and waiting for you."

"What did you send me? And how did you get my add . . . You know what, I don't want to know. I just started to like you; I don't want to have to arrest you." For what now seemed like the millionth time, he thought, *God, this man is frustrating.*

"Rest assured, it's something you want. I might go so far as to say you've wanted it your whole life."

On that enigmatic note, Picaud walked down the steps onto the path in the gently falling snow and out of sight, leaving Bill to wonder about what he could possibly mean.

Bill made it home the following day. Waiting for him in his home office was a large brown box. He opened it up to find a stack of large leather-bound notebooks that looked like they'd recently been polished to a bright new shine.

He opened up the first and began to read.

When he read the name, he did a double take. When he was sure of what it said, he began to read in earnest and didn't stop until he went through the entire stack.

The *real* last piece of the puzzle slid into place, and Bill couldn't help but laugh at the knowledge of where Picaud's fortune had come from.

At least it had gone to good use.

Edward decided that he was going to go for a walk around the area. His ship was being loaded with everything he needed for the journey ahead, and he had some time to kill. As he walked down to the public parking lot, he knew it was time to do his last bit of business; he couldn't move forward until he did.

He knew around which area Cory was rumored to be. His favorite spots to hang around were near the marina or the beach house. He was aware of Cory's situation, but nothing could've prepared Edward for the sight waiting to greet him behind one of the beach bathrooms next to the dumpsters, barely hiding from view.

As Edward turned the corner to look for Cory, he startled the two men out of the act in which they were engaging. The large, muscular man zipped up in a hurry as the dirty homeless man wiped his scraggly, bearded mouth.

The first thing to hit Edward before realizing the homeless man was Cory was the smell. As he stepped forward, he walked into an invisible wall of putridity.

Edward was spared having to chase away the other man, who ran off in embarrassment. He walked forward to get a better look at the man sitting on his knees, propped up by one arm while the other tried to protect his eyes, which were squinting against the sun to look at who had interrupted his business.

"See something you like? I'll do what you want for the right price!"

When Edward's eyes looked upon what Cory had become, he felt disgusted; but with himself. He'd taken his revenge too far.

Then something snapped, and Cory's manner changed completely. He was now smiling. "Why didn't you say you were from wardrobe?"

Edward said nothing.

Cory looked up at the figure still blotted out by the sun. A look of embarrassment came over his face. "Sorry about the mistake; lot of crazed fans have been getting through lately. Think I'm going to have to have a word with the security around here."

Cory made his way to his feet. Edward fought with his nose as he took a good look at Cory. His lips were white and cracked, dirt caked onto every inch of skin and clothing. It looked like he was wearing the same clothes he had been in in his rant video. It was hard to say for sure because they were so tattered and frayed.

Edward felt the best way to go about getting Cory to do what he wanted was to play into his madness. He called for a limo to come pick them up.

With real tenderness in his voice, he said, "Mr. Tovin, there's been a bit of a location change for the next scene. A car is on its way to take you; they'll touch up your hair and makeup there."

Cory's head swiveled around. "I wasn't told about this."

"It just happened, sir. I was sent to relate the message as well as escort you there."

When Cory saw the limo pull up, a green-and-yellow grimy smile lit up his face. He adjusted his clothing and even pressed his hair down as Edward opened the car door to let him in.

The closest rehab facility was only minutes away, but for Edward, it was one of the longest rides of his life, second only to the one that had landed him in this mess in the first place.

When they arrived at the center, two men who'd been briefed of the situation were standing to meet Cory and to take him inside. When Edward saw that they played along, he made sure they received a generous tip.

Just before Cory was to be escorted into the facility, Edward stopped the orderlies. He walked up to Cory, placed his hands on his shoulders, and waited for Cory to look him full in the face.

When he finally did, he saw that Cory had locked onto his blue eyes. A spark of sanity, and perhaps recognition, passed there, if only for a moment.

"Cory, I want you to know that you have suffered enough. I forgive you . . . and . . . I'm sorry. I'm not sure anymore what you deserved, but it wasn't this." Tears began to well in the corners of Edward's eyes as Cory was taken off to the treatment center.

Edward filled out the necessary paperwork and called Jake. He couldn't take back what he had done any more than his bullies could, but he could try to set things right. He made it clear that he wanted Cory to be taken care of. He was to be transferred to the best rehabilitation center there was, and all of his medical bills were to be covered by the company until he was once more deemed sane, if that day ever came.

Chapter 24

A SECOND CHANCE

On the island of Maui, close to the western shoreline, there stood a restaurant named PattyRicks. A small building right on the beach, surrounded by tables stuck in the sand. Facing the tables and ocean beyond was a bar underneath an awning made of old palm fronds. Behind the bar lead to the kitchen and the hostess area, where a woman was making everything ready for opening before the lunch rush.

She stopped for a moment to survey her restaurant. The place was small but in a great location and had the reputation of some of the best food on the island. She was always busy with both tourists and locals alike.

A crack of thunder rolled through the air. She looked up to the sky and saw it was gray.

Perfect, she thought. *Gonna be one of those days.*

Rain on the islands came and went frequently. Even though she usually retained customers who would shelter underneath the umbrellaed tables, it was better for business when the rain went on its way.

She looked at her watch; it was only a couple minutes to eleven. She looked around at her staff, saw they were ready, and nodded for the hostess to open them up for business.

It wasn't unusual to have a line waiting to get in, so when she saw the small mass of people flooding through the entrance, she picked up a handful of menus and helped seat everyone.

Move, move, move, that's what she told herself. *Got to get it done and people served.* She therefore took no special notice of the singular man toward the back of the line when she sat him.

One of her waiters called out last-minute, and once the bulk had been seated, she switched her role to fill in.

When she made her way over to the man sitting by himself, she was still in a hurry to get everything done. After the briefest of glances down at the man nose-deep in a menu, she stuck a notepad in front of her own and asked if he wanted anything to drink.

"Jack on the rocks and a water would be great," the man said with the slightest trace of a tremor in his voice.

He was probably on a blind date waiting for the mysterious other to appear. Being in this business, you got to see many stages of romance, from the plethora of first dates to the Sunday early-bird special where the silver-haired couples kept their dating game alive and well. Every time she saw it, she felt her heart soften, then a pang of sadness.

She rushed off to put the order in at the bar and continued on to her other customers. When she finally made her way back to pick up the jack and take it to its destination, she had hardly set the glass down on the table when the man snatched it up and downed it in one large swig.

With the glass still at his lips and his head tilted backward as if clearing the way for the amber liquid, she said, "Nervous about the date?"

He lowered the glass and looked up at her. Sharp blue caught her attention.

"You have no idea."

Their eyes locked together. Brittany lost herself in those small oceans and felt as if she were drowning in them, but peacefully.

Shaking off the feeling to try and get her bearings back was hard. She was swimming against the current. There was something remarkably familiar about those eyes. Then the man smiled.

Eddie smiled.

EPILOGUE

Off on the farthest reaches of the ocean's tides, a large pirate ship with the name *Quiet Storm* sailed along in the bright blue surroundings with a smiling sun and calm waters.

Edward sat in a chair next to the helm as his two sons, Westley and George, made-believed they were real pirates. It was one of their favorite games.

Nikki, the oldest, was down below with her mother, finishing up her lessons for the day.

Edward watched his boys laugh as they swung foam swords at each other, grateful that they would tire themselves out. Later on that evening, all five would gather before bed as he would read aloud one of his many precious books. It was everyone's favorite part of the day.

Placed in his lap was a large white folder he would paw through frequently. He was doing the same now, but today was a special day. They'd gotten their mail at their last port. Jake had sent a newspaper clipping of Bill taking down yet another big name in connection with the famous "Little Black Book." Edward read it and the many other clippings like it before the new one took its place in one of the clear, untouched sleeves.

With each entry in the white folder, Edward not only felt it was money well spent but also that it was helping to erase some of the damage done to the world by adding pages to a certain blue folder all those years ago. It was true that the damage could never be fully erased, but every little bit helped.

Edward was startled out of his thoughts by a light touch of a delicate hand on his shoulder. Before he turned around to look at his wife, her scent wafted past the salt on the air and enamored Edward's lungs as he breathed deeply to take it in.

Brittany held out a bottle of Ol' Creek, and Edward took it gratefully.

"Gene wants to know what you want for dinner tonight."

"Why does he bother asking me? He knows I always enjoy whatever he picks out."

"He probably just wants to continue the illusion of you having a choice . . . you know, like when I decided you were going to marry me." She said it with such a bright and tender smile that Edward's heart was full to bursting at the sight of it.

She pulled him in close for a kiss. "So," Brittany said, "we've been all over the Caribbean, South America, even brushed against Antarctica. Where are we off to next?"

"To wherever the wind may take us. Life's a mystery, and I'm tired of trying to plan it through. As long as I have you guys, I'm happy. I say we let fate take us to where we're needed next."

She smiled with one raised eyebrow. "Uncertainty and the spirit of adventure. You sure you weren't a real pirate in a former life or something?"

"I'm a pirate now. But my treasure isn't gold or doubloons. I seek new knowledge and experiences, not to mention that booty!" He emphasized his last point by grabbing a handful of Brittany's backside.

She smiled and lightly slapped his chest in reply, causing him to spill a little. "Ashton called—said she and Westley are flying down to tour the Galapagos and wouldn't mind some company."

Edward was drinking and choked a little in surprised excitement. He swallowed and yelled, "To the Galapagos!"

He handed the bottle over to Brittany, who smiled and drank deeply.

NOTE TO THE READER

Thank you for coming on this journey with me. Your time is your most valuable asset, and I greatly appreciate you spending it with me. Hopefully you enjoyed it as much as I did and will come along with me on the next adventure! If you'd like to, I'd appreciate it if you'd leave a review wherever fine books are sold—and spread the word!

For more information, visit https://philiplacroix06.wixsite.com/author or follow me on social media at

https://www.facebook.com/search/top?q=philip%20la%20croix

https://www.instagram.com/philip.lacroix_/

ABOUT THE AUTHOR

Philip La Croix is a thirty-three-year-old knight at Medieval Times in Scottsdale, Arizona, and is looking to expand his talent beyond his use of the sword and lance. He graduated from California State University Fullerton with a BA in theater and has been an entertainer all his life. He is channeling his many experiences into telling new tales. *The Best Laid Traps* is the first of hopefully many books to be sent out into the world.

Made in the USA
Las Vegas, NV
04 March 2023

68536395R10229